Songs Of The Dead Road

Carolyn Newton

Seek Beauty —
Carolyn Newton

Copyright © 2026 Carolyn Newton

The right of Carolyn Newton to be identified as the Author of the Work has been asserted by her in accordance with the Copyright, Designs and Patents Act 1988.

First published in 2026 by Bloodhound Books.

Apart from any use permitted under UK copyright law, this publication may only be reproduced, stored, or transmitted, in any form, or by any means, with prior permission in writing of the publisher or, in the case of reprographic production, in accordance with the terms of licences issued by the Copyright Licensing Agency.

All characters in this publication are fictitious and any resemblance to real persons, living or dead, is purely coincidental.

www.bloodhoundbooks.com

Print ISBN: 9781917705592

To Callie, David, and Laura
I loved you when you were but a twinkle in my eye and every day since.

War is not the vilest form of evil, not the most evil of evils. An unjust trial, for instance, that scalds the outraged heart, is viler. Or murder for gain, when the solitary murderer fully understands the implications of what he means to do and all that the victim will suffer at the moment of the crime. Or the ordeal at the hands of a torturer. When you can neither cry out nor fight back nor attempt to defend yourself. Or treachery on the part of someone you trusted. Or mistreatment of widows or orphans. All these things are spiritually dirtier and more terrible than war.

— ALEKSANDR SOLZHENITSYN, *THE RED WHEEL*, OCTOBER 1916

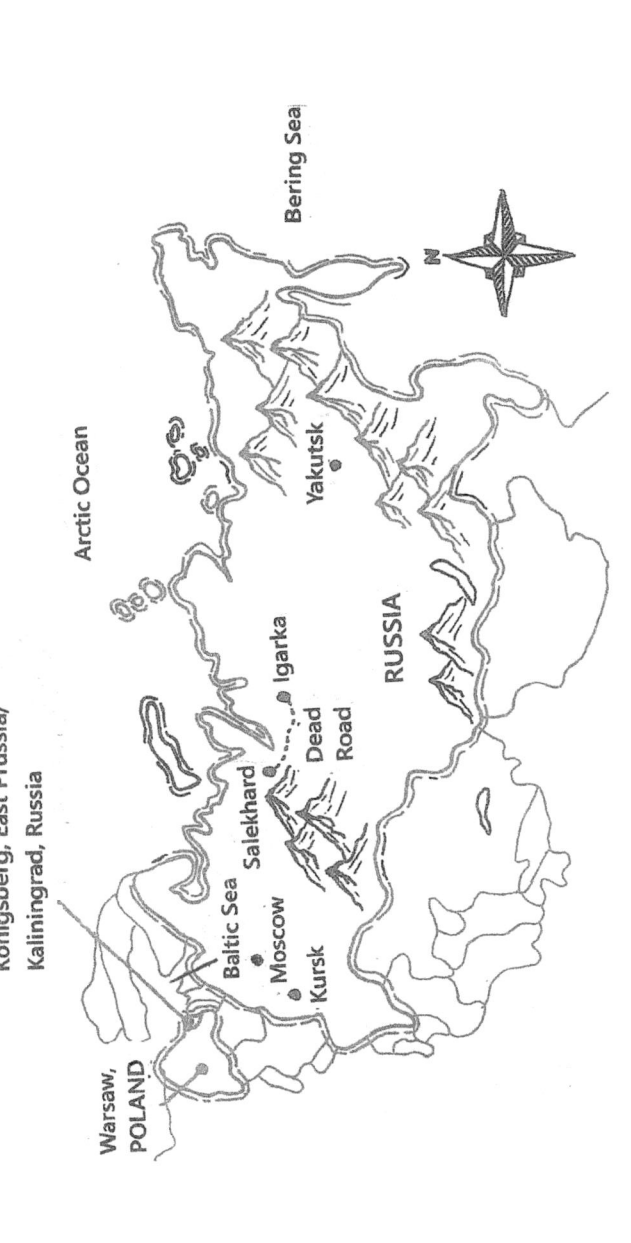

Part One

Chapter 1

Song of Loss

Warsaw, Poland
June 1939

Ján marched down the thickly carpeted stairs, matching the rhythm of his footsteps to the beat of the band as he neared the festivities below. *"Jeden, dwa, trzy, cztery, pięć,"* he counted, and the numbers began to dance in his head to a tune that bubbled up from his imagination. Years later, when he would think on this night, he would remember the exhilarating energy of the crowd brimming with laughter and the confidence of wealth. At the time though, as he navigated the gracefully curved treads, he was focused only on the burden of expectations he alone carried.

He reached the landing and paused, waiting to be acknowledged by the glittering crowd. Smoke from cigarettes held aloft in ivory and silver holders drifted up and mingled with the laughter of people accustomed to having the world bend to their liking. Women in sleek satin dresses, their finely coiffed hair sparkling with jeweled combs, hung on the arms of well-fed financiers, politicians, and celebrities, and gazed at their companions, absorbing the men's conversation through the gauzy filter of their martinis and gin fizzes.

Ján's blonde, curly hair was plastered back, coaxed into sleek compliance with the water from his bath and smelling pleasantly of his mother's lavender soap. He fiddled with the sash of his cashmere robe and tugged at the collar of his starched pajamas.

"Ján, darling!" his mother called, "come down and play for us!" as though his arrival was serendipitous rather than meticulously planned. "My beautiful boy is off to Königsberg tomorrow to continue his studies at the academy there," she announced to the oohs and aahs of a fawning audience. She swept toward the stairs, her sapphire blue dress swirling at her ankles, and reached up to lure him down.

All eyes were on him now. He took a tentative step towards her, registering the moment his fingers left the handrail as though he was now untethered and hurtling through space. His mother captured him, grasping his hand and flinging his arm aloft while commanding the attention of her guests in tribute to her treasured boy.

She smelled of exotic flowers and tobacco, a sweet and savory combination that he would recall often through the years when he thought of her and her luminescent charms. This night, he was aware only of his desperate desire to please her.

"Play something for Mama, dearest. Mozart, just like you practiced," she whispered in his ear as she installed him on the thick, velvet cushion of the bench set before the gleaming piano, a concert grand ordered especially for him from Blüthner in Leipzig. He was a small lad, and his legs dangled as he inched forward to set his hands gingerly on the keys. Most thought him much younger than nine years of age, a miscalculation that was not helped by the pajamas, his mother's idea. A hush settled over the tipsy crowd, and they chuckled when he turned to them and bowed his head.

"Wolfgang Amadeus Mozart's *Ah, vous dirai-je, Maman* in twelve variations," he announced, and the audience chuckled at his solemnity. His fingers began to stroke the keys, and the guests extended their most generous indulgence as they settled in to listen to a child's interpretation of the French folk song.

Then he began to play the variations. He deftly maneuvered from the whimsical to the melancholy themes, the melody ever-present as it tipped from his right hand to his left. When he reached the rousing conclusion, they erupted with applause and raised their glasses in a toast. "Bravo!" they shouted.

His father hoisted him onto his shoulders and carried him, the conquering hero, through his adoring fans and back upstairs where he handed him his stuffed bear and tucked him into the crisp linens of his enormous bed. "That's my boy," said his father gently as he kissed him on the forehead.

Ján lay still and listened as the party continued late into the night. He thought not of Mozart and the frolicking tune, but of the melody that was composing itself from magical fragments of the evening. The clink of crystal, the sharp tap of high heels on marble, the throaty laughter, and the swoosh of the service door as a platter of perfectly arranged confections emerged from the kitchen, all brought together in a feast of chords and rhythms. Bright notes inspired by his mother's elegance grounded by a strong beat redolent of his father's reassuring presence. The music assembled itself in Ján's mind as a remembrance of all he held dear, and he nodded off, content in the knowledge that he had brought them joy.

The chaotic platform at Warsaw's Główna railway station still reeked of the fire, a construction mishap that had damaged large swaths of its ambitious art deco design. Passengers and porters jostled each other as they navigated an obstacle course of workmen, equipment, and caution banners. Despite repairs and ongoing construction, traffic in and out of Poland's capital city remained steady, and the entire Balik family had come to see their golden boy off on his journey.

Ján shifted from foot to foot and tugged at the stiff collar of his starched linen shirt. The train before him idled with equal impatience, its massive cars filling with passengers and luggage. Ján tried to tamp down his uncertainty over how he might manage this adventure all on his own. This time last year when he went to visit his Aunt Ada and Uncle Erik for the summer, his nanny had accompanied him, but this year was diffcrent. Distracting talk of Hitler and Germany filled the wealthy salons of Warsaw, and as a point of pride to him, Ján was nine and a half years old, too old to be traveling with a minder.

Hanna, the elder of his two sisters and the more serious-minded, thrust a basket of food in his hands. "You need to carry this; it's rumpling my dress."

His mother, watching the exchange, hurried to his side and retrieved the awkward parcel. "Hanna! We have servants to stow this in Ján's seat. I can't bear any stress on his hands!" And with that, she snapped her fingers, and their chauffeur appeared with a trolley of trunks and bags. He spirited the basket and luggage away, leaving Ján to the ministrations of his mother and sister.

Ján's other sister, Magda, sauntered over, ogling the soldiers massing on the platform. She offered a sly smile and twirled around her fingers the blue ribbon dangling from her straw hat.

"For heaven's sake, Magda, stop flirting with the soldiers," exclaimed Hanna. "It's embarrassing!"

"Who else should I flirt with?" Magda challenged her older sister. "You're such a gloomy old soul. Try having some fun for a change." She tilted her head toward a young man standing nearby. Hanna rolled her eyes as the young man tipped his hat in Magda's direction.

Ján watched them bicker with mild amusement. He would miss his sisters. Their antics livened up the house and deflected some of the attention that was routinely showered on him. At nineteen and seventeen, they were young women with thoughts of university and marriage, and they usually treated him like a pet. Mama had often told him that he was her blessing baby, a treasured boy long anticipated, but Ján had also overheard the servants refer to him as the oopsie baby, and while he didn't exactly know what that meant, he understood that it wasn't particularly nice.

Ján's mother waved the girls away. "Listen to me, Ján. This is the opportunity of a lifetime, and you need to make the best of it. Your aunt and uncle are generous to a fault to have you study with them for the summer. I can only imagine how skilled you will be after another term in their care!"

Ján nodded. He knew what was expected of him, and he remembered his last summer with his relatives in Königsberg. Up at dawn for calisthenics followed by breakfast, morning music theory drills, lunch, piano lessons in the afternoon, and two hours of practice after dinner. The lessons and practice didn't bother him so much—it all came rather easily to him—but he longed for the companionship of friends. Aunt Ada and Uncle Erik didn't have any children, the serious students at the academy were all much older than he, and his schedule didn't allow him to meet any of the younger students who were brought by their nannies for afternoon lessons.

Just as when he was home, he had only adults and servants for the odd times when he wished to play. Aunt Ada was a charmer and loads of fun, but Uncle Erik was different. Surly and ill-tempered, he was scary, and Ján did his best to avoid him.

The whistle blew and black smoke billowed from the stack into the warm June morning. Lara Balik bent low and cupped her son's face in her gloved hands. "You are meant for great things, Ján. You are my gift, and you must pursue beauty and joy. Seize your destiny." She kissed his golden curls, quickly turning her head to fuss with her hat, hoping that he didn't see the tears in her eyes.

Artur Balik, a man at ease with his wealth and standing, issued crisp instructions to their servants and wrapped his arm around his son's shoulders. He guided him on board the train, slipping the attendant a neat stack of bills as he led his son to his compartment. "Be good, Ján, and mind your aunt and uncle. Don't ever make anyone glad twice, you know, glad to see you come and glad to see you go!" he teased with a wink. Then he leaned down and whispered in Ján's ear, "And try to make time to play. See if you can goad that stuffy uncle of yours into helping you make friends."

Ján breathed in his father's scent of rich cologne and sweet cigar tobacco and leaned into the smooth touch of his freshly shaved cheek. He wanted to throw his arms around his father's neck and squeeze tight, but he held his arms at his side and practiced being a man. "Yes, Father," he said solemnly with a slight tilt to his head.

Artur cuffed Ján on the shoulder and stood up, fighting the catch in his own throat. "On your way, lad, and make us proud!"

Ján pressed his face to the glass and watched his father rejoin his mother and sisters on the platform. His mother leaned into his father's strong embrace, and Hanna offered her a lace handkerchief as Magda focused her attention on a cluster of young men sporting university ties. The whistle blew a final time as the train lurched forward, gathering momentum and gaining speed. Ján remained at his post as his family receded from view, growing smaller and indistinct before disappearing behind a puff of smoke. His last sight was of his mother, a bright spot of petal pink silk among the dull sooty grays of the station.

Ján shared his first-class compartment with two elderly sisters from Königsberg, dashing his hopes for a companion close to his own age and requiring him to make small talk for hours. He escaped to the toilet so often for some peace and quiet that the ladies began to root through his basket for the cause of his apparent stomach troubles. Their thorough investigation involved tasting the delectable apple cake that the Baliks' cook had carefully packed in a tin, and they rationalized that they were doing him a favor by saving him from a potential source of gastric distress.

When they finally fell asleep for their afternoon nap, Ján was grateful for the respite from their chatter despite the irritation of their arrhythmic snoring.

The flat countryside rolled past, and Ján pressed his nose against the glass, watching the workers hunched over their plows while cajoling their mules. Accustomed as he was to city life with lively markets, clanking trolleys, and packed concert halls, he pondered what life was like for the men and women toiling in the fields, their movements repetitive and unhurried. He thought he might like to try a spell in the country, just for a bit, and imagined himself with dirt on his hands. He knew it was an idle wish. His mother would never approve. He chuckled to think of Lara Balik with chapped hands, a plain homespun dress, and straw hat. No, that would not suit her at all.

Close to dusk, the train pulled into Königsberg's grand station, a modern structure with an imposing entrance befitting a city designed for royalty. Ján was relieved to see Aunt Ada waving enthusiastically from the platform. She was his mother's identical twin with the same thick golden hair, sparkling blue eyes, and dramatic mannerisms, but where his mother was waifishly thin, almost brittle, Aunt Ada was plump and relentlessly cheerful. Ján adored her.

"Darling boy, you must be exhausted!" she said as she pulled him into a crushing embrace. "I have been counting the days until you arrive." Her Polish was crisp and lightly accented from her years in East Prussia.

Ján politely asked after Uncle Erik and was pleased to learn that he was at the academy and would not be available to greet Ján until tomorrow morning. That meant he had Aunt Ada all to himself for the evening. They corralled his luggage and the piles of gifts from his mother and paid the porter a handsome fee to deliver the parcels to the house.

"My little man, surely you brought half of Warsaw with you! What was Lara thinking?" Ada chuckled as the man hauled the baggage cart away. Thus unencumbered, Ján and Ada set out to tour the town. With Ada behind the wheel and the top of the convertible folded down, they traveled a circuitous route crossing two of the bridges over the Pregel River, zipping past the Brandenburg Gate and the Polish church before stopping to get ice cream in full spectacular view of the castle backlit by the summer's evening sun.

Finally, as dusk settled around them, they motored past the academy and into the leafy neighborhood where Aunt Ada and Uncle Erik lived in a stuffy but commodious house. It had none of the elegant trappings of his home in Warsaw with its bustling supply of discreet employees. Ada and Erik had only two servants: Liesl for housekeeping and Karl for maintenance. Nevertheless, Ján remembered it fondly. It had a tidy garden, a warm and cozy kitchen with a sweets jar that was always full, and the most extraordinary room with a heavily embellished Bechstein grand piano, a generous music library, and huge windows looking out over the leafy lawn and the cottage next door.

As they completed the final leg of his journey, Ján spied the house at the end of the street, and then his exhaustion took over. He nodded off against the leather seat and barely roused when Aunt Ada carried him into the house and tucked him in bed.

"It's easy to forget that you're just a little boy," she whispered as she slipped off his jacket and shoes and pulled up the covers. "Sleep like an angel, Schatz, and sweet dreams."

The following morning, Ján awoke to bright light streaming in the window of his compact bedroom. Tucked in the attic with a single dormer window, it was furnished simply with a creaky iron bed, a plain dresser, a small desk, and a rather wobbly chair. Someone had left a tray with a carafe of water, a biscuit, and a note in Ada's extravagant handwriting. *Good morning, Schatz. Join us.*

Ján smoothed out the wrinkles in his shirt and put on his shoes, then he balanced on the chair and looked out the window. Elderly Karl was slowly trimming the back hedge while Uncle Erik and Aunt Ada sat on the terrace, eating breakfast. Uncle Erik's nose was buried in the newspaper, and Aunt Ada was chattering away between bites of generously buttered pastries.

Ján slipped down the stairs and through the parlor where he stopped in front of the open door to the garden. He watched his aunt and uncle, waiting for a moment to interrupt.

Finally, Erik spied him standing in the doorway. "Don't dawdle there like a ghost! Come out and say hello!" he bellowed.

Ján walked over to the table, grateful for Aunt Ada's broad smile as she cleared a spot for him to sit down.

Erik sat back and adjusted his ample torso in the small wrought-iron chair. "You took your merry time coming down this morning. Half the day is gone! Don't expect to keep this schedule up!"

"No, sir." Ján responded, remembering the strict instructions that his mother had given him. "I am eager to begin my studies. Thank you for inviting me again this summer."

"Well, that's good at least. You haven't grown much since last year, have you?" his uncle observed. "You don't look a day over six."

Truth was, Ján didn't spend much time with other children his age, so he had no idea how big nine-and-a-half-year-olds were supposed to be. He was accustomed to being the smallest in the room and generally didn't question whether he was somehow deficient. "No, sir, I suppose not," Ján responded blandly.

"Speak German, son, you'll find your Polish is not welcome here. It's enough for me to have to explain away Ada's Polish roots to my friends. I shan't be saddled with a foreign nephew that can't speak the language. Best to get in the habit now."

Then Erik Richter, maestro, headmaster, and disciplinarian, folded his paper, set his knife and fork on his plate angled at exactly the four and eight o'clock positions, and stood up with a flourish. "Ada, bring Ján to the academy this afternoon for his first lessons.

I'll see you after lunch." Without waiting for a response, he turned and strode into the house.

Ján addressed himself to his studies as thoroughly as a prodigious nine-year-old could. Each morning, he met Karl in the garden at sunrise for calisthenics while Erik observed from the terrace, sipping his first cup of coffee for the day. Poor Karl suffered through the exercises despite his creaky knees and unreliable balance, and Ján endeavored to put on a display for his uncle that would give credit to Karl's geriatric coaching. After breakfast, Ján would don his suit and meet his uncle in the foyer. Liesl and Ada nodded in approval at his punctuality and decorum before each of them planted a kiss on his cheek and slipped him a sugary treat for his pocket.

Days at the academy were filled with lessons and tutorials. His piano teacher, Herr Kippels, was a patient, yet demanding mentor, and Ján blossomed under his guidance. He was so impressed with Ján's progress by early July that he proposed adding the boy to the list of performers for the concert scheduled for the end of the summer, an annual event for which most of the other musicians had been preparing for months. Erik, who insisted that Ján call him Meister Richter when on academy grounds, was hesitant to allow this craven display of nepotism until Herr Kippels, unbeknownst to Ján, invited him to observe one of the boy's lessons.

Ján was delighted when his teacher suggested that they move his afternoon session from the cramped studio to the grand concert stage of the academy. He had only visited the exquisitely appointed hall once and had wondered what it must feel like to approach the piano on the stage with an audience hushed in eager anticipation. He was so captivated by the sight of the magnificent Bösendorfer piano basking in the stage lights that he didn't notice his aunt and uncle sitting in the back row. Ján climbed onto the bench, and both he and Herr Kippels laughed when they realized that Ján needed a bit of a boost to properly address the keys. They scrounged behind the curtain and found a quilted piano cover that they fashioned into an extra cushion.

Once Ján was properly situated, Herr Kippels withdrew sheet music from a leather binder and arranged it on the piano stand. "Now I know you haven't seen this piece before, but we have been practicing tempo and interpretation. Let's see what you can do on your own. I know you can play these notes, but can you make them leap and soar in the hearts of your audience?"

Ján peered at the arrangement. It was his gift that he could look at lines and squiggles on the page and hear the notes come alive in his head. He sat motionless, while in his mind, the lively mix played out as joyful and bold. He nodded slowly.

Herr Kippels explained, "This is Johann Sebastian Bach, Suite No.2 in B Minor, The Badinerie. It means that it is a quick, light movement in a suite. Let's see what you can do with this." He set the metronome ticking and then sat back with his hands clasped in his lap, signaling for Ján to start when ready.

Ján shifted slightly on his padded seat, his feet barely reaching the gleaming pedals, and studied the sheets in front of him. He did not put hands on the keys, though. His eyes feasted on the notes in front of him, and he considered the different ways that he could approach the piece. He was oblivious to anything in the room but his hands, the music, and the elegant instrument before him. In the back of the hall, Ada was perched on the edge of her seat, barely breathing, while Erik fidgeted. They both watched their nephew, and to their eyes, he was simply staring at the pages. After what seemed an interminable wait, Erik harrumphed and started to stand, but Ada's hand shot out, and she urged him back in his seat.

"Wait. Just wait. Look at him. He's transfixed," she whispered.

Finally, Ján's hands lifted, gently caressing the keys. He closed his eyes momentarily and then he leaned forward and poured himself into the music. The notes danced from his fingers, his right hand leaping across the keyboard and his left keeping pace. Ján's head bobbed as his hands worked their magic. The notes were crisp, and Ján kept an exuberant pace.

Then suddenly, inexplicably, he struck a sour note. It ricocheted off the stage and fouled the room. Herr Kippels clenched his jaw; Ada gasped; Erik squeezed his fists; yet Ján was undeterred. He remained focused on the arrangement. He lifted his hands only a fraction of an inch off the keys, tilted his head and recentered himself, going deep in his thoughts to conjure up the melody once more. He pictured his fingers lightly caressing a few notes and then bearing down to draw out the very marrow of others.

He began again. The merry melody frolicked in his interpretation. He was confident and inspired, each note truer than the last. It was a short piece, complex to play with a small hand, and even more difficult to attain the variations in tempo that gave the suite its depth, yet Ján immersed himself in the performance, coaxing out the bold notes and providing subtle nods to others. When he finished, he held his hands on the keys, letting the strings quieten and the music fade away.

"*Gott im Himmel,*" uttered Erik.

Ada stood and applauded loudly, and Ján swiveled his head in surprise. He peered into the lights and waved meekly at his enthusiastic audience.

"Well done, lad," remarked Herr Kippels, and Ján knew that was high praise indeed.

It was decided that Ján would indeed perform in the concert. He was slated to take the stage first to avoid stealing the limelight from the other artists. Erik wanted the audience to focus on Ada, a classically trained mezzo-soprano performing "Wo in Bergen du dich birgst" from Wagner's *Die Walküre,* accompanied by Eduard von Habel, Erik's prized pupil. Erik remained convinced that Ján's participation amounted to little more than a circus sideshow, but Ada, who had keen business instincts in addition to her wealth of musical talent, was adamant that they showcase Ján's extraordinary talent. "Think of the mothers lining up at our door with their children for lessons after they see our little prodigy, Erik! We might end the year with a profit after all!"

Erik scoffed at his wife's silly ideas, but he was intrigued with the notion of acquiring a bit of coin. He grumbled and complained as Ada made plans for Ján's big debut. The concert was scheduled for the first Saturday in September, so Ada hastily wired Lara and arranged for Ján to stay in Königsberg an extra week. Then in a rare break from his lessons, Ada and Ján visited the tailor to order a bespoke tuxedo. "Fit for the little prince you are, Schatz!" crowed Ada.

The day of the dress rehearsal on the eve of the concert, Ján awoke at his usual time and dressed for calisthenics with Karl. The early morning sun was drying the dew off Karl's prized roses, and Bismarck, the neighbor's hound, had escaped with some poor soul's shoe, which he was enthusiastically shredding by the back gate. Besides the hound and a couple of playful rose finches, Ján was surprised to see that there was no one about. He sat down by the breakfast table on the terrace, folded his hands on his lap, and waited.

"Ján! Silly boy, I'm afraid we've forgotten all about you!" Liesl rushed into the garden, drying her hands on her apron. "You must come with me." Flustered, she glanced at the stone wall that surrounded their back lawn, hoping none of the neighbors were snooping.

"May I please have some breakfast?" Ján asked, but Liesl didn't hear him. She shooed him up from the chair and nudged him toward the door.

"Your aunt and uncle are in the music room. You should go there." She scurried back to the kitchen, talking to herself in low but emphatic tones.

Ján remained where she had deposited him, staring across the hall at the door to the exalted room. Normally, it remained shuttered during the day. He was allowed there only after dinner for practice with Ada, never alone, always adhering to his rigidly scheduled sessions.

He tiptoed to the door and discovered it was slightly ajar. He knocked softly, and the door swung inward. Ján could see his aunt and uncle sitting side by side in front of Erik's beloved Volksempfänger, the German radio with a sturdy brown case featuring the menacing authority of eagle and swastika stamps. Normally, concert music from Berlin or Vienna sputtered out of the device, but today an announcer spoke urgently. Tears ran down Ada's face, and Erik was stiffly patting her back.

"There, there, Schatzi. All will be well. You'll see. Perhaps it is for the best. All of us in one big Germany," Erik said as Ada's tears became a torrent of grief.

"Aunt Ada?" Ján was frozen in place, feeling like an intruder and wishing that he were back in Warsaw in his own home with his parents and sisters.

"Oh Ján, my dear boy!" Ada rushed over and wrapped her arms around his shoulders. "It will be alright, I am sure. Warsaw is a long way from the border. They'll be alright."

Ján looked to Erik for help. "Uncle Erik? What's wrong?"

Erik cleared his throat, uncharacteristically at a loss for words. "Well, Ján, it's hard to tell really, but the announcer on the radio is saying that we—that is, Germany—have been attacked by your people, the Poles." Erik avoided looking directly at Ján. He stared at the carpet and hesitated for a moment before pressing on. "The long and short of it is that Germany must now defend itself and has declared war. The German army is now in Poland. Now I'm sure your parents and sisters..."

"I want to talk to my mother," Ján interrupted in a quivering voice. Aunt Ada's tears were quite contagious now. "I...I...just want my parents."

"Oh, Schatz, of course you do. But you see..." Ada seized on an idea. "Let's try to call." She wiped her face and clasped Ján's hand, pulling him with her to the credenza in the hall. She began dialing the number.

"Ada!" said Erik. "What are you doing?"

Ada ignored the question as she brought the receiver to her ear and waited for the operator.

"Yes! Thank you. Finally!" Ada said in her deepest and most regal voice. "I need to place a call to Warsaw."

Ján could not understand the chirpy voice leaking back through the phone.

Ada stamped her foot impatiently. "I understand that some things might be *down*, as you say, but surely you can try." Another pause. "Well now I must insist that you try! NOW!" Erik came up behind Ada and clutched the receiver. She glared at him, but he teased it out of her hand and hung up the telephone.

"You won't get through. Not today. Lara will contact you when she can." Erik turned to face Ján. "You must be brave, do you understand?"

Ján sniffled and nodded at his uncle.

Erik continued. "What your mother and father would want is for you to carry on. They wouldn't want you to fret or worry. They would want you to go about your day. Worry never bought anyone a reprieve. Let's get you ready for rehearsals."

Ján choked back his tears and followed Erik, endeavoring to hold his shoulders square and his head high. They motored to the academy, and when they arrived, Ján could recall little of the drive over. He moved as his uncle's shadow, one foot after another, pulled by an invisible need to be close to someone familiar.

They proceeded through the front entrance of the forbidding brick structure, which had always reminded Ján of a haunted house with its dark wood floors and intimidating echoes. Today, the building's gloom consumed him much like a hungry beast demolishes its prey. As if to underscore his solitary misery, pupils and professors darted about gleeful and giddy in equal measure.

"Meister! Come this way, the Führer is getting ready to speak," said a voice from within a side parlor.

Erik and Ján moved toward the open door to find a room full of men and a few women crowded around a radio. They jostled for a space, and Erik let go of Ján's hand to push his way toward the front. Ján remained sandwiched in the back, his view consisting entirely of the backs of the men huddled in front of him. His stomach gurgled, and he had the fleeting thought that he still hadn't eaten.

The voice of the announcer from the Reich Broadcasting Corporation came through the radio, and a hush settled over the room. The Führer was in the Kroll Opera House in Berlin and had begun to address the politicians and dignitaries assembled there. Ján listened intently, trying to decipher the German as Herr Hitler shouted out his speech. What little he heard was enough. *Bombs will be met with more bombs. The Germans will carry on the fight regardless of the size of the resistance.*

Ján looked around for his uncle but with his limited view, there was little that he recognized. He retreated from the room and sought refuge on the bristly horsehair sofa in the hallway. He thought of his mother and his sisters in the lush garden of their home. Were bombs falling there? He thought of his father behind the massive desk in his office at the bank. Would the Germans drop bombs on banks too? Did these people hate him because he was their enemy? Cheering from inside the room interrupted Ján's thoughts. These people wanted Germany to win, and that meant his family had to lose.

"Ján!" Uncle Erik barreled into the hallway. "Ach—don't disappear on me like that! You have a rehearsal to attend!"

He was promptly whisked away as if nothing was amiss.

By the evening of the concert, Ján was consumed with worry. News reports continued to extol the might of the German army as it swept into Poland. The port at Danzig was under German control, and, according to all that Ján heard, the Polish army was incapable of repelling the superior German forces. There had been no word from his family in Warsaw, and Ján fantasized that they were on a train right now speeding across the countryside, his sisters bickering, his mother sipping her tea, and his father smoking a pipe while reading the financial news. He clung to the thinnest thread of hope. Surely if anyone could outsmart the Germans, it was his parents.

Standing in the wings of the concert hall, Ján tried to tamp down his nerves. His knees shook and his stomach roiled.

Ada came up beside him, her voluminous ball gown swishing with each step, and gently laid her hands on his shoulders. "You can do this, Schatz. Think of your dear mama and papa. They would love to be here to hear your music and to see you shine."

"But, Ada," Ján sniffled. "What if they're not alright? What if they are scared?"

Ada sighed deeply. "Ján, I am sure they are scared, but I am also certain of one other thing. Your mama will hear you play in her heart. Your music will touch her and comfort her, my little hero. We cannot help them right now, but she will hear you, and it will bring her joy."

Uncle Erik appeared behind them resplendent in his own tuxedo, his gray hair combed back and his spectacles polished. He nodded briefly to Ada and Ján, strode on stage, and drew the curtain aside to face the audience. A hush fell over the crowd.

"Good evening, ladies and gentleman," he intoned in his theatrical voice. "I am Meister Erik Richter, president of the Academy of Music, and I welcome you to this performance in the name of our institution and in celebration of our dear Führer and our Motherland, the glorious Germany!"

Thunderous applause erupted in the hall, and the audience was quickly on its feet. "Heil Hitler!" they called in unison.

Ján locked eyes with Ada, his thoughts a chaotic jumble of fear and shock. *Uncle Erik was celebrating?*

Ada knew what fresh terror gripped him. She was equally

troubled and choked back tears. "He has to say that, Schatz. We are in Germany, and they are separating us into patriots and enemies. If we must play along to be safe, then we will. It's the reason you are listed in the program as Jan Richter tonight. You and I, we must be German, and Erik is just keeping us safe. Try to remember that and take comfort that we know what is in our hearts."

Ján listened to the rest of Erik's introduction but he heard none of it. His mind was on his mother and the gift he would send to her tonight. The curtain parted, and Uncle Erik stepped back and gestured to Ján.

Ada leaned down as much as her gown allowed. "That's your cue, Schatz."

Ján strode onstage and approached the piano. There was a smart leather cushion on the bench now, and Ján pulled himself up, flipping back the tails of his tuxedo. The audience laughed, but Ján didn't hear. Once again, he was conscious of only his fingers, the music in his head, the black and white keys before him, and tonight, the image of his mother as he best remembered her, diamonds glittering at her ears and a thick, shiny fur stole wrapped around her shoulders.

He played to her as his notes cascaded toward the heavens. The melody was designed to impart the exuberance of a lively dance, but to Ján it was an urgent entreaty to his mother to be safe, to be waiting for him. It was a plea to God to allow him to be reunited with his family and to be home and to find it as solid and secure as he had left it.

His part of the program was short, designed to showcase his talent without distracting from the more seasoned performers. When he concluded his performance with a flourish, the audience roared with approval. Ján slipped off the bench and faced the crowd, his expression solemn and his movements much too stiff for a boy his age. He bowed low once and then a second time to acknowledge the patrons' enthusiasm before walking rigidly offstage.

As soon as he was behind the curtain, he collapsed into Ada's embrace and sobbed.

Chapter 2
Lara's Song

Königsberg, East Prussia
Autumn 1939

The news was grim, and Ján's anxiety over the safety of his family began to take a toll. He complied with Erik's admonitions to apply himself to all his lessons, but he was sullen and drew even more inward.

"Eat, Schatz!" Ada pleaded. "Liesl made the sausage especially for you."

Ján set down his fork. "Please, Aunt Ada, I think I would like to practice." When she frowned in response, he followed up quickly, "I will eat later, I promise." He waited for permission. She shrugged and, after a dismissive wave of her hand, he slipped off his seat and disappeared into the music room. Minutes later, he began to play.

"It's not healthy for the boy," Liesl insisted. "He never comes back to finish his food, and," she lowered her voice and hissed, "he is having *accidents*. He tries to hide it, but I must wash his linens every day." She clicked her tongue, a sure sign of her disapproval, and retreated to the kitchen leaving Ada alone at the dinner table.

Erik had gone to see an acquaintance, the leader of the local Hitler Youth groups, to inquire as to whether Ján might join a club for the younger boys called the *Deutsches Jungvolk,* DJ for short. Ada was alarmed at Erik's plan but relented when he explained to her that he was hearing reports of ethnic Poles being rounded up for work camps.

"A nine-year-old boy? They would send him to a work camp?"

"I think yes, they might. And just think how that would make us look!" Erik mused. "A camp for children possibly, and..." his voice trailed off. Ada knew he was keeping something from her, but she was afraid to ask for details.

They hungered for news, gathering around the radio for the popular show *Hans Fritzsche Speaks* while holding their collective breath for a glimmer of hope. With soul-crushing consistency, Herr Fritzsche offered only high praise for the Germans and gloomy prospects for the Poles. The Soviets had invaded from the east, sealing their partnership with Germany and spelling certain defeat for the Poles. Ada anxiously followed reports as the German army rolled across the Polish countryside, growing ever closer to Warsaw. *Blitzkrieg.* That was the word on everyone's lips and the one that she struggled to keep from Ján's ears.

For the Germans who had suffered an ignoble defeat in 1918, the news arrived with the explicit expectation of full-throated patriotism. Ada kept to the house, declining invitations and growing increasingly morose. Erik nursed a not-so-subtle grudge over having to suppress his glee while in the company of his despondent family. He also chafed at the thankless burden of diverting prying eyes and ears away from his mirthless household.

The month of September ended with the family restless and unnerved. They'd had no word from the Baliks in Warsaw, which only compounded their fears. Ada worried about Ján, and the morning began dismally when she and Erik quarreled about his relentless insistence on maintaining appearances.

"Erik, he's just a boy! We can't force him into the DJ. Perhaps we can send him home after all?" Ada pleaded. "His family are important people in Warsaw. Surely, they are working to get him back as we speak!" She simply couldn't imagine Ján, as talented and sensitive as he was, marching around town with the DJ, all of them acting like serious little soldiers.

"You and Ján, by virtue of your questionable lineage, are in danger!" Erik snapped when challenged. "It is a stain on me too! It threatens all we have ever worked for."

"Me?" Ada struggled to breathe as fear inched closer to panic. "Why would they want me? I'm your wife. We've lived here for years!"

"And you will always be Polish in the eyes of the law. I can protect you only if you do as I ask. You have a reputation, a degree of fame, and frankly an association to me, but Ján? He has nothing. He is nothing but the enemy. His family is likely fighting against our soldiers right now!" His face bloomed with red patches as his anger erupted. "You have put us in terrible danger by having that boy in our house, so you will *not* defy me when I try to Germanize him and keep us all safe. He will go to school and attend the clubs like any other dutiful boy." Without waiting for a response from Ada, he jammed his hat on his head, grabbed his walking stick, and slammed the door behind him.

Ada didn't move from the dining table, her mind a jumble of thoughts and her emotions raw from the angry exchange with Erik. From the music room, the sounds of Ján's frenetic playing suddenly stopped, and the silence was more difficult to bear than his clamorous practice. Ada abandoned her cold toast and walked to the closed door, but as soon as she wrapped her hand around the knob, she heard Ján's sobs. She listened for a moment and then backed away. There was nothing she could do or say at this point. Might as well let the boy cry himself out.

Erik returned home in sour spirits. His friend had denied Ján's entry into the DJ on the grounds that the boy lacked the required paperwork to prove an impeccable family history, and furthermore, he had gone on to ask some unnervingly specific questions about Ján's parents. Erik worried privately that he might have put a bullseye on Ján's back, and thus his own, but he certainly wouldn't give Ada the benefit of acknowledging she might have been right. As much as he was annoyed by the boy, ensuring his safety was the simplest way of keeping trouble away from his doorstep. Erik was adamant that Ján's Germanization process must proceed without delay.

At dinner, Erik surveyed his doleful family. Ada and Ján silently picked at their food as Liesl served the pork and potatoes in ill-concealed annoyance. He cleared his throat loudly.

"Today, I arranged for you to have a tutor at the academy, Ján. You will start tomorrow morning."

"Whatever you wish, Uncle Erik." The boy ventured a nervous glance. "Are you dissatisfied with Herr Kippels?"

"Yes, well you will continue your music lessons, of course, just as always, but now you will have lessons in German, literature, mathematics, history, and science." Erik was starting to feel rather clever about his scheme. "We'll make a good German boy out of you in no time!"

Ján said nothing, but his eyes filled with tears, and his chin began to shake. He eased off his chair, bowed his head slightly toward Erik, and dashed from the room.

As his feet pounded up the stairs, Ada turned on her husband. "You insensitive fool! How did you think he would react? With joy? Leaping up and hugging your neck with gratitude?" Ada glared at Erik, but he showed no emotion as he concentrated on slicing a thick chunk of pork and stuffing it in his mouth.

He chewed slowly and swallowed deliberately. Then he took a generous gulp of his beer before pointing his fork at Ada. "When I married you, I knew it would be taxing at times because you are not German. I was dazzled by your talent and your beauty, and of course your youth. I was prepared to put up with your extravagant nature," Erik waved his fork around to emphasize his point, "but make no mistake, Ada dear, my patience with your tedious nephew is growing thin. If we cannot put that boy on a train and send him back to Poland where he belongs, which is utter folly, then you have two choices. You can send him to school and encourage him to learn to be a proper German lad, or you can find another family who is willing to take him in."

He picked up his dinner plate and carried it into the music room to listen to the radio. He was not going to entertain any more of Ada's objections. By turning his back on his wife, he decreed that the conversation was over. This was his house, and anyone who lived in it would abide by his wishes. Besides, it was time for the much-anticipated broadcast of the Berlin Philharmonic. He fiddled with the dials on the radio, and soon the strains of Beethoven wafted through the fractured house.

Ada was left alone at the dining room table, mulling over untenable options and fighting the same sense of doom that had clouded her morning.

Liesl hurried to clean dishes and tidy up the kitchen so that she could go home and escape the tension.

As the music from the radio became louder and more strident, Ada prepared to unleash her most vehement protest on Erik. She paced back and forth by the dining table, muttering to herself and crafting an argument. She would take the boy back to Warsaw herself. They would pack his things, get in the car and start driving. She had lived in Germany long enough to pass for a native. Warsaw had surrendered, and soon the Poles would be brought under the German government. As soon as possible, Ada was sure she would be reunited with her family. They would all be Germans now.

She clenched her fists and took a deep breath. The music from the radio had stopped, so this was the best chance she would get this evening. She stomped toward the door. "Erik! We need to talk."

The phone in the hallway rang, alarming at this time of night. Ada froze, her hard-won bluster dissipating with the interruption.

They rarely received calls in the evening. In truth, they rarely received calls at all, since so few people had telephones in their homes. It was only due to Erik's stature in the community that he had been allowed this privilege. He hoisted himself up from the chair and moved to pick up the receiver. He spoke softly, and Ada strained to comprehend the gist of the call. The ringing echoed in her ears, and she feared she would faint. She was holding on to the back of Erik's chair, steadying herself when he returned, his face ashen.

"That was Peter," he said quietly.

Ada looked up, confused. Her head was pounding, and she was unsure if she was hearing properly. "Peter, who? Someone from the Academy?"

"Yes, Peter, my student. He took a huge risk calling here. He was on tour in Kraków, got caught in the invasion. He is now in Warsaw, trapped, yet finally under the protection of the army. Conditions are bad." Erik faltered. "Ada?"

Ada was frightened to see the look on Erik's face. It was as if he were pleading with her, his hands held out, either to embrace her or catch her, she wasn't sure.

"They are rounding people up in Warsaw, Ada. First it was the soldiers and politicians, but now it is the lawyers, professors, and bankers. They're gone, Ada. Lara, Artur, the girls. They're gone."

"Gone where?" Ada felt the tears well up, and she began to shake. "Where did they go, Erik? Who took them?"

"Nowhere. They didn't go anywhere. They're dead. All of them. Shot."

Ada clung to the back of the chair, willing herself not to fall as the walls seemed to sway around her. Beautiful Lara. Hanna and Magda. Talented Artur. Surely it was a mistake. In the chaos, it could all be a horrible mistake. Then Ada caught sight of Ján standing in the doorway. He stared at Ada and then at Erik. They remained that way, paralyzed in the moment, unmoving, until he screamed, a raw, primal shriek that came straight from his soul. Ada put her head in her hands and collapsed.

Herr Kippels knocked on the door the following morning, and Liesl answered with a scowl on her face. With the exception of this dismal house, people everywhere were celebrating the spectacular performance of the German army, and she longed to join them. After the theatrics of the previous evening, Erik had left early, Ada was nursing a headache, and Ján had not appeared. She decided that she worked in a tomb.

"If you're here to inquire about Meister Richter, he has gone to the academy," she said brusquely.

"No, Liesl, I am not here for Meister Richter. I am here for Ján. He did not show up for his lesson today, and he needs to be there." Herr Kippels pulled his hat off his head, looked around to see who might be lurking on the sidewalk, and nervously tugged at the brim. "People are asking," he whispered.

Liesl clicked her tongue and pointed to the music room where Ada sat in Erik's large chair.

"My apologies, Frau Richter, for this intrusion on your day. Your husband told me this morning. Well, I am aware—" Herr Kippels searched for the right words, but nothing occurred to him.

"That my sister and her family were murdered? Yes, Herr Kippels. Apparently, that is what we are told." Ada talked softly, keeping her hands in her lap and her eyes downcast.

"Frau Richter, I know it is a difficult time, but they are asking questions about Ján. I managed to persuade them that I had arranged a private lesson here today, but I fear that there are those who feel he doesn't belong, in Königsberg, that is." The man paused to make sure Ada was registering the import of what he was trying to say. Getting no reaction, he pressed on. "I need him to return for his lessons. To show that he is one of us."

Ada lifted her head and faced the thin, balding man standing nervously in the doorway. "Why do you care, Herr Kippels?"

"Because he is a boy of immense talent who is scared and alone right now. I lost my own father when I was quite young." Herr Kippels gathered his courage and stood a bit taller, more assured. "Frau Richter, I was never blessed with a family of my own. I would appreciate the chance to help my young friend."

"Indeed, Herr Kippels. Please tell me how you might accomplish that."

He convinced her that Ján should return to the academy in a bid to ensure his safety, and together they hatched a plan. Rather than try to hide him, they would feature him, make him visible to help bolster his chance for survival.

The following morning, Ada watched as Ján walked out the door dressed in his suit and with his blonde hair neatly combed back. He gave every appearance of going about his day like any other young scholar, but he had dark circles under his eyes and struggled to quiet a quivering lip.

"One step at a time, Schatz," she offered, hearing the impotence of her words.

Time was no balm for the boy. The fraught days stretched into weeks, and while Ján's anguish hardened into his every thought, his talents provided him, for the moment, with a secure cover. Under Herr Kippels' care, he excelled at the piano and was soon playing for audiences who lined up to see him. He was the wunderkind, billed publicly as Jan Richter. Erik arranged for tutors to ensure that Ján completed his academics and used the generous proceeds from the boy's engagements to pay for the bespoke schooling that became a prohibitive luxury as teachers disappeared from the classroom and took up weapons to defend their nation at war.

Ján did as he was asked without rancor or enthusiasm. He spoke politely when addressed but offered little conversation of his own. His German improved, and he was quick with his studies.

Likewise, his piano recitals were technically superior, if lacking in soul. Audiences marveled, but Ada and Herr Kippels worried. They had seen Ján at his best, and they were witnessing a hollowed-out version of the boy.

After the capitulation of Poland, there was little news, and winter arrived in Königsberg amidst euphoria over Germany's demonstration of strength to the world. Ján worked steadily throughout December at festive concerts and as a featured performer at several holiday parties hosted by the city elite. The presence of Nazi officers in their intimidating uniforms terrified him, and on more than one occasion, his fear sent him racing to the toilet in a fit of nausea. Were any of these men present when his family died? Did one of them pull the trigger?

Each night, Ján lay in his bed and summoned images of his family. If he closed his eyes hard and squeezed them especially tight, he could hear their voices, but their faces were beginning to blur and take on the static lines of the photograph that Ada had placed on his dresser. He realized he was recalling the picture and not the people, and the thought of losing them in his memory brought on fresh waves of grief. For months, he had held on to the hope that they would magically appear in Königsberg, laughing that the news reports were all a big mistake. Every day that passed made a mockery of that dream.

On New Year's Day, Ján marked his tenth birthday with little fanfare. Liesl had baked a cake, scrounging the local market for suitable ersatz ingredients for the rationed items, and Ada presented him with a jumper that she had knitted herself. One arm was a little short, and the neckline was rather droopy, but he wore it all day to please her, even to the Academy. Herr Kippels gave him a fountain pen that had belonged to his father.

"He would be honored to know such a talented lad was caring for it now," he insisted with glistening eyes. He took out his handkerchief and blotted his tears.

Ján appreciated his gifts and the effort that went into them, but in his mind, he was back at his ninth birthday, celebrated with a lavish party at his home. There he had been surrounded by his sisters, his parents, and their friends, and they all marveled at the antics of a pair of camels from the Warsaw Zoo who made funny footprints in the snow. His parents loved birthdays and planned elaborate celebrations designed to impress even the most jaded of Warsaw's elites. At the time, he thought he hated being the center of attention, but he would give anything now to revisit that moment and soak in the revelry that seemed to surround his mother.

Winter yielded to a shy spring, slow to arrive. When at last the raucous blooms and sunny afternoons appeared, they were greeted with much relief as an antidote for the dreary winter doldrums. There was another concert scheduled for the academy, this time with Ján as the featured talent, and as usual, he arrived early for his rehearsal. So many of the students had been called for military service that the academy's ranks were desperately thin. Erik and Ada hoped that Ján's appearances would help them expand their children's lessons.

"It'll only be toddlers and old men left soon," grumbled Erik, and Ada bit her tongue. Her husband was openly scornful of women's contributions. Time was that Ada could sell out a big concert hall all on her own, but Erik seemed to have forgotten that. Ada was too weary to suggest a women's study program. She reserved all her dwindling strength for Ján.

Ján walked onstage and peered around the empty hall. His footsteps created a melancholy echo that amplified his tiny presence in the cavernous room. He approached the stately Bösendorfer and caressed its satiny wood finish. It was a beautiful instrument, and it reminded Ján of his mother. The first time he performed on this stage, he had done so for her. He had pushed through his grief and pounded out the notes, hoping that they could fly across the miles and sprinkle down on her in Warsaw. It had been his love note to her, her absence unthinkable to him at the time. Ján stared at the empty seats in the hall and pictured his mother, father, and sisters sitting in the front row. He closed his eyes and bowed to them, their applause all too real in his thoughts.

He seated himself on the bench—he was tall enough now to forego the cushion—and looked at the keys with their bold boundaries of black and white. No grays, no uncertainties. A melody began to play in his head, mournful yet gentle, leading to a few quick chords that captured his mother's energy and passion followed by somber rhythms that spoke to his grief and remembrance. He put his fingers on the keys and began to play, the notes spilling out into the great hall. Tears ran down his face, unchecked and raw, but the music didn't stop. It just kept flowing from his heart to his fingers, unbidden and cathartic. When it was finished, he dropped his head into his hands and sobbed freely.

A handkerchief was pushed into his fingers. Startled, Ján looked up and stared into the kind eyes of Herr Kippels.

"That was extraordinary, my boy. I've never heard anything quite like it, and I have never seen you play with such passion."

"It just came to me," Ján said. "I couldn't stop it, and I didn't want to. I needed to play."

"Yes, I can see that. It is your gift and, perhaps, your curse. You know that, ja? Can you write it down? Capture it?"

Ján nodded.

Herr Kippels ducked behind the curtain and returned with a sheaf of manuscript paper and a pencil. Ján sat on the stage and gripped the pencil, spreading the papers out before him. Then he closed his eyes and sat so still that Herr Kippels was worried that he had fallen asleep, but then Ján looked up, past the seats, the curtains, the walls. He saw instead his home in Warsaw and the faces of his family. Their images were so clear, and he could feel their presence and their love. The music came back to him. He scribbled furiously, one note after another. The pencil danced across as the pages were filled with notes and annotations. When it was complete, Ján wrote one simple word at the top, *Mama*.

Herr Kippels sat on the stage beside him and gently patted his heaving back. Exhausted, Ján battled for each breath. "You wrote that for your mother?"

"No, Herr Kippels." Ján looked directly at his teacher with a ferocity that startled the older man. "She told it to me. It came from her."

Herr Kippels nodded. "So, it did, son. So, it did." He hesitated, unsure of how much to push the boy, then he plowed ahead. "Can you play it at the concert? Can you share your mother's voice?"

Ján dropped the pencil and gathered the papers, holding the neat stack reverently. "Yes, sir. I think I must."

Herr Kippels confided in Ada what had transpired on the stage, and she was eager to hear the composition for herself. She urged Erik to join her backstage, but he not only rejected her invitation, he also scoffed at the notion of any deviation from the published program. Lurking in the shadows alone, she listened to Ján play the pieces that Erik had chosen, the ones printed in the program, and she marveled anew at the maturity and depth of his skill. Such elegance in a child so young!

Herr Kippels then put the sheet music that Ján had written in front of him. Ján reached out for it, stacked the pages neatly and set them reverently by his side. He then began to play the notes exactly as written, but straight from his heart.

Ada listened in awe as she heard her grief interpreted so lovingly back to her. As many times as she had felt an emotional response to music, she had never experienced such a deeply personal reaction to a collection of notes before. This piece not only evoked the grip of her loss, but in it, she heard her sister's voice calling out to her in comfort, and she struggled to contain her tears.

The evening of the concert, Ada noticed a change in Ján. She reckoned that it was barely perceptible to others, but to her, it was striking. He was calm and more at peace than she had seen him in months. Just before they left the house, while Erik pulled the car around to the front, Ada pressed a package in Ján's hands.

"For me?"

Ada nodded. "Open it, you'll see."

Ján carefully peeled away the colorful tissue to find a black leather book filled with pages of exquisite paper for transcribing music. His music. On the spine, an unknown craftsman had tooled Ján's initials, JAB, and the year 1940, a flawless mark of distinction.

Ada didn't wait for him to speak. "I heard, Ján. I heard the piece that you wrote for Lara. This is for the music that comes to you. You can write it down and keep it close."

Ján clutched his treasure and gave Ada a spontaneous hug as Erik impatiently blasted the horn outside.

Later in the concert hall, in his usual manner of reverence and restraint, Ján strode on stage wearing his tuxedo and looking remarkably self-possessed for his tender years. His eyes were directed at the Bösendorfer, but what he saw was his family, standing behind the piano, urging him on. He began with Mozart's Piano Concerto No. 21 and then executed pieces by Bach and Brahms with technical precision. The audience clapped and cheered as Ján stood and bowed to acknowledge their praise. Then he returned to the bench and gently laid his fingers back on the keys. A hush fell over the audience. The only sound was the rustling of programs as the patrons searched in vain for the title of this unexpected piece.

Ján spoke directly to the audience. "I wish to conclude this performance with an original composition."

Erik stood by Ada in the wings. He was shocked by the boy's provocation, and as the Maestro, he abhorred surprises. He moved to charge onto the stage, his mind racing to think of a way to end this gracefully before Ján made a fool of them all.

Ada stepped in front of him and put her hand on his chest. "Don't," she said, and by then Ján had started to execute his spellbinding piece. The composition began simply with a sorrowful tune that evoked a deep well of emotion. The rawness gave way to a gentler dirge that transitioned quickly to sprightly chords of joy and laughter. The audience was captivated, and Erik stood in the wings taking in the scene. It had been a very long time since he had been caught off guard by talent, and by God, this boy had more talent than even he had imagined.

The score was technically uneven, but that paled in comparison to the intense emotion that the arrangement of notes evoked in the listeners.

When Ján finished, the audience was once again on its feet. Ján stood and bowed low. The sounds of their applause dimmed in his head, replaced by the voice of his mother. *Well done, dearest*, he heard her say, and he allowed himself to smile.

CHAPTER 3

ADA'S SONG

Königsberg, East Prussia
January 1945

Ján emerged through the weathered door of the academy with his hand wrapped around the leather-bound journal that was tucked deep inside his coat. He and his music were constant companions, and the melodies he wrote were as necessary to his daily existence as food and shelter. They were a balm for his anxieties, particularly now that he was a thief attempting to break out of an official building. On that account, there was scant chance of retribution for him to fear. The German army was in retreat, and they had bigger worries than a boy snooping around an abandoned building. Nevertheless, Ján's heart pounded, and he moved with caution, keenly aware that danger lurked in many forms.

Snowflakes swirled in the frigid air and settled on a desolate patch of frozen mud, a sad remnant of the lush garden that had graced the entrance to the school before the war came to Königsberg. It was a city holding its breath, awaiting the invasion that was certain to come, cowering against bitter winds sharpened over arctic waters.

Ján listened for nature's syncopated rhythms, the patter of ice against spindly branches and the whistling air dancing with the few stubborn, brittle leaves. A melody formed in his head. He committed it to memory as he searched through the dense fog of his ragged breathing, hoping to spy Ada waiting for him nearby. Seeing only his own footprints, he pulled his woolen cap down to his eyebrows and resolved to head straight for home.

As he trudged back through the streets where dirty piles of well-trodden snow hid under a thin veneer of fresh whiteness, Ján tamped down his fears and looked for signs of encouragement, some little anecdote that he could share with Ada to lift her spirits, particularly since his visit to old academy buildings had been fruitless.

Searching for snippets of normalcy was a game they played to quell their worries. "Frau Weber got a letter from her son today. She thinks he must be in Africa!" or "A crowd gathered at Herr Schneider's when a rumor started that he had a clandestine radio and captured a signal from France!" Today, however, was bleak, and there was little to report. Hope was increasingly elusive, a privilege of the delusional.

A butcher lingered inside his shop, surrounded by bare shelves. Meat had long ago disappeared from kitchen tables in Königsberg. The proprietor, his white jacket smeared with the ancient stains of long-ago cutlets and roasts, glared at Ján and offered a crisp Nazi salute. Ján replied by waving his arm in an ambiguous gesture and then quickened his steps.

Next door, at Braun and Son Newsagent, a sign dangled, warped and peeling from years of exposure. Ján could remember a time when the portly Mr. Braun stood out front, tempting shoppers with sensational headlines and convincing them to splurge on a tin of coffee or a bag of sweets. That was in the days before his son had died near Stalingrad, and the old man had given up after that. Thieves, or those driven by desperation, had stripped the store bare long ago, and bombs had ripped apart the picked-over carcass.

Farther down the street, remnants of Frau Winkelmann's bakery remained with a ragged hole in the roof and the interior blackened with ashes from the fire. The shattered window still bore traces of the crudely drawn Star of David and the torn, yellow placard that warned shoppers away from the Jewish-owned business. Ján shivered, less out of cold than foreboding. The city lay gutted, exposed. Fear clung to every encounter, and those he passed on the street mirrored his own furtive movements.

The deprivations had been later in coming to Königsberg compared to other cities closer to the fighting, but the benefits of isolation couldn't last forever. The bombings of the previous summer had laid waste to many of the city's monuments and grand structures. The magnificent bridges that had defined Königsberg's grandeur were rubble, save one. Despite the government's insistence that citizens stay to defend their city or face severe reprisals, the state of general despair was such that many people were contemplating defiance and organizing means of escape. The Russians were coming, and they were close. Every day, a bit closer.

The academy had closed in '42, a victim of conflict and conscription that had robbed the city of much of its vibrant talent. Those whose gifts lay in artistic endeavors had been forced into muddy foxholes and reeking U-Boats to hold weapons with their tender hands. Its campus became a hostage of the military who stripped the performance spaces for use as grimy warehouses and cluttered offices. Now the polished wood floors and intricate moldings of a building once dedicated to creative endeavors bore the scars of a callous army in disarray.

Ján had been back only one other time when he and Ada had slipped by the guards to disperse Herr Kippels's ashes. His death was seen as just one more unremarkable loss, barely noted as an inevitable cost of war, too many nowadays to honor with funerals. Illness, the official paperwork claimed, but Ján knew better. His teacher and dear friend had been felled by grief, his weary heart broken when the soul of his city suffocated in the absence of beauty.

Uncle Erik was in the Home Guard along with all the other old men, teenaged boys, and invalids, shivering in the snow somewhere on the outskirts of the city and armed with kitchen knives, ancient hunting rifles, and rusty shovels. It was a testament to Ján's diminutive stature that he was not with his uncle. He had recently turned fourteen, the age of compulsory service, but he appeared much younger. It was a small blessing for Ada that he hadn't been conscripted. In the absence of the army, scattered in an ignominious retreat, the Home Guard was the last desperate bulwark against the Russian invasion.

Quietly nursing his umbrage over Ján's ability to evade duty, Erik had petulantly demanded several specific books to ease his discomfort at being away from home. Ada had sent Ján to search what remained of the academy for the titles, but he found no trace of his uncle's library in the weary old house. The army had stripped the building of any remnants of its past life and departed, leaving only battered metal file cabinets and cheap office furniture. The magnificent concert hall was only a treasured memory. It had been leveled the previous summer in the British bombing raids and the stately Bösendorfer had been smashed to kindling.

Daily life revolved around survival, and rituals had been reduced to their barest functions. Food, any food, was an extravagance along with shelter and warmth. All activities were in pursuit of the pared-down essentials. First Liesl and then Karl had left. There was no money to pay their wages, and there were no ties of endearment to bind them in unpaid service. They disappeared into the gray mass of Königsberg's inhabitants, all battling for a small share of the dwindling resources.

The Richters' one blessing was their home, a luxury in the

decimated city. They had burned much of the furniture for heat, and the cupboards were empty, but they had managed to stay, unlike many of the rootless refugees who wandered the streets, hungry and freezing. Each day, Ada sent Ján out on errands to queue for bread or scrounge for supplies, and he traversed streets clotted with desperation. The deep emotions that welled within him—fear, horror, sadness, revulsion—became dirges that he faithfully added to his notebook, elegies composed of notes rather than words to honor the lives lost. In the evenings, he and Ada would light a precious candle in the music room, stoke up the fire if they had fuel, and Ján would play for her.

As Ján neared the main road that separated the hollowed-out shops from the residential district, he felt the vibrations a split second before he heard the rumbling of the convoy. The grinding gears and the screeching brakes assaulted the muffled hush of the deserted marketplace, and Ján scurried into an alley to avoid being seen. He spied a tailor across the way peeking out of his door. The man motioned for Ján to join him, but it was too late. The trucks roared into view, and Ján watched the lumbering convoy take possession of the streets. Russians. They had arrived.

Ján could hardly breathe. He thought of Ada, alone in the house. As the last truck hurtled past, its canvas roof flapping in the frigid air, Ján put his hand on his coat to secure his journal and leaped out from the shadows. He took one more look at the tailor, who was frantically signaling at Ján to cross the street to safety, but the boy never hesitated. He darted onto the sidewalk and made a dash toward home. The deep snow gripped his boots and snarled his progress, so he ventured out into the middle of the street where his feet could find better purchase in the icy ruts. He slipped and fell, bloodying his hands and knees, but he righted himself and pressed on toward Ada and home.

Ada heard the rumblings and felt the tremors. When Ján burst through the door, he found her in tears, pacing the hallway. She saw the blood on his gloves and trousers and cried out, but Ján ran into her embrace and hugged her fiercely enough that she knew he was alright. "They are here," he said.

That evening, they huddled together on the music room floor, fearful of letting any light escape from the windows. Ada drew the curtains tight and mended Ján's britches and gloves by the stingy glow of smoldering coals. Ján couldn't risk the sound coming from the piano, so he hummed his new melodies to Ada as she worked.

"The concert hall is a pile of rubble, and there is nothing left of the academy. None of Uncle Erik's books. Nothing," Ján recounted.

Ada merely nodded. With Erik in danger and the Russians at their door, she couldn't move past her fear of the present to conjure memories of a treasured past.

They passed two days like this, sequestered in the music room, nibbling cold scraps and playing games to distract themselves from the cold and their hunger. On the third day, they had run out of food. Ján refused to leave Ada behind, so together, they bundled up and prepared to go out in search of anything edible. Ada scribbled a note on a piece of stationery and handed it to Ján, grasping his hand and pulling it toward her heart.

"Listen to me, Schatz. We don't know what is ahead for us, so keep this with you. There's an address on here. In Griefswald. It's Erik's sister, a sour woman, but she's family. It's all we have, and if we get separated—" She broke off at the mention of the unthinkable and turned to hide her face, fighting to control her fear. She peeked behind the drapes and surveyed the street. No sign of trucks or neighbors. They were in their own bubble with little to guide them.

Ján stuffed the paper in his pocket and secured his book under the layers of his thick coat. He was ready. Ada adjusted the belt around the waist of Erik's ample trousers, pulling the folds of fabric tight around her emaciated body, and checked her pockets for their identification papers and the useless ration coupons. They opened the front door and stepped out just as a truck rounded the corner and barreled down the street. It was a smaller transport, less thunderous than the convoys Ján had seen, but equally threatening with the insignia of the Soviet army painted on the side. Ján and Ada dashed back in the house, but they knew they had been spotted.

They hid in the music room and cowered behind the sofa, afraid even to breathe as thick boots advanced up to the stone stoop. The pounding on the door rattled their nerves, but neither moved. They stayed crouched, willing the soldiers away. They were relieved when the knocking stopped and the boots retreated down the stairs, but the respite was short-lived. The boots thundered back up, and the door crashed inward, slamming against the wall and shattering the mirror behind it. Shards of glass skittered across the dusty floor.

There were three of them, two young men and one more seasoned and grizzled. The soldiers stood inside the wreckage of the door for just a moment to get their bearings, and in the quiet of their hesitation, Ján imagined them turning back, disappointed. But the older man rubbed his chin, grinned through his rotten teeth, and motioned the other two forward. They held their guns loosely at their sides, the posture of victors, and strode into the house, bantering openly as they moved toward the kitchen. Surly and impatient, they flung open cupboards and plundered drawers.

Ada flinched each time a dish shattered on the floor. The men came for food and sport. In the absence of food, they turned to sport.

They entered the music room, throwing back the drapes and smashing several window panes with the butts of their weapons. Ján and Ada felt every assault to their sanctuary as though it were their own bodies receiving the blows. One of the young men sat down at the piano and hammered on the keys, laughing. His companion raised his pistol and took aim. Pop, pop, pop. Three shots at the magnificent Bechstein as wood and ivory exploded.

"Stop!" Ján jumped to his feet and screamed. He didn't realize what he was going to do until he was already standing, staring at the shocked faces of the three men.

They immediately pointed their guns in his direction and two shots rang out, both hitting the smooth wood paneling behind where he continued to stand, frozen with fear.

Ada pulled herself up beside him and gathered him in an embrace. "What do you want?" she asked. "It is just us, a woman and a boy. No one else."

The older man stepped forward and motioned with his weapon for them to come out. Ada and Ján walked to the middle of the room with their hands held high as the three men snickered.

The older man looked at Ján and pointed to the piano. "You—play!" he spit out in heavily accented German. Ján sat on the bench and ran his hand across the three angry holes. The instrument was irreparably damaged. The man came up behind Ján and set his bristly face right next to Ján's ear. "Play!" he screamed, and Ján hurriedly produced the semblance of a melody, pushing splinters away with his fingers.

The older man then gave his weapon to one of his companions, and he turned to Ada. Grabbing her by the waist, he began to swing her around in a crude dance, pumping his legs up and down in a frenzied display.

Ján balled his fists and screamed at the man. "Stop! You're hurting her!"

The soldier pushed Ada away and charged at Ján. "Play!" he screamed again, and one of the young men put a gun to Ján's head as the man set Ada back to spinning.

The men took turns careening Ada around the room, their movements becoming increasingly raucous and erratic. If Ján slowed the music or objected in any way, one of the soldiers would threaten him with his weapon. Ján played on. The young men pushed Ada roughly between them, making lewd jokes that sent them into spasms of laughter. When the older man regained his turn, the younger men goaded him, their taunts turning malicious. He pushed Ada roughly to the sofa and pulled at her clothes.

Ada's sobs turned to pleading, and the laughter of the men died suddenly, replaced with cruel insults. Ján stopped playing, and for a moment, the men didn't notice. They were fixated on Ada, their eyes wolflike. Ján reached for the iron poker by the fireplace and swung it at one of the younger men. The impotent punch barely landed, and the man crumpled to the floor more off balance than injured.

"Leave her alone!" Ján shouted valiantly, his voice sounding small and plaintive.

One of the men wrestled Ján to the floor and put the gun next to his head. Ada screamed, "Stop! Let him go. Please God, let him go. He's just a boy." She spat the words out and pushed back on the older man hovering over her. He responded by grabbing her hair and twisting it to the point of pain. She cried out, and the man nodded to his companion holding on to Ján.

A shot rang out, and Ján felt lightning explode in his head. The soldier pulled him up and tossed him out of the room into the hall. The door slammed after him followed by an ominous click. Ada cried out, and Ján writhed on the floor, his head roaring and blood pooling beneath him. He drew himself up unsteadily and dragged his body back to the door but it was locked.

Ada screamed again, and jeers followed, a guttural sound of evil and hatred. The shouts tangled with the ringing in Ján's head, a sickening collision of pain and terror. He leaned against the door, willing himself to move, to stand. Deep nausea welled up within him, and he retched, fighting to keep his wits about him. He finally managed to haul himself upright, lean against the wall, and put his hand to his head. He couldn't feel his ear, only a pulpy mess of skin and blood mingling with his hair.

Ada's screams had stopped, replaced with a low moaning. Ján tried to throw his fists against the door, but he lacked the strength to lodge an effective assault, and nothing would move the lock.

Shock tore at the edge of his consciousness, and he fought to stay alert. Keys. He needed keys, and he remembered that Karl had a spare set. He staggered through the dining room and into the kitchen, searching through the mayhem of shattered glass and porcelain strewn across the floor. He spied them where Karl had left them, hanging on the hook by the door to the garden.

He lurched back to the music room and tried to open the door. His hands were slippery, shaking, numb. He fingered each key as best he could but none would slip into the hole. He began to panic, his heart racing as he hurried to get to Ada. He had a key halfway into the lockset when the door suddenly swung open, pulling him back into the room. One man was holding on to the knob, and the other two sat on the rug next to Ada's motionless body. Ján ran to her as the two men stood, casually adjusted their trousers, and moved to join their comrade. Right as they reached the hallway, the older man turned, smiled at Ján, and raised his pistol.

Ján used his last ounce of strength to throw himself across Ada's body and then waited as the man snickered and holstered his weapon. Ada didn't move. She was already dead.

Ján stumbled along the highway. Fresh snow had fallen overnight, and the road was hidden under a pristine layer, untouched at this early hour. He couldn't remember how he got here; the searing pain in his head blotted out his balance and his memory. He had spent part of the night curled up next to Ada's body, warm for a while, but the cold and rigor had crept in quickly. He felt duty bound to stay close by, out of loyalty and pain, but he couldn't bear to face her glassy eyes. The splintered piano mocked him, and the house smelled of evil, the odor of the soldiers' unwashed bodies settling over the debris left in their wake.

Hours before dawn, he staggered out the front door and into

the snow, seized by an urgent need to find Erik. He had no idea where his uncle was, only that he was camped on the outskirts of town. Pushing one leaden foot ahead of the other, he hobbled down the deserted streets until he had cleared the abandoned shops and houses, heading east along the road that skirted the Pregel River.

The side of Ján's head was raw, crusted with dried blood, and the ringing in his ears throbbed unabated. He still couldn't hear in his one good ear, and he lacked any assurance of balance as he wobbled over gouges in the road. He leaned on trees when he could and stopped often to put his head in his hands, trying to quell the pain. He saw phantoms. Ada standing in the distance coaxing him on; his mother calling from deep within the trees. He was pulling himself up when the trucks roared around the bend.

"Erik," he muttered, and spasms like shards of glass shot down the side of his face when he tried to talk. He lurched out into the road and waved his hands, hoping his uncle would see him.

The lead vehicle screeched to a halt, spewing dirt and blackened slush from its massive tires. A second truck following close behind was forced into a skid to avoid a collision. They idled like powerful stallions, eager to be on their way as steam poured from under the hoods. Ján stood in the roadway, facing the pair of menacing machines and willing his uncle to appear.

Instead, it was a Russian soldier who clambered out of the lead truck, waving his weapon and shouting in words whose meaning was a mystery but whose intent was clear. He stormed up to Ján and knocked him down with the butt of his rifle. Another soldier, this one with wild red hair and a gash on his face, jumped down from the second truck and joined the fray. The two men exchanged a terse volley of Russian and then the red-headed soldier laughed. He reached down and picked Ján up, tossing him in the cargo area as though he were a bag of rubbish.

Ján hit the floor of the truck with a dull thud. His shoulder absorbed the impact before his head smacked against the rough boards. He whimpered as his wound reopened, and he brought his hands to his face to quell the roaring in his head. The convoy resumed its journey, and he lay as he was thrown, plagued by nausea and the distant but incessant staccato of rotten canvas flapping in the frigid wind.

Ten minutes or two hours later—time ceased to hold meaning—the truck bounced over a crater in the road, and Ján was thrown forward into another body, this one warm and small, a child. She was alive, but she didn't cry out. She lay against her mother who was crumpled on the floor. He pushed himself up and peered into the interior of the truck, taking stock for the first time.

Women and children in various states of injury and distress were strewn across the floor. Two soldiers also rode in the back of the truck with them, one a hulking bear-like man with a scruffy black beard and the other a thin man with angry blisters forming a seeping constellation across his face.

Other than the soldiers, Ján counted nine passengers in the truck with him, most in shock. Then he spied the girl. She sat toward the front near the cab, and she was enveloped in a huge red cape that she was attempting to spread across as many people as possible. He was mesmerized by her. She was frightened, but unbowed. She looked directly at Ján, and he noticed a steely determination in her face, an uncompromising directness that startled him. A boy lay on one side of her with his head on her lap, and a woman in torn and soiled clothes on the other. The girl reminded Ján of an illustration in a Polish book from his childhood in which Mother Earth, taking the shape of a tree, spread apart her knotty trunk to provide shelter to the children and animals in the forest.

This memory of his family brought a fresh wave of grief, and he closed his eyes as he thought of Ada lying on the floor of the house with no one to attend to her.

They rolled back into Königsberg, and Ján spied familiar sites through the holes in the canvas covering. It wasn't long before he knew where they were going: the massive train station on the southern edge of town. The towering beehive-shaped window that dominated the façade had once welcomed him with its modernist design, but today it reminded him of a monster's jaw, waiting to swallow him up.

The scene in front of the station was chaos on an unimaginable scale. Trucks were parked haphazardly along the road disgorging injured and stunned people—women, children, old men—some barely able to stand. As the convoy slowed to a halt, the soldiers on board jumped down, stepping on and over the people lying in their path and tracking through the dirt and blood that covered the floor. They began yelling for everyone to get out, but few moved. Either out of fear or injury, the collection of broken souls stayed rooted to the floor, preferring the thin illusion of safety in the back of the transport to the bedlam outside.

Ján inched toward the back and tumbled out, trying to quiet the pounding in his head. People were being herded into groups. Soldiers used threats and the butts of their weapons to empty the convoys, but the dazed and weary were slow to move. Shots rang out, and a woman fell. Then people began to rush, tripping over each other, children losing their mother's grip and being trampled in the exodus.

Ján glanced back at the girl in the red cape. She was trying to rouse the woman whose head lolled in her lap. She managed to enlist the boy, her brother perhaps, to help scoot their mother to the edge of the truck bed, but the woman, though barely conscious, was resisting. She murmured in low tones, pushing her children away, but the girl was undeterred. She locked eyes with Ján.

"Please," she said. "We need help."

He moved to the woman's side and held on tight as they pulled her down from the truck, and Ján winced when he saw the extent of her injuries. They half-dragged, half-carried her to an area near the platform where they were allowed to sit. The trucks rolled away, leaving them in a sea of damaged people clustered in groups like compliant sheep.

Women with buckets of water and baskets of bread moved solemnly among them, their faces emotionless and unreadable. They offered sips from giant, rusty ladles and pressed slices of hard bread into outstretched hands. Ján gobbled his tasteless portion. He hadn't seen food in days, but it did little to quieten the unrest in his stomach. The girl was attempting to coax her mother and brother to eat. She softened up bits of bread in her own mouth before prying open her mother's jaw and forcing bits in her mouth. *Just like a momma bird and her baby*, thought Ján. The woman gagged, and the girl gave up, offering the remainder of the thin slice to Ján and her brother. Ján accepted the extra portion.

"Let me see your ear," she said. He slowly turned his neck, and was ashamed when she gasped.

"Does it hurt?" she asked.

He nodded. The question was absurd but kind. She cared and that was something.

She reached under her skirt and tore a long strip from the bottom of her petticoat. She took care with wrapping it around his head. It didn't alleviate the pain, but it helped cover the wound and provided a meager measure of warmth to his head.

"That will keep it from getting dirtier at least. What is your name?"

He cast his eyes down, unwilling to answer her. His name, spoken aloud or whispered furtively, would anchor him to terrible place, and he wanted only to run away, escape this nightmare, and return to Ada and the music room. He would try again to summon Erik. The girl continued to stare at him, and he ignored her. Hugging his treasured book to his chest, he gobbled the remaining piece of the gifted bread and hoped that the girl would forget about him.

A shrill whistle sent a ripple through the crowd as a train roared into view and stopped next to the platform. It hovered on the track like a wily predator stalking its prey, and Ján wondered how he could ever have been excited at the prospect of boarding such a malevolent machine. Of course, the last time he rode on a train, it was in a first-class carriage, a far cry from the demon of iron and steel hissing in front of him now. These were cattle cars, crude boxes fashioned of wood siding and iron nails. No glossy window for the view or padded seats for a nap. No servants whisking luggage away or placing tins of apple cake in his seat. Soldiers moved through the crowd prodding people to their feet with the butts of their weapons.

"Make a line!" someone ordered in heavily accented German. "You will be taken away from the front lines to safety. Stay together, and board quickly!"

Ján searched frantically for his escape route. As people began moving in the direction of the tracks, he pictured himself disappearing into the masses, gliding stealthily backwards toward freedom, away from this teeming pit of misery. Shots rang out inciting panic in the traumatized throng. Fear seized them, and like a stampede of spooked animals, they set on each other, pushing and shoving. The weakest among them fell as the strongest trampled over them. Ján froze, unable to separate himself from the mob that swept him forward, his thoughts disconnected from his feet.

The girl was protecting her brother and mother, entreating them to move away from the madness, speaking firmly but with a tenderness that drew Ján back from brink of his fear. She caught his eye, challenging him, and he noted her resolve. It was as if she were reading his mind, and he latched on to her strength. They both knew that this train was not taking them to safety, yet they had no choice but to press forward.

He fell in beside her, helping to ease her mother along while keeping an eye on the wide-eyed little boy teetering on the verge of shock. They scrambled into the cattle car and clung together as others jostled their way in behind. Ján helped the girl steer her mother to a spot along the wall next to the door. Bloodied and bruised, she collapsed onto the rough wooden floor, and the boy snuggled in beside her.

Ján and the girl stood on either side, guarding their group and serving as a buffer against the crush of people pushing their way in at gunpoint. The stench of desperation and fear pervaded the crude box. Ján pressed his nose up against the cracks in the wall to draw in fresher air.

People jockeyed for space as the car filled. They pushed up against those around them as more souls were herded in behind. It was so crowded that no one could fall. They all stood or leaned against each other as the giant door was slammed shut, plunging them into darkness as the train shuddered underfoot. After a terrifying delay, it lurched forward and gathered speed as a hush fell over the crowd, a combination of hopelessness, injury, and fatigue. A baby whimpered weakly, and several people began coughing, but the silence of despair was taking over.

Shivering and achy, Ján eased himself down to the floor and scrunched up against the wall of the car with his knees pulled tight to his chin. Dirty bits of straw were scattered about between the crush of bodies. As the train settled into a rhythm, Ján's ear throbbed, and his fiery joints rebelled against any movement. Clackety, clackety, clackety, the vibrations of the rails created a pernicious rhythm, and the sound turned into a cacophony of discordant and disturbing notes. He buried his head in his hands, willing the frightening melody to stop.

The girl screamed, and Ján was jolted alert. Her mother's head lolled on his shoulder, eyes lifeless, her body slumped. The heat of her fever began to dissipate in death's grip. The girl shoved against those around her and tried to pull her mother back up, beating on her and anyone else who tried to help. She thrashed and screamed until the boy cried out. Then she sat back, breathing raggedly while she searched for her brother's face.

"Otto!" she called as she grasped at sleeves, trousers, arms, legs, seeking his familiar face. When he reached out, they leaned into each other in grief, cradling their mother's lifeless body between them. Ján turned his head to distance their sorrow from his pain. The melody building inside him wouldn't go away, a haunting loop in his fevered mind.

Clackety, clackety, clackety. Cries in the car erupted periodically over the din as death reached in to claim the weakest and most injured. Cold air and the last remnants of daylight poured in through cracks to numb the living into a defeated complacency. Ján pitched forward, trying to ignore the pricks in his legs and the searing aches in his joints. He felt an insistent tap on his shoulder and looked up to see the girl holding out a sweater. She pushed it toward him, and he accepted it gratefully, confused at this sudden appearance of warmth and kindness. She had regained the determined fire in her eyes, her grief overruled by desperation.

The sweater was meant for a man, way too big for Ján, but that was a consideration for a different time. He pulled it on over his coat, ignoring the protests in his limbs and checking as always that his book was secure under this new layer of warmth. The boy similarly pulled a sweater on as the girl rifled through a curious bag full of odds and ends.

What was she doing? She tugged at her mother's body and removed stockings and jewelry, wrapping them around her own body. He watched as she wiggled herself upright, using her hands to feel around the door to the train. By now, her movements attracted the attention of the other passengers, and Ján was certain that she was losing her mind, succumbing to hysteria. Some swiveled to watch her, and others called for her to stop. She ignored them and turned to Ján. Through the darkness in the fetid car, he could feel the intensity of her eyes on him.

"We can jump out," she said, her words hurled at him, urgent and provocative. "There is snow along the banks, and if we can jump far enough out and away from the train, we can get away."

Ján felt a smidgeon of hope. She wasn't crazy; she was making a plan. He helped her pull Otto to his feet and leaned in attentively as she explained her idea.

"They didn't lock the door," she said. "Do you understand? We can push it open and jump out."

Ján nodded; the sharp pain returned but he pushed it down. He was tasting freedom.

She reached for Ján's hands and gripped with more strength than Ján would have credited to her thin frame. Together, they put their shoulders to the rough boards. It moved only a few inches, weighted down by the bodies leaning against it. She put her shoulder to it again and grunted as she pushed with all her might. The door lurched a bit more, knocking her off balance and drawing in the assistance of others who clawed and pushed it farther along on its track. A narrow gap opened, and cold air rushed in. Those standing nearest grumbled as they hurried to cover their faces. Others eagerly leaned forward because, for the first time since leaving the station, they could see where they were. The sun was setting over a dense forest where bare branches whizzed by in a blur of spindly grays, blacks, and browns. Thick piles of coal-stained snow were heaped along the tracks, blue shadows reflecting traces of dying light. Menacing scavenger birds patrolled overhead.

The girl didn't hesitate, wedging herself through the small space. She turned to face Ján and Otto and with her right hand, she grasped the handle inside to steady herself and allowed herself a hopeful smile. Ján positioned himself behind Otto, waiting until she jumped so he could get her brother to the door quickly.

Suddenly, the train lurched around a sharp bend. People spilled onto each other, crying out. The momentum caused the door to slam shut. Ján was knocked aside by the woman next to him, and Otto was tipped across the body of his mother.

"Her hand! Help!" someone cried, and Ján noticed that three of the girl's fingers were trapped between the door and the siding of the car. Arms reached out and clawed as the train continued to careen around the curve, pulling them away from the girl's trapped hand. Feet slipped on the filthy slime covering the floorboards.

Ján fought to put his shoulder to the door but he didn't have the strength to push through the people who had fallen in front of him. The train rounded out of the curve and everyone fell back in the opposite direction. The door slipped slightly, and the girl's fingers fell away as she dropped. They steeled themselves for the jolt of running over her body, but felt nothing. The train barreled onto a bridge crossing high over a river. Ján sank to the floor as Otto screamed.

Chapter 4

Song of Monsters

Deep inside the Soviet Union
January 1945

In Ján's feverish dreams, he was at home. He was standing in his garden in Warsaw where the sloping lawn smelling of freshly-cut grass was bordered by plants bursting with spring blooms. An imposing fountain splashed with tumbling streams accompanied by a twittering chorus of playful songbirds. His sisters reclined under the shade of the big willow tree that dipped its curtain of leaves down to the stately reflecting pool while his father sat on the large terrace smoking a pipe. His mother and Ada, reclining on the upholstered swing, tilted their heads together and laughed, beckoning to Ján. "Join us dearest!" they called in their matching, lyrical voices. He wanted to go to them, but he couldn't move. As they urged him on with smiles and winks, his leaden legs held fast to the stones, and the fountain grew louder and more insistent, drowning out their entreaties. Splish, splosh, splish, splosh, clackety, clackety, clackety, louder and louder until Ján was jolted awake. Verdant landscapes were replaced by the sooty walls of the cattle car, and birdsong became the moans of passengers clinging to life.

The train charged forward in Stygian darkness carrying within it the scent of death and the fear of living. How long had they been sealed up in this dungeon? Hours? Days? Ján vaguely remembered a stop when the soldiers came in, scarves covering their faces against the stench and guns held aloft, as if any of the passengers might summon the strength to fight back. They carted out some of the dead, threw scraps of bread about, and locked the door on their way out. They had missed Otto's mother. She lay as she died, propped against the wall of the car with vacant eyes. Otto leaned over her, shielding her from the soldiers, and Ján was pressed into her other side, cold and unyielding. The soldiers had passed right over them.

The pain persisted in Ján's head, daggers and fire attacking him under his skin. His wound seeped through the makeshift bandage, and he drifted in and out of consciousness. The dreams were his salve, for in this respite, his family would appear. They stood before him as he remembered them, yet he was older and more afraid. They reached out and called for him. He yearned for their outstretched hands and broad smiles, but he was rooted to the rotten boards of the train, chugging along this desperate corridor.

In brief moments of lucidity, Ján was mindful of the boy Otto who, in the short time that Ján had known him, had lost his mother and his sister. Ján felt a tug on his sleeve and rolled his head slowly to find Otto sitting up, staring at him with tear-swollen eyes.

"Do you have family?" he asked, and Ján said no. It was all he could muster and all he had to say. He had nothing and no one. By now Erik had probably found Ada's body, and Ján wondered if his uncle was worried about him. More likely happy that he was gone. No, he had no one. Ján reached out his hand, and Otto clasped it.

"You're very hot."

"Yes, but I am here." Ján shivered as he fought to sit upright. "I am here, and we are here together. We will be family now."

Thirst kept him awake, a raw lust for water. His tongue was swelling, and his joints screamed. Every movement of the car, every curve they rounded, and every switch they encountered brought on fresh waves of torment. When the train slowed and rocked over a convergence of tracks, Ján wept in half-conscious misery.

His mother spoke to him. *Water, my sweet boy, the snow outside is water.*

"Mama," he cried.

Get some water, my boy.

The train screeched to a halt, the whistle cutting through the air like a knife stabbing at Ján's one good ear. A pair of weak hands pulled him to his feet and propelled him forward. He felt the big door rattle followed by a rush of cold wind, and when he leaned toward the fresh air, he fell onto a platform. Others ventured out of the train, timidly picking their way over and around him. Although it was in the dead of night, the lights on the platform burned their eyes, and they held their hands over their faces as soldiers yelled at them to get in line.

Now rough hands, strong and well-fed, pulled Ján to his feet and thrust him into the flow of people moving in haphazard clusters. "*Schnell*! Quickly!" the soldiers screamed in thickly accented German. Ján was sandwiched, driven forward with the movement of the crowd. His feet sometimes took a step, but mostly, he was dragged along. Then they stopped. He wobbled on feverish legs and reached his hand out to find something to lean on. There was nothing except other people, a line of freezing, terrified souls, barely alive.

Otto. The image of the boy flashed in Ján's head, and he panicked. Where was Otto? Did he leave the train too? Ján couldn't remember, couldn't recall what happened. He turned to go back, but another whistle rang out, and the entire mob of half-starved souls around him began to plod forward. One step after another off the platform and into the woods nearby, Ján was carried along, powerless to resist. He tried to call out, but no sound emerged. Otto was lost.

Ján had made it deep into the woods and far away from the chaos of the station when his legs gave out. The serpentine line of people had begun to spread out as they numbly followed the soldiers' instructions and marched forward. They stopped briefly for their captors to walk up and down the column, taunt the captives, and push them into formation. Alone and consumed with fever, Ján saw brilliant flashes of light before he keeled over, his head meeting the snow with barely a thud. He heard shouting and felt a boot to his stomach. A loud pop and the ground exploded around him. Then it was quiet.

The snow is water, my dear boy. The snow is water.

Just as the sun broke free of the horizon and tinted the sky with a muted wash of pinks and oranges, a man and a woman plodded on the path alongside a cart pulled by a sullen mule. It was early and the earth teetered at the delicate point where day and night danced, one ascendant and the other fading. The man and woman thought only of the task at hand. They were neither poets nor dreamers and aspired only to pass one day at a time. Despite the charms of this magic hour, they shuffled along with their eyes downcast. The ice under their feet held fast to the deep blues of moon shadows and crunched to the rhythms of the squeaky wagon wheel and the mule's occasion snort.

"For once it is not snowing," he remarked.

"Just wait," she replied. "It will start again."

The pair bantered amiably despite the bitter cold and the grim nature of their work. This was their daily chore, unpleasant but a job nonetheless.

It must have been a difficult night, the woman observed. Yes, the man agreed. Two bodies already and they had barely left the station. As they were paid per head, this was promising to be a lucrative day. They picked up the frozen corpse of a woman, still clutching a delicately embroidered handkerchief, and laid her in the cart on top of the two bodies already lumped there. The man pried the handkerchief out of the woman's hand and examined the workmanship. He noticed two spots of blood and tutted in disapproval. A shame to mar such delicate stitches. He handed it to the woman who stuffed it into the deep pockets of her oversized coat.

Ján felt their rough hands pull at his torso. They picked him up and tossed him in the cart. When he fell against the frozen body of the woman, he grunted and moaned.

"What's that now?" the man asked.

"Appears he's not dead, that's what," the woman replied as she hauled herself up on the back of the cart and turned Ján over. "He's breathing, not much, but he's still alive," she offered, unsure of how to proceed. They had always been dead before. She'd never found one still alive.

The mule pawed at the ground impatiently as the man moved to the back of the cart. He poked at Ján's feet as the woman felt the front of his oversized sweater. She reached through the layers of clothing and pulled out Ján's composition book.

Ján's hand lifted, weak but determined, and his fingers closed around the journal. His eyes fluttered open and then shut once again, but his hand stayed wrapped around his cherished collection of music. The woman called the man over, and he struggled to discern the features of the book through his rheumy eyes.

"Saints among us!" she exclaimed and pointed to the bullet lodged in the soggy leather cover. She quickly made the sign of a cross over her chest. Something was protecting this boy, and she was loath to run afoul of such powerful forces. They bickered briefly about what to do. Toss him back in the snow? Take him to the prison where he had been heading?

The man was adamant. They would push him to one side and continue collecting bodies. He might die yet, and they needed the money he would bring them. If he did have a guardian angel and was still alive when they reached their destination, they would turn the boy over to the authorities. The woman conceded the point but insisted on making a dedicated space at the front of the cart to shield him. She wasn't going to provoke whatever forces were fond of this lad. They pushed him off to the side and covered him with coats and sweaters taken from the truly dead. In this way, Ján made the journey slightly north and away from the line of damaged souls and the gulag that had been waiting to receive him.

Wake up, sweet boy. Ján heard his mother and wanted desperately to see her. Everything was gray and fuzzy, and a strange tinny echo lay underneath her voice. Hands gently prodded him, and a sharp pain split his head. *Wake up, sweet boy*, he heard again as he fought against his slippery consciousness to bring her face into focus.

The woman leaning over him was not his mother, and she was not entreating him to wake up. She was winding a bandage around his head with practiced efficiency while a younger man stood by and watched. Ján reached reflexively for his book, but the spot next to his heart was empty. He began to flail about, calling for help. He needed his book.

The woman tried to calm him with brisk but kind words.

The man reached under the bed. Ján opened his eyes to see his journal held over his face by the soft fingers of one who works with his brain and not his hands. The man, wearing an expression of amused curiosity, was clad in a smart jacket and had a stethoscope looped around his neck.

Ján couldn't understand a word of what either of these people said. He clutched at his journal and cradled it to his chest. It was waterlogged and featured a hole in the leather cover, but it was his, and he needed to hold it.

The man spoke slowly and Ján stared at him. His voice was bland, and he seemed to pose no threat, but he spoke neither Polish nor German, the two languages Ján knew.

"My name is Ján Balik," he whispered in German, hoping that this man would know how to respond.

"Ján?"

He nodded slowly, the pain throbbing anew.

The man pointed to himself and replied in rough German, "I am Dr. Dobrow. You are in a hospital in the Soviet Union. You will get better."

Dr. Dobrow and hospital. Ján understood that much. He wanted to ask him about Otto and the train, but the words wouldn't come. The room began to spin, and he closed his eyes to quell the nausea. When he opened them again. Dr. Dobrow and the nurse were gone.

Ján remained in the hospital for two more weeks. The beds around him were occupied by a rotating cast of various ailments whose hosts seemed to arrive and then disappear with disconcerting regularity, either walking on their own or being rolled out under a sheet. There were few visitors, and no one took any particular interest in him. He observed this new world from the horizontal perspective of his thin cot, attempting to glean as much information as possible from the few clues that wafted into his peripheral vision.

The only constant was the nurse, an efficient woman who smelled of carbolic and cabbage and who seemed to regard Ján's injuries as a personal affront to her war on germs. She bathed him, delivered meals, and changed his bandages without making eye contact or tempering her permanent scowl. Ján's condition slowly improved under her relentless care. The frostbite on his cheeks where he had lain in the snow began to heal, and the carnage around his ear reassembled itself into a bundle of gnarled scar tissue.

His journal slowly dried, and he took great care to dislodge the bullet, smooth out the buckled leather cover, and separate each page. The hole that remained was bored deep into Ján's collection of melodies. The bullet had skewered his first composition, the one inspired by his mother, traveled right through the heart of his tribute to Herr Kippels, and halted at the études prompted by his walks through Königsberg under siege.

New haunting melodies returned to Ján when he thought of Ada and Otto, pieces he imagined in minor keys with jarring discordant notes to invoke the horror and despair. They were still too painful to revisit and he vowed never to write them down, but they returned over and over in his dreams. He knew he would have to surrender and capture them one day. A song for the girl, Otto's sister, emerged. This one started with dissonant notes but persisted in yielding to something less caustic, more hopeful. Perhaps she survived her fall? He would never know.

A fortnight after his arrival, Ján awoke to find a woman standing by his bed, talking in low, clipped tones to Dr. Dobrow. The nurse lurked impatiently in the background. The woman's black dress featured an insignia, and she carried a sheaf of papers with her. She was thin and tall, all angles and bones, and she wore a pair of oddly square pince nez, balanced low on her nose. She leaned over Ján and peered under the bandages around his head, frowning at the sight of his mangled ear. She opened his mouth and examined his teeth, nodding more approvingly at his general well-being from that angle. She and the doctor exchanged a quick volley of conversation before she walked away. Ján could hear the clack of her heels against the hard concrete floor long after she had left his field of vision.

"Mrs. Kotova will be coming back to fetch you tomorrow," he said. "She will take you to your new home."

Ján was left alone to ponder what that new home with Mrs. Kotova might be.

The journey proved to be a long ride of uncertainty. The No. 15 Special Home for Children was a considerable distance from the hospital, but Ján knew nothing of their destination when Mrs. Kotova whisked him away from the hospital. He sat on the cold, stiff seat of cracked leather, shivering in the unheated car. He was back to wearing the clothes from his journey out of Königsberg. He had brought nothing else with him and nothing was given. His jacket now featured a ragged hole from the bullet and was woefully inadequate for the frigid Russian winter even with the addition of the sweater that the girl had gifted him on the train. None of the items had been washed but at least they had dried during his convalescence. His journal was tucked under all the layers, which even bundled over his thin frame were insufficient to ward off the icy air whistling through the car windows. He watched Mrs. Kotova and the driver, whose name Ján surmised was Dmitri. Both had woolen blankets draped across their legs, and Mrs. Kotova was cocooned in a thick fur coat. They said little to each other and nothing to Ján.

He observed the puffs of vapor from their silent, frozen breaths and noticed they fell into a pattern. Dmitri's were quick and shallow, and Ján wondered if he was nervous. Mrs. Kotova's were slower, deeper, more controlled. The pattern made Ján mindful of Herr Kippels' metronome, and a plainchant came to mind, repetitive hints of contrasting notes. He tried tamping down those thoughts. The days of music for him were gone. Survival was everything. Artistry was frivolous. He felt a sharp pang of sorrow as he remembered his mother's pride in his destiny. There was no room for joy in this bleak and forbidding place.

He turned his gaze to the passing countryside and endeavored to summon more comforting thoughts, but the icebound landscape offered no respite. They drove through villages where stooped men pushing carts hustled off the mud-stained icy roads to avoid the speeding sedan, and they motored past white-blanketed fields and pastures, dormant during the winter months. Snow and ice, punctuated by coal dust and dirt, stretched across every vista and crunched under the speeding tires. At length, they came to the outskirts of a larger settlement dominated by a factory belching smoke accompanied by a busy railway station with a labyrinth of tracks surrounding the shunting yards.

Dmitri made a left turn, and the sedan began climbing a hill. After they crested the rise, they drove through a stone entrance, and just below lay a chapel, long abandoned and surrounded by a series of imposing yet deserted buildings, each fashioned as architectural companions to the church. A statue of a priest peered down over the chapel door and presided over the courtyard, the craggy man's hands forever frozen in a gesture of blind supplication and his face worn down by time and the elements to an expression of benign indifference. As the sedan roared past, Ján examined buildings for signs of life. Seeing only vacant windows, he shuddered to think of the ghosts within those ancient walls.

At the end of the lane, the car approached a cluster of more recent structures. What they gained on their surroundings in youth, they lacked in charm. Ján saw what appeared to be an administrative structure, a former house perhaps, flanked by low rectangular outbuildings, each featuring windows high along the walls and covered in bars. Ján struggled to make sense of the arrangement. Were these for livestock? A puzzle since no other living creatures, human or otherwise, seemed to be on the premises.

The sedan stopped in front of the main building, and Mrs. Kotova addressed Ján for the first time since they'd left the hospital. She motioned him out of the car, and her intent was clear. He was to follow her inside. He climbed out of the car with achy limbs and a full bladder. They had not offered him the opportunity to eat or relieve himself on the long ride.

They walked into a central reception area where two women

sat up at attention and greeted Mrs. Kotova. She ignored them and led Ján into a small, charmless office where she took off her hat and coat and adjusted her glasses before sitting wearily in a chair behind a metal desk. Ján noticed that she was younger than he had thought, but any assets of her youth were clouded by a churlish demeanor. On the wall behind her desk hung a large poster of Stalin dressed in white and surrounded by fresh-faced children. The edges of the paper were curled, and there was a large brown water stain covering most of the top, but Stalin's face beamed through signs of wear with tenderness toward the adoring children. She motioned Ján to a chair opposite her own.

"Sit and answer my questions. Nothing more, nothing less," she commanded in impeccable German.

"Name?"

"Ján Balik."

"Age?"

"Fifteen."

"You are too small. You do not tell me the truth. What is your age?"

"I am fifteen. I was born on January 1, 1930."

Mrs. Kotova sighed in exasperation. "If you do not tell me the truth, you will be punished. Where were you born?"

"Warsaw. In Poland."

"What happened to your ear?"

Ján lifted his chin and looked directly at her. "It was shot off by Soviet soldiers."

She glanced down at the papers in front of her and scribbled a note. "And will this cause problems for us here?"

"No."

The interview proceeded in staccato fashion until Mrs. Kotova had documented the required details of Ján's young life. He didn't trust her, and although he answered all her questions truthfully, he was grateful he didn't have to reveal details. He was a Polish refugee from Königsberg, and his injuries occurred there. That's all he shared. Mrs. Kotova was not interested in his parents or his pedigree. She set down her pen and stared at him with an unsettlingly direct gaze. "Do you know where you are?"

"Only that I am in the Soviet Union." Ján attempted to project defiance; in truth, he was confused and terrified.

"Yes, you are, and you will remain here. This is a home for waifs and misfits such as yourself. It is known as a *detdom*. Do you understand?" Ján understood it was a rhetorical question and simply nodded as she continued. "It is here at the No. 15 Home that we rehabilitate deviant children, those who do not know how to function in a modern society such as ours. You wouldn't be here if you weren't somehow a conniving little vagrant," she said, "and while your injury has spared you the work camp, you will be expected to behave yourself here and earn your keep if you stand a chance of leaving as a productive member of society. Do I make myself clear?"

Ján nodded and continued to hold his tongue. The realities of the interview threatened to overwhelm him, and he feared that he would burst into tears any minute, yet he was determined not to cry in front of this woman. He would find a way out. Surely there was a way out of this place.

Ján cried precisely one time while at the *detdom*. His mother's voice had come to him again in a dream, and he woke up sobbing. The boys who shared his mattress in the room full of bigger boys hauled him up and dragged him to the toilet where they held his head under the rank, frigid water and laughed at his misery.

He never heard his mother's voice there again. That was the way of this place. Weakness was the original sin and had to be avoided at all costs. There was a feral quality to life at the No. 15 Special Home. Despite a semblance of rules—boys slept in communal rooms on the left, girls on the right—the children were largely left to their own devices unless one or more of them upset the workings of the adults who were nominally in charge. Then there was hell to pay.

Official reports extolled the virtue of education and emphasized the children's attendance at the local school, but there was no transportation and many of the children lacked the clothing for participation. Instead, in a nod to the redemptive role of labor, the children were assigned chores and farmed out as free workers to the surrounding community. Clad only in the thin and threadbare garments, they shoveled snow, hauled coal, and collected precious metal shavings at the armaments factory in town.

At the home, they were responsible for tidying up their quarters and cleaning after meals, but the sleeping spaces were cramped rooms with barred windows high in the walls. The only furniture was a collection of filthy mattresses strewn about. No linens, few blankets. As for meals, Ján observed trucks entering the yard. Crates of cabbages and bags of flour were carried into the main building with astonishing punctuality, yet the small fleet of vehicles assigned to the home also left fully laden with corresponding regularity. At each meal, one or two a day, the children were served a lukewarm paste of porridge or a thin turnip soup. Ján learned that there was an official schedule for assigning the children to kitchen duty and general garden maintenance but the reality was that with little equipment or supervision, the benefit of labor remained a virtue extolled if not exercised. The children were hungry and cold, and most, like Ján, were victims of great unacknowledged trauma.

If weakness was the crime, then strength, brute strength, became the prize. Bigger boys regularly pummeled the smaller boys. The smaller boys took their revenge out on the girls. The youngest and weakest spent the days cowering in the corner, trying desperately to evade a thrashing. Ján had never learned to fight, but thanks to Erik's relentless emphasis on calisthenics, he was stronger and sturdier than his size might imply. After his initial dunking in the commode, he took to arming himself with a long rusty nail he found on the grounds, and at least he was left alone most of the time. Thanks to the train girl's enormous sweater, none of the boys knew about his extra jacket layer underneath, which provided a meager measure of warmth and a buffer against the occasional stomach punch.

Thus, Ján spent the remaining days of that winter plotting his escape. At first, he had to stay close to his assigned building. There were four others just like it huddled together in the shadow of the main house, all packed with children aged anywhere from toddler to adolescent. Ján visited each building and found the same conditions, children sitting listlessly on their mattresses, some playing improvised games, others spoiling for a fight.

During a brief unseasonable thaw, the road that seemed to stop in front of the complex revealed intriguing possibilities. Ján discovered that what appeared to be a terminus was, in fact, merely a bank of dirty snow. As it melted, he could see that the road narrowed to a small lane and continued on past the structures, curving around a thick copse of fir trees. Ján made a mental note to explore it.

For now, he was busy making himself indispensable in the main house. Most children avoided their keepers, often with good reason, but Ján had long experience with adults, and he preferred their company. While the adults were generally up to no good, there was a thin veneer of civilized behavior that was missing in the squalid quarters where the children acted like wild, trapped animals.

At first the collection of secretaries, cooks, and handymen shooed him away, physically pushing him to the door and slamming it behind him, but he persevered and soon discovered that the ladies in the reception area found him useful to avoid doing their work. He couldn't speak Russian, and they assumed he was younger than he was, so they figured that he was likely to ignore any incriminating conversations they might have. They viewed him as something of a pet and began giving him small tasks that kept him dawdling in their vicinity.

Ján soon picked up enough Russian to understand a few conversations, and he gradually became invisible to the few adults who strode in and out of the building. Mrs. Kotova was the exception. She was to be avoided at all costs. One particularly frigid day, she found him helping the secretaries. As punishment, she ordered Dmitri to drag him outside and tie him to a stake near a small outhouse where he remained for hours. He was rescued by one of the ladies who worked in the kitchen. Lesson learned.

Spring arrived cloaked in mud and dusted with coal ash. The warmer temperatures lured the children outside where they improvised simple games to pass the time between occasional chores. Ján ignored the scrum of shifty boys circling around a wide-eyed newcomer and ventured around to the back of the main house. This was the best vantage point from which to spy on the road that led from the house to whatever was beyond the cluster of fir trees. A line of smoke in the near distance spooled in the air over the treetops, and the mud held a fresh set of tire tracks. Ján leaned against the wall outside the kitchen in the area that he knew to be a blind spot from the steamy window. From there he watched and plotted a foray down the lane. One day he would set off without turning back.

Vera, a scrappy girl who was just a bit younger than Ján, sauntered over to join him. Ján ignored her.

Undeterred, Vera scooted close and nudged him with her shoulder. "One of the workers dropped this on her way out yesterday," she said as she pulled out a small tin containing a pack of matches, tobacco, and rolling papers. Vera expertly assembled a cigarette and struck the match. She passed it to Ján who inhaled deeply before doubling over in a fit of coughing.

Vera laughed and patted his back. "You never smoked before? Try again."

Ján managed a long drag, then he attempted a sophisticated exhale and ended up in a spasm that left him gasping. He tried to recover a sliver of dignity with distraction.

"Where does that road go?" he asked, pointing down the lane with the cigarette.

Vera shook her head. "Nowhere special, I think. Trucks head back there every now and then, but nothing else. I guess it's where they burn trash. I'd stay away, if I were you. Mrs. Kotova would have your hide if she found you back there." She reached for the cigarette and put it to her mouth. She closed her eyes and took a deep draw before blowing out little smoke rings.

Ján was so mesmerized by Vera's sophistication that he didn't notice when a window opened behind them. One of the kitchen workers, a man with a grim scar on his face, stuck out his head. "Get away. You hear me? Go away before I come out there and thrash you!"

Ján pushed away from the wall and turned to say goodbye.

Vera chuckled. "You're not leaving, are you? That's Ivan. I heard he was taken prisoner during the war. He yells a lot, but it's all talk and no action."

Ján was torn between his desire to avoid trouble and his sudden interest in Vera. "How long have you been here?" he asked.

Vera stared down at her toes for a few minutes before answering. "Long enough. This is at least my third winter. My brother and I were brought here when my parents were arrested."

"Arrested?"

"I don't remember too much. My mother is in the gulag near Kaluga. I don't know anything about my father."

"Which one is your brother?" Ján couldn't remember ever seeing Vera with another child.

"I'll answer that if you tell me what happened to your ear."

Ján pushed away from the wall and started to walk away.

Vera stubbed out her cigarette on the mud-flecked toe of her boot. "Wait!" she said.

Ján paused but kept his back to her.

She carefully stored the remnants of her cigarette in the tin and stuck her hands in her pockets. "I'm pretty sure my brother died not long after we got here. We were separated. Dima was a sweet boy, but he was simple, you know?"

Ján didn't know. "Simple how?"

"My mother used to say that Dima was soft in the head, that he would always be a little boy." Vera shrugged. "I don't remember much more than that. Some woman told me that he had gotten adopted out. She said it was for the better."

"Did you see him?" Ján asked.

Vera stared at Ján, trying to decide if he was making fun of her. "Well, no. No one asked me to or told me I could."

"Then how do you know? That he is dead, I mean. Maybe he really did get adopted or something."

"Who, Dima? Nah. Nobody wants kids like Dima. He's dead, and I'm still here."

The window behind them flew open again, but this time, a rush of scalding water hit the tops of their heads.

On a day when the snow mixed with ice and rain in a battle between a recalcitrant winter and a determined spring, Ján sought refuge in the main house. He had observed Mrs. Kotova climbing into the back seat of her car with Dmitri at the wheel, and they had driven out of the complex toward town. Ján seized the chance to escape the cold, leaky barracks.

He found the housekeeper curled on the floor with a mop and a bucket by her side. A morose woman, she had been drinking heavily all morning. She spied Ján and pointed toward the stairs before nodding off. Ján hauled the supplies up the steps and set to work finishing her chores only to hear car tires crunching over gravel outside. At the No. 15 Special Home for Children, the sound of Mrs. Kotova's car evoked the same terror as the roar of a lion or the howl of a wolf.

He abandoned the bucket and slipped inside a closet, pulling the door shut. He would not risk discovery. He crouched low, too fearful even to breathe, and was relieved to hear a deep voice. He pressed his good ear to the thin floorboards where he could pick up bits and pieces of the conversation.

A man had arrived and was demanding to speak with Mrs. Kotova, something about a visit from Moscow and missing paperwork.

Nina, the younger of the two women in the office, tried to stall the impatient man, but he screamed, reducing her to tears. The man was a bully, but he was unlikely to care about Ján's whereabouts. Best to slip out and return another day.

Ján tried to twist the latch, but the door was jammed. He pushed and pulled on the rickety knob, but the door wouldn't yield. Memories of the train raced back, and he felt the claustrophobic grip of the car filled with stench and despair. He had to get out. He clawed at the door until his fingers were raw, but it remained resolutely stuck. Breathing heavily, he slumped to the floor and felt around for a tool he could use to pry his way out. He was in a long, thin storage area surrounded on both walls by floor-to-ceiling shelves, and as his eyes adjusted to the dusky interior, he spied a single light bulb hanging from a thin line over a collection of boxes. Ján teetered on an overturned crate and grasped the cord. One good tug, and the bulb buzzed on, casting a harsh, sulphureous glow in the narrow space.

Ján pulled down the box closest to him and lifted the lid. Inside were neat rows of files, each with a child's picture affixed to the front. He opened the first file. "Rosina Smetova" was written on the label. The picture showed a rosy-cheeked toddler with pudgy arms and huge dimples beside her smile. Her hair was festooned with a large ribbon, and she wore a lovingly embroidered dress. The rest of the paperwork was indecipherable, apparently a collection of official notes and letters. Ján looked at the last page where there was another picture, this time of a girl, gangly and emaciated. She lay on the floor with bulging eyes and a protruding belly. It was hard to tell if it was the same girl whose picture Ján had just admired. Stamped underneath in bold black ink was *Умер в апреле 1945 г.* Ján recognized the word "*Умер.*" He had seen Nina write it out last week on a report about the rabid dog that had been shot on the property. She told him then that it meant "death." Ján's heart began to race, and he put the folder back in the box and snapped the lid shut. *Please God no,* he thought.

He could hear the argument escalating downstairs between Nina and the man from Moscow. Katrine, the elder of the two women, had now joined in, and the three were having a loud debate. Ján pulled out more boxes. The files took on a pattern, a photograph of a healthy child followed by what appeared to be evidence of an illness. In the last few boxes, the pictures on the front showed children with physical or cognitive anomalies, some mild and others profound. He thought of Dima. Was his picture on any of these files? He leaned his head against the door and tried to calm his breathing.

When he heard the arrival of a second car followed by the unmistakable sound of Mrs. Kotova's footsteps, he leapt to his feet. This was not where he wanted to be found. Better to admit to helping the housekeeper and suffer the consequences than to answer to his discovery of these files. He tried the door again, but it still wouldn't budge. Seeking a good hiding place between the shelves, he switched off the light and ventured deep into the closet, using his hands to help guide him in the dark. He discovered a small break in the shelving and tried to squeeze into the tight space. He wedged himself between the supports and pulled one foot in. He took a deep breath and began to maneuver his second foot back, but he lost his balance and tipped to the side, sending the shelves crashing forward. Boxes and files tumbled to the floor in a mighty racket.

There was a pause in the conversation below and then footsteps scurried toward the stairs. Ján frantically began picking up boxes, creating more of a disturbance. Leaning forward to pull shelves back upright, he spied a thin shaft of light on the floor. He felt around with his hands and discovered that the light was coming from an adjoining room and that he was crouched in front of a second door, one that had been blocked by the shelves. He ran his hands up the plain wooden surface and found a simple latch. The door easily swung open into a room he had never visited before. Broken furniture was piled against the walls and piles of old books and religious vestments were stacked under a window. The door to the hallway was cracked just a sliver, and in the opposite corner, under an old blanket, stood an upright piano. Ján stared at the instrument with equal parts excitement and dread.

Mrs. Kotova's heels clacked up the stairs followed by another set of footsteps, heavier, more assertive. Ján's heart was pounding, and sweat soaked his collar despite the cold air pouring in through the gaps in the window. As the pair advanced down the hallway toward the room, Ján eased the closet door shut, pushed a box of robes in front of it, and pulled the blanket off the piano. Dust motes swirled in the weak sunlight, and a mouse skittered along the baseboard as Ján stared at the keys. It was like seeing an old friend after a long absence, but both Ján and this piano had suffered.

Mrs. Kotova paused in front of the other room. She picked up the mop and moved the bucket of water. She seemed oddly calm and even-tempered. The steely edge to her voice had been replaced with a more convivial tone. She made a comment about children and chores, and moved back into the hallway, the second set of footsteps following her voice.

Ján closed his eyes, gently caressed the dusty keys, and began to play. The piano had not been tuned in years, and animals had nested in its case amongst the strings and bridges, yet as Ján coaxed the instrument out of hiding, the soothing notes of one of Chopin's nocturnes filled the room. The quaggy strings wavered, and a tinny sound emerged, but the melody was unmistakable. Ján poured all his angst into his fingers, and the notes filled the small room. He heard Herr Kippels in his head. *Don't overdo, my lad! Less is more.* Feet scrambled up the stairs, and a crowd gathered in the hallway. Mrs. Kotova charged into the room.

Ján ignored the sudden appearance of his audience and continued to play. He was prepared to grab the instrument and hold on with all his might, but no one touched him. Instead, when he came to the final dramatic sweep in the cadenza, the beleaguered piano valiantly responded to his insistent coaxing, and he heard clapping. He turned to see Nina smiling broadly as she celebrated his performance. Katrine followed, and soon the hallway was filled with applause. Finally, Mrs. Kotova brought her hands together in a begrudging gesture of acknowledgment.

She turned to the man behind her, and said, "Comrade Novikov, this is Ján Balik, one of our newest residents." She walked over to Ján and ran her hand over the keys. "Ján, Comrade Novikov is from the People's Commissariat of Enlightenment, and he is here to inspect our home, a rather unanticipated visit." She tilted her head toward Novikov and offered a forced smile.

Ján detected the note of displeasure in her voice. The woman he knew was lurking right under the surface of this act for their visitor.

"Ján has a remarkable talent, and we are looking for opportunities to make this gift part of his rehabilitation," she explained to an appreciative Comrade Novikov and a stunned group assembled behind him. "He has been with us such a short time that we are still trying to find ways to showcase his talents." As she spoke, she placed her hand on Ján's shoulder and squeezed until he was tempted to cry out.

Comrade Novikov nodded appreciably and addressed Ján. "How old are you and where did you learn to play, young man?"

Ján answered him truthfully, describing his studies at the academy in Königsberg. Comrade Novikov listened intently and then pulled Mrs. Kotova aside. They spoke in low tones, but

Comrade Novikov was animated, gesturing and smiling broadly. Twice he pointed to Ján, and Mrs. Kotova nodded. He then tipped his hat and walked briskly out of the room, maneuvering around the assembled crowd to make a beeline to his waiting car.

"So, Ján," Mrs. Kotova said, her words laced with vitriol, "aren't you the goose that laid the golden egg? Quite a little show you put on there. Comrade Novikov will be here to collect you tomorrow."

Chapter 5

Song of Friendship

South of Moscow, the Soviet Union
Summer 1945

Comrade Novikov turned out to be a complex character easily wounded by criticism, often distracted, and more than occasionally ill-tempered. Initially, Ján found him intimidating, particularly at the way he cowed Mrs. Kotova, but time revealed a crippling insecurity under the man's crusty demeanor. Ján was amused to discover that the man talked a lot but accomplished very little.

They stood together just offstage in the renovated auditorium in Oryol, a city southwest of Moscow. Comrade Novikov produced a small comb from his pocket and tried without success to tame Ján's clumsy haircut.

Ján was too caught up in the excitement of the show to protest. He couldn't see the audience, but from the telltale chorus of creaky seats and rustling paper programs, he sensed a full crowd of spectators eager to hear the young musicians perform. Billed as the triumph of childcare under the Soviet State, this concert by rehabilitated waifs, dubbed The Besprizornye Musicians, was a highly anticipated event.

While Comrade Novikov seized credit for the inspiration behind the production, it was in fact the brainchild of Helena Shmetlana, a jolly dumpling of a woman who served as a sort of jack-of-all-trades at the People's Commissariat of Enlightenment, the agency otherwise known as Narkompros. Seeking to remedy a flurry of bad publicity over graft and corruption within the State system, she had cheerfully suggested to Comrade Novikov that during his inspection rounds, he should scout out candidates for a public relations tour, a chance to show off bright, shiny, and talented children to the general population. His efforts had been lackluster at best, but his serendipitous discovery of Ján changed all that. The boy was brilliant. Novikov made quick work of instructing Miss Shmetlana to call in favors and assemble the troupe of performers.

During their weeks of rehearsals in the dimly lit warehouse in Kursk, the children had become a little family of sorts. In addition to Ján, there were a dozen other boys and girls of various ages and skill levels plucked from a collection of State homes. Among them were singers, a trumpet player, a flutist, three violinists, and a cellist. Ján was undeniably the star of the show.

Most of the children hadn't held an instrument in months, if not years, but they practiced with relentless enthusiasm and developed a fierce camaraderie with a competitive edge.

Miss Shmetlana served as their overindulgent chaperone and source of inexpert haircuts, and Comrade Orlov, a pedantic theatrical director on loan from the Ministry of Cinema, was tasked with assembling the motley troupe into a traveling band of performing propagandists. He stumbled into the rehearsal space with sheafs of party-approved musical selections, a collection of instruments seized from enemies of the State, and a shiny whistle that he used to cajole the children toward a semblance of routine.

For their part, the children would have performed anything in exchange for the tasty meals and warm bedding that Miss Shmetlana provided. With just a few weeks of proper food in their bellies, they began to exude a look of rosy-cheeked, milk-and-honey good health. Loose teeth and pesky skin lesions from recent, leaner times became a little less obvious. Comrade Novikov had arrived only recently to preview the show in Oryol and was so charmed with their progress that he doled out hugs and insisted to their amusement that they all call him Batya Alexi.

"Batya Alexi?" Ján finally bristled under the constant combing and tried to get his mentor's attention. "Batya Alexi!" he said louder.

Novikov dropped the comb in alarm. "What is it, Ján? You won't be nervous, will you?"

"Not at all, Batya. It's time for you to go onstage." Ján pointed to Comrade Orlov who was standing in the wings opposite, flapping his arms at Novikov and pointing to his timepiece.

Novikov searched his pocket for his notes, then he strode onstage and addressed the microphone. Applause broke out at this sign that the performance was imminent.

After Novikov's verbose introduction, Irina was the first performer, prancing onstage with her long, blonde hair plaited and tied with gleaming satin ribbons that matched her red dress. The violin was much too big for her, but she carried it reverently and deftly placed it in first position before holding her bow just over the strings. With a nod from Comrade Orlov, she began to play. The audience quieted, transfixed by the contradictions of her youthful innocence and the bold notes that she teased from the strings.

Borya followed, then Leo, Maria, and Emil. Ján watched each with a mix of awe and pride. He had seen them all in rehearsals, of course, but their charisma and poise in front of an audience took a special grace, a kind of showmanship that Ján had only seen before in adults.

The prime spot on the program belonged to Ján, and he

delighted the audience with *Precipitato* from Prokofiev's Sonata No.7, one of the War Sonatas and a selection known to be favored by Stalin. Comrade Orlov had saved the skittish piece with its frenetic pace for last as a patriotic tribute. Ján was ambivalent about the appeal of the selection, but his previous repertoire of German music and western classical pieces would hardly be appropriate for this crowd, and the thrill of playing in front of an audience had him soaring.

He walked onstage and offered the spectators a slight nod before taking a seat on the bench. He closed his eyes and thought back to his performances on the Königsberg stage when he had needed cushions to properly address the keys. He allowed himself a brief smile at the memory while putting his hands in position on the keys. Once he began to play, everything melted away but the sounds of the piano and the memories flooding his thoughts. The audience reveled in his performance and leapt to their feet at the conclusion of the piece. Ján stood and acknowledged them with a deep bow, yet the applause continued unabated. Comrade Orlov hustled on stage, waving to the crowd as he sought to confer with Ján.

"They're demanding an encore!" he shouted above the clapping that was growing more raucous as the audience sensed its power. "What have you got?"

"Rachmaninov?" Ján suggested.

"Don't be an idiot," Orlov shot back. "Who else? Lourié?"

Ján shook his head. Tonight, he would play to the glory of Poland. Before Orlov could object, Ján returned to the bench with his thoughts on the day he found the piano at the orphanage. It was his fellow Pole, Frédéric Chopin, who had brought him here. The crowd began yelling at Orlov to vacate the stage, so he scurried to the wings in a state of unease over what Ján might produce and how much trouble it would invite from the authorities. He cowered behind the curtain as Ján signaled to the audience to sit down. He then stretched his fingers, rolled his shoulders just a bit, paused with his hands hovering over the keys, and then produced the very same nocturne that he had pounded out on the decrepit piano at the No. 15 Home.

This time, the Russian Becker piano, despite its age, was in excellent condition, and as Ján's fingers danced over the keys, the cool, detached notes of Chopin's most famous piece began to temper the crowd. The wistful melody created a melancholy air, and Ján was transported back to the first time he had played this piece at his home in Warsaw. As he hammered out the last few notes, the audience was tamed, and Orlov had recovered his composure and stood ready with the other children to whisk them on stage for the final bow. Novikov rushed on ahead of him to claim a bit of the limelight for himself.

They settled into this pattern for the next few months. Traveling, rehearsing, performing, then traveling again. They buckled down to their lessons under Miss Shmetlana's insistent care and Comrade Orlov's jittery perfectionism, but they also giggled and played and fought like siblings.

Ján composed a special piece full of lively notes and gleeful chords to celebrate this newfound sense of camaraderie, and he carefully transcribed this composition into his fragile book.

October 1946

Comrade Novikov rejoined the band of musicians for their concert in Moscow, and the audience was once again wildly enthusiastic. Stalin did not attend, but high-level party officials were in the hall, and Ján overhead Comrade Novikov discussing with Orlov rumors of their certain promotions. Both men seemed especially obsequious this evening. Ján decided to seize the moment.

"Batya Alexi?" Ján tugged on Novikov's sleeve after the final curtain call.

"Yes, lad, what is it? You were exceptional tonight, truly magnificent!"

"Thank you, Batya, but I wonder if at the next concert, I could play one of my own compositions?"

Nonplussed, Novikov stumbled around his response. "Well, um, probably not. We need sophisticated music, you see…A child's ramblings…well I am sure you understand."

"I'm not a child. I'm sixteen." Ján returned to the stage and seated himself at the piano, pausing just long enough to control his breathing. He pictured his mother, and he then thought of the concert hall in Königsberg, and of Herr Kippels, and Ada. He began to play, and as his fingers caressed the keys, his tribute to his mother filled the venue. In Ján's mind, he was back with his family, and in his remembering, they encircled him and reclaimed him as their own. The notes captured his mother's vibrant personality and commanding presence with bold rhythms and harmonious undertones.

Small pockets of patrons who were conversing on their way out stopped at this unexpected performance and made their way back toward the stage. Ján played with a full heart, pouring himself into the familial love that inspired him to write the piece. When he finished, he sat at the piano for a long time, the echoes of the music still playing out in his mind.

Applause broke out amongst those still in attendance, and several of the patrons rushed the stage to pat Ján on the back. They thrust their programs in his face and demanded an autograph, interrupting his reverie. In the dizzying crush, Ján glanced up just as the flash from a photographer's camera blinded him for a few minutes. Comrade Novikov was pressed with questions about Ján and attempted to turn the focus back on himself, while Comrade Orlov, visibly annoyed at the sudden attention lavished on a boy, charged the stage and spirited him off. He cuffed Ján on the side of his head.

"I don't know what Western bourgeois artist you stole that from, but it stops now!"

Amidst the commotion, Comrade Novikov hastened to his side, and Ján sought his reassurance. "I wrote that piece! Batya Alexi, you believe me, don't you?"

"Well, um, I am sure you *think* you wrote that. It's quite sophisticated for a boy your age. You probably heard it somewhere and remembered it. It's a moot point anyway, no more performances. We're done! The tour was a grand success, and we're finished!"

"We're *done*?" Ján blurted. "Done with what?" The elation he felt was dissolving into horror. Irina and Emil ventured over to see what the commotion was about.

Comrade Novikov, sensing dissent in the ranks, puffed out his chest in an effort to wrest control over the situation. It simply would not do to leave the hall with a band of simpering children after such a stellar performance. "Look, Ján," he said, "it couldn't last forever. These things have seasons, and this season is done. Kaputt, as you would say. We need to take a break and let the enthusiasm build up again." He smirked and waved his hands dismissively. "There will be more, perhaps next fall. We can organize a new round of engagements then, but in the meantime–"

"In the meantime, what?" Ján demanded. It was dawning on him what Novikov was trying to tell him. "What do we do now?"

Novikov bristled at this challenge. Ján's insolence right at this hour of his triumph was infuriating. Novikov grabbed Ján's arm and pulled him aside. "Now? Now we take you back to the home. That's what. And if you behave yourself, we'll come get you when we have a new schedule." Ján opened his mouth to interrupt but Novikov cut him off. "You are a star, and we *will* be back to collect you. Sometime, but not now, unless you cause a fuss, then you're done. Do you understand?"

Clackety, clackety, clackety. The train rumbled through the night. Ján sat by the window and watched the darkened forms of the nocturnal landscape drift past the window. Comrade Novikov, in the seat beside him, snored with gusto and murmured in his sleep, but for Ján, slumber was elusive. The last time he had been on a train, Otto sat nearby. The sound of iron wheels on rails and the car's rhythmic swaying would forever live in Ján's memory alongside the stench of death and the fear of uncertainty.

A newspaper was folded in Comrade Novikov's lap, and Ján glanced at it, surprised to see his own face. The picture, nestled in the bottom corner of the front page, showed him blinded by a flash and surrounded by admirers. The photographer had captured the side of his face with the missing ear, and the scar was ugly and exposed. The concert however, had been a resounding success, and Ján was the face of the triumph, albeit a damaged one, an apt metaphor for the times, according to the article.

For Ján, it was a bitter pill. Comrade Novikov, who had abandoned all pretense of familial warmth and now only answered to his more formal title, was returning him to Mrs. Kotova and the grim realities of the *detdom*, the No. 15 Home. Ján wished he had never been on tour, never met Borya or Irina, because now having tasted escape, this forced return to a feral existence was crushing.

With the first inklings of dawn and the promise of weak autumn sunlight, they pulled into the station, and Ján spied the hill in the distance. Beyond where the road disappeared over the rise, Ján knew that the forsaken remnants of the convent clung to the meadow with the No. 15 Special Home lurking behind. The train entered the bustling railyard, and they were jolted from side to side as the car navigated over the switches.

Comrade Novikov stirred and looked around to get his bearings. "Ah, we are here. Now that wasn't so bad, was it?"

Ján didn't answer. His heart was pounding, and he struggled to breathe. He clutched the small bag of meager possessions that he had accumulated on tour and felt under his thin jacket for the book that stayed close to his chest.

"Listen, young man," Novikov continued, "there is no reason to pout. In fact, you should be grateful that I accompanied you here in person. Your lack of appreciation does you no credit."

Ján turned to look his ruddy-faced companion in the eye. "Excuse me, comrade, but what exactly am I supposed to be grateful for? I played for you and your friends and your audiences. I watched you and Orlov accept the praise that was due to me and Leo and Irina and Emil. Now we are just being discarded." Ján's eyes filled with tears, and he averted his face to get his emotions under control. Out of the train window, he spied Mrs. Kotova's car with Dmitri standing beside it, smoking a cigarette. He did not want to get in that car and return to the home. "Please, Comrade Novikov, don't make me go back! I didn't mean to appear rude," he begged.

Novikov stood and brushed out his rumpled suit coat and trousers. He wore his indignation as easily as a scarf or a top hat. "You just don't know how good you have it, Ján. It's a shame that you cannot shed your elitist attitude and recognize how much others like Mrs. Kotova and I have done for you."

A few of the passengers began gathering their bags to depart the train, and Comrade Novikov moved to join them. "Come, Ján, it does no good to sulk."

Ján's desperation was crushing him, squeezing the air out of his lungs and turning his knees to wobbly jelly. "Don't make me–" Ján hesitated, afraid to say much more.

"Nonsense! Quit making a scene. Move along, boy! Now!" The other passengers were starting to observe the confrontation between the two, and it amplified Novikov's anger.

Ján reached out and grabbed Novikov's hand. "Please! You don't understand, there's danger at the home. I've seen it with my own eyes." Once he had started, Ján's story poured out of him.

"Children are ignored! They go missing, and no one pays attention."

Novikov stared at Ján in disbelief. "What are you saying, boy? Are you out of your mind?"

"No, comrade! I've seen pictures. Dozens of files of children! Who knows what happened to them? I can show you!"

"Well then," Novikov acquiesced, recognizing an opportunity to get Ján off the train, "you better get up and show me then."

Mrs. Kotova was waiting by the car. Her greetings to Comrade Novikov were devoid of warmth but offered with sufficient deference to deflect any offense. To Ján, she simply nodded to acknowledge his return. Novikov kept up a lively banter as the car climbed the hill.

"Mrs. Kotova, you would be proud indeed of your young charge here. Ján was the star of the show and left a trail of admirers all along our tour route." He showed her the newspaper article with the photograph of a stunned Ján on stage in Moscow. She reached out with her gloved hand and took the newspaper, folded it carefully, and slipped it into her handbag.

Once they had driven around the desolate convent and followed the road to the cluster of buildings that comprised No. 15 Home, the car came to a halt. Dmitri walked around to open Mrs. Kotova's door, and Comrade Novikov and Ján climbed out on their own.

Mrs. Kotova approached and put her hand on Ján's shoulder. She addressed Novikov. "Comrade, you have made a long journey, and I know you are eager to get on your way. I will take Ján from here and get our little celebrity settled back in amongst his friends. Dmitri will take you back to the station."

Novikov held up a finger as Dmitri moved to get behind the wheel again. "Not so fast, Mrs. Kotova. Before I leave, I'm afraid that I must investigate a very serious accusation that Ján has leveled against you and this home."

Mrs. Kotova's grip on Ján's shoulder tightened, but her face gave nothing away. "Accusations? Whatever about?"

Novikov explained to her what Ján had just told him about files of children. "You see, Mrs. Kotova, reports of missing children make for serious accusations that I must resolve before I can leave Ján in your care. I am sure you understand."

Ján felt the earth pitch uneasily under his feet, and he steeled his knees in the hopes he wouldn't pass out. He struggled to breathe. He was fully exposed now with no avenue of retreat while Mrs. Kotova's hand on his shoulder was squeezing tighter. He winced in pain.

Novikov motioned to the front of the building. "After you," he said to Mrs. Kotova, and they entered the reception area. Nina and Katrine smiled and called out when they saw Ján, but when they noticed the tension in the group, they returned to their typing.

"So, Ján, where to?" Novikov inquired testily. "Show me these files."

Ján pointed to the stairs and motioned for Novikov to follow him. Mrs. Kotova stayed close behind. With leaden feet, Ján climbed up each tread and led them down the hallway to enter the room that he had offered to mop so many months ago. He approached the closet door and pulled on the handle. It was stuck, just as Ján remembered. He planted his feet and pulled with all his strength. The door resisted at first, but as Ján continued to apply pressure, it popped loudly and swung open.

They all moved into the dark, cramped space, and Ján could feel Comrade Novikov's breath on his neck. He reached up to clasp the light cord, thinking of all the boxes and files that were likely spilled across the floor. When he gave a tug to the string overhead, the harsh light flickered on, and Ján stared at the interior of the closet. Rows and rows of empty shelves. Nothing here. Ján advanced deeper into the closet where he knew the other door connected to the room with the piano. He pushed it open, in a panic now, and discovered this room to be unchanged. Boxes of musty ecclesiastical robes were stacked against the wall, and the blanket had been returned to its perch across the ancient piano.

Ján turned to face Novikov, his eyes pleading. "Batya Alexi, you must believe me. They were here. Boxes of files with photographs and proof." Ján's voice broke as a sob threatened to destroy what little remained of his composure. "You must believe me," he pleaded.

Novikov turned to Mrs. Kotova. "My apologies, madam, for this unconscionable intrusion. I will be on my way now, and I leave this nefarious lad in your capable hands." He then addressed Ján. "And after all I did for you. This is a disappointment indeed. Shame on you. I trust you will apologize appropriately and make amends to this fine lady here." He offered Mrs. Kotova a quick bow and strode out of the room.

Ján and Mrs. Kotova were left alone as they listened to Comrade Novikov's footsteps retreat down the stairs and out the front door. Car doors opened and shut, and gravel crunched under tires as the sedan rolled back down the lane toward the train station.

Ján's fear was turning to anger, a toxic mix of raw emotion and desperation. "I know what I saw," he said simply.

"I have no idea what you are talking about," she replied coolly, arching a thin brow, penciled in harsh black lines, "but I certainly have an idea of how we can help refresh that memory of yours. You will not win this deceitful game, Ján Balik." She pulled the newspaper out of her handbag and looked at the photo. Without a word, she ripped it into pieces and allowed them to fall to the floor.

Ján walked into the fading afternoon sun and squinted. His legs shook, and he wrapped his arms around his chest to guard against the cold. Autumn was fading into winter's icy grip, and arctic winds were stripping the last of the leaves from the trees. His eyes watered as they adjusted to the thin light. Two weeks. That is how long he had cowered on the floor in the locked shed. Two weeks of cold and dark with mere scraps of bread until he finally relented and wrote the letter to Comrade Novikov retracting his statements from the train and confessing that he had concocted the story of the files. For good measure, Mrs. Kotova insisted that he also admit that he was now happy to be back at the No. 15 Home and had no desire to return to the tour if Comrade decided to schedule another round of performances.

Ján had willed his fingers to stop shaking long enough to push the letter through the miserly crack under the door, and then he retreated into the far corner, pulling his legs to his chest and holding his body in a tight ball. After some time, he heard the rustling of paper and the screech of a rusty bolt. The door opened just a crack, and a shadow passed through the shaft of timid light that leaked across the floor. Someone was moving about outside. Ján cowered in the darkness and waited until he was sure the person was gone.

He crawled out slowly into the deserted yard and struggled to stand while the world teetered precariously around him. He reached out to steady himself against the wall, unsure how long his legs would hold. After a time, he gathered his courage to let go, to keep walking, one foot followed by the other. Habit took him to the rear door of the house where he knew Lana, the cook, labored just inside. He tried to turn the handle, but it was locked, so he rapped three times before he slid down in a heap on the top step. The door inched open, and Lana's fleshy face peered out. Ján began to push himself up, but Lana shook her head.

"No more, Ján. We can't let you in. Go on now. Get away before we are all in trouble." She quickly closed the door, and he heard the lock click back in place.

Back on his feet, he wobbled and swayed to the nearest

building where he collapsed on the mattress just inside the door. He lay as he fell with one arm pinned and one leg splayed out on the floor. As exhaustion claimed him, he was once again visited by the dream that had dogged him over the long days in confinement. He was riding on a train, the car tipping back and forth. Panicked, he ran along the narrow corridor shouting for help and banging on the compartment doors. Otto beckoned to him from the far end of the car, and Ján fought against the erratic pitches of the car to rejoin his companion. Despite his exertions, he was unable to reach Otto before his friend disappeared in a blast of steam. Ján mounted a frantic search for a way out.

In a new twist to his delusion, Lana appeared, shaking her head no and pushing him back. Erik yelled for Ada somewhere in the murky depths of the train, and Ján heard but could not see Comrade Novikov laughing. Then they were all laughing, a tinny sound of cruelty and blame.

A blast of cold air jolted him awake as a trio of young girls burst into the room. He feared that they were a part of his imaginings until they fell on him and tugged at his arms and legs.

"This is the girls' room," one of them said. "I'm Katia. We heard you were back." She helped Ján stand and guided him across the hall to the boys' side.

"I need to talk to Vera," he said.

"Vera is gone. She got adopted."

"Did you see her leave? Did she tell you her plans?" Ján's breathing quickened, and he felt lightheaded again. *Where was Vera?*

"None of us saw her, but that's what they said up at the house. She left with a family, and they said we wouldn't see her again."

Ján hobbled to the exit. The biting air rushed in, and his eyes once again strained to adjust from the rancid darkness of the hut to the low autumn sun. He peered down the lane that ran behind the copse of trees to where the thin line of smoke slithered toward the cluster of clouds overhead. *Vera was gone. Did she go in search of her brother?* Ján wanted to celebrate her freedom, but he was dogged by the certainty that something had happened to her, something dark and evil.

His gaze followed the muddy tracks back toward the main house as they merged into the ruts of the drive toward the convent. As his eyes swept past the house, a cloud passed in front of the sun and tempered the reflection on the windows, revealing Mrs. Kotova's scowling face. She locked eyes with Ján and slowly crossed her arms over her chest. His heart pounded, and he fell back into the dank hallway. Defeat settled into his bones.

April 1947

Maxim Vasiliev arrived at the No. 15 Home in the same manner as most of other the children: in the back of Mrs. Kotova's sedan. The spring thaw was underway, and Ján was with a group of boys replacing rotten boards on some of the sheds when they heard tires crunching gravel accompanied by whining brakes. They all watched as the newcomer emerged from the car and followed Mrs. Kotova toward the main house. With his sunken eyes, sharp cheekbones, and telltale sores around his mouth, he looked like all the other malnourished children that Mrs. Kotova collected like stray dogs.

Dmitri drove off, and Ján watched the car motor down the muddy lane. A quick movement off to the side caught his attention. The boy pitched forward, almost falling on top of Pushka the cat's heap of rodent conquests before catching himself and stumbling back upright. Mrs. Kotova glanced back briefly, but refused to break stride to accommodate. The boy regained his footing, quickened his steps, and caught up with the matron as she climbed the stairs.

Ján watched him slip something into her handbag. He then turned and smiled at Ján, giving him a cheeky wink. He followed the unsuspecting Mrs. Kotova into the reception area before the door slammed shut. Ján laughed quietly to himself. This new boy showed promise.

The boy emerged from the house after a long stint of enduring Mrs. Kotova's interview. He looked about, unsure of his next steps but projected a measure of confidence that was a rare sight at the No. 15 House. He glanced in Ján's direction, exposing a deep red handprint on his cheek.

Ján dropped the rotten board he had just peeled away from the hut and went to investigate. He pointed to the boy's face. "I'm Ján. What did you do to deserve that?"

The boy chuckled and stuck out his hand. He was a full head taller than Ján with a deep voice. "I'm Maks, and the delightful Madam Kotova was rather angry to find a dead mouse in her bag." Maks's bright blue eyes crinkled as he laughed. "Entirely worth it. I'll enjoy finding ways to vex her." He took in the full measure of the compound and sighed. "Well, as we Russians say, visiting is good, but home is better."

Ján had never had a friend like Maks. He had never had a true friend of his own at all, so he basked in Maks's self-assured attention. Maks was only seventeen, just a few months ahead of Ján, but he could easily be mistaken for a much older boy, almost a man, really. He was from Pskov, which he helpfully showed Ján on a tattered map. His parents were both teachers at the pedagogical college and had been arrested as enemies of the State. Maks bounced from house to house as relatives offered him shelter before one by one turning him out to fend for himself. The taint of the accusations against his parents followed him everywhere.

Just before his uncle and aunt had put him out on the street nearly a year ago, he overheard them discussing how his mother had been at a transit camp near Kursk. He had been living on the streets, carrying the stolen papers of a much younger child, and working his way back to her. He almost made it before he had been arrested as a vagrant at the train station and turned over to Mrs. Kotova. It took him only minutes to earn her contempt.

Ján, wrapped in a thin blanket, ventured out into a day where a late spring snowfall was dusting the patches of dirty slush with a fresh covering of unsullied white. Maks had been hauled before Mrs. Kotova three days ago, and Ján suspected that he was shackled in one of the outbuildings as punishment for his habit of needling the woman. For the first hundred feet or so, Ján would be visible from the house, so he had to hope that no one was watching out of the back windows for the few minutes it would take him to cross to the other side of the yard. Throwing the blanket over his head, Ján hurried out into the swirling mix and covered the hard ground quickly. Lana briefly looked up from the window in her kitchen and saw Ján dart by, but she held her tongue. Better to see nothing and say nothing.

Ján pulled on the door of the first shed he came to, and it easily swung open. Pushka scampered out, leaving a few mouse bones scattered across the dirt floor. Nothing else here. Same with the next two sheds. At the fourth shed, Ján saw the lock on the door before he attempted to open it. He had been held in this same one before and knew that the shackles were on the back side. He lay on the ground and put his eye up to a small crack in the siding.

"Maks?" he whispered. "It's me. Are you alright?"

Rustling leaves and scraping boots were the only signals from inside. Then a low moan.

"Maks? Are you alright?" Ján repeated. He knew how cold it got inside these malevolent places, how disorienting the experience was, and how terrifying it was to be left here. "Maks!"

"Steady there, my friend, no need to holler." Maks offered in a weak voice. "You don't want to get yourself tossed in here with me. I must say though, it's pretty nice. I've never been warmer or better fed." He coughed deeply and moaned again.

"Why are you in here? What did you do?"

"I underestimated Dmitri's sense of humor when I plugged his tail pipe with a rag." He laughed and then dissolved into a fit of coughing. "I can only hope that I prevented Mrs. Kotova from offering her hospitality to some poor child. Then it will be worth it."

Ján was worried by the sound of Maks's cough. It was deep and relentless once a bout started. "Hang on, Maks. I'll be right back."

Maks started to protest, but Ján was already on his feet. He walked back to the edge of the yard and peered around the side of the first shed. Lana stood in front of the window, wielding her knife against some unseeable carcass. Ján deliberated only a minute before walking toward the house in full view. He approached the window and stood where Lana was forced to acknowledge him. She motioned with her knife for him to leave, but Ján stood firm and pointed to the shed. Lana knew what he was asking, and she silently cursed him. He had the ability to worm his way into her wounded heart. Seeing no one about, she ladled a generous portion of beef broth into a cup, opened the back door, and set the cup and a long spoon on the stoop. She closed the door and returned to her chopping.

Ján took the broth to the shed and lay down against the thin siding. He used the spoon to chisel away at the rotten boards and create a portal near where Maks could position himself. Then he waited for Maks to inch his way over so that his face was level with the tiny opening. In this way, Ján fed Maks as much of the warm liquid as he could wedge through the board. Maks's coughing began to quiet.

"Well done, Ace," said Maks. "I owe you one. Don't risk yourself again. I'll see you soon."

When Maks stumbled into the communal hut a day later, he was feverish and prone to prolonged bouts of coughing, but he was alive. Ján commandeered a pile of random bits of clothing from the other boys and tucked Maks into as warm a cocoon as he could manage. He then walked into the yard to stand once again in view of Lana's kitchen. He could see someone inside but the steam prevented a closer look. Ján reached down and picked up a pebble that he threw against the window. The figure inside moved closer to the glass but backed away before Ján could see who it might be. Presently the door opened and Ján walked toward the steps, but he stopped abruptly when Mrs. Kotova appeared wearing an apron and holding a large spoon.

"I should have known it was you," she said icily.

Ján stood his ground. "My friend Maks is ill. He needs something warm to drink."

"It is I who decides who needs what and when. Maks will be taken care of, but not by you. Do you understand?"

Ján stared back at her, neither speaking, nor attempting to leave.

"Run along, Ján, there is nothing for you here." She wiped her hands on a towel, and when Ján didn't make a move, she leaned toward him and pointed with her spoon. "Lana is no longer employed here. So, you best move along before you find yourself kissing the floor of your own cottage."

When an unexpectedly warm day coincided with an improvement in Maks's condition, he and Ján ventured outside and sat in the sun for a bit. Deep shadows lurked below Maks's eyes, and his voice remained raspy. Ján leaned his head back and began to hum a joyful tune that he had composed in the company of his fellow Besprizornye performers. Those happy memories seemed a lifetime ago. Maks tapped his toes in rhythm with Ján's humming.

"It's good to hear some happiness, even if it's just a ditty coming from your scrawny brain," Maks teased.

Ján smiled and began to whistle another tune, but Maks resumed his coughing and Ján was pulled out of his reverie. "Are you going to be alright?" he asked. It was more of a wish than a question.

"Ach, of course. It's just a struggle at the moment." Maks used the back of his hand to wipe his mouth.

"Why haven't you ever asked about my ear?" Ján demanded suddenly. "You're the first person here who never asked about what happened to my ear."

"Do you want to tell me?"

"I would rather not talk about it. I just wondered why you never asked."

"Oh, I noticed it, if that's what you're wondering. It's ugly, and there's a story there. But you need to know that we all have our ugly scars and our stories. Yours just happens to be more visible than most. If you want to tell me your story, I will listen, but I don't need to hear it to know you are brave." He pointed toward the smoke curling up and over the black tree tops beyond where the lane curved behind the copse of trees, and added, "One thing I truly must know, where does that road go?"

Ján told him about the cars and trucks that disappeared around the bend, the constant smoke, and the boxes of files, and Vera.

Maks listened intently while Ján talked, then he reached across and lightly punched Ján's arm. "You and I are going to walk down that lane and see what is on the other side."

"No, it's too dangerous," Ján protested, but Maks was already struggling to stand.

He reached out to coax Ján up. "What's the worst that could happen?" he asked with a twinkle in his eyes.

Ján started to list all the grim possibilities, but one look at Maks's face told him that his friend was going with or without him. Better that they go together. With a glance over their shoulders to see who might be watching, Maks leaned on Ján and they began to walk. The lane was an obstacle course of frozen mud threaded with deep ruts and slippery patches of ice. Both boys were wearing thin-soled shoes that were too small to allow them to walk quickly, so they plodded along making measured progress.

When they reached the bend, they heard a truck approaching, rapidly by the sound of the tires chewing through the frozen mud and popping layers of ice. The boys fell into the underbrush and crouched down where the scrubby frozen plants offered limited protection. The truck roared past, and Ján risked a peek at the transport. He thought he could see the profiles of several passengers behind the canvas flap in the back. Once the lumbering vehicle rounded the bend, Maks tapped Ján on the shoulder and motioned for him to follow. Ján hesitated, glancing around to make sure they were out of danger, but leapt to his feet when he saw that his friend was already lurching unsteadily in pursuit of the truck.

Past the cover of the trees, the lane began to amble up a low rise, and Ján realized that the smoke was farther away than he had suspected. Too intrigued to stop now, the boys leaned into the chilling breeze and managed to hobble up the hill and through another small grove of aspens. As they neared the edges of the tree line, they spied three long, low huts similar to their own quarters and clustered around a central building with a large chimney, the source of the smoke. The truck had pulled to a stop, and the driver was helping two women climb out of the back, each holding two small children. All of them disappeared inside the central building.

Ján tugged on Maks's sleeve. "Vera never said how old her brother, Dima, was. Maybe he was really young, and they brought him here?"

Maks shrugged. "Maybe. Only one way to find out." Maks crept forward, making slow progress while leaning on Ján for support. Since the adults took the children into the center building, the boys decided to peek inside one of the three outbuildings.

Ján had a nagging feeling about this place. If these huts were full of little children, why was the place so quiet? Why were these huts so secluded? On a day like this when the weather warmed even slightly, shouldn't the children be allowed outside? Instead, there was only the idling of the truck, the cracking of the ice, and the occasional caw of a scavenger bird circling overhead.

They reached the first hut, but the door was locked. They moved around to the side, and Maks cupped his hands, signaling at Ján to climb up. Teetering in his friend's feeble grasp, Ján pulled himself up to the windows mounted high on the rough wooden siding. Dirt was caked on the glass, and ancient spider webs hung in sheets, catching leaves and an assortment of dead insects. Ján rubbed a peephole in the window with his fingers and used his jacket cuff to wipe away the dirt before he pressed his face up against the glass. The glass was just as dirty on the inside, and at first Ján thought the room was unoccupied.

"Nothing here!" he whispered to Maks and began to climb down, but a slight movement within caught his eye. "Wait!" he insisted. With a grunt, he pulled himself up again. Ján shielded his face with his hands and peered back in again. There it was, something moving. A cat maybe? His eyes were beginning to adjust to the inner gloom, and vague shapes were starting to form into recognizable images of children. Rows of cribs lined the walls, and in each, there was a child. No one else seemed to be about, and there was scant light coming through the filthy windows to illuminate the room. A putrid odor seeped through the cracks in the sill. Ján gasped so hard that he almost toppled from his perch.

"I can't support you much longer!" Maks whispered. "What is it?"

"Oh God, Maks!" Ján blurted in horror, forgetting to lower his voice. "It's children, dozens of them. Some are barely moving, others are...I don't know. I can smell them better than I can see them. It's awful! They are just lying there. One or two sitting, but still. None of them are moving or playing. I can see some eyes open, but I just can't tell if they are alive or—"

Maks's grip gave out, and he tumbled back, bringing Ján down with him. They collapsed in a heap on the frozen ground, knocking out their breath and leaving them stunned. They heard the truck's engine roar back to life. Ján scrambled to his feet and positioned himself against the side of the building that gave him a view of the vehicle in the lane. Maks rolled over on his elbows, gasping for air.

"What do you see?" he asked despite a searing pain in his chest.

Ján responded without taking his eyes off the truck. "The

driver is in the cab. Now the two women are coming out and getting in the front with the driver. They don't have the children with them anymore. They're just sitting there."

"Go get in the back of the truck. You can go into town, get help," Maks said.

"No, I'm not leaving you." Ján turned to look at his friend and noticed that blood was trickling from Maks's nose. "I can't leave you like this."

"It's exactly why you have to go! Get help for me and those children inside—the ones that can be saved anyway. You have to leave. Now!" Maks hissed.

Ján looked back at the truck, still idling.

"Go! I'll never make it. Bring help back!" Maks insisted before he dissolved into a painful bout of coughing.

"Hang on then, I'll be back, I promise. I won't leave you here," Ján assured his friend before slowly moving around to the front of the building. He had a full view of the truck now, and presumably, anyone inside the central building or the truck could now see him. He kept his movements calm and slow so as not to draw too much attention to himself and, after unbearably long and tense minutes, he reached a small fir tree at the edge of the drive.

He was close enough to hear talking from the cab, and he decided that the driver was likely distracted by the two women inside. Crouching low, he sprinted to the rear of the truck. He could see Maks peering around the corner of the hut, and he waved. Then he hoisted himself up and into the rear cargo area. The floor was empty except for a few broken toys and a dirty blanket.

New voices emerged. A door opened and closed. Ján strained to understand the banter as the voices grew closer. Ján thought he heard "*delivery*," but he wasn't sure and he had little time to react when he realized that whoever was speaking now stood just on the other side of the canvas. He wedged himself in the corner and held his breath. A pair of rough hands pushed several boxes through the rear flaps. Ján squeezed his eyes shut and prepared to be caught, but the boxes, simple in construction and without markings, remained just inside the opening as the hands withdrew. A bit more banter and the truck jolted into gear and began rumbling down the lane, back toward the No. 15 Home. Ján arranged himself on the floor and lifted the flap just enough to see Maks lying on the ground.

"Please God," thought Ján, "please let me make it to someone who can help."

The truck bumped and shook as it rumbled over the deep, frozen ruts. Ján watched the trees at the bend in the lane recede into the background, and soon they passed the No. 15 Home. A few more children had ventured out into the yard, but otherwise it was quiet. Ján spied a boy standing by a shed idly snapping a long stick, and he thought about calling to him to go and get Maks but decided that it would be futile. He had no way of explaining where Maks lay. His only hope was to get to town.

Ján leaned back against the canvas siding and settled in for the ride to town, plotting his move once he knew where the truck was going. He would have to find a soldier or a detective, and he had no ideas about how to accomplish that. Before he could mull over any possible scenarios, the truck stopped, and the driver's door opened and closed. Ján peeked out from under the canvas flap. They were in front of the abandoned convent. Puzzled, Ján lifted the flap just a bit higher to get a better sightline when a pair of hands reached in and grabbed him. He tried to wriggle free, but the hands had a firm grip on his arms. The canvas flap was thrown aside, and Ján stared into the driver's startled face. Mrs. Kotova's steely gray eyes peered at him over the man's shoulder.

She didn't say a word, simply motioned with her head for the driver to yank Ján out of the truck and onto his feet. As the man pulled him down and forced him to stand upright on the ground, Ján screamed, "Maks is hurt. You must help him."

She made no response other than to tell the driver to take Ján back to the main house. Ján glared at Mrs. Kotova. "You are evil!" he shouted. She ignored his cries and turned to question the two women still sitting in the cab. "You are evil!" Ján shouted again, and Mrs. Kotova met his eye right before the driver's fist slammed against Ján's head.

Chapter 6

Song of Wood and Wire

Northern Siberia, the Soviet Union
August 1952

Ján tugged at the brim of his hat, a wool Lenin-style flat cap. It was entirely unsuitable for brutal Siberian heat, but beggars like him couldn't be choosy. Its previous owner had keeled over months ago during a forced march, and the poor man's fellow prisoners had mourned his passing while they scrambled to strip him of his possessions. Ján couldn't bring himself to scrap over spoils, but when two desperate inmates came to blows over the hat, it had launched into the air and fallen in Ján's lap. Possession being nine-tenths of the law, the wool oddity now belonged to Ján. It was all he had to protect him from the enormous midges and mosquitoes, plagues of the summer months in the taiga, boreal forests with acre upon acre of pines, spruces, and larches.

They were just three hours off the boat, having been brought from Igarka down the Yenisei River toward Yermakovo. Single-file, they trudged through the swampy, insect-ridden forest to their new camp. Ján had heard rumors that this march was to be about twenty kilometers, but he could never be sure. The guards were rarely forthcoming. Ján had learned many hard lessons about trust and dependability, and he took nothing at face value.

Alban plowed his way through the dense underbrush to walk alongside Ján. Breathless, he pulled at his trousers to show Ján deep red welts along his backside. "I stopped to pay nature a visit, and this happened. We'll be eaten alive before we reach the camp!"

Ján examined the oozy bites. "You're telling me you don't have these giant, blood-sucking insects in Yakutia, eh?"

"Oh, lots and lots, there's no getting away from them. My people have a deep reverence for the natural world, but these little suckers are hard to love," Alban replied with a smirk. He shifted the weight of his rucksack and fell in line with Ján, the two keeping a companionable silence between them.

They had been unlikely friends for five years, ever since Ján had been removed from the No. 15 Special Home, classified as an enemy of the State, and sent on a prison barge to the far north of the Siberian wilderness to labor on the Transpolar Mainline. Envisioned as a 2,400km rail corridor connecting northern ports from Salekhard to Igarka, the project depended on the mass mobilization of undesirables, victims of political retribution, and ethnic purges as slave labor to die in service to Stalin's folly. This impossible mission was aptly nicknamed "The Dead Road."

They were an unlikely pair. Alban, a political prisoner from the far eastern region of Yakutia, was a member of the Sakha people, an indigenous community native to Siberia. Muscular and compact with striking dark hair and deep-set, hooded eyes, he was blessed with a persistent smile that imbued his face with radiance that even his present circumstances failed to diminish. He was Ján's elder by eight years, but the two had met on the treacherous journey north, and they had bonded easily over a shared sense of survival. Ján was buoyed by Alban's constant sense of awe and wonder, persisting even after the trials that they had endured moving from one labor camp to the next as the railway lines progressed.

Alban was intrigued by Ján's taciturn demeanor, and he was eager to know more about his thin, pale friend whose refined resilience seemed at odds with his scars. Alban patiently tolerated silence as the response to his questions about Ján's history and cobbled together scraps of information that escaped Ján's miserly sense of privacy into intriguing clues. Alban knew that Ján was a talented musician. He had also gleaned that Ján spoke Polish, German, and Russian with ease, but he could not identify which part of the world Ján considered his home. Nor did he know how Ján had lost one of his ears or what traumas prompted the nightmares that caused him to wail in his sleep.

Alban was confident that when the time was right, he would learn the story behind his friend's injuries as well as the fates of Vera, Dima, and Maks. Those were the names Ján shouted in his dreams then later professed not to know.

For their crimes against the Soviet regime and the threats that their personhood posed, both Ján and Alban had been sent as expendable labor in service to section 503, the farthest north and east of any part of the doomed project. They hacked and clawed their way through dense coniferous forests and ancient stands of birch and aspen, laying timbers to build fragile corduroy roads over the swampy terrain so that the first vehicles could gain access to areas that until now had likely been seen by more birds and bears than people.

They laid railway lines over spongy permafrost and watched those same tracks heave and buckle as the weather turned from soggy in the summer to frozen in the winter. They built bridges over recalcitrant rivers and constructed massive embankments to try to shield the project from the inevitable whims of the arctic climate. They watched their fellow laborers die of dysentery, typhus, exposure, and unrelenting depression. Then they arose each morning with the prospect of doing it all again. Five years and counting of beating the grim odds.

They arrived at the Barabanicha Labor Camp at the end of a work shift. The line to enter the camp was long, and some of the men and women reporting back from their work shifts were injured. Ján and Alban stood in the unrelenting heat alongside their fellow marchers and waited while old prisoners then new were meticulously checked in by the guards and passed through the disinfection huts, an exercise in collective misery.

"Can you believe the size of this place?" Alban tried to wander out of line to get the full measure of the camp before he was shoved at gunpoint back to the group. "It's like a whole city here!"

Indeed, compared to the other camps where they had been interned, this was a massive undertaking with rows of wooden buildings watched over by precipitous guard towers above and bellicose dogs below, all surrounded by barbed wire fences. Despite the expansive workings, Barabanicha had only one main entrance with an arched gateway constructed of wood and a single guard's office to govern all the goings and comings.

One by one, Ján, Alban, and the rest of their group had to submit to interrogations about their identity, their crimes, and the length of their sentences. Then they surrendered their clothing for disinfection, all of it thrown in a pile for cleaning. Ján clung to his precious book of songs through steam baths and painful haircuts from an oddly engineered shearing machine, assaults that were followed by full body shaves to deter lice. Ján noticed that the welts on Alban's backside were swelling and resolved to find him some help, but they were pushed along before he could ask. Alban was joking with their fellow travelers, and Ján wondered anew where he found his deep well of joy amidst all the deprivations.

Once established in their barracks and wearing the random bits of clothing that had been handed to them, Ján's too large and Alban's comically small, their wanderings confirmed that the camp was indeed extensive, far bigger than Ján had seen during his five years' servitude on the rail project. There were rows of barracks surrounding the administrative building, each marked with its own special interior color, another curiously personal imprint and a reminder that this bleak and desolate place carried the touch of humans and the weight of their suffering.

Ján's and Alban's barracks featured splashes of purple paint inside and held a single stove to warm the fifty prisoners that it was intended to house. Bunks were solidly built with shelves underneath for the few personal items each inhabitant could claim. Other barracks in the vicinity were smaller and moderately better appointed, and there was a clear delineation of the men's and women's quarters through the strategic placement of ample coils of razor wire. There was indeed an infirmary, a luxury that hadn't existed in other camps, and the accompanying hut was blessed with two stoves. Peering through the barred windows, Ján and Alban decided it was for the doctors and essential staff, a small perk in their bondage.

Mixed in with the barracks were carpentry shops, washrooms, disinfection huts, a massive dining hall, kitchens, a bath house, storerooms, dog kennels, and the ubiquitous solitary quarters for punishment. That feature was a constant in all the camps, and Ján shuddered when he passed by, noting the metal-clad doors punctuated only by peepholes for guards. Both he and Alban had done their share of time in solitary often for the most menial of perceived infractions, and they dreaded their inevitable introduction to this particular lodge. It was about control, they knew that well, and there was no avoiding it. Escape was a self-imposed death sentence.

They returned to their barracks after a meal of coarse bread and thin soup. Tomorrow, they would receive their work orders, and they pondered what fresh hell awaited them. As they approached the long hut, Ján stopped and tilted his head.

"What's with you?" Alban asked impatiently. "I'm in a hurry to get off my feet."

Ján held up his hand and pointed to the door of their quarters. "Music. I hear music." Ján closed his eyes and absorbed the muted sounds that wafted through the open door. A tired instrument and a novice player, but to Ján's ears, the piece was beautiful.

"Well don't just stand there, let's go see," urged Alban.

At the far end of the hut, a lone man held a battered guitar. Ján had not seen an instrument since his tour with The Besprizornye Musicians so many years ago, and this one had clearly been through its own desperate journey. Water-stained and out of tune, the guitar transported him to a time when he was surrounded by the luxury of song. Memories of his parents, Aunt Ada, Herr Kippels, and even Uncle Erik flooded his thoughts, and he choked back a lump in his throat. He clutched his prized book, as always lashed to his waist, and watched the young man fumble with the strings. Ján had never been taught to play a guitar, but he had a sense of how to tease a tune out of the instrument. He approached the man and sat on the floor opposite.

The man looked up and grinned. "Sorry for the noise, I've never actually played one of these before. I was a trumpet player before all of this," he said as he waved his hand to highlight the rows of bunks and the primitive conditions. "I'm Sergei, by the way, welcome to Barabanicha."

Ján introduced himself and Alban, unable to quell his curiosity. "How did you come by the guitar?"

Sergei rubbed his chin, "It belonged to a fellow traveler named Yuri. He brought it all the way with him from wherever he called home. Carried it through the ice and snow and hauled it through the swamps. He took better care of it than he did his wife, God rest her soul, and he played it for us each night. We kind of got used to it. He died this morning, and they just came to take his things. The guards either didn't see this or just left it behind, so I thought I would try to learn a chord or two."

Sergei chuckled. "We'll miss the music a lot more than we'll miss Yuri. He was an old coot, full of anger and complaints, but this guitar settled him down, and he could play like an angel."

Ján reached out and Sergei handed him the instrument. The wood was warped, but to Ján, it was magnificent. He plucked a fragile string and produced an ornery note, flat and warbled. Ján adjusted the tuning key gently, and Sergei and Alban watched as he entered an inner world, oblivious to all but the guitar. One by one, Ján delicately twisted each of the tuning keys, listening carefully for the best tone and pitch. Then he sat back, closed his eyes, and strummed, placing his fingers on the frets to tease out the notes. It would never be perfect, but it sounded better.

A ruckus erupted near the door and broke Ján's spell. A herd of men barreled between the bunks led by a thick-headed brute with piercing blue eyes. "What's this now?" he asked. "Old Yuri's not cold in his grave, and we've got the new pups clamoring for his treasures."

Ján swiftly handed the guitar back to Sergei and stood up. He wasn't looking for trouble on his first day. He extended his hand. "I'm Ján. The guitar is not mine; Sergei here was kind enough to let me try to tune it, that's all."

The man laughed. "No need to explain. I'm Edgars and we all hated the old geezer. Sorry to say it, but he's better off wherever he is now. Hoping someone can play that thing though."

Sergei began to strum out a tune, a lively song with hints of decadent jazz that soon had the men tapping their feet. Alban grabbed a metal bowl and spoon and began to pound out a percussive rhythm, and Ján clapped along.

Edgars whooped and danced. "That'll do just fine! Yes, sir, that'll do!"

Word spread in the camp that the purple barracks had a fledgling musical troupe forming, and visitors began appearing at the door each evening as the workday was done. Ján played occasionally, but Sergei with his experience performing in underground jazz clubs in Moscow had already acquired a version of a fan club.

Other musicians began to come forward. Andras, a baritone from Vilnius, Jozef, a violinist from Stalingrad, and Imrich, a tuba player from Leningrad. They had makeshift instruments to accompany the guitar, and each night featured a lively mix of singing and dancing in the different languages of the camp, usually all at the same time. They came in from the construction sites, endured the disinfection routines, and with their bellies at least partially satiated with meager portions of bread, soup, or porridge, they gathered to make merry.

As the summer months faded into fall, the dreaded insects diminished but cold weather set in. As bad as the midges were, exposure to the extreme temperatures was worse, and the men knew that they would not all survive. Ján tried in vain to warm his hands as he paced back and forth in front of the solitary cells. Alban had been gone for two days now, and Ján was worried about him. The guard sat outside whittling a piece of wood down to a nub. He looked up to see Ján loitering nearby.

"Get along, you have no business here!"

Ján held up his hands. "I mean no disrespect, but I am checking on my friend here. Alban Tuluukov."

The guard grunted. "He'll be sprung soon enough and you'll see him. Wait any longer, and I'll toss you in there with him." He held up his knife and pointed at Ján. "I said GO!"

Two more days passed before Alban wandered into the barracks after dinner. He was pale, his head had been recently shaved, and he wore clothes that were several sizes too small.

"By all means, don't wait for me. Play on, gentlemen!" he announced.

Ján glanced up and smiled. "It's about time. We missed your horrible sense of rhythm."

The ensemble was six men strong tonight. Always Sergei and the guitar in the lead with an assortment of cobbled together instruments in accompaniment. They launched into a spirited version of "Kalinka Malinka".

As was traditional with the beloved folk song, the men sang the chorus three times, each repetition faster than the last, but when it was time to launch the next verse, a strong baritone voice rang out. It didn't come from within the assembled group, but rather from outside the window.

Sergei played on, but most of the men ran to the door and peered out. The guard who had been watching over Alban sat in the dirt on his haunches, his head thrown back in song.

Alban explained, "Well, we got to talking through that blasted metal door. Turns out, he was studying opera in Petrograd before being ordered into the army. He let me out in exchange for the chance to sing with us. It's just tonight, I promise."

The guard looked up and tipped his hat. Ján nodded his head in a show of gratitude and led the men back inside.

As the days got shorter and the temperatures plummeted, the men became accustomed to their Russian baritone harmonizing from the other side of the thin wall. The guard, Egor Zaitsev, never asked to enter the barracks, and the men never invited him in. Music was a common thread that joined them, but it couldn't surmount the imbalance of power.

The men shuffled back into camp from the worksite, intent on finding their way through the blinding snow. The gelid landscape was obscured by the swirling flakes, whipping in and around the ice-clad trees. The wind howled, and they lined up to shield themselves, their hands on the shoulders of the men before them and their visibility limited to the length of their battered arms. One foot in front of another, over and over. The sound of a dog barking signaled their proximity to the camp, and then the guard tower gradually came into view overhead. The line paused at the gate for permission to re-enter. Each in turn was checked in, and then he was sent on to the disinfection hut. Today marked the ten-day rotation for Ján, Alban, and their group to submit to the steam bath and shaving routine. They surrendered their clothes and huddled in the hot room, the sudden change from freezing to heat both painful and welcome.

Ján was shocked to see the bruises on Alban's body. Big purple splotches rimmed in black littered his pallid skin. His coughing had never abated, but somehow it seemed less notable as all the men succumbed to ravages of the extreme elements. Coughing in the hut was as ubiquitous as breathing these days. The bruising was new.

At night, the dreams came to Ján. Unwanted guests who wouldn't leave, they took root in his subconscious and gnawed at the threads of his sanity. Ján was slipping into melancholia, unable to shake off the sense of his own culpability in his fate. To avoid the dreams, Ján lay in his hard wooden bunk and fought sleep. In the night, tossing from side to side, listening to the snores, sneezes, and coughs of his fellow laborers, he relived his removal from the No. 15 Special Home in acute detail.

He remembered being shackled in isolation as his punishment for going down the lane with Maks and attempting to ride out on the truck, but Ján knew there had also been deeper suspicions of him because he possessed incriminating information. He remembered shivering on the hard-packed dirt floor, his joints aching. He remembered Katia drawing up alongside the wall, the sound of her voice in his head clear despite the passage of years.

"Ján!" she whispered. "Are you alright? Mrs. Kotova told us you were away, but I had a feeling you were here."

"Go away, Katia. You don't want to get into trouble. I'm here. You can tell the others, I'm here." Ján struggled not to cry.

"What happened? You must tell me."

"No. Leave me alone, Katia. For your own good, leave me alone."

"Suit yourself, but do you need anything? Anything that I can do?"

"One thing. Do you know where Maks is? He was hurt, and I am worried about him."

Silence.

"Katia?"

"Ján, he's dead. The men went into the forest and found him. Mrs. Kotova gathered us together to say that you and he ran away, but that he didn't make it. He died in the woods. I thought you knew."

Ján remembered his sobs erupting, shaking his thin body against the unforgiving ground. His tears puddled in the dirt as he lay in the mud formed by his grief for Maks and his anger at having put his fearless friend in danger.

And then came the night of his release. The door opened and two armed guards stood just outside. Torchlight shone harsh and accusatory across Ján's prone body. He stared into the light, marshaling every shred of energy to defy his jailors, but he couldn't tell who was there until he heard Mrs. Kotova's voice.

"Here he is, boys. All yours. He is too old to be here and is proving to be a bad influence on the children."

Mrs. Kotova stepped aside and covered her nose against the stench as the guards reached in to unlock the shackles and haul Ján to his feet. He was taken to a prison overnight and put on a train, then a wagon, then a barge. Weeks of travel with no hint of his destination until they reached the first labor camp. He remembered meeting Alban and adjusting to life on the work crew, his hands covered with calluses as he hacked away at the swampy permafrost and battled the intractable forest.

At last, the spool of memories would fade as sleep claimed him, but then dreams began. Maks appeared on a bridge just built, luring Ján to the edge. "Come over," he would taunt, "you deserve to be with me. It's simple. Just step off and fly."

Vera joined Maks, and they accused him. "You lived, and we died. You hold the secrets, and you do nothing."

Sometimes the dreams featured Aunt Ada, shaking her fist.

"You were just supposed to play, Ján. If you had just stayed at the piano, none of this would have happened."

Other times, it was the pictures of the children in the files, taunting him.

Alban began coughing so hard in the bottom bunk that he jostled Ján awake. Ján sat up, sweating in spite of the frosted room. He leaned over and peered down at his friend. "You sound worse. I'm worried for you."

Alban wiped his mouth with a rag and quickly stowed it under his pillow. "That's a fine accusation coming from you. You were at it again, you know. The names you yell out each night. They haunt you."

The following evening, Sergei gently lifted the guitar from under his bunk and settled himself on the floor. The men fed the furnace with the abandoned possessions of the dead and settled into the music as Sergei played. The mood in the hut was subdued, and amidst the sniffles and coughs of the men, Sergei strummed a simple folk song.

Ján watched Alban. He lay on his bunk with his head nestled in the thin blanket. His eyes were closed, but a smile was forming at the corners of his mouth as he strummed his fingers along with Sergei's song. He had struggled on the work detail today. Ján had stood by him, catching him when he stumbled and putting part of his efforts into ensuring that Alban met his work quota for the day. They wouldn't be able to sustain that for long. They both knew it. The icy grip of winter was setting in, and blizzard conditions were once again becoming the norm.

Ján stepped back from the men, wrapped his blanket around his shoulders, and quickly slipped out of the hut. The cold air hit him and knocked him breathless for just a moment before he recovered his equilibrium. The dark figure huddled under the window.

"I thought I might find you here. I hoped I might," said Ján.

Egor turned to face him. "Not enough voices in there to cover up my presence out here, eh?"

Ján drew closer, and pulled his blanket tighter against the wind. His teeth were rattling so violently that it was hard to talk. "I need your help. With Alban."

Egor drew up straight and tall. He had the luxury of his thick woolen coat and fur ushanka hat with the earflaps. He also had a significant and intimidating size advantage over Ján. Now he was no longer Egor, the fellow musician, but Sgt. Zaitsev, the camp guard. "What is it that you think I could or should do?"

"He's dying, and he won't last long. He needs to see a doctor and he needs a different duty assignment. Do they need help in the infirmary, or the kitchen, or the carpentry shop? If he goes out on the detail tomorrow, he will die."

Egor stroked his chin with his thick gloves and pondered Ján's request. "Tell me why I should. You know you are brought here to die. All of you. Survival has never been the goal."

"Yes," Ján said, "but you are a human, as am I, and so is Alban. You must help him."

"I can get him assigned to a preferred duty, but it will cost you the guitar. I want it, and if you get it for me, I will see to it that he is pulled off the detail."

Ján felt the pain of defeat in his chest. "It is not mine to give. Please tell me that there is something else."

"What could you possibly have that I would want? Meet me with the guitar here at midnight, or you both go out tomorrow, same as always. You're a clever man, Balik. You'll figure it out." And he strode off in his big black boots and voluminous coat of warmth and privilege.

Ján returned to the hut. The men were clustered around Sergei, harmonizing softly. Alban had fallen asleep, clutching the blanket. Ján noticed that a spot of blood was collecting on the mattress under his nose. Ján climbed into his bunk over the top of Alban's and curled into a ball. He could not sleep, and he couldn't get Maks out of his mind. What would he have done to save him? Anything.

The guard came to get Alban in the morning darkness, just as the men were waking up and trying to stoke a thin wisp of warmth from the stove. Ján used the spade to break the icy seal on the water bucket and splashed his face. His beard was scraggly but every little protection against the cold was welcome.

"Alban Tuluukov!" the guard announced. Alban rolled over in bed and rubbed his eyes. Everyone but Ján tried to look busy.

Alban coughed and pulled up the blanket. "What have I done now?" He was groggy and confused.

"Gather your things, Tuluukov. You're coming with us."

Alban began to throw his few possessions on his blanket. Ján approached and helped him pile up his gloves and scarf.

"It's alright. You're getting resettled. Go with them and get well," Ján said quietly.

"What do you know? What have you done?"

"Shhh. Go. I'll come and visit you."

The men returned from the disinfection hut, a cursory exercise at best in the frigid winter months, and collapsed on their bunks. Sergei warmed his hands by the stove and reached under the bed, already humming the bars of a gentle folk song. He stopped when his hands met the cold floor. "What the devil? It's gone! Someone has stolen our guitar." He looked up, the anguish in his eyes. Edgars began ripping the threadbare blankets from the beds as Jozef lay flat on the floor, peering under other bunks. Panic was setting in.

"I gave it to Egor," Ján said quietly.

Jozef rolled over and stared at Ján. "You did what?"

"I gave it to Egor. In exchange for Alban. He was dying. It was the only way I knew to save him." Ján began to shake, his fear of losing Alban and now his fear of losing these friends overwhelmed him.

Sergei thundered across the room, his face turning crimson as his anger mounted. "You had no right! It wasn't yours to give. It belonged to all of us, and all of us should have made that decision." Sergei inched up to Ján's face. "Why Alban, eh? Every one of us needs saving. Who told you that you get to decide who lives and dies?"

Ján swallowed hard. Sergei was right of course, and there hadn't been time. He was searching for words, an explanation, when the first blow landed on his back, right at his kidney. The pain knocked his breath away, and he fell over on the floor. Boots rained down on him, kicking, shoving. He heard Jozef pleading for them to stop and then a pop when his ribs cracked. He tasted blood, and his last thought before losing consciousness was that today was as good a day as any to die.

The tiny metal window slid open again, and Egor's face peered through the small aperture. "Balik! Are you dead?"

Ján moaned but did not open his eyes. Egor jangled his keys and pulled back the big door. A wave of fresh air rushed into the tiny chamber, and Egor followed with a cup of warm water and a slice of bread. "You smell like shit." He dipped the bread in the cup and forced a small bite into Ján's mouth. "I am getting tired of being your nursemaid. Here, drink this." He held the cup to Ján's parched mouth and poured a bit of liquid down his throat. Ján began to cough, and it set off such pain that he just wanted to drift off into oblivion. He had no desire, no strength left, to battle this world.

Egor set down the plate and unshackled Ján from the bindings. "It's your lucky day. You are finished serving your punishment for starting the fight."

Ján groaned, gasping for air. "I didn't start a fight. You know that."

"Perhaps, but the men in your hut said you did, and you weren't talking. C'mon, I'll help you up." Egor reached down and pulled Ján to his feet. Ján screamed and passed out.

He awoke to the sounds of clinking glass and the hushed tones of a whispered conversation. Keeping his eyes closed against the pain, he tried to process where he was. His chest ached, and he was shivering, a feverish cold. Even through the ringing in his ears, he could tell that this room echoed differently than the hut. It was smaller, and fewer people were clustered about. He lay quietly, absorbing the warmth of the space and gathering his wits.

As his consciousness developed more clarity, cherished memories flooded his thoughts—his mother, Aunt Ada, his fingers on the piano keys. Piano. The image jolted him out of his comforting reverie, and his hands reached for his midsection where his book of music stayed strapped to his waist. He felt nothing. Panicked, he tried to roll over, and he knocked into a small table. A metal cup of water tipped over and fell, clanging against the hard wooden floor. Footsteps hurried his way.

"Settle down, my friend. You are safe."

Ján opened his eyes, and a sharp pain seized his head. He struggled to focus.

"It's Alban, don't try to say anything. You are quite ill, but you will be alright."

At the sound of Alban's name, Ján shut his eyes and reached out his hand. The pain took hold in his chest.

Alban clasped his hand and patted it gently. "You are in the infirmary. You have broken ribs from the beating Edgars meted out, and you have typhus from God knows where. Probably that evil isolation room."

"My book, my music...I must have it. Where is it, Alban? Please tell me!" Ján's panic was rising again. He needed his hands on the book.

"Settle down, my friend. You're lucky I was here when Egor brought you in. They stripped you down and gave you a thorough scrub. Your clothes, they burned, but I saw the book and your stupid hat on the pile and saved them for you. Your book is here, under the bed, probably infected."

Ján continued to thrash about until Alban placed the book on his chest. He wrapped both his arms around his treasured possession and melted into the mattress, his body defeated, but his mind sparking with unrest as his tortured memories settled on the faces of his family.

Alban pulled up a chair. "I know this is my doing," he confessed. "Because of you, I get to work inside, in the warmth, and even get a cupful of bone broth every now and then," he shared conspiratorially. "Soothing but God only knows where it comes from."

Ján tipped his head forward to acknowledge Alban's point.

"You will tell me one day, eh? What this book means? You are a fool, Ján Balik, but I am glad you are my friend."

Ján received Alban's compliment as an accusation. Was that the sum total of Ján's worth now? Alban's friend? He was a grown man now, and he was not the man his parents had envisioned. No home, no family, no education, no country even. Certainly, no destiny to spread joy and beauty. Why couldn't he have just died on that floor? He thought again about the children in the orphanage. How many survived? In that moment, Ján's heart shattered. He wailed, a deep cry of pain and rejection. His faith had been wrenched away long ago, and in the void, his soul cried for release from guilt.

Alban reached down and gathered him into a tender embrace. He pulled Ján's emaciated frame into his lap and rocked him until his outrage was spent and the crying ebbed. Others in the room scurried to the edges like cockroaches in the light to see two men embrace in love and pain. Alban ignored them.

He spoke softly into Ján's ear, "I am of the Sakha people, and we have a truth, 'the tree doesn't move without the wind.' You and I are the wind, brother, and we must blow to change this world. We will not be defeated, and we will not let them steal our spirit and our love. Do you hear me? My people live in the harshest place on this earth, and we survive because we live in harmony with nature. We revere the sun. We respect the icy winds. We thank nature for abundance and for scarcity. We are not like these fools who try to conquer and rule. They tried to destroy our language, our spiritual traditions, yet they will only bring destruction on themselves. This work we do now for them? It is for a dead road, built with hubris and arrogance. It is bound to fail because we are fighting nature, and nature always prevails."

Alban rocked Ján back and forth. As if he heard Ján's thoughts, he said, "You have not lost your family forever. They are still all around you. The soft breezes of spring, the biting sleet of winter, the flowers, the trees—your family is a part of all that."

He began to sing, but it was unlike anything Ján had ever heard before. Haunting and beautiful, jarring and melodic. Ján yielded to Alban's embrace and allowed himself to be enveloped in the music. Alban's voice became a rush of wind blowing down from the mountain. It became the reindeer and the birds as they answered the wind. Then it became a human cry, calling out to nature with reverence and respect. Alban had burrowed deep into the chant, summoning the spirits for strength and resilience. The room was quiet save for Alban's exhortations, and it seemed that they were all wrapped in a mystical spell. His singing gradually became softer and gentler until it was barely a whisper, yet Ján could feel it flowing still from Alban's chest. Then he was quiet.

He carefully placed Ján back into the cot and smoothed the covers. "I will not let you go, brother," Alban assured him. "I will not let you go to that dark place."

Ján reached out and clasped Alban's hand. He nodded and turned to walk away, but Ján stopped him. In a timid voice, he asked, "Will they ever forgive me for the guitar?"

Alban paused. "You don't know?" he asked. "But of course, how could you?"

"Know what?" Ján tried to sit up, and the pain shot through his chest again.

"The day after they beat you up, after Egor hauled you to the isolation room, there was an accident on the work crew. The snow, it was blinding, and the men were trapped. Andras survived, but he suffered severe frostbite. He lies just over there. But the rest, Sergei, Edgars, gentle Jozef. The rest, they didn't make it."

Chapter 7

Anna's Song

Kaliningrad, formerly Königsberg, the Soviet Union
Autumn 1953

Ján shifted in his seat, trying to relieve his aching backside on the unyielding wooden bench. The woman squeezed against his shoulder glared at him and harumphed with displeasure. He put his hand on his knee to quell his tapping foot and forced himself to concentrate on the view as the soft patterns of the rural landscape rolled by the train windows.

The rhythms of rail travel put him in a fraught state of mind, and the placid cattle and gently undulating pastures did little to ease his discomfort. His journey was almost complete after months of scrounging for any means to move west, and the closer he came to Kaliningrad, the greater the uncertainties loomed.

Stalin was dead, and along with his demise came the end of the Dead Road project. Ján and Alban had received their release notices within the same week. Alban had thrown his cap into the air and whooped. Then he had grabbed Ján and twirled him around. "I am going back to Turul!" he had shouted. "I will find myself a wife and together we will make fat and happy children. My mother will be a grandmother!"

Other prisoners had joined in, clapping and hugging each other. Ján had laughed at their exuberance. Alban had won. Despite all their hardships and deprivations, the loss of their friends, and the crippling toll on their bodies, their jailors had not succeeded in robbing his friend of his joy and his zeal for living.

Yet in the quiet moments that came later, Ján had been forced to confront what this meant for him. He had no home, no papers, no country of allegiance, and no family anticipating his return. His scars were frightening, and Ján doubted that any woman would consider him as a suitable husband and father to her fat and happy children. He had no real education beyond the refined music halls of Königsberg, and he hadn't touched a piano in years. He was forced for the first time to acknowledge that this camp was the closest thing to home that he knew. He had nowhere to go.

His roiling emotions found expression in a melody, one that was both somber and nostalgic with morose chords and cautious rhythms. He reached under his jacket for his book and penciled in the notes under the title, "Barabanicha on the Dead Road" written in German, then after a pause, he added the title in Russian and Polish, such was his sense of dislocation. This book chronicled all the tumult, aching disappointments, and fleeting moments of joy from the past years, and he thumbed through the pages revisiting the memories of those he cherished. Only two of these pieces had ever been played on an instrument. The rest existed only on the page and in Ján's heart. He closed the book and rubbed his thumb over the cracked leather cover, scarred, pierced, and water-stained, before securing it under his belt. He tried to find fault with his reasoning for this journey, but with few options, he inevitably arrived at the same conclusion. Soon, he would know if he had chosen wisely.

The exodus from the camps back toward points west meant that all methods of transport were brimming with displaced people, the few among the millions exiled who were happily or anxiously plotting a return to an uncertain future. They had been savagely uprooted from their communities and had long dreamed of returning, but years had passed, and there were no assurances that anyone familiar would be left to greet them or help them re-establish themselves. They were marked as criminals and undesirables, and it would be impossible to stitch back the lives they had left behind. Ján had endured months in transit via barges, wagon rides, trains, and on foot. He was frightened and hopeful in equal measure.

Alban had begged Ján to accompany him to Turul. "We'll get you some kind of job, and you can live with me until I find a wife!" Ján was touched by Alban's offer, but either pride or pragmatism prevented him from agreeing. Why would Ján go farther east? His roots were in the west, and he was drawn back there by tenuous memories and the promise of familiar sights. They parted ways and promised to keep in touch. Alban slipped Ján a piece of paper with an address on it. "Just in case you change your mind," he had said with a wink.

"Kaliningrad! Next station, Kaliningrad!"

Ján sat up straighter, tilted his head back, and stretched his weary shoulders. He felt in his pocket for the identification papers Alban had stolen for him from the burn pile at the infirmary. They marked him as Evgeni Baburin from Gorky, and although they were singed, all the information was intact. Ján carefully folded the documents and smoothed out the damaged corner. *You and me both*, he thought, *a bit rougher around the edges than we used to be.*

Ján resolved to charge forward into his new life and hoped that Evgeni, poor soul, would open the door for his return to Königsberg, now Kaliningrad. It was the only place that he remembered with any clarity, but when he had been forced out of the city, it was a German town. Now it belonged to the Soviet Union, and all Germans had reportedly been expelled, arrested, or killed. Polish Ján Balik was unlikely to be admitted. German Jan

Richter was certainly forbidden. Evgeni from Gorky just might have a chance.

He had no guesses about what he would find here, but at the least, he planned to say a proper goodbye to Ada. He owed her that.

The train pulled into the outskirts of town, and Ján spied few familiar sites. The station that had welcomed him fourteen years earlier as a young boy bore ugly scorch marks and evidence of vandalism. In the vestiges of the once impressive façade, he spied the large window that looked like a giant beehive. It was at once recognizable and sadly altered, but a sign that he was indeed back in the city that he had once called home. He closed his eyes and cherished for a moment the memory of Ada waiting for him at the platform. There would be no such greeting today.

Alighting from the train, he adjusted his rucksack and submitted his papers for scrutiny. The young soldier stepped aside to show his documents to a superior, and they consulted for a moment. Ján's heart thumped, and he focused on holding his sweaty hands still. He would not be able to answer any questions about Evgeni's family or the city of Gorky with confidence. They could put him back on the train or haul him right to prison. The possibilities were grim, but after a time, the soldier returned. Summoning his most authoritative voice, he warned Ján to register with the police and keep them informed about his movements. Evgeni Baburin was a known enemy of the State and required monitoring. Ján simply nodded and walked away. One success.

As he strolled along the busy thoroughfares, he summoned memories of the pleasures he had experienced in this place with Ada. He took his time to wander the streets by the castle and revisit Ada's favored shopping district. The signs in German were long gone, all was in Russian now, but Ján saw an ice cream shop near the castle that he recognized, and he meandered across the one familiar bridge that had withstood the barrage of bombs in years past. Many of the grand boulevards of gracious homes and lively cafés had been replaced by the ugly concrete buildings favored by the Soviets. The city was a drab imitation of its former self.

The building that had once housed the academy was gone, replaced by a boxy, utilitarian school. Ján walked up the circular drive to watch the children of the Russians elite play on the grounds oblivious to the story of the place where they now frolicked. The location of the concert hall was a grassy park with paths and fading flowers designed to entice families out for a casual stroll.

Ján thought of his years of servitude in the Arctic, the bitter cold, the grim conditions. All that time, this park that held echoes of his past performances had been a place of peace and contentment. He felt cheated and dwelled for just a moment in self-pity, a nod to the years lost and the people he still mourned.

Ján resumed his journey. He knew he was procrastinating, and it was time to confront the most painful of his memories. He walked down the tree-lined avenue of the familiar neighborhood, a riot of glorious yellow, red, and bronze leaves in a spectacular autumn display. Ján had expected for everything to seem bigger, more impressive than the bleak surroundings of his recent past, but in truth, the houses that remained seemed smaller than he remembered and all appeared worn and diminished. He thought back to the last time he had walked this street, terrorized by Ada's death and seeking a protected path through the ice to warn Uncle Erik. Then he was only a young boy, and now he was a man. The world was a different place indeed.

At the end of the street, the house stood much as Ján remembered it. The gardens, once trimmed to perfection under Karl's care, were overgrown with the last of the fall flowers. Birds flitted among the red berries in the untrimmed shrubs, and blue swaths of late-season lobelia competed for sunlight with heady yellow chrysanthemums nestled in the vague outlines of the former flower beds, the weight of their fat blooms bending the stalks low. As Ján approached the house, he noticed that the paint was brittle and chipped, but otherwise it showed signs of care.

He walked up the stairs and stood by the door, wracked by fear and indecision, but as his heart settled and his resolve stiffened, he raised his hand and knocked. There was no immediate response, yet he waited. He scrutinized every brick and stone for signs that he was welcome here, but the house remained mute.

After a few minutes, as Ján raised his hand to knock again, he heard movement inside. A slow but steady gait advanced closer to the front entrance, and a woman called out in Russian, "Be patient, I'm coming!" She opened the door, and Ján stared at a stranger. An old man coughed somewhere in the shadows of the house.

"My family lived here once. My aunt and uncle."

Confusion clouded her face, and she stepped forward while adjusting her thick glasses. Her mouth pinched into a tight frown, and she put her hands on her hips. "German scum."

"My aunt died here." Ján pointed past her to the music room door, looking much as it did when he last pounded against it.

She didn't invite him in, but rather moved to plant her feet more firmly to block his path. "I don't know anything. This house is ours. Go away."

Ján bit his bottom lip and worked to keep his anger in check. "May I just come in and say my peace? I'm not here to argue with you. Truly after all that has happened, I do not want to argue with you. I would like to pay my respects, that is all."

"There is no respect that German scum can offer in my home. You are not welcome. Leave!"

Ján put his hat in his hands and slipped past her into the foyer. "I mean you no harm, but I came a long way and will say my peace."

She screamed at him as she shuffled to the kitchen, her distress punctuated by the sounds of cabinet doors slamming and utensils clattering to the floor. The old man called out, complaining about the commotion.

Ján stood before the music room, focused only on his memories of Ada's plaintive cries, as clear now as when he was a young man pleading with the soldiers through this very door. "Rest with peace, Ada," he said in Polish. "You were kind to me, and I will always remember you with love."

The woman returned brandishing a wooden rolling pin. "Get out of my house! I will call the police! You will regret this!"

Ján fled from her and the house, running away with as much speed as he could muster. He would never return here, and as he scarpered around familiar corners and well-remembered streets, he relinquished any sentimental ties to the house and consigned it to the evil that had stained it. He was certain that Ada's spirit had long ago separated from that place.

He wandered aimlessly, his stomach growling, his pockets empty, and his emotions on edge. Had he really believed that Erik was still here, waiting to welcome him back and help get him on his feet? It was a delusion brought on by desperation, and now he had to make the best of the situation in a place that was at the same time familiar and wholly foreign. He had no money for food, much less for a ticket out of town. He had been warned to register with the authorities wherever he decided to stay, but while it seemed futile to stay here, it was just as unthinkable to start over somewhere new. Where would he go?

Returning to the business district, he meandered by the storefronts, most repaired and sporting new signage in Russian. He scanned the crowds seeking a familiar face, but no one glanced his way. He spied a row of refuse bins in an alley and ducked in to rummage among the debris for a morsel of food.

"Hey, you, go away!" a man shouted, brandishing a knife as he charged out of a door. Ján grabbed a paper parcel and scurried away. The man retreated but not before screaming obscenities over his shoulder. Free of his pursuer, Ján slowed his gait and unwrapped the paper to find a collection of chicken bones. Smiling at his good fortune, he sucked each clean of marrow, savoring each morsel that he was able to glean from the delicate offering. He tried to remember when he had last eaten meat and failed to recollect.

The sun was setting as he wandered across the lone surviving bridge and through the old part of town. He saw now that evidence of the bombings still marred the face of the city much the same way his body had incorporated the assaults he'd endured. It was a part of who he was whether he liked it or not, and in his reckoning, it branded him as damaged and undeserving. The city wore its scars with more dignity than he could muster.

A biting wind blew off the river, and he wrapped his thin jacket tighter as he watched lights shutting off in the storefronts one minute and then flickering on shortly after in the living quarters above. He thought of what it must be like to have a home with a bed, a cozy fire, a full larder, and a companion to share it all with. Shadows moved behind curtains, and Ján grieved in his solitude.

Someone somewhere was playing a piano, and Ján paused to take in the sound. Like an insect summoned by a light, he turned a corner down a narrow street and followed the notes to an unimposing little café. Hints of bright lights from hidden spaces leaked onto the sidewalk in front. The jaunty rhythms, clearly the work of an amateur player, danced in the night air, and Ján stood transfixed. How long had it been since he had been in the presence of music? The guitar. It had been that blasted guitar.

A man approached him from behind, but Ján was so intent on listening to the music that he didn't notice. The man swerved on unsteady feet and slammed into Ján's shoulder, knocking them both off balance.

"*Mne zhal*—I'm sorry," he slurred in Russian, hastily brushing off Ján's jacket.

Ján tried to hold the man back, assuring him that no harm was done when both men wobbled to their feet and faced each other. There was just enough light in the alley for Ján to see the man's features, and his heart skipped a beat. "Eduard? Eduard von Habel, no? From the academy!"

Eduard tried to focus his inebriated eyes to peer into Ján's face. "Yes, that is me. Who are...wait! No! It couldn't be. You're the boy, the wunderkind. The Richters' little prodigy, right?" Eduard wiped his nose on the sleeve of his jacket and attempted to hug Ján. "It's wonderful to see you! A bit of a connection from the old days, eh?" Eduard leaned back unsteadily. "You must join me for a drink, that is if you can treat me to a spot of good cheer." He made a show of turning out his pockets to reveal threadbare emptiness.

Ján's hopes were dashed when he realized that he and Eduard were fellow vagrants. "I'm afraid that I am equally bereft, my friend. Perhaps you can guide me to a spot where I can rest tonight?"

Eduard chuckled. He wrapped his arm around Ján's shoulder and smiled. "I have a better idea. Follow me!" Like a field marshal leading his troops, he gestured ahead and took a bold step only to collapse on the pavement. Ján reached down to help him up and noticed Eduard's prosthetic, a crude wooden semblance of a leg.

"The war?" he asked.

Eduard fumbled, trying to regain his composure. "An explosion, those damned U-Boats." He brushed the conversation away, and pulled himself up. "I suspect you know nothing of such traumas. Erik Richter's golden nephew would not have to stoop to such indignities."

Ján moved in front of Eduard and pulled off his cap, exposing the scars where his ear should have been. "I have no desire to compete with you for the saddest story. I share this with you only in solidarity, and I am sorry about your leg." He pulled his hat back on his head and put his arm around Eduard's shoulder, "How have you come to be here? It seems that all Germans have been banished and replaced by good Soviets."

"Indeed," slurred Eduard, "and thus my dirty little secret. German father, Russian mother. Isn't that a lark? The war was rather awkward for my family." He laughed to himself and then gave in to a fit of coughing. "I had to make a choice, no? Joined up with the Ivans, and to my utter ash-stoshishment—" He paused and made a show of enunciating his words. "Astonishment, I ended up on the winning side. I don't think your uncle would like me much now, no? We're more alike than you think, my little wunderkind friend, both homeless mongrels."

"Then perhaps you can share that good idea with me."

They headed toward the light, and it turned out to be coming from the recesses of the little café. Eduard fiddled with the door and escorted Ján inside past a scattering of tables covered with cheerful, red-checked tablecloths. The menu board was folded neatly to the side, and the chairs had been cleaned and arranged in preparation for the morning's breakfast patrons. The kitchen door had a circular window, and light gleamed from within. The music was growing louder, and Ján could feel the vibrations from the floor. He was propelled forward by the magnetic pull of the notes. His fingers twitched and tingled.

Eduard beckoned him down a narrow passage behind the pantry to a small staircase leading to a cellar. Light, music, and the sounds of conversation and laughter flooded up from below. They followed the merriment and emerged into a smoky basement club complete with a bar and a small stage graced with an old upright piano. A woman wearing a bright red dress with lipstick to match was improvising a tune, a mishmash of folk songs and jazz that was oddly appealing. A smattering of patrons sat at the rickety tables and drank from an assortment of bottles. They broke into applause when they saw Eduard, and he responded with an exaggerated bow.

The woman quit playing, clearly annoyed that her audience had been usurped. She stepped off the stage and lit a cigarette, dramatically ceding the spotlight to Eduard and retreating to the bar. Eduard hobbled up to take her place and fumbled his way onto the bench at the piano. He was still woozy from his afternoon bender, but it had little effect on his performance. The audience roared with approval as he launched into an American ragtime tune, which delighted Ján with its complexity and dangerous associations. American music was forbidden now that the area was under Soviet rule. The audience egged Eduard on, bolstering his confidence and composure.

Ján moved to the side to watch. Leaning against the bar, he marveled at Eduard's skill. The last time he had seen him play, the man was dazzling an audience with Liszt's La Campanella, a remarkably difficult and acrobatic piece of music. Now, he seemed equally in his element with subversive tunes, a mix of loose honky-tonk rhythms rendered with technical skill. Despite his semi-inebriated state, his handwork was flawless, and he maneuvered the pedals with one foot while his prosthesis splayed out to the side.

The woman sidled up to Ján and offered him her cigarette. He accepted and took a long drag before he handed it back. She was young with wavy brunette hair and brilliant green eyes. Her fingernails were polished with stark red lacquer but raggedy and chewed to the quick. Ján thought she was beautiful.

"I'm Anna," she said, speaking in Russian, sticking out her hand.

"Ján Balik," he offered back, gratefully accepting her gesture with a handshake. "Do you come here often?"

She rolled her eyes. "Is that the best you can do?"

Ján blushed. He could build a railroad bridge over a raging river, but he had no experience striking up a conversation with a woman. He opened his mouth to try to interject something witty and memorable when he noticed that the audience was now turned in his direction, clapping and urging him on.

Anna pushed him forward. "Eduard just introduced you. Apparently, you're something special."

Ján stared at Eduard, who was standing on stage urging him

forward. "My friend, the prodigy Ján Balik, all grown up and missing an ear. Step forward Ján and show us what you can do!"

Ján's fingers ached to touch the keys, but not like this with a rambunctious audience eager for a rollicking performance.

"Get on up there," Anna urged. "They might even buy you dinner if you please them. You look like you could use some fattening up."

Ján offered a timid wave and approached the piano with reverence. Eduard clapped him on the back and stumbled off the stage, motioning to the crowd to encourage Ján with their applause. Ján sat at the bench and regarded the piano, a solid German model. The ivory was stained and chipped, but as he scrutinized each key, they whispered back to him. Someone shouted at him to hurry up and play, but Ján was focused only on the instrument in front of him.

The excitement and trepidation that he felt in the moment reminded him of joining the children's orchestra, a time of friendship and hope. He had written a song then to celebrate his joy, and while it was duly recorded in the book strapped to his chest, he still knew every note by heart. He closed his eyes, and placed his fingers on the keys. In that moment, he was whole again, without pain or knowledge of cruelty and loss. He knew only the notes in his heart, and he began to play.

Although he had written this piece as a teenager, it was a mature composition requiring stamina and agility to accomplish the ambitious jumps for his right hand with the energetic tempo. He had composed a tribute to the personalities of all his friends: frantic Leo, generous Maria, troubled Emil. His music paid homage to them all, and when he was done, his hands dropped to his side. It was only then that he registered the whoops and cheers from the club's patrons as they jumped to their feet and rushed the stage. They hugged him, patted him on the back, and pressed food and drink into his hands. Then they forced him back to the bench to play more, and he was happy to oblige.

Ján rolled over and took a long pull from the cigarette that Anna dangled in front of him. The late afternoon light cast harsh shadows across the floor of the storeroom and illuminated the soft curves of Anna's freckled shoulders. Ján ran his fingers along her arm and pulled her toward him for a long kiss, but she pushed him away, laughing.

"Konrad will be looking for me to set up the bar, and he'll be looking for you too," she said, climbing up from the pallet that served as Ján's bed on the floor amid piles of cans, sacks of flour, and kegs of beer. "You know, one of these days he's going to come in here looking for a jar of pickled cabbage and find us."

Ján reached over and tried to pull her back. "I don't care who finds us. Don't go. Stay just a few more minutes."

Anna broke free and reached for her clothes, and Ján leaned back to admire her. He was smitten, and she knew it. She buttoned up her blouse slowly, deliberately egging him on. When he groaned, she leaned down to give him a soft kiss, and then, adjusting her apron, she slipped out of the door.

Ján lay back and finished the cigarette, tracing the red lipstick stains and contemplating his good if fragile luck. He had gone to the authorities as Evgeni Baburin to register as required, but as a convicted criminal, he was barred from the few jobs that were available. In the eyes of the State, he was a traitor, regardless of circumstances or time served. He spent several days walking about town inquiring about work. He would have taken anything from janitorial duties, dock worker, to farm hand. He thought he had some promising leads, but it was illegal to hire workers without official approval, so he was repeatedly turned away.

His saving grace had been his evenings playing the piano for food and board in Konrad's illicit bar. Since the first night when he appeared with Eduard, the patrons had clamored for him, and he happily obliged, learning more of the forbidden American tunes that seemed to rouse the audience into ordering extra rounds of food and drink.

Word of Ján's nightly performances had spread, and Konrad's establishment was now filled beyond capacity each evening that Ján appeared. Some of their best customers were the authorities charged with shutting down such illegal businesses, but they looked the other way so long as Konrad was willing to reward their patronage. In return, they asked no questions about Ján's past. Konrad agreed to give him a place to lay his head, a hot meal each day, and the chance to earn a few tips as long as he stood on the stage each night and entertained the crowds into a buying frenzy.

Ján stubbed out the cigarette and surveyed his tiny corner of the world. He thought back to the tribulations of laboring through the cruel conditions of the far north and wished he had known then that one day, he would be sleeping with a beautiful woman surrounded by abundant piles of food. He pulled down the coffee tin and emptied his stash of tips. He carefully stacked the coins and smoothed out the bills. Another month or two, and he would have enough money to buy Anna a ring and ask her to marry him. Perhaps he could earn enough that she could quit her job at Konrad's and focus only on a home for the two of them. He imagined them in a place of their own, and he laughed at the thought of a few chubby children running between them. He remembered Alban and wondered if he had found his wife yet.

The snow was falling in thick, fat flakes, and business in the café was unusually slow as patrons who might have stopped in for a cup of coffee and a pastry hurried home to ride out the storm. Ján was just finishing up restocking the bar when Konrad poked his head down the stairwell and told him they were closing for the night.

"No one is coming in this weather except the drunks with no money and less sense. Might as well close up early. I'm sending Anna home, and you can have the night off."

Ján reluctantly agreed, frustrated by the loss of tips. He moved to shut off the taps and lock up the cabinets when he had a thought. Anna was going home early. This was an intriguing opportunity. Usually, Konrad insisted on walking with Anna when her shift ended in the wee hours, but today, she was leaving on her own. Ján was curious to see where she lived. She never shared anything with him about her family or her home, and he wanted to know, especially since he was getting closer to a proposal and would need to approach her parents soon.

Ján threw on his coat and ventured out into the storm. He waited in the shadows for Anna to depart the café, and then he followed her. She meandered through the alleys, stopping at the newsagent and then at the butcher before she left the business district and, balancing her parcels, crossed into a residential section featuring sizable homes with expansive gardens. They were the only pedestrians braving the frigid weather on this quiet street, so Ján was grateful for the curtain of snowfall as he struggled to keep up with her without giving himself away.

After a long walk, she stopped in front of a stately stone house with an elaborate wrought-iron gate at the drive. Ján remembered this neighborhood. It was where his Uncle Erik's wealthy patrons had lived, and he had performed at elegant parties in some of these homes. Although there were changes where the bombings had ravaged the privileged enclave, it was clear that much effort had gone into restoring it for the elite Soviet officials who were living here now.

But why was Anna here? Ján thought she must be working a second job as a housemaid or nanny to a wealthy family. All the more reason to marry her and help her settle into a home of her own. He watched her root through her bag and produce a key to unlock the heavy barrier. A car approached on the road, cautiously creeping by and obscuring his view. When it had passed, Anna was gone.

Eduard joined Ján for a beer at the bar. He still visited the café and performed on occasion, but he had secured a position as a music teacher at the local primary school, and he was trying to piece his life back together. Ján could look at him and find traces of the formidable musician he had once been, and he hoped that his old friend would find happiness. Eduard was in a somber mood as he swirled his drink and watched the foam bubble at the top of his glass.

"How much longer can you live on the floor of Konrad's storage room?" he asked.

Ján drained his mug and moved behind the bar to tidy up. He was glad to have Eduard's company and needed his advice. "Not much longer, I hope, although I have appreciated Konrad's hospitality."

Eduard nodded. "Oh, I am sure you have. We were quite a pitiful pair when we stumbled down the stairs that night, but you have to admit, your current situation cannot go on forever."

Ján debated how much to tell Eduard. He was glad to have a friend but he was unsure of their boundaries. He decided to take a chance. He reached under the bar and pulled out his jacket. From the pocket, he drew out a small box and opened it to reveal a simple gold ring with a tiny stone, a black-market purchase that had cost him dearly. "I am planning to ask Anna to marry me, then we will find a home of our own." He smiled at the thought that he had been nurturing these many months. "Spring is approaching, and I have saved up a bit of money."

"Are you out of your mind?" Eduard looked alarmed. "You can't possibly–"

"Can't possibly what?" Ján challenged, angry at Eduard's reaction. He snapped the box shut and jammed it back in his coat pocket.

"Listen, Ján, don't get me wrong. I like you a lot, but Anna... She's way out of your league. How much do you know about her, really? You are an ex-convict here on a stolen identity. Your chances of getting a decent job are nil! How could you do that to her? Even if she would agree to this crazy plan, which she won't."

Ján slammed his fist against the bar, angry at himself for trusting bonds of friendship that apparently never existed. "You are just jealous that for once in my life, I have found a sliver of happiness," he said, ignoring the petty edge in his voice. He grabbed his hat off the peg and stormed out. He heard Eduard calling after him, but he pressed ahead. He wasn't interested in explanations or excuses. There was only one person who understood him, and Ján was determined to see her before she left home to come to the bar.

The afternoon was clear and crisp with high, floating clouds in a brilliant sky, a day that hinted at spring and hope. Yet Ján strode through long shadows cast by the winter sun and saw storm clouds lurking. He made his way to Anna's home and stood before the tall, iron gates, attempting to control his heavy breathing while he mustered the courage to step into this hushed, private world. In the stark light of day, the stone house loomed as a more foreboding structure than he remembered from viewing it through the cascading flakes of an evening snowstorm. There was a time, a lifetime ago, when he would have been at ease in this world, but that boy had died on the Dead Road, and he now surveyed the spoils of wealth and power with jaded eyes.

The gate was unlocked. Ján pushed it open and walked up the drive, his feet crunching on the icy path. He had been stewing over Eduard's betrayal as he stormed his way here and now faced the realization that he hadn't given any thought to what he would say to Anna. Rejecting Eduard's thin appraisal of his prospects, he decided to take a chance on blunt honesty. He needed to hear Anna confirm her feelings for him, an attachment that he never questioned because of her enthusiasm over their clandestine trysts.

He grasped the gleaming brass lion mounted on the expansive front door and started to knock when he heard music. It was a simple folk melody he had heard Anna play on occasion at

Konrad's, and he smiled to think that she had privileges of using the piano in this grand house, likely a very expensive instrument and a rare treat for an employee. He wondered if he might be allowed to play it before he spirited her away, but his thoughts were interrupted when the music stopped and Anna's laughter echoed across the palatial formal rooms.

He relaxed his hold on the knocker when he spied her walking across the polished marble floor. He tapped on the window, and caught her attention. She hurried to the door, but rather than invite him in, she joined him outside, wrapping her sweater around her shoulders and casting furtive glances around the grounds to make sure they were alone. Ján moved to embrace her, but she stepped back.

"What are you doing here? How did you find me?" she demanded. There was anger under her harried questions.

"Well, I, uhm, I followed you one day to make sure you arrived home safely in the snow. It has been some time, but I knew you lived here. Or perhaps you work here too? May I come in? I have something I need to ask you."

"Ján, this is terribly awkward. I can't invite you in. My– He doesn't know about you, and now is just not the time."

Ján felt the earth fall away from under him. His thoughts were reeling, and his voice took on a pleading tone. "But, Anna, I love you! I have known this for some time, and I have been planning for us." Before she could react, he pulled the box out of his pocket and got down on one knee. "I want you to marry me. We can have a life together."

"Oh, Ján, no!" Anna recoiled. "What we have...we're just having fun. I thought you understood!"

"Having fun?" Ján's hands shook, and his head throbbed. "How can you possibly be–" He stopped short of accusing her and searched his scattered mind for what to say. His head screamed betrayal, but his heart clung to the myth of her devotion. "How can you deny what we've meant to each other?"

"Silly boy, I adore being with you, but I could never *marry* you!"

Ján spied movement through the leaded sidelight when an older man strolled into the hall. He wore a uniform with gold epaulets looped across his shoulders and broad stripes decorating his sleeves. He stopped and listened, then picked up a newspaper and studied the headlines. Anna attempted to position her body to block each man's view.

"Why are you keeping secrets? I see your father. Let me speak to him," Ján demanded, gesturing to the man inside.

Anna jerked him away from the door, pulling him into the thick shrubs that ringed the house. "Secrets? That's rich coming from you, Evgeni Baburin, or Jan Richter, or whatever you decide to call yourself tomorrow. Why do you assume that I owe you anything? That man is not my father. He is a part of the government here, an important official, and we have...Well, we have an arrangement. Do you understand?" Anna glared at Ján, her frustration growing.

"An *arrangement*? What kind of arrangement? If you're living here, why are you working in Konrad's bar?" Ján was struck by a sudden insight, a gutting sense that everyone was in on the joke but him, and that clarity made him sick to his stomach. "But of course!" he laughed cruelly. "You're a spy. You're sharing information on Konrad, on Eduard, the patrons, and me. No wonder Konrad's shoddy bar never gets raided. God, how can I be so stupid? And how can you do that to Konrad?"

Anna scowled, her once beautiful features marred by the seediness of truth. "Konrad knows every bit of what I am doing, you idiot. You are a convict, a scrapper who plays tunes for pennies! Don't talk about things you don't know anything about and don't mistake a little fun for love. It's really quite charming but terribly naïve."

Ján reached behind her neck and pulled her face toward him, pressing his lips on hers and forcing her into a rough kiss. Anna pushed him away and slapped him hard as he stumbled back. She ran the back of her hand across her face, taking in desperate, ragged breaths, and he stood stunned and motionless while his heart shattered.

"Don't ever do that again, you hear me? You're better than that, Ján Balik. You really are." She reached down and closed his fingers around the ring box and pushed his hand away. "Bye, Ján. You'll find the right girl. I hope you do, but I'm not the one, and you mustn't ever come back here again." She turned and went back inside, closing the door firmly behind her.

Ján wandered aimlessly, trying to piece together how his brief glimmer of happiness had soured into such humiliation. After walking for hours, he found himself back in the alley in front of the café, a familiar scene where warm light streamed through the window and across the smooth stones of the alley. Eduard was playing the piano inside, a rich repertoire reminiscent of his earlier successes. Konrad was most certainly working behind the bar. It was such a simple tableau that he had taken it for granted. It smacked now of nefarious dealings. Ján couldn't face the stage or the crowd. He retreated to the storeroom and burrowed into his pallet, listening to the revelry below. Music of his own pain came to him, an ode to his disappointment meant to purge his heart of Anna and her duplicity. He grabbed a bottle off the shelf and gulped a generous swig. His gut stung, and it felt right for the moment. Punishing and brash.

The notes coalesced in his mind. He tipped the bottle back for another deep draw, then he fumbled for his book with the intention of adding to the patchwork of melodies. As he thumbed through his compositions, seeking a fresh page for this newest entry, a small scrap of paper fell out. Ján picked it up and focused on the handwriting, instantly recognizable.

Find me anytime brother
Alban Tuluukov
Petrovskogo, 181
Turul

Ján tucked Alban's note back in his book, grabbed his rucksack with his coffee can of meager savings, wedged the bottle under his arm, and walked back into the darkened café.

Eduard had begun playing a round of sentimental songs, and the audience was singing along. Ján paused to listen for just a moment, then he slipped out the door and headed to the train station.

Part Two

Chapter 8

Song of the Piano

Turul, Yakutia, Russia. Land of the Sakha People
1991

Sofya leaned over the chipped kitchen sink and peeled the last of the potatoes. The jarring notes coming from the piano in the next room were vexing to her patience, and she bore down on the knife, attempting to rectify the disharmony with her own rhythmic scraping of the soft skins. She tipped the potatoes into a pot of water and took her basket out into the garden to seek some peace.

Lifting her chin to the sun and soaking in the warmth, she sought to hold in the rays to tide her over the coming months. This was the short but blissful interval between the scorching Siberian summers and the brutal arctic winters. In this seasonal respite, the leaves rustled softly, the clouds floated regally, and the world seemed to slow ever so slightly to enjoy these few precious weeks of cool mornings and warm afternoons. She closed her eyes to cherish a measure of autumn's embrace.

Sofya heard the squeak of the door hinges. Little Alexei Turgenev emerged followed by Ján who leaned down and spoke softly, eliciting a broad smile from the young lad. Freed from his lessons, Alexei bolted away, dragging his canvas satchel in the dust behind him. Sofya chuckled at the boy's glee over his release, thinking to herself that she was probably more delighted with his departure than he was. The poor boy's dedication was offset by his ham-fisted technique.

Still, she couldn't bemoan the joy that these lessons brought Ján. She might not be able to distinguish the difference between Prokofiev and Pashkevich, but she had grown up steeped in the musical traditions of her Sakha ancestors, and the sound of her beloved husband's voice and his tender affections to his students were sacred melodies to her. He didn't have to give these lessons, didn't have to endure the tedium or the grating assaults on the keyboard. She knew his talent was wasted in this little town, and yet, even the clumsiest of students seemed to bring him immense satisfaction.

Dzikusku pushed the door with his nose and padded out into the garden to join her. He plopped down beside her and rested his head on her lap, his long legs tucked beneath him and his soft gray fur nestled against her legs. "My little savage. Even you need a bit of peace and quiet yourself, eh?" she asked as she scratched him behind his ears. She hoped that Ján would join them, but she spied Alban's blue truck as it turned into the lane. He parked on the side of the road and climbed out, waving to Sofya as he made a determined beeline to the door. Ján emerged, holding a bottle of vodka. He clapped his friend on the back and shut the door behind them. Sofya set aside the basket she had been cradling in her lap, her eagerness fading. He was drinking.

Sofya pushed herself to her feet and crooked her elbow around the handle of the basket. Dzikusku groaned at the interruption, but Sofya's mind was a whir of emotions, and the dog's complaints elicited no sympathy. Ján's drinking signaled the dark spells that often overcame him. With a bit of vodka, he became more pensive and withdrawn than usual, and she knew it was a sign that he was reliving his secret traumas. She spied her sister Tuyaara just over the gate.

"If you see Ján, please tell him I've gone for a walk!" Sofya called out.

Tuyaara flicked her hand in Sofya's direction, and the damp shirt she was pinning to the line crumpled to the ground. She scoffed. "And what makes you think your husband will come out to chat with me, eh?" Tuyaara had a habit of seasoning her comments with ample helpings of derision.

Sofya wasn't interested in her sister's usual gripes. "Just telling you in case he asks. Alban is here, and I don't want to disturb them."

"You don't want to disturb him after all that racket we've been listening to?' Tuyaara bellowed, her indignation growing, but Sofya ignored her. She whistled for Dzikusku, and they set off down the lane.

Sofya's walk ended in the cemetery. Out of breath and with sweat glistening on her forehead, she raised her hand to shield her eyes from the sun so she could better greet the two simple markers. Their two children, neither long in this world. Next to little Artur lay wee Lara, their firstborn. Sofya accepted that they would not be blessed with children, and it was her determined choice to be content.

Dzikusku padded up behind her and nudged her hand with his cold, wet nose. Sofya reached down and stroked his thick fur. "Artur would be twenty-five today, 'Kusku. Hard to believe, eh?"

He tipped his head to the side and twitched his ears in response.

"I'm sure you can read my mind," said Sofya. "Let's see you work your tender magic on Papa. He would never admit it, but he is sad today, thinking of his little boy."

When Sofya and the dog arrived home, Ján was pacing in the garden. He greeted her arrival with a mix of mild panic and profound relief. "You left without warning! I didn't know what to think," he said.

Sofya looked over at Tuyaara who was tending to another load of washing, and her sister shrugged. "He never asked!"

Sofya linked her arm in Ján's and guided him into the house, casting a reproving glance in her sister's direction.

She sat him in a chair and offered him a glass of water. "I just went for a short walk. I needed to acknowledge Artur's birthday. Look! My basket is still hanging on the sergeh. Nothing is amiss."

Ján followed her hand to see the sacred, ceremonial post that marked the bounds of their garden. The sight of her basket, such an ordinary sign of the pattern of their lives, quelled his agitation for the moment. This was a pattern they repeated often since their marriage over thirty years ago. Sofya was equal parts patient and persistent. She doubted that he would ever offer her an explanation of the root of his anxieties, but she was determined to love him beyond his demons into a better place. Never once had she given him reason to doubt her loyalty, but with Ján, there was always this lurking sense of loss and betrayal.

He said softly, "Please forgive me. We are both minding our losses today."

Sofya moved to pull him into a fierce embrace. She could never stay cross with him for long, especially today of all days. This was as close as he would come to saying Artur's name. If only he would open up, but didn't they all live with secrets and scars? Some folks wore them like badges of honor, and others? Well, Ján was the type to hold it all in and push forward. She pulled his face to hers and gave him a tender kiss.

They had met soon after Ján's arrival in Turul in the summer of 1954. He had shown up on Alban's doorstep like a vagabond, carrying a frayed rucksack and shouldering the weight of a lifetime of tragedy. His clothes were tattered, and his flaxen hair with the impish curls was long, matted, and tied with a leather cord into a loose knot.

With him was a wolf pup, a scruffy ball of black fur who had latched onto Ján during his travels and seemed to regard him as her pack. Together they had walked along the desolate path across the taiga and into the village, and by the time they arrived in Turul, they had become inseparable. Ján had named his companion Schatzi.

Ján was a mystery in the small village, a welcome source of intrigue and gossip among the townspeople. Families in Turul had known each other for generations and most were related through a complex web of connections, so a stranger was a pleasant diversion and a source of good-natured speculation.

Quiet and thoughtful, Ján was an enigma. He said little about his past and deftly deflected probing questions about his heritage. Thin and slight of build with a tangled mop of blonde hair and deep blue eyes, he stood out among the sturdier, dark-haired Sakha people, yet with Alban's enthusiastic patronage, he was quickly embraced by the community.

If asked, the town's residents would have easily identified Ján's unassuming generosity, humility, and kindness as his most dominant traits. He moved among his new friends with profound gratitude for the tiniest token of friendship and warmth, and for a community so recently ravaged by hateful purges, they agreed that Ján's quiet charm was a felicitous balm against the uncertainties of life. The fair-haired man and his dark-furred companion were soon a fixture about town.

Alban's bride, Ayta, took on Ján's social life as her special assignment. She pressed him with food and attention to tease out the nature of his burdens, a mission that was wholly unsuccessful. Ján proved to be impervious to attempts to glean much of his history, and his secrets only added to his appeal. Ayta took pride in educating him in the Sakha traditions that she and Alban treasured. It was all a bit bewildering to Ján at first. He learned to love the local cuisine that featured jellied fish casseroles or raw white fish drawn from the nearby Lena River and served with apricot buns or vegetables seasoned with vinegar. He embraced the indigenous reverence for the natural world, and he welcomed the familial rhythms of small-town life.

Ján had intended to stay in Turul only for a short time. He needed to see his friend and shake off the heartache from his return to Königsberg. As he walked about the dusty lanes and admired the simple charm of the colorful frame houses, each surrounded by tidy, wooden fences, he was reminded of the care and kindness that pervaded the people's relationship to the land, which was often punishing and vindictive in return. He felt the edges soften around his urgency to keep moving.

He had met Sofya the first time he entered the town's general store. After overstaying his welcome as a guest in Alban's home, Ján had insisted on contributing to Ayta's pantry and set out to acquaint himself with the only purveyors of supplies in town, brothers Michil and Gerasim Popov. Michil was a charismatic giant of a man with a broad chest, large ears, and an outsized personality. His brother Gerasim was equally loud and imposing, but considerably less charming. Together, they provisioned the village out of a modest establishment, which was stocked with seasonal produce and wild game supplemented by canned goods imported through connections in Yakutsk, the nearest city.

The store, a two-level wooden structure covered with a patchwork metal roof, sat at Turul's main crossroads adjacent to the village's only school. The establishment's bright green paint made it a beacon in the constant snow and ice of the winter months, and over the short summer season, it featured a yard with clucking hens and well-tended window boxes of bright flowers. Inside, the ceilings were low and the walls were covered with shelves that sagged under the weight of the merchandise.

Ján walked among the crates and boxes, searching for items that he knew Ayta would like. Schatzi stayed close to his heels.

"You can't have that wolf in here," a voice boomed from the back.

Ján reached down and grasped Schatzi's collar. "My apologies," he responded. "This is my dog, Schatzi, and she won't leave my side."

Michil wedged his ample girth between the stacks of canned goods and stood in front of Ján, sizing him up. "If that's a dog, then I'm the long-lost tsar. You're Alban's friend, eh? I've heard about you and that wolf that follows you around. Welcome to Turul! And if your Schatzi even so much as nicks a can in here, you're paying for it." Michil smiled broadly and stuck out his hand. "Do we have a deal?"

"I believe we do," said Ján. He noticed Sofya standing behind the counter, and he waved. "Hello."

Sofya looked first to Michil and then returned Ján's greeting with a silent and timid wave. She turned away and disappeared behind a curtain.

"My wife, Sofya," Michil said matter-of-factly. "She doesn't say much."

They were an odd couple. He was brash and outspoken, and she was shy and young enough to be his daughter. Ján couldn't help but notice that she was quite pretty with raven-colored hair plaited in a long braid and dark eyes framed with long lashes. Not pretty in the film star way his mother had glimmered, but just as lovely in a gentler way. Sofya had the allure of someone who was oblivious to her striking features. Extraordinary. There's a story there, thought Ján, but wasn't that the way of this broken world?

Ján quickly made his purchases and departed, mulling over his encounter with Michil and Sofya. He released his grip on Schatzi and started walking back to Alban's when she spied a chicken and dashed after it. The plump bird darted under a fence and into the adjacent school with Schatzi in full pursuit. Ján scurried through the school's open door, calling for his pet and hoping that he would find the chicken still alive. The sound of panicked clucking lured him deeper into the building.

He passed by classrooms filled with neatly arranged desks until he came to the last room off the hall, a slightly bigger space, but compact nonetheless. There he found the chicken sitting atop a dusty old upright piano that was covered with a bright red tablecloth. Schatzi was jumping wildly, trying to get to the frantic fowl. Ján raised a window, scooped up the chicken, and tossed it back into the yard. He shut the window and scolded Schatzi. "You will get me in trouble one of these days! You have to decide—are you a dog or a wolf?" Schatzi sat on her back legs and wagged her tail, prompting Ján to forgive her instantly.

Crisis averted. Ján looked around the building to apologize for barging into the school. Finding no one about, he returned to the piano and peeled back the cloth. It was an old, tired instrument with a boxy design that was obviously assembled with speed rather than care. He ran his hands across the rough wooden cabinet. *OKTABA* was stenciled on the fall in faded gold paint, barely legible under years of grime. A Red October piano, a Soviet brand. It was scratched and worn, a far cry from the Bösendorfer of his performance days, but Ján thought it was beautiful.

He sat down on the bench and examined the instrument, relieved to see that it had all its keys. *That is a plus,* he thought. He played a chord, and the notes wavered, slightly off-key. Undeterred, Ján repositioned himself, rubbing his palms against the coarse fabric of his trousers before placing his hands on the keyboard. He played the Chopin nocturne by memory. The strings were soft and the hammers needed work, but the music flowed from his fingers in a torrent of emotion.

Schatzi sat by the bench, enchanted by the sound and the intensity of Ján's dedication to the endeavor. When Ján played the last stanza, he left his fingers on the keys for just a moment to feel the fading vibrations, and he closed his eyes to let the moment linger.

"Where did you learn to do that?"

Ján whipped his head around to find Sofya standing in the

back of the room. "Please pardon me," he stammered, "I...I... didn't intend to make myself at home. It was the chicken..."

"Yes! The chicken and your hungry wolf there. Might I say that is one lucky chicken. When your beast is a bit older, that chicken won't have a chance," Sofya said, and they both laughed. "You didn't answer my question," she added.

"I'm sorry, but what was your question again?" Ján asked.

"You know what I said. I think you just don't want to answer. That's okay, I understand, but you should come here more often. I've never heard anyone play that thing, and I'd love to hear more." Sofya blushed. From out in the yard, Michil called her name, and she disappeared as quickly as she arrived.

In the coming days, Ján found himself inventing excuses to meander by the school, looking out for a chance to slip inside and play, and hoping to see Sofya again. She intrigued him, and yet, he had to remind himself that she had a husband, a big burly one that was up to all kinds of nefarious activities if Alban was to be believed.

Ján had a route he followed that took him first by the store and then in front of the school. No chickens emerged to entice Schatzi in for another chase, so Ján lingered in the hopes of securing an invitation. He looked around a bit, and seeing no one, he wandered away. Running after Schatzi to save a chicken was one thing, but bold breaking and entering seemed a step too far.

One day when the cold weather had arrived for good and a few flakes scattered about in the air, Ján stopped by the store to buy a few provisions, and Sofya was waiting at the counter. After they exchanged a few pleasantries, Ján fell silent, unsure of what to say. Sofya wrapped his purchases in an old newspaper and handed the bundle to Ján. He thanked her quickly and started for the door.

"Would you like to play the piano again?" Sofya said to his back.

He turned, and she could see the joy in his eyes. "That would be very nice," he said simply. "It's been a long time since I could play regularly."

"Follow me then," she said, and she untied her apron and pulled her sweater closer. "I'm going to the school for just a minute," she called out, but Ján couldn't see anyone else within earshot.

She led him next door and entered through the front of the school. Ján and Schatzi followed along, the wolf's paws clicking on the worn linoleum floor. This time, the building was filled with the sounds of children in the tiny classrooms. The walls covered in flaking paint displayed their work. Laughter and chatter echoed throughout the building. Sofya led him down the hall, but rather than entering the room with the piano, she turned to the opposite side. There through an open door, they encountered an old man, his face defined by a crooked pair of glasses and a thinning crown of white hair.

"Mr. Marikyanov?" asked Sofya softly, and the old man lifted his head to peer at his visitors. Ján noticed that his glasses' thick lenses magnified his eyes and blurred the edges of his face.

"Yes, yes! Who is here?" He scrunched up his eyes and thrust his head forward. "Ah, Sofya, my dear. What brings you across the lane? Did I forget to pay the school's account again?"

"No, Mr. Marikyanov," she said, "you and the school are just fine with Michil. I came to introduce you to someone special. This is Ján Balik. He is new to town and he would like to play the school's piano. He's really quite good."

"Mr. Balik! Such a pleasure to make your acquaintance. I have heard about you from our mutual friend, Alban. You can play our broken-down piano, can you?"

Ján took off his hat and extended his hand to Mr. Marikyanov. "It is nice to meet you as well. As for the piano, yes, sir, it's in pretty good condition, and I can play it. With a few tools and some tuning pins, I can fix it for you, if you would kindly allow me to practice on it every now and then."

They walked across the hall followed by Sofya and Schatzi. If Mr. Marikyanov noticed the wolf, he did not remark on her presence. Ján sat down on the bench, lifted the lid, and began to play. He chose one of his childhood favorites, Prokofiev's *Peter and the Wolf*, because it seemed fitting for a children's space, but also to gently tease Mr. Marikyanov about Schatzi's presence. Once again, despite the sad condition of the instrument, Ján was able to coax out a solid, if twangy, rendition of the treasured tale. Sofya beamed as Mr. Marikyanov danced a jig to the music, and soon, teachers and children began filling the back of the hall, intrigued by this unexpected gift of music. The children joined Mr. Marikyanov in his joyful prancing and swaying. Sofya leaned over the back of the piano, spellbound by the motion of Ján's fingers and the vibrations of the timeworn hammers hitting the strings upon Ján's commands. Schatzi sat next to her, her tail wagging in time to the music.

Ján reveled in the chance to have an audience, so he finished up the Prokofiev and launched immediately into "Aquarium" from Saint-Saëns' *Carnival of the Animals*. The children stilled as he ran his fingers up and down the keys, evoking the satiny flow of water and the slightly mysterious tone of the piece. When he finished, the room was full, and everyone broke into an enthusiastic mix of applause and cheers. Schatzi joined in with a well-timed howl, and Mr. Marikyanov laughed as he realized the wolf had been there the whole time. Ján waved at the children, and they formed a line to approach the piano and thank him for the spontaneous concert. When the room was cleared, Mr. Marikyanov pulled up a chair and sat facing Ján.

"Young man, I can't remember a time when we have had that much cheer in this space. For that I thank you. I almost gave this piano away to Michil for firewood last year, but there is the matter of this unwieldy metal frame. So here it sits where no one has touched it in years. Needless to say, I am glad that we kept it."

Ján tapped his hands against his trousers, itching to get his fingers back on the keys. He looked kindly at the older man, so gratified by his response to the pieces. He said, "Well, Mr. Marikyanov, I should be thanking you. I haven't had this much fun in a long time. I hope that you will allow me to return and play again sometime."

Mr. Marikyanov stood and rubbed his chin with his hand, deep in thought. Ján was worried. He hoped he hadn't pushed his luck and asked too much of the aged headmaster. An uncomfortable silence followed as Mr. Marikyanov shuffled out of the room. He turned left and disappeared down the hall.

Ján looked at Sofya in alarm. "Did I say anything to offend him?"

She shrugged and helped him cover the instrument with the dusty cloth. The two walked out of the school with Schatzi close on Ján's heels. They spied Mr. Marikyanov deep in conversation with Michil next door. The headmaster was gesturing with his hands as Michil stood towering over him, his hands on his hips.

"Oh, this can't be good for you or me," said Sofya warily.

Eventually, the old man turned and made his way back, followed closely by Michil.

Ján stepped forward. "Mr. Marikyanov, please pardon me if I said anything to cause you distress. Truly, I do not want to inconvenience you at all."

The old man looked up in alarm. "Mr. Balik, quite the opposite! I am inspired by your gifts." He glanced at Michil for approval before continuing. Michil nodded, and the old man said, "I, well we, would like to make you an offer. Michil here tells me you are still living with Ayta and Alban. Do you wish to have your own home?" He didn't give Ján a chance to answer before he pointed down the lane and plowed ahead. "You see, we have an empty cottage over there. It belongs to the school, which really belongs to Michil here. It used to be my house, but since the death of my wife, it just didn't feel like home. I moved in with my daughter several years ago and the house sits empty now. Mind you, it's a tiny place, don't get too excited, but we would like you to live there and work at the school. The piano needs tuning, the halls need painting, there are places where the floor is rotten, and that's just the start of it. If you could take care of repairs and maintenance then you may play as long as you wish. Why, you may even give lessons to the students if that would bring you a measure of happiness."

Ján agreed immediately with tears in his eyes and a lump in his throat. He reluctantly offered up the complicated fact that he had no official papers, only a stolen identity. He hoped that it wouldn't sour the deal, but Michil only laughed and waved his hand. "We don't stand on ceremony here, lad. Besides, Alban told us all that already."

The three men shook hands. Having no possessions other than the items in his rucksack meant that for Ján, moving was a simple affair. Ayta and Sofya joined forces to gather basic furnishings and supplies, and together they created a cozy bedroom and a serviceable kitchen for him. One chair would have to suffice for now. They positioned it close to the bulky brick oven that dominated center of the cottage between the kitchen and the sitting area. He also had access to a large barn behind the cottage in case he decided to purchase a wagon and a horse. All dreams for later.

They brought Ján in on a Saturday and showed him his new home. Alban, Ayta, and their babies joined by Michil and Sofya, Mr. Marikyanov, his daughter, and the three schoolteachers all crowded into the tiny house to bless it with food, friendship, and good luck. As each bid him good evening, Michil and Sofya were the last to leave.

"I don't know how to thank you enough," Ján said, his voice choked with emotion.

Sofya nodded her head, markedly reserved in Michil's presence, and scurried out. Michil clapped Ján on the back. "Good to have you for a neighbor. Mind you, Sofya's sister, Tuyaara, and her husband, Dabyn, live just next door." He pointed to a blue frame house just over the fence. Smoke curled from the chimney, but no other evidence of its occupants was visible. "You'll not be thanking me for their company. That woman is a sharp-tongued wench if you ask me." He laughed. "Can't always choose your neighbors or your in-laws. Just glad we have you as a buffer." And with that, Michil departed and left Ján alone in his new home.

Ján felt like a king. He had a roof over his head and a piano at his disposal. He reached in his rucksack and pulled out the leather book of his songs. It was stained and creased, and the bullet hole remained, but the music inside was intact. He placed it on a shelf and leaned down to rub Schatzi's fur. "We are home now, my little family. We are home."

Chapter 9

Song of Remembrance

Turul, Yakutia, the Soviet Union
1955

Ján applied the final coat of paint to the hallway in the village school. The children would return for the fall term within the week, and he was scrambling to complete the last items on his list. He had pulled up the cracked boards and installed new floors that were better suited for the months of unrelenting snow and ice.

The classrooms gleamed with scrubbed windows and sturdy desks, each of which Ján had inspected and repaired. Outside, he had repainted the fading wood siding and repaired the roof in anticipation of the season's first snowfall.

He stood outside and assessed his work while Schatzi sniffed around the border of fading flowers. *It'll serve the children well*, he thought, not allowing himself too much praise. He was more enthusiastic about tackling the next project. With the school building in tip-top shape, he could concentrate on tuning and restoring the piano. He dreamed of the instrument at night, and in his mind's eye, it was bright, shiny, and refurbished. Likely it would take him all winter, and he was eager to get started.

He had worried about securing the supplies that he would need in this frontier village, but the Popov brothers turned out to have quite a network of connections. Ján suspected that the tiles for the floor and the endless cans of paint that appeared at the school had their origins in Michil's and Gerasim's shady business dealings. There were items in the store that Ján was surprised to find in a town that was reached only over muddy, narrow roads in the summer and across a frozen river during the winter. *Just don't ask,* warned Alban, and Ján turned a blind eye, concentrating only on keeping his own dealings on the straight and narrow.

He crouched down behind the building and washed out his paint supplies, eagerly anticipating the time he could now devote to playing the piano. It would be his own private opportunity for remembrance, and he could play as long as he wanted once he secured the building for the night. In remote Turul, the locking up was less a protective measure against thieves than a way to ward off unwanted animal visitors. He and Schatzi walked from room to room, checking the windows and closing the doors.

Ján tensed when Schatzi perked up her ears, emitted a low growl, and moved to stand beside him. Someone was in the building. He followed her as they crept down the hallway, peeking into the classrooms. Ján gently rubbed Schatzi's head and repeated "It's alright, girl, everything is fine" as they neared the sound of muffled sobs. He peered through a doorway and was surprised to discover Mrs. Omukova, the teacher responsible for the older children. He had been certain that the building was empty, yet here she was, hunched over a desk with her head in her hands. In front of her was a letter.

Ján sat nearby and waited until she was ready to talk. He knew she sensed his presence, and he was prepared to wait. She looked up with red-rimmed eyes, and he leaned forward. "Can you tell me what troubles you?"

She shook her head no, but he didn't move, choosing to wait.

He watched her twist a handkerchief between her fingers and recognized that she was fighting an inner battle. Finally, she spoke. "They came for us late at night. It was always late at night when the soldiers showed up. We were living in Yakutsk then. My husband was a teacher, and we had just gone to bed. There was a loud banging at the door. My husband let them in, and they hit him. They said that he had conspired against the State and that he was preaching anti-Soviet ideas. It was a lie, of course. We were told to pack quickly, both of us. I was guilty by association, you see. What do you pack when you have less than an hour and you do not know where you are going and for how long?

"There were many of us they collected. We were all taken down the river on a barge and then by wagon to a train station. None of us knew for sure where we were. We pulled into a station in the middle of the night, and they told us all to get off. The men were separated from their families and the women and children put back on the train. It started moving again, and I watched my husband fade into the distance. It happened fifteen years ago this month, and I have not seen him since."

She paused, and Ján sat quietly, thinking of Otto and the train. The years collapsed, and once again, in his mind, he was being propelled forward in the onward march of scared people, his feet hitting the platform and being pushed again, forward, away from the train, and then the realization that he had left Otto behind.

Mrs. Omukova didn't know his past and how easily he could imagine the scenes she was describing. He smelled the smoke, the unwashed bodies, the fear, and the residue from discharged firearms. He knew the feeling of waking up face first in a bank of snow and ice. But he told her none of that. This was her story, and he was here to listen.

She took a deep breath. "The women and children were taken to a fishing camp where we were ordered off the train and told to get to work. We had to build our own shelters and provide for our own survival, and all hours every day, we worked sawing giant holes in the dense ice so we could pull up the fish. If we were sick or injured, they ordered us to the factory for processing and canning the catch for export. We never got to eat any of the fish that we shipped out. Maybe scraps of the undesirable parts, but to us, any food was survival.

"We were told that the men had been taken to the mines, and that they would join us when their re-education was complete. They were doctors, lawyers, teachers like my Nurgun. We worried about them, but letters never came, and we lost track. I was released three years ago, and I came back here because this is where my husband grew up. This is his home. I hoped that if he had to look for me, he would start here."

Ján absorbed her painful memories and added them to his own. He asked, "What is in the letter?"

She pushed it towards him. "My husband died ten years ago. Ten years of me writing letters, asking questions, and dreaming of what I would say to him when he found me here." Her voice trailed off, and Ján read the letter. Indeed, the letter confirmed that Nurgun Aydynovich Omukov died in a camp in northern Siberia in February of 1945.

Ján chose his words carefully. "Mrs. Omukova, I am sorry for your loss. Your loss of your husband and this loss of hope. Will you tell me about Nurgun? What were his favorite songs? What was he like?"

She told him how they met and married. That his family in Turul, long dead now, had been against the marriage. "They thought I was flighty," she said. "They should have seen me gutting fish in a canning factory." She said that they had one daughter whom they had buried a month before they were shoved on that barge. "For the best, really. She had a heart condition and wouldn't have survived in the Altai. We got to bury her in Yakutsk, together."

Her words worked their way into Ján's thoughts, a melody that captured the spirit of Nurgun Omukov, a teacher and a father and a husband and, at the end, a man alone and imprisoned. When she had summoned all the words that captured the memories of her husband, Ján invited her to step across the hall. He arranged a chair by the piano, and then he said, "Mrs. Omukova, this is how I heard you describe your husband. You shared words, and I will give you notes. I hope this pays tribute to him and your memory of him."

Ján began to play a musical translation of the man who had been gone for years but whose death was only today being mourned. The melody captured the symmetry and depth of Nurgun Omukov, a man who loved order, tidy spaces, and the reliability of math. There was a movement intended to depict him as a father with sweet and strong notes to honor his and his little girl's time together, and finally a more somber melody to mark the barge and the goodbye.

"But we never said goodbye," she said.

"Didn't you though?" asked Ján. "Every night you dreamed of him and said goodbye, and every morning you awoke to thoughts of him and said hello."

She said nothing at first, but the taut lines around her mouth began to relax. "You captured the spirit of Nurgun. When you play and I close my eyes, I see him. I can hear his voice, and I can sense his strength. Thank you."

Ján promised to write the music down and play it for her any time she wished. "My gift to you," he said.

For just a moment, they sat together in companionable silence. She stood and laid her hand on his shoulder. "You know, Mr. Balik, there are a lot of us here. Former prisoners or families of prisoners. We carry this legacy of unresolved pain. Do you mind if others come to you?"

"It would be an honor."

She walked out the door clutching the letter that had imploded the thin veneer of hope that she had nurtured all these years.

Ján ran his hands over Schatzi's back. The weight of memories lay heavily on him. "Let's go home, girl." He closed up the rooms, turned off the lights, and exited through the front door. His stomach growled but he didn't have the energy to prepare any dinner. Sleep first, then food in the morning. He watched Schatzi chase a rabbit into the mossy expanse between the school and his home. A bundle of repressed energy, she was no longer a puppy. She had bonded with Ján and lived only to please him, and he was grateful for her company.

As he reached the stoop of his home, he was so lost in his thoughts that he didn't see Sofya sitting in the shadows. He whistled for Schatzi and put his hand on the door knob when she spoke up.

"Don't let me scare you; you seem preoccupied. Is everything alright?"

Ján was indeed startled. "You shouldn't sneak up on people like that!" he said more stridently than he felt.

Sofya smiled. "I didn't sneak up on you, I was sitting here the whole time. I saw the lights on in the school and thought you might need something to eat. Do you? Need something to eat?"

Ján noticed that she had a plate covered with a linen towel in her lap. His stomach growled again. "That would be nice, I'm actually really hungry, but," he looked around, "where's Michil?"

"He and Gerasim have gone to Yakutsk. They'll be back tomorrow or the next day."

Ján noted that she didn't seem particularly interested in his return. "Are you sure?" he asked.

"You're hungry, and I have food. Seems like a winning combination."

Sofya accompanied him inside and set the plate on his kitchen table. As he ate, she sat in the chair by the brick oven, and Schatzi followed her, nudging her arm with a paw each time she stopped stroking the fur on the wolf's chest. When Ján finished, Sofya took the plate and bid him farewell. He watched her walk across the moonlit yard to the store and then waited until he saw the light come on in the second-floor rooms above.

"Good night," he said quietly, and he crawled into his bed, falling asleep to unsettled images of trains and goodbyes. He woke up in the middle of the night and retrieved his leather book, adding the notes he had dedicated to Mrs. Omukova's husband. Then he nodded off to sleep with thoughts of Sofya, her beautiful face and generous spirit.

Word spread quickly. Mrs. Omukova brought her neighbor to the school to hear Ján play the piece he wrote about Nurgun, and soon, he had more visitors, a neighbor of a neighbor or a cousin of a friend, each of whom sought Ján out to help them resolve the unresolved or make peace with a tragic loss. In the years after Stalin died, some families found their way back together but more often than not, remnants of a family had to reconcile themselves to the loss of time and memories. Deaths and injuries haunted the living yet the act of survival held its own perils of guilt or regret for desperate choices. Ján had a gift of taking people's tragedies and creating a musical blanket that surrounded them with peace and provided a sense of closure, a reminder that they had done something to keep the memories alive. It buoyed Ján to bring comfort to others, but it often served to bubble up the pain he had buried deep inside his own heart.

"Mr. Balik! Mr. Balik!" The little boy was bundled so tight that it was difficult to lift his little legs above the deep snow. He fought his way through the drifts to Ján's door and knocked softly with his mittens. "Mr. Balik, come quick!" He stood impatiently on the stoop waiting for Ján's reply.

Schatzi barked inside the cottage, and soon Ján peered around the door. "Hello, Elley, what brings you to my home? It's early, and besides, today is not the day for our piano lesson."

Little Elley pulled down his scarf to reveal a gap-toothed smile. "Oh, I know, Mr. Balik, but my grandpa is at the school with Mr. Popov, and they want you to come and see."

Ján threw on his coat and followed Elley to the school. There he found a small crowd gathered in the hallway. They pushed their way through to the music room and found Mr. Marikyanov with Michil and Gerasim, all of them smiling from ear to ear.

"Ján! Finally," thundered Michil. "We're just back from Yakutsk, and look what we have. Books! Boxes of them for the school. Mr. Marikyanov here was complaining about the state of our school supplies, and look what we found!"

Mr. Marikyanov was pleasantly flustered. He reached into the first crate and drew out an early reader. He rubbed the cover reverently. This would have been banned under Stalin just a few short years ago and was likely dubious still, but it was a gift to have these supplies. "Where can they all go? We need a library that the children can visit, but there is no room." He turned to Ján. "Perhaps you can build some shelves for the hallway?"

Ján walked around the crates, sixteen of them brimming with books old and new, a treasure trove for the school. He shook his head. "The hallway is narrow as it is. The best solution is to add a library onto the school, build an addition. We can start in the spring thaw and have it ready by the beginning of next term."

"Right, right, right," exclaimed Michil impatiently. "But what about now? We went to considerable effort and expense. Called in a few chits to be honest. We can't have them sitting in boxes for months."

Mr. Marikyanov walked around the music room, rubbing his chin with his hands. "Actually, I have an idea," he said as he looked straight at Ján. "A much better idea. We're going to give this piano to you, and we're going to help you carry it over to your house. You can play it as much as you like, and you can have your music lessons there. This room," and for emphasis he extended both arms as if the space were cavernous rather than a slightly bigger than modest classroom, "will be our library."

Ján wasn't sure he was hearing correctly. The piano was his? He would have it at his house to play whenever he wanted? "That sounds like a wonderful plan, Mr. Marikyanov. I will take good care of it; you can count on me."

"Well of course we can. You're the only one who *can* take care of it. Now we have a solution."

The piano was dispatched immediately. Ayta, Sofya, and Tuyaara fluttered around Ján's cottage, debating how they might squeeze the instrument in while the men stood in the cold holding it aloft over the snow. They stamped their feet and cursed under their breath as they waited for a final decision. Red October pianos with their steel frames were notoriously heavy, and Alban hollered to the women to find a spot pronto. "Ayta! I'm going to lose a finger if we can't set this beast down soon!"

The women scrambled to clear out a storage alcove intended for wintering supplies, tossing firewood into the kitchen while the men, intent on warming their hands, wrestled the piano into the sitting area. Despite the women's best efforts, the clunky steel and wood box still wouldn't fit. Alban stomped outside and returned with a sledgehammer. With a series of well-placed blows, he widened the storage space enough that the men could hoist the piano over the rubble and slide it up against the wall. The rest of the cottage resembled a disaster with bits of the broken wall and piles of firewood littering the floor.

"And there it stays for all eternity," announced Alban, holding out his reddened and cramped hands for Ayta to fuss over. "I'm not lifting that beast ever again! But no worries, Ján, I'll be back tomorrow to help tidy things up."

Ján wasn't the least bit bothered by the gaping wound of a wall. He wanted only to shut out the world and spend a day alone with his treasure, but the piano was left to stand silently in its new niche. It kept company with the lone chair and the valiant brick oven as Ján reluctantly trod back to the school and addressed himself to the task of uncrating books to create a library.

In short order, he had corralled enough precious boards to build a series of shelves, some tall, some short, to house the fledgling literary collection. Alban and Ayta stopped by with their children in the afternoon to help while assuring Ján that Sofya and Tuyaara were in his cottage imposing order on the mess. Mr. Marikyanov spent hours sorting the books and organizing the collection in neat piles in the middle of the room.

As darkness fell, Alban took his family home, and Mr. Marikyanov hurried after them so that his daughter wouldn't worry. They left Ján on his own to marvel at what many hands could accomplish in a single afternoon.

Resolved to have the project finished, Ján lit several lanterns and unpacked the last remaining boxes. He was eager for the teachers and students to arrive in the morning to find a world of literature all ready for them. He had the design carefully laid out—biographies here, science books there. A whole section of small shelves tucked under the windows held the books for the youngest learners, and the taller, higher shelves had the titles destined for older students. There were many books that would appeal to adults, and Ján organized the library with the entire community in mind.

He pondered Michil's and Gerasim's ability to put their hands on exactly what was needed. On the surface, it was a magnanimous gesture, but as ever, Ján detected an undercurrent of intrigue to their dealings. They were often away, and occasionally, Ján saw men appear at the store who had unfamiliar faces. He had quizzed Alban yet again about the source and motivation behind their largesse, but Alban had brushed the question away. "Don't ask too many questions about their dealings, my friend. They do much good for the community if only we look the other way. It has been going on a long time."

Working in the empty school with only Schatzi for company,

Ján sorted the last box and hurried to get the shelves filled. He pulled out the volumes and noticed that most were history books or large special interest volumes, and he was amused to see that these books came in an odd assortment of languages. *Great Circuses of Europe* trumpeted one title in English that Ján was fairly sure would not pass muster with the regional Soviet authorities. Another volume was dedicated to the Great War, told from a Russian perspective and focusing on the glorious revolution that eclipsed the conflict and created the Soviet State. Ján shelved them in the older reader section, dutifully scribing in the makeshift card catalog the author and title in his precise handwriting. He carried the lantern back and picked up the last few books in the crate. A history of the Roman Empire in French, a biography of Karl Marx in German, and a volume on birds in Russian were all dutifully stored.

Ján picked up the next book on the stack. He caught his breath when he saw *Warsaw: Style and Design*, written in Polish and published in the early 1920s. The book, full of large glossy pictures and edgy, art deco-inspired graphics, featured the interwar lifestyles of the Polish elite. Photographs of thin socialites emerging from shiny automobiles gave the impression of a city in awe of itself and offering a carefree life of riches and excess. Businessmen in expensive suits and fancy hats or the idle rich wearing dark sunglasses and trendy casual wear graced the pages of this fantasy edition. Ján was fascinated by these photographs of his hometown. How did this little treasure end up in Yakutsk?

A few of the buildings looked familiar, and he was gripped by nostalgia for afternoons in the garden, sitting under the willow tree, or watching the fountain rippling to the chorus of birdsong. He feasted on the captions with words whose shapes and spellings were a gift after his long separation from his mother tongue. He savored the pages, searching each for a snippet of recognition. A large spread was devoted to the Warsaw Zoological Garden with models in furs and feathered headdresses posing beside caged animals far from their native habitats.

Ján flipped to the next page, and the image before him sent a shock through his heart. He brought the book closer to the lantern where dancing light flooded the picture. "The Exquisite Villas of Mokotów" read the banner and underneath, Ján recognized the creamy stone façade of the elegant mansion from his childhood. A white touring sedan with a black canvas roof and sporty red spokes was parked on the circular drive leading to the expansive front entry. Clustered around the decadent car stood a family, posed as if preparing to motor off for a day of recreation. The caption read, "Warsaw financier and noted philanthropist Artur Balik, his wife, Lara, and their daughters, Hanna and Magda, plan to explore the city in his Rolls Royce."

Ján pressed his fingers to the picture and traced the tiny faces of his parents and sisters. They were relaxed and carefree, confident in their social standing and their wealth. Hanna was a shy toddler, peeking out from behind her father's protective embrace, and Magda was an infant, safely cocooned in her mother's arms. *I was not even a glimmer in their dreams,* thought Ján, and he was engulfed by an overwhelming wave of loneliness. They were a family that existed before him, and they all perished without him. He tried to remember the sound of his father's voice and his mother's laughter, but nothing came to him. They had become as indistinct to him as they were in this picture. Fuzzy images frozen in time.

He was overcome with jealousy. He was the outlier, the one who didn't get to be with them at the beginning or at the end. Why couldn't he have died with them? Ján had long since abandoned religion, but he was sure that somewhere they were together, past their pain and without him. He hugged the book to his chest as tears streamed down his face. His family. Gone all these many years, and look at him. Alone, managing one day to the next in a wilderness town. He cried for the family he'd lost, for the bitter pain that was welling in his chest, and for the life he never got to live. He remembered his mother's words even if he had lost the sound of her voice. *You are meant for great things, Ján.* He lay on the hard floor and curled around the book in a tight fetal knot.

Schatzi approached him warily and poked at him with her cold nose, but Ján was paralyzed in sorrow. She whimpered and nudged him with her paw. Getting no response, she curled up behind him and laid her head on his shoulder. He sensed her warmth and reached out to stroke her fur. He felt an urgent need to be with his mother, to see his father, to hear his sisters' bickering. He closed his eyes tightly, but nothing came to him, just the smell of musty books and the strong beat of Schatzi's heart.

He eased himself upright and tucked the book in his jacket. He knew what he needed to do. He crossed the snowy yard to his home. Schatzi followed noiselessly, staying close on his heels. He sat down at the piano and positioned his fingers on the keys. From memory, he played his very first composition, the melody in honor of his mother. He followed that with a piece he had written to his father, and then the two songs for his sisters. Hanna's was an elegant and stylish piece; Magda's was full of contradictions and sharp edges, but beautiful in its own way. When he finished, he put his head in his hands and closed his eyes. He had sent them everything he could, and he only hoped that they remembered him and loved him still.

He ached for some kind of response—thunder, the howl of wind—and the silences were cruel. He took Schatzi back out in the cold where she darted off in search of a hare or a fox. It was then that he saw Sofya standing in the path. She tilted her head and smiled at him, but he was too raw to know how to respond. He felt abandoned, and at the same time, he just wanted everyone in this backwater town to leave him be. They could never understand him, and he was terrified of loss. Better to keep them at bay and plot his escape.

"I heard you playing," Sofya said. "It was beautiful."

Ján nodded but he would not meet her eyes. He whistled for Schatzi and turned to walk back toward his home. Just a few more steps, and he could close the door on everything and everybody.

"Are you alright?" Sofya asked. When he didn't respond, she walked behind him and continued. "Tuyaara and I cleaned up the mess inside. It's not perfect, but better." Still no reply.

They reached his house, and he turned to her. "Sofya, I am not in the mood for company tonight. I will see you tomorrow."

She didn't move. "You don't seem alright to me. What happened?"

"Nothing happened, please, Sofya. Go home to Michil. I'll be fine."

"Michil is away. Michil is always away. I am not leaving you alone, not in this state."

Ján stepped into the house and left the door open behind him. Schatzi padded in and curled up in front of the fire. Sofya followed, gently closed the door, and proceeded straight to the kitchen where she scrounged in his cabinets for some food. Loose tea, a block of cheese, a loaf of old bread, and tinned fish were the sole inhabitants of his pantry. She set the pot on the stove and soon she had a scalding cup of tea and an open-faced sandwich for him. She took it in the front room where he was sitting on the floor, staring into the fire and rubbing Schatzi's back.

"Are you going to tell me what happened today?" she asked.

Ján said, "No. It is for me alone to hold inside."

Sofya reached out and placed her hand on his face. Her palm was warm, and he leaned into her touch.

"Sofya, please go," Ján insisted. "This is wrong, we cannot be here together like this."

She pulled her hand back and laid it in her lap. She asked, "Do you want me to leave to allow you to wallow in your own pain? You confuse me, Ján. I am trying to help."

He turned to her with a fierceness that alarmed her. "No, Sofya, I don't wish you gone. I love having you here with me. I want nothing more than to be here with you, now. Just the two of us, but you are married. You are not supposed to be here alone with me, and I cannot, tonight of all nights, control what I say or do. You should leave."

She leaned forward, grasping his face in both of her hands, and she brought her lips to his and kissed him lightly. Ján melted into her embrace. Her warmth softened the edges of his pain, and he took her in his arms and kissed her tenderly and deeply. She ran her fingers across the scars on his ear, and said ever so quietly, "You do not have to bear your pain alone."

Ján picked Sofya up and carried her to his bed, closing the door on Schatzi's protests. They spoke little while they cautiously endeavored to give each other comfort, delighting in the intimacy and surrendering to sensual touches and kisses. They lay in bed for a long time while Ján twirled his fingers around Sofya's glistening black hair, and she twisted her leg around his in playful intimacy.

A crash jolted them out of bed, and Ján threw on a shirt and ran into the front room. He laughed to see Schatzi covered in tea as she licked the plate clean. Sofya walked up behind and wrapped her arms around Ján's waist.

"I never got around to eating the dinner you fixed for me," he said, "but it looks like Schatzi enjoyed it. I'll take her out and rejoin you in just a few minutes if that is alright?"

Sofya put the kettle on and walked back to the bedroom. It was morning, but the sun would not be up for a few more hours. She lit the lamp and leaned over to tidy the clothes strewn about the floor. She spied the book which, when she picked it up, fell open to a specific page. The spine was cracked where Ján had gripped it. She looked at the picture and the caption. The Polish meant nothing to her except that she saw the name, Balik. She gasped and brought a lantern closer to the picture. She saw a massive house with an expensive car and an impeccable family. Artur, Lara, Hanna, and Magda Balik. *Oh God,* she thought. *Ján. What happened to you?*

When Ján and Schatzi returned, Sofya had tidied her clothes, carefully placing the book back on the floor where she had found it. Ján climbed into bed, the bitter cold from outside still clinging to his skin. "I need to warm you up," she teased, and she was quite as good as her word.

The town held a special ceremony to bless the new library. Michil was fêted as the guest of honor, and the villagers were effusive with their appreciation before wandering through the renovated space to explore the collection for books of interest. Ján observed the festivities from the shadows, eager to put some distance between him and Michil's smug appetite for praise. He tried to find Sofya in the crowd, but there were too many bodies jostling for space around him. The room was even more compact now that the walls were lined with shelves.

Despite the limited space, the mood was festive. Ján was gratified to see men and women file through, some without children of their own. He was especially pleased to see Mr. Marikyanov in such high spirits directing attention to particular titles and recommending books to the children who scampered in from the hallway. Sofya arrived and stood beside Michil. She wouldn't meet Ján's gaze as she hovered at the edge of the crowd with her shoulders hunched and her eyes downcast. They had not spoken since the night they shared their treasured intimacy, and Ján longed to have her to himself again.

As guests began to depart, Michil yawned and stretched his arms out wide, forcing others to squeeze out of his way. "Well, well, that was a nice little chance to treat the villagers to some fun." He clapped Ján on the back dismissively and pushed his way toward the door. Sofya remained in the shadows. Ján's heart stung to see her so diminished. Michil barely glanced her way as he snapped his fingers at her. She left the room without a word. Ján listened to the rhythm of her footsteps as she scurried down the hallway.

Michil watched Ján for a moment and then moved to stand next to him, his height and girth amplified in comparison to Ján's slight build. He spoke slowly into Ján's good ear, his words at odds with the smile plastered on his face. "Don't think I don't know what happened between you and my wife. Keep your distance, Balik. I won't ask again. I doubt you want to see any harm come her way." He sauntered out of the room without waiting for a reply.

Chapter 10

Sofya's Song

Turul, Yakutia, the Soviet Union
Spring 1956

The sun emerged from its stingy winter orbit, and the resurgent trees created a swath of pale green that announced fresh beginnings. Ján experienced nature's awakening as impending loss. He had spent the interminably bleak winter staring at the windows above the Popov store and thinking of Sofya, wishing for a moment alone with her but doing his best in such close proximity to stay away. He convinced himself that his only option was to leave, and he had waited through the days of eternal darkness and deep cold for the thaw that would allow him to make his exit. Every budding branch and every morning greeted by birdsong were signs of his looming separation from a place and a people that he had come to love.

Ján sat at his piano and softly stroked the keys. He had packed his few belongings in his rucksack, and it was sitting next to the door. Schatzi lay on the floor at Ján's feet as he said goodbye to his beloved instrument. The wolf sensed his trepidation and pushed her head up under his hands, insisting that he respond by stroking the thick fur between her ears. They were startled by a crack outside the window followed by flickers of light across the worn floor. Schatzi growled but Ján shushed her. "Just the thaw, girl. The melting ice is telling us it's time to go."

He closed the piano and rested his head against the cool, smooth wood. "Farewell, my friend," he whispered. He produced two envelopes, one for Alban and the other for Mr. Marikyanov, and propped the thin paper against the music stand, running his hands over the top of the instrument one last time.

Fragments of memory crowded his thoughts. Disturbing recollections of leaving Ada behind and venturing out into the hostile battleground that had been his last home. He pushed the panic down. He reminded himself that he was leaving now of his own accord. He could stay here and he would live, but it would be a hollow life without Sofya, and he couldn't risk whatever punishment Michil might devise for her. It was best to keep moving and hope to find healing somewhere else. He shouldn't have gotten so attached to this far-flung place, anyway.

Ján led Schatzi away, and the two struck out across a hushed field accompanied only by the hoot of a lone owl in the distance and the crunching of their steps through the brittle ice. When they cleared the barren edges of Turul, Ján stopped for a moment. "Which way, girl?" Schatzi dashed off in pursuit of a rabbit, and Ján rubbed his beard. "Looks like west it is."

The weak sun cast their shadows across the ice in muted blues, and although they encountered small stands of arctic trees, most of their journey took them through endless vistas of unbroken snow-covered tundra. They trudged until the afternoon when the world around them began to sink into darkness and Ján stopped at a protected spot. He curled up away from the wind, cushioned only by a thick, second-hand blanket and Schatzi's warmth. They fell into a fitful sleep driven by bone-weary fatigue.

He awoke to a gray dawn where a meager promise of sunlight lurked below the horizon. There were noises in the distance:

ardent voices and the clang of metal against recalcitrant ice. Schatzi emitted a low growl, her fur on edge as she prepared for intruders. Ján wrapped his arms around her and made shushing noises by her ear. As his eyes adjusted to the dusky morning, he was relieved to see Alban and his son, Feodor, trundling toward them in their sled.

Schatzi leaped out of his arms, barking and wagging her tail as she dashed toward their friends, launching her thick paws against Alban's chest and covering his face with affectionate licks. Ján scrunched his eyes to get a better view and waved as Alban pulled up alongside.

"No sneaking up on you, is there?" Alban laughed as he ruffled the fur on the wolf's head. He turned his attention to Ján. "Where the devil are you going, Balik? I've been chasing you down for hours." He held up Ján's note. "Running away? Without a word?" Alban shook his head and stuffed the note back in his pocket.

"Don't try to talk me out of it, Alban. It's hard to explain."

"No it's not. You act like I haven't watched you pine over Sofya all winter. But this? Running away? I thought you were smarter than that."

"Easy for you to say, Alban."

"Perhaps, and we can listen to your sorry whining another day, but there's something you need to know. Michil is dead."

Ján was certain he was hallucinating. "Michil dead? How? When?" A sickening thought occurred to him. "Does anyone think I had anything to do with it?"

"Yes, dead as a man gets and no, you're the last on anyone's mind. Come with us, and you'll see for yourself."

They arrived back in town to find a crowd gathered around the entrance to the store. Ján pushed through the rabble to force his way inside. Clusters of curious people milled about in the cramped aisles, their heads tilted together in muted conversation. Ján caught sight of Ayta and she pointed to the living quarters above, so Ján wound his way around boxes of unpacked goods toward the stairs.

He emerged to see Michil's body laid out on the dining table, covered to his chest with a sheet. Ján had seen death too many times to be alarmed by the ghoulish pallor of Michil's skin and the rigidity of his muscles. Sofya sat on a chair in the corner, her presence ignored by the men hovering close to Michil's body. Despite the gauzy black veil covering her face, Sofya held her head high, asserting her presence to the men who snubbed her. Ján brushed past the gawkers and knelt by her side.

"Sofya? What happened?" he asked gently.

"Greed," she replied as she turned her head slowly to look directly at him with eyes that were startlingly fierce. "This was always the way it would end. He wanted everything he could conquer. Risk just made the chase more exciting. The reward was always worth it for him. The rest of us be damned."

Ján nodded. "Gerasim?"

"Alive, but injured. He will recover. The wagon fell through the ice, and Michil was trapped. They knew better. We all know better than to trust the river this time of year."

"I'm sorry for your loss," Ján offered meekly, not knowing what to say.

She glanced at Michil's body with a dismissive calmness. "Turul's loss, maybe. That is all."

Sofya's defiance pained and confused him. Ján avoided the store for the next several days, unsettled by her curious detachment. He could understand some combination of grief or relief, but there was something lurking behind her impassive numbness. It was as though she were a loaded spring ready to snap. Ján decided that she felt some sort of twisted remorse over having betrayed her marriage vows, and he didn't want to cause her further distress. He had promised Alban he wouldn't leave, not just yet, anyway, so he watched the villagers come and go, bringing her food and leaving small gifts, while he stayed cloistered in his little house. He took solace in the company of his piano, avoided any contact with Sofya, and poured his trepidation into endless hours of playing.

Sofya watched Ján out her window, yearning for his company but mindful that he was keeping his distance from her. She was mired in grief, not for the brutish Michil, but for the loss of Ján's friendship and the tenuous nature of her survival as a widow. As Michil's wife, she was a nobody, nothing but a punching bag for his derision, but she could also count on food for her table and a roof over her head. The abuse seemed a necessary price to pay for survival in such a stark place. Now with Michil gone, she expected his family to toss her to the wolves. She had nothing to count on, no safety net, not even Ján's affection, and this was the deepest cut of all. She convinced herself that their night together had been a momentary temptation for him, some impulse to distract him from his own pain. She didn't want to court further embarrassment by assuming an attachment that he didn't feel.

Two weeks after Michil's death, she emerged from the store toting a hastily packed cardboard suitcase and strode past Ján's house to arrive at her sister's doorstep. Tuyaara saw her coming.

Sofya hung her head low. "Gerasim took over the store. He said I am not welcome anymore."

Tuyaara chuckled softly and put her hands on her hips. "Well, your fortunes have certainly taken a turn for the worse. Maybe it serves you right for putting on airs with that Popov family."

"That's a mean thing to say even for you, Tuyaara. You know better than anyone exactly how I came to be married to Michil." Sofya swallowed her anger. This wasn't worth dredging up, and she had nowhere else to go. "Will you let me stay? I'll not be a bother."

Tuyaara's husband Dabyn was loath to take Sofya in, but Tuyaara prevailed. "She can work for her keep," she promised, savoring the chance to humble her sister. Sofya was given a pallet in the corner of the room where the five children slept.

Sofya was hanging washing on the line when she heard Ján playing the piano. She was not schooled in the finer points of music appreciation, but she could imagine that what she was hearing was a very complex melody to play. The composition was frantic with notes falling over each other in distress. It was a doleful song, equal parts heartbreaking and sinister. Tuyaara walked out with a basket full of wet linens and dropped it at Sofya's feet.

"All hours we hear that racket. Dabyn has been over more than once to tell him to stop, but the man doesn't listen. I guess he can't with only one ear." Tuyaara giggled at her own joke. "And if that music weren't torture enough, one of these days, I'll do something about that furry nuisance."

Sofya turned to find Schatzi nose down, digging furiously in the garden in pursuit of a miscreant critter. She ignored her sister's acidic humor and coaxed Schatzi to her side. "I'll take the pup back."

"Tell him to stop his racket and control his wolf."

Sofya waved back at Tuyaara and urged Schatzi along, having no intention to comply with the tart request. The music was calling her over. In the sorrowful notes, she heard a reflection of her own pain.

She walked to Ján's door and knocked. He played on, and Schatzi pushed the door open with her nose. Sofya followed the implied invitation and tiptoed in where she could observe Ján, amazed at the machinations of his hands as they raced about the keyboard. The music stand was empty, so whatever he was playing was pouring from his memory in a disturbing and raw melody. She absorbed the punishing rhythms feeling like an interloper in his private world, yet she was unable to pull herself away. It was as though he were peering straight into her soul.

Ján played the last notes and then rested his calloused fingers on the keys. He tipped his head forward slightly as if in prayer, and Sofya began to back away, mindful of just how mortified she would be if he caught her eavesdropping. She almost made it to the door when she bumped into Schatzi. The wolf yelped, and she froze as Ján spun around in his seat. As soon as he recognized Sofya, his shoulders relaxed and he gifted her with a broad smile.

"I...I...I am so sorry," she stuttered, unable to conjure a satisfactory explanation for her actions. Schatzi wagged her tail, forgiving her instantly.

"Hello," he said kindly. "I've seen you at Tuyaara's." He motioned to the lone chair. "Please stay."

They observed each other in an awkward silence, both hoping for insight into the other's thoughts. Ján spoke first. "It's good to see you. To be truthful, I knew that Gerasim had taken over the store, but I didn't know how to help. Are you alright?"

Sofya shrugged her shoulders. "I am glad to be useful even if Tuyaara and Dabyn complain about my being there." She quickly changed the topic. "I was outside, and I heard you playing, and I had to come closer. That song; it's haunting and beautiful."

"I'm glad you came by."

"Are you? I was afraid you were avoiding me. Maybe that you regretted what happened," she stammered. "Between us, I mean, if we're both being truthful now."

"What? Oh no, Sofya!" Ján jumped up from the piano seat and motioned for her to sit with him on the rug. "I never regretted a thing. In fact, I thought of you every day, every minute, hoping that we could be together again. And then when Michil died, well," he paused, unsure how to proceed. "I don't know, Sofya. I guess I decided it was you that regretted what happened."

She cocked her head and looked into his eyes. He searched her face for clues, hoping for a sign of warmth or affection, and was rewarded by a long, slow kiss.

"That's how I feel about the night we shared," she said.

They began a courtship of sorts. Whenever Sofya heard the piano, if she were able to step away from her chores, she would walk around the fence and slip into Ján's house. He always knew when he heard her footsteps at the door, but he kept on playing, and she pulled the chair over to watch. As the days got warmer, and life on the tundra turned greener and more vibrant under the summer sun, Ján's music became less fretful and more hopeful.

One afternoon, Ján watched until he saw Sofya emerge from the house with her gardening tools. As she tended to the vegetables, he opened the windows wide and sat down at the piano. The melody for today was his newest composition, and he took a deep breath before laying his hands on the keys. The notes began softly with a gentle rhythm. There was a reticence to the score, a shyness about the melody that gradually yielded to a more cheerful and forthright celebration of joy. As he hoped, he heard squeaky hinges and light footsteps. She stood in the doorway holding a trowel, transfixed. When he finished, he turned to face her, and tears were running down her face.

"It's beautiful, Ján. So different from anything I have ever heard you play," she said. "It gives me hope."

He slid off the bench and crossed the room, reaching for her hand and holding it gently. "I wrote it for you."

She dropped the trowel and kissed him with a hunger borne of loss, love, passion, and friendship. "Is it too soon after Michil's death for me to tell you that I love you?" he whispered as he kissed her ears and caressed her neck.

"I did not love Michil. I never loved him. I did not wish him dead, but I wished myself unmarried to him," she replied simply.

Ján led her inside where he pulled her down to the rug beside him and drew her into an embrace, whispering in her ear, "I think I need to get a new chair for you so we each have a place to sit." She laughed softly, and he leaned back and gazed at her with gentle eyes. "I am not one to judge and do not wish to question you. I wonder, though. If you did not love Michil, how did you become his wife?"

She placed her hand over his and brought his fingers to her lips, kissing them tenderly. She looked away, nervous about revealing too much and fearful of how he might perceive her if she told the truth. He tilted up her chin and smiled. "Sofya, I love you. You cannot shock me, and you needn't fear my reaction. We are survivors, both of us."

She searched his face for hints of trust and acceptance, challenging him not to judge her. "My father sold me to Michil to pay off a debt. The same father who didn't remember my name when he was drunk and who died an alcoholic. I could've defied my father, refused to marry and left home, but he would've gone to prison for what he owed, and Tuyaara and I would have been shuttled off to work in one of the camps. I was scared that none of us would survive if he was sent to one of the gulags." She hesitated for a moment, and then asked, "Do you think I am a coward?"

"I think you are very brave."

She intertwined her fingers with his. "Now I get to ask a question. What happened to your ear?"

"Russian soldiers shot at my head."

"Surely there is more to tell."

"It was a long time ago when I left Königsberg. That is all."

She didn't react, say she was sorry, or express outrage. She simply raised her hand, pushed back his long blonde hair, and tenderly traced the scar. Then she kissed him, and he kissed her back. She found it easy to accept that he was an enigma, a closed door who nevertheless had an open heart. She could live with that.

They were married in early fall. Sofya wore a dress she made for herself, and Ján borrowed a linen shirt from Alban to wear with his everyday work trousers. It was too big, of course, but Sofya made some temporary alterations, and he looked very handsome. Schatzi hovered between them as vows were exchanged. After the wedding and a dinner hosted by Alban and Ayta, Sofya retrieved her cardboard suitcase from Tuyaara's and walked around the fence, entering the cottage that was now their home together.

The next morning, before the autumn sun had peeked over the horizon, Sofya left their bed and tiptoed into the kitchen to light the stove. Slipping soundlessly out the back door and followed closely by Schatzi, she crept around the fence into Tuyaara's garden, a small plot with a few stubborn stragglers from the summer vegetables that Sofya had teased out of the harsh tundra. She plucked a few stalks of flowering heather and returned to the bedroom with two cups of steaming tea, two slices of thick bread, homemade jam, smoked white fish, and a jar with the heather sprigs.

Ján slept deeply, a smile teasing the corners of his mouth. Sofya set down the food to watch him as he breathed in and out, mumbling a name or two as he dreamed. In the weak dawn light, she could see that his missing ear was just one of the many assaults on his body. His arms, covered in soft, blonde hair, had telltale signs of cuts, bruises, and burns. She knew what frostbite did to fingers and toes, and she saw evidence of that too. What she didn't know was how many of these bruises he carried in his heart.

"One of these days, Ján Balik, you will tell me your story," she whispered.

She walked around the room, furnished with cast-offs and a chest of drawers that Ján had built himself. Sofya wondered if Ján would mind the addition of a few touches of her own, a pillow here, a picture there. Her toes bumped into a pile of Ján's clothes, hastily tossed to the floor in their zeal to celebrate their marriage, and she smiled with the memory. For her at least, it was only the second time she had ever made love. Sex was a well-worn path, but never before had she known love like this. Ján was tender, kind, and ardent, and she had felt every bit the blushing bride.

She reached down to gather his clothes, lovingly folding his trousers and setting his undergarments aside to wash. She opened the large trunk at the foot of the bed, intending to put his clothes away, and she spied the book of photographs she had found earlier. She reached in and ran her hands across the cover, thinking of the family inside and wondering again what happened to them. The book moved a bit with her fingers, and she spied a second spine peeking out from underneath.

She teased it out of its hiding place and discovered a book with a hand-tooled leather cover. Clearly it had once been very expensive and quite a treasure. Now it was covered in water stains, and the leather featured cracks and significant scars, including a deep injury in the front. Sofya plumbed the hole with her little finger. It was a couple of centimeters deep and precise, most certainly from a bullet.

Ján grumbled a bit in his sleep and rolled over. Sofya held her breath, but he slept on.

She took the book into the front room, curled up in the worn chair. Holding a candle close, she caressed the cover. The book was black, thick, and expertly bound. The cover was decorated in an elaborate pattern embossed into the leather, and on the spine, she saw the markings, JAB 1940. She caught her breath. Ján must have had it since he was a child.

She opened the cover and examined the pages inside. They were crinkled and stained, and the bullet had bored through the first third of the book. Sofya recognized Ján's practiced penmanship and she felt a lump in her throat for she was looking at music that he had composed. The first page was written in a boy's handwriting and featured a flurry of notes with a single word at the top, "Mama."

Following were more pieces, each seemingly dedicated to a person or an event, and later entries carefully written around the savage hole in the paper. Sofya could not decipher much of the alphabet or Ján's notations to read the titles. She thumbed through piece after piece until she found a section that she could read. Ján had switched to writing in Russian. She saw compositions to Vera, Dima, and Miss Shmetlana, among others. One to Maks was hurriedly composed in clumsy, almost sloppy handwriting. A large ink bloom stained a corner of the page, and Sofya wondered. *Was this caused by tears?*

In a more refined penmanship, she saw dedications to Alban, Sergei, and Jozef. Four more compositions followed, and here Ján had reverted to another language. German? Sofya couldn't read it once again, but the piece dedicated to Anna alarmed her. Here Ján had neatly scribed a song, the melody simpler than many of his other compositions. The notes undulated on the page, so it seemed to Sofya that it was a gentle song. So why did he savagely strike it through? Was this Ján's reaction or the work of someone else who had gotten hold of his book?

She quickly thumbed through the other pages and saw no other pieces that had been so angrily excised. After this, the writing reverted to Russian again, and here Sofya realized that these were people from Turul. Her heart fluttered to see her own name followed by a song painstakingly written with notations in the margins, *gentle* written here, *kind* written there. *Beautiful* was boldly scribed and underlined, and Sofya brushed away a tear. She knew of no one who had ever judged her as beautiful before. There were more, each to someone specific either a person dear to Ján or a melody written to ease someone's pain. She closed the book and held it close to her heart.

"You found my treasure."

Sofya was startled to see him standing in the doorway, cradling a lukewarm mug of tea.

"I woke up and reached for you, but you were gone. The breakfast is delicious, but I would honestly rather have you," he said. There was only affection and generosity in his voice.

Sofya relaxed. "I was putting away your clothes, and I found this. It's beautiful. It's all yours, right?"

Ján knelt before Sofya and carefully took the book from her hands. "It was given to me as a child when I wrote this first piece to my mother. The grief–" he shook his head, parsing his words carefully. "It is too much for a child, and yet, children seem to hold sorrow differently than adults." He sighed and collected his thoughts. "It helps me when I am feeling sad or happy or grateful or bereft to put my thoughts into song. Music has always been my original language."

Sofya put her hand over his and looked into his deep blue eyes. "The bullet hole?" she asked simply.

"Ah yes, this book rescued me in more ways than one." He hesitated, deep in thought and his brows knitted together in concentration. "Until I met you, this was my most valuable treasure." Then the corners of his mouth twitched, and the beginnings of a smile formed. He leaned over and kissed her forehead and said, "This, my dear, is what I write when I am happy." He took the book to the piano and opened it to Sofya's page and began to play. The notes started off like a delicate spring wind, rollicking across the tundra in a welcome rush of warmth and sunshine. The melody became richer, at one point incorporating a tune most familiar, her Sakha song, the one her mother created especially for her. When had he been listening to learn that? It was exquisitely rendered, and she was overcome with love to think that when Ján considered her, this expression of joy is what he created.

She went to him and wrapped her arms around his back, holding him tight. "You are a gift, Ján Balik. My gift."

He carefully set the book on top of the piano, and they returned to the bedroom as the remains of breakfast, lovingly prepared, became Schatzi's feast.

Part Three

Chapter 11

Moscow, Russia

September 1992

Harper Burns pushed her way through the frenzied crowd exiting the Tverskaya Metro Station and emerged into the heart of Pushkin Square. She hurried past the street vendors selling sausage and cabbage pies and darted into McDonald's, an unthinkable fixture just a few short years ago, but now a glaring sign of the new Russia. She ordered a coffee for herself and turned to leave before dashing back to the counter to pick up a second cup for Tom Rainey. It was still her first week on the job, and she was eager to get off on the right foot with her new colleague.

The newly refurbished offices of *The Moscow News*, Russia's oldest English language newspaper, were situated just off the square. Harper entered the bustling reception area just as the elevator door dinged open. She charged forward and collided with a man wearing a bespoke suit topped with an elegant cashmere coat.

"I am so sorry!" she exclaimed in English while biting her lip against the sting of hot coffee seeping through her clothes. She thrust a handful of cheap paper napkins at his sleeve, horrified at her clumsiness and praying that she hadn't splashed him too. Switching to Russian, she continued to offer a stream of apologies.

The man grumbled and brushed by her as he hurried toward the door. Alina, the receptionist, arrived with a damp cloth to help Harper tidy up.

"You sure know how to make an entrance," Alina laughed.

"Who is he?" Harper dared to ask as she peeled back layer after layer of soiled fabric.

"Alexander Stein, the chief editor," Alina said with a wink.

"Shit," Harper shot back. "How good of a memory does he have?"

"Pretty good. Mind of a steel trap, actually. Now get on that elevator and work your magic up there. No one knows that you just humiliated yourself in front of the boss." Harper pointed to the blooming stain on the front of her shirt, but Alina nudged her towards the elevator. "It's nothing. Our little secret."

Harper stepped into the domestic newsroom juggling her worn leather briefcase with a soggy bag of coffee while tugging her blazer over her soiled white shirt. The sight of the storied newsroom, a frenzied hive with phones ringing and typewriters clacking under the thick haze of stale cigarette smoke, banished worries over the morning's fiasco.

She adored the controlled chaos, the purposefulness of this space. This was history in the making, and there was nowhere she would rather be. Even with an impressive resume for such a young journalist, she was eager to prove herself, show off her dogged determination. No one had ever accused her of being patient.

She paused at the framed copies of front pages lining the office walls and steadied her breathing. "For you, Papa," she whispered, "today's the day. Storm the ramparts, take no prisoners." Thus emboldened, she made a beeline for her desk and stored her valise, making space amidst tidy piles of paper, a finicky Soviet-made typewriter, and freshly sharpened pencils.

"Good morning, sunshine." Tom Rainey's lyrical voice

grabbed her attention. He was a tall, garrulous, silver-haired Texan, and his smile was infectious.

She handed him the half-filled cup. "I picked up a coffee for you but I'm afraid that I'm wearing most of it. A girl has to stay warm somehow. I might just have dumped the rest on Mr. Stein."

Tom laughed. "Well yee haw, I guess. Don't fret, Miss Burns. At least you've made yourself memorable."

Harper allowed herself a peek down the long corridor.

"Oh, she's here alright," Tom offered. "You'll be fine. I haven't seen her bite anyone yet."

Angelica Turner commanded her newsroom with a mixture of intimidation and mystique. An exacting editor with a remarkable eye for detail and little tolerance for nonsense, she was a woman who wielded language with precision. "Miss Burns, your question?" she asked when Harper appeared at her open door.

Harper took a deep breath and squared her shoulders. Angelica was attacking a sheaf of papers—someone's earnestly written story—leaving a trail of aggressive red pencil marks. Harper waited for her attention. Without looking up, Angelica said, "Miss Burns, I'm getting old waiting for you to speak. You are lurking with a purpose, I assume?"

Harper's idea came tumbling out. "Yes, yes. I am! A story about propaganda and the myth of a happy childhood under Stalin. Something that *feels* pressing with all the documents coming to light since the fall of the soviet government."

"Feels pressing or is pressing. Be specific."

"Of course. *Is* pressing. The legitimization of the Soviet State relied in part on insisting that Stalin was a benevolent father figure. My own father grew up under Stalin's rule. After my grandparents were arrested, he was shuttled between State homes and orphanages until his aunt could arrange his release to the UK. He met my mother when they were both in domestic service and neither ever spoke of his past, but even as a child, I could see that he suffered crippling insecurities. They haunted him for the rest of his life. It appears that for millions of children—"

Angelica interrupted. "Take a breath, Miss Burns. I get your drift, but you're a bit close to this topic to be an objective source."

Harper responded before her brain could urge caution. "I disagree, Miss Turner! I think my father's experience—what little I know of it—gives me a special angle and a determination that other reporters may not be able to channel." She watched Angelica for a reaction. The woman was still making mincemeat out of the piece in front of her.

Angelica finally set the red pencil aside and looked up. "And? Is that the gist of your argument? Your determination?"

"Miss Turner, my father died last year. He was an incredible man but he suffered from headaches, nightmares, and fears that he battled in secret. He took his pain to the grave. There are so many others like him out there, people who were robbed of their innocence and whose trauma got passed to the next generation. It's not personal redemption for me. It's a way to expose the harm and hold the perpetrators accountable for their fealty to a corrupt system and a cruel dictator. I want to uncover the true nature of what life was like for children under Stalin, peel back the propaganda."

Angelica tapped her pencil on the table. "Solzhenitsyn's work is hot right now; people are eager to see an insider's view. This might tie in well, sort of a corollary exploration into the notion of political imprisonment and its ripple effects." She charged out of her office, and Harper hurried down the corridor after her. They stopped in front of Tom's desk.

Angelica didn't wait for acknowledgment. "Rainey, Burns here has an itch to follow up on adults who suffered an abusive childhood in the Soviet system of orphanages, victims of Uncle Joseph as it were. Poke around with your contacts, see what you can dig up, and let's revisit this at Monday's meeting when you have the bones of a story."

Harper blurted, "But, Angelica, er, Miss Turner! I was hoping that I could take this one on!"

Angelica pointed to Harper with the well-worn end of her pencil. "Miss Burns, I appreciate your shiny enthusiasm, but I decide who does what in this newsroom. Rainey will take the lead on the investigation around the myth of the happy childhood. If there's anything there, he will find it. I have something special for you."

Tom offered Harper a sly wink. "I'll get on it right away. And, Miss Burns? Let's put our heads together, okay? I want to hear your vision for this piece."

Angelica handed a brochure to Harper. "The Moscow Winter Festival begins mid-February. Months away and arguably more of a piece for the arts and culture folks, but considering the tumult of the times, the paper wants to focus on a renewed sense of national pride. There will be a music competition in advance of the festival. A bit of history combined with a taste of the new Russia, as it were. You are to contact the organizers, get a bead on what they are hoping to create, and feature the contestants during the buildup to the festival. You play the violin, don't you, Miss Burns?"

"Well yes, but..."

"Excellent. You're perfect then. Contact the organizers, sit in while they make their selections, and focus on the contestants. Find someone that will win the heart of the new Russia. And, Miss Burns?"

"Yes, Miss Turner?"

"Keep a spare shirt in your desk drawer."

Harper dangled the brochure from her fingertips as if it were a stinking piece of rubbish. Pictures of bright lights, ice sculptures, and frigid outdoor chess games indicated a lively affair, but hardly the type of event that required a gritty reporter. "Hard-hitting journalism my ass," she grumbled.

"Cheer up, it's not the end of the world," Tom drawled. "Let me do some digging into Papa Stalin, you write that little ditty about the competition, and then I'll share what I have. You gotta pay your dues, Miss Burns."

"Fine but can we just stick with Harper and Tom? I hear 'Miss' and I think of old school marms."

"Duly noted."

Harper investigated the details of the festival. She visited the venue and spoke with the organizers, then she sat at her typewriter with her notes and pounded out an announcement designed to entice contestants to enter in droves.

```
Tchaikovsky, Rachmaninoff, Shostakovich,
Rimsky-Korsakov, Prokofiev all honored
Mother Russia with their musical genius.
Who is the next great Russian musician?
The organizers of the annual Moscow
Winter Festival are launching a
celebration of Russia's rich musical
heritage. Seeking artists performing
traditional classical or folk songs as
well as composers of original scores,
they hope to present a rich tapestry of
Russian cultural and regional
traditions.
```

Her article profiled a sampling of contestants before outlining the most exciting news.

```
Ten winners will be chosen to represent
different regions and styles of music.
Winners will each receive a prize of 400
rubles as well as an all-expense paid
trip for two to Moscow in February to
perform at the festival.
```

She wrapped up by sharing the submission details and deadlines.

Harper dropped the finished piece in Angelica's tray and rushed to Tom's desk with the hopes of finding out about his research.

"You look like you could use a good story," he said.

"Always in the mood for that. That last piece was boring even to me, and I wrote it. Hit me with something extraordinary."

"Your instincts about the myth of Soviet childhood story are good. Others have tried to investigate, of course, but the difference now is the timing. There were some high-profile prosecutions during the Soviet era of officials whose jobs dealt with child welfare but who were exposed for running scams. They were brought up on charges of neglect or corruption, but nothing systemic was ever exposed. With the Soviet Union dissolved and a wave of reforms unfolding, documents are coming to the surface and more people are willing to share their stories, people like your father. There's a goldmine of information out there just waiting for someone to come along and ask the right questions."

Harper's pulse was racing. She knew she had her teeth into a powerful story. "Papa never told me much, but the sadness was always there, lurking just under the surface. What else have you found out?"

Tom explained that it was still early in the investigation, but he had managed to uncover leads on contacts who might still be alive to testify to their experiences. "It all boiled down to State control—fear of groups who can disrupt the revolution, either because they are seen as not sufficiently committed to the cause or because they resided on land that the Soviet government wanted. Children got caught in the crosshairs." He pulled out an old photograph and placed it in front of Harper. In it a smiling Stalin holds up a young girl as she embraces his neck. "Does this look familiar to you?" Tom asked.

"It does, but the details are sketchy. Fill me in."

"The girl is Gelya Markizova. Engelsina Markizova, to be precise, named for none other than Friedrich Engels. She accompanied her father, a member of the Buryat-Mongol delegation, to see Stalin in 1936. The story goes that Gelya, who was only seven, traveled with her father all the way from Siberia to the Kremlin.

"She was allowed into the meeting but was bored by all the speeches, so she grabbed a handful of flowers and hopped up on the stage to hug Stalin. Remember, the propaganda of the time posited him as the most visible symbol of the USSR's benevolence, a campaign that was blasted across the country on posters that featured well-fed, happy children. Anyway, little Gelya hops up on stage trying to stir up a bit of fun and hugs the evil dictator. The press went wild."

Harper stared at the girl whose severely cropped hair and endearing overbite elicited such a warm reception from Stalin. "This is quite a cozy scene. What happened to her? You said she traveled with her father, and that he was a communist, right? She must have been one of the lucky ones."

"Well, not so fast. She did, in fact, travel with her father, who was by all accounts loyal to the fledgling government and eager to do his part, and because of this photo, she became instantly famous. Stalin gave her a pricey gold watch, and she was showered with gifts from across the Soviet Union. In a sad twist, her father was arrested not long after and charged with spying for Japan. Despite Gelya's letters to Stalin pleading for his release, he was shot in 1937."

"Oh God, that's awful!" Harper exclaimed.

"And that's not all," Tom continued. "In 1938, her mother was arrested and sent to Kazakhstan, where she too was murdered, all denied of course. And to add insult to injury, the official record of the event in this photograph was changed to substitute another child's name for Gelya's. It simply wouldn't do for Stalin to hobnob with the daughter of the people's enemy."

Harper ran her fingers across the grainy picture. "Such a tragedy! How many more like Gelya and my father?"

Tom admitted that no one likely knew how many children had been killed or traumatized as a result of accusations against their families. The criteria for being designated an enemy changed with the times, an amorphous and capricious definition of undesirables. "The purges took place largely between 1918 and 1953, ending abruptly with Stalin's death," recounted Tom, "and the children who survived? They run the gamut from stalwart communists to traumatized souls living in a cocoon of silence while nursing their guilt."

Harper realized that she had been so consumed in little Gelya's story that she had cracked her pencil in half listening to Tom describe the scope of the tragedy. "Tom, you really *must* let me help you with this. I just filed the silly music piece. I can stay on top of that story, really! I want in on this one too."

Tom chuckled. "Don't worry, Angelica will lump more on your plate, but I'd love your input on this one. It only seems fair. Let's review the notes together and see where we go from here. Divide and conquer."

It was dark when Harper left work. The street vendors had departed, and the cold wind had died down. Now in the glittering lights of Pushkin Square, tiny bits of ice mixed with the soft rain to turn the wet pavement slippery, sending the pedestrians indoors. Harper passed restaurants and bars where she could see patrons mingling over savory suppers. The light from candles and sconces spilled out across the sidewalk through broad windows foggy with cozy warmth. She descended back into the chilly warren of the metro station to return to her little studio apartment. When she finally slipped her ancient key in the big brass lock, all she wanted was to take a warm bath and sit with her thoughts.

She gathered her kit and trundled down the hall to the communal washroom in the fusty boarding house. Harper thought often that her idea of heaven would be a new apartment with a private bath, but that was impossible to find in Moscow on her meager salary. She ran the water well past the stingy fill line painted on the chipped porcelain, grateful for the warmth of a functioning water heater this evening. She lay still, processing the emotion of the day until the water cooled and a loud knock on the door announced the annoyance of a neighbor, waiting to use the space.

She wrapped herself in her bathrobe and, after mumbling a quick apology to the hirsute man pacing outside the door, she scurried back to her private quarters. She poured herself a glass of wine and picked up the framed photograph that sat on the side table. Her father stood tall and thin, his tie slightly askew while the elusive Scottish sun gleamed on his bald head. Her mother leaned toward him in her signature style of a full-skirted dress and fake pearls that completely ignored the Twiggy-fueled 1960s and stood firm against the polyester-soaked 1970s. Wedged between them was Harper with dark, choppy hair cut too short and a grin defined by the recent loss of her front tooth. She was a grown woman now but still sported the short, black hair that framed her striking blue eyes.

"Here's to you, Papa and Mama," she said aloud as she lifted her glass. She looked into her father's eyes, fuzzy and indistinct behind his thick black glasses. "What can you tell me, Papa? Where can you lead me?"

She reached behind the chair and pulled out the violin case. Elegant and expensive in its day, it was cracked and scarred now from harrowing journeys and years of wear. On the side near the clasp was a small brass plate engraved with the name of Harper's grandfather, *Rudolf Romanovich Bychkov*. Since her own father anglicized his name, the instrument was all she had to connect to this distant man, a musician in the sparkling yet doomed days of the Tsar and a man destined to end his life as a prisoner of the new regime.

She opened the case and ran her hands across the worn spruce, imagining the violin in its polished heyday. Then she picked up her bow, positioned the instrument, and played a Russian folk tune that her father had taught her. She closed her eyes and recalled holding the same violin as a child, her father standing behind. "*Find the G set, ah! very good. Now full step to B, da! da! and a half set to C. Well done, my dear!*"

She laid the bow in her lap but kept her chin resting against the same smooth wood that had felt the warmth of her grandfather's hands then her father's. She whispered, "I won't give up on the story, Papa. I promise. I won't give up."

CHAPTER 12

SONG OF BETRAYAL

Yakutia, Russia
June 1992

Dust billowed up as the convoy from Turul bounced along the rutted road toward the outskirts of Yakutsk and the festival grounds at Us Khatyn. The corrugated dirt thoroughfares that followed the paths of the original Sakha horsemen gradually gave way to paved highways as the procession neared the city built on unforgiving permafrost and Siberian dreams. The travelers from Turul joined clusters of other conveyances—cars, trucks, wagons—all making the trek to mark Ysyakh, the holiday honoring the magic of summer solstice.

Undaunted by the gritty breeze and the relentless insects, Sofya waved a horse-hair fly swat and searched the horizon for signs of the festival. Many in the village had acquired cars over the years, mostly older Japanese models that were oddly better suited to the cold than cheaper Soviet vehicles, but for this trip across the muddy terrain and thawed rivers, they preferred their wagons drawn by hardy Siberian horses. The squat mares plodded along, unflappable in the controlled chaos of automobiles and scooters zipping by.

Sofya and Ján had joined Tuyaara's family with adults and children wedged together and straddling bags and supplies as they endured the jolts of a ragged journey. Alban's wagon rolled in front, close enough for Ayta and Sofya to call out to each other and point out the sights.

"There it is!" squealed Sofya as she grabbed Ján's arm and gestured toward the tiny dots of color barely visible at the far edges of the field. He smiled and squeezed her hand as he tried to channel some of her enthusiasm. Travels were fraught for Ján. As the endless permafrost and stands of ancient trees passed by, he thought of previous journeys, thick with scars of banishment and loss. He reminded himself that this occasion was meant to be jolly.

During Ysyakh, Yakuts gathered to honor nature deities and the gifts of renewal and rebirth during the brief reprieve from punishing winters. This was their sacred holiday, and families journeyed from across Yakutia to feast, compete, and reconnect. Venues for music, sports, feasting, competitions, and dancing surrounded the thousands of Yakuts massed in the large open area.

On these long days of near constant light, interrupted by mere hints of nighttime, children ran for hours squealing and laughing between the brightly hued yurts in a village that resembled a collection of broad-bottomed beehives. Babies were cherished by adoring relatives with each auntie and uncle opening their arms for a cuddle. The adults reminisced; dined on stuffed perch, pancakes, and horse meat; and sipped kumis, a drink that Ján politely declined having never acquired a taste for the fermented mare's milk. Older children were particularly solicitous because their help translated into coveted blessings from their family elders.

Amidst shouts and greetings from extended kin, the caravan from Turul trundled into the campground. Ján pulled the components of their tent out of the back of the wagon and carried them over to where Alban was setting up his family's accommodations. Dabyn had taken the horses to water at the lake and then disappeared into the crowd as soon as the convoy halted, leaving Ján in charge of getting Sofya's family settled. Alban and Feodor pitched in to assist, and the men had the camp arranged well in time for their wives' critical assessments.

Ján was pleased to see Sofya so deeply rooted in her extended family's embrace. Having only tart-tongued Tuyaara around for most of the year was a burden that she bore without complaint, but to see her among her scattered siblings and cousins was a delight. Ján mostly stayed on the fringes. The family was generally kind to him, but he shared little of their history. His fair skin and blonde, curly hair set him apart in a sea of dark-haired Sakya in-laws, and in truth, this yearly ritual always made him wistful for his own kin. He wondered what Hanna's and Magda's families might have been like if his sisters had survived the war. They would be grandmothers now, and Ján was certain that all their children would have been beautiful, generous, and talented. He mourned the knowledge that his family, the sparkling stars of pre-war Poland, would die in obscurity with him.

He watched Sofya embrace one of her niece's babies, and his heart ached to see her squeeze his chubby fists and plant kisses on his rosy cheeks. They tried not to dwell on their losses, but at times like these it was hard, especially now that their friends were not only parents, but also grandparents, the generations around them swelling with potential.

At night, Ján held Sofya close. Despite the late hour, the persistent sun shone outside, casting the interior of their simple tent in eerie patterns of muted light. Ján ran his fingers across the soft folds on Sofya's belly, and he leaned in to kiss her tenderly. "Are you content?" he asked.

"As ever," she replied as she nuzzled into his shoulder. "We are indeed blessed."

The next morning, the family assembled for the walk to the opening ceremonies. The children giggled and frolicked, chased by

Dzikusku and other family dogs, while the adults walked in groups, chatting excitedly about the day's events. As they neared the festival grounds, they were greeted by women wearing traditional Yakut dresses and bestowing blessings on the gatherers. As if to challenge the ubiquitous dust, Sofya, like many of the other women, was dressed entirely in a white dress she had painstakingly sewn and embroidered by hand just for this event. Keeping with tradition, they were each given a handful of horse hair, which they dipped in oil and then fed to a nearby pyre as an offering.

The opening ceremonies featured armor-clad riders atop muscular Yakutian horses re-enacting the arrival of the first settlers to the region. They paid homage to the blessings of nature that had sustained them over the centuries. Ján and Sofya stood in the crowd tens of thousands strong and strained to see all the elaborate performances.

After the official opening was complete, they gathered in a large circle, linking hands for the Osokhay dance. Their circle was swiftly enclosed in other concentric loops as the crowd moved around a cluster of tall wooden sacred *sergehs* and chanted in Yakut, their ancestral language. Over the years, Ján had learned to appreciate the rituals, even though as warmly welcomed as he was, he couldn't shake off the sense that he was an interloper, weaseling his way into a tradition that was not intended for him to experience fully.

Sofya luxuriated in her community of sisters, cousins, and nieces. When they departed to visit the kiosks featuring delectable dishes and finely crafted artistic endeavors, Ján and Dzikusku wandered off to explore the festival events.

They found Alban huddled with a group of men on the fringes of a large circle drawn in the grass of an expansive field. Two men, stripped to their waists and wearing their most ferocious expressions, faced each other inside the circle, their fists balled and muscles tightly coiled. Spectators were massing on the sidelines, cheering on their relatives and teasing the opponents. The air crackled with a palpable desire for a bruising match.

"A good diversion for the men, eh?" Alban mused.

Ján pointed to the bigger of the two competitors. Like Alban, the man was of modest height but solidly built. "Isn't that your cousin, Mahad? The horse herder?"

"Aye. Never been beaten. Every year, he gets older, but he still wins. You should feel bad for that other fella. He's going down."

Ján crossed his arms and settled in to watch. The two men squared off, and the crowd urged them on, delighted that the match was finally under way. It was clear from the outset that the earnest opponent was destined for failure, but Mahad played along with him to heighten the tension and whip the crowd into a frenzy. After taunting the man and pretending to reel from his futile attempts to drag him down, Mahad tired of the charade and, with one swoop of his arm, he flipped the man over and pinned him to the ground.

The crowd cheered. Mahad released his victim and helped pull him back to his feet. He looked over at Alban and smiled, revealing a gap-toothed grin. The erstwhile rival limped out of the circle, shaking his head, and Mahad turned to the crowd again. "Are there any other takers? Who thinks they have the strength to best me?" he roared, and the men in the crowd hollered back as they pushed a skinny young man into the ring.

"Ayhal! Ayhal! Ayhal!" The crowd chanted the young man's name as he sought his bearings from being thrust so suddenly into the limelight. He stripped off his shirt to reveal a thin chest and scrawny arms.

This is going to be ugly, thought Ján.

Mahad approached the lad and shook his hand. He pretended to wince at his opponent's grip, and the crowd tittered with laughter. Gathering his wits, Ayhal ducked and charged at Mahad, seeking to knock him off balance, and the older man swayed in mock surprise. Despite Mahad's jesting, Ayhal was not easily deterred and offered up a tenacious commitment to the fight. After a couple more bold attempts, Ayhal pulled back his arm and landed a swift punch, connecting with Mahad's eye. The crack of bones was audible to the crowd, and they roared once again. The referee moved to castigate the young man for his illegal move, but Mahad was faster. He reached around and grasped the lad around his waist, tossing him to the ground like a rag doll. Game over.

"I do not believe the strong man will be bested today."

Alban and Ján turned toward the voice, surprised that they had company. Two men: one tall with close-cropped, blond hair and his shorter, stockier, red-headed companion. When had they approached? Ján recognized them as frequent visitors to Gerasim's store where he had observed them arriving and leaving at odd hours. He had never tried to interfere, remembering Alban's advice to turn a blind eye when it came to his neighbor. This encounter was another matter entirely, almost certainly not a coincidence. Dzikusku growled, and Ján wrapped a wary hand around his collar.

Alban offered the strangers his hand, eager to get the measure of the pair. "My cousin will most certainly remain undefeated if that is all the competition that he will face. Perhaps you might like to take a shot?"

The tall man ignored Alban's gesture and shook his head. "I think not."

Alban kept his hand extended but narrowed his eyes. "I'm Alban Tuluukov. My friend, Ján Balik. And who might you two be?"

The stockier of the two men laughed. "My associate, Diak, has no manners; forgive him. You are just the man I am looking for. My name is Burdy. We work for a man named Vasiley DuBoff, and we were told to seek you out. We have a proposition for you."

Alban crossed his arms over his chest. "Do you have family names or is it just Burdy and Diak?"

"Burdy and Diak will work for today."

Intrigued, Ján and Alban walked a distance with the two strangers and listened to their business proposal. Their boss, Vasiley DuBoff, was a scrappy native of Siberia who, though born poor in Omsk, was an enterprising man who found himself in the right place at the right time. With the collapse of the Soviet regime, DuBoff had leveraged his connections to obtain valuable oil and natural gas leases from the new Russian government.

"Mind you, Vasiley is not a highly principled man." Burdy laughed. "He just wants to be on the winning team. So here we are, ready to make something of this opportunity. We need an engineer with knowledge of the local terrain. Our mutual friend Mr. Popov led us to you."

The men handed over a packet of papers and shook hands with Alban and Ján. They promised to contact Alban within the week and then departed as quickly as they had arrived. Alban eagerly tore into the envelope to see what was inside, yet Ján watched their mysterious visitors walk away, unsettled at this unexpected encounter.

"Why the sour face? All this crazy turmoil in Moscow and now a chance to make some profit suddenly lands at our feet! A man can at least look!" Alban said as he pulled out a sheaf of documents.

Ján started to reply just as Mahad ambled over to join them. One of his eyes was swollen shut, but he waved off any concerns for his injury and clapped Alban on the back. "Who are they? I saw them lurking about during the matches."

Ján scrutinized Mahad's face with its fresh wounds and ancient scars. He had seen similar assaults on the Dead Road: broken bones, missing teeth, twisted noses. He assumed there must have been many violent punches over the years to cause all that damage.

Mahad noticed Ján's stare, and he chuckled as he leaned down to scratch Dzikusku's head. "Your ear and my face. We could entertain each other for hours." Ján reddened to be caught staring. Mahad guffawed and punched Ján on the shoulder. All in good fun apparently. He reached out a big paw and gave Ján a bone-crushing handshake.

Ján cradled his hand. "I can only hope the blood starts flowing in my fingers again," he teased, but there was no reaction from Alban. He was still staring at the papers, his thoughts far removed from the friendly banter.

"Alban?"

He snapped to, a big grin splayed across his face as he stuffed the packet under his arm. "Yes, yes! I am here. Let's go celebrate Mahad's victories, eh?"

That evening, Alban sat with Ján in the yurt, papers spread out between them. Ayta and Sofya had gone to stand in line under the late evening light to press themselves against the ritual pillar and pray for miracles and grace. Alban sipped his kumis, and Ján took measured swigs from a bottle of vodka. Ján found Alban's ebullient mood oddly unsettling, and he kept his counsel, trying to temper his resistance to Alban's excitement.

Alban had smoothed out a large map with Turul circled in red. He pointed to a spot just north of their village. "These papers indicate that DuBoff owns the rights to the oil and gas reserves here. Apparently Gerasim is cozy with him, and that's not exactly a recommendation, but who knows? According to this letter, DuBoff wants to hire me to work with the team from Moscow to design and build a network for moving the gas to market." Alban ran his hands through his short, dark hair, now graced with silver streaks at his temples. "Everything appears to be in order, and the gas will flow one way or another, with us or without us. If we sign on, the work can help our families, improve the whole town."

"Can you trust him?" Ján asked quietly, trying not to trample on Alban's optimism.

"He's a Siberian survivor, just like all of us in the village," Alban said. "I think we have no choice but to proceed with caution."

Ján focused on the small writing and powered through reading the entire document. The gist of the proposition didn't make sense to him. The idea that exploring for natural gas would result in such a rosy outcome for the village as the documents promised seemed far-fetched. He scanned the contracts, documents, and letters from government officials. They appeared to be in order, but Ján had scant experience with matters of business. He had plenty of experience with dubious people, and he was slow to trust. There was something about this deal that just seemed too easy, too fortuitous to be believed.

Alban was elated over this turn of events for his clan. He and Ayta were endlessly scheming ways to keep their family in Turul, especially now that their son Feodor was mulling a move to Yakutsk in search of more opportunities for his growing family. Alban looked at this proposal and saw jobs for the young people who were rapidly shedding the traditional way of life and customs. He talked about using the profits to build a medical clinic to serve the people and offer more services to make life bearable in the interminable winter months.

As Alban talked, Ján listened while pondering his own misgivings. He wondered about the line between seeking progress and selling your soul. Finally, he had to admit that he was unconvinced. "What about the damage to the land, to the way of life that you seek to protect? Isn't that what this festival is all about? Reverence for the Earth?"

"Reverence is all fine if your family is safe and well-fed," snapped Alban, and Ján reverted to silence.

Ján had promised to meet Sofya to greet the rising sun at the big copper *sergeh* atop the hill, and he dutifully made his way there, nursing his disquiet over the day's events. He meandered by the barn where the horses were dreaming of victory in the coming day's races, then around the shuttered kiosks, and finally past the jaunty illustrated sign enticing visitors to the next round of mas-wrestling, a popular attraction. He walked with his head hung low while he mulled over the conversation with Alban. Something had shifted between them, and Ján replayed his role, wondering where he had gone wrong.

He found Sofya with Tuyaara and Ayta standing in a dense crowd around the massive ceremonial *sergeh*, eagerly watching the horizon. The sun had dipped for a brief spell after midnight, and the sky was vibrant with bold pink streaks shining across the muted blue washes that passed for darkness in the Siberian summer. Billowy clouds were tinged in the palette of the heavens, hinting at the proximity of the sun lurking just out of sight.

As the sky began to brighten, a murmur of excitement grew in the crowd, and Sofya reached for Ján's hand, drawing him into her reverence and anticipation. But where the crowd lifted their hands to embrace the heavenly display of warmth and energy and welcome the glowing sun as it peeked up from the horizon, Ján saw only storm clouds, massing at the edges of their lives.

Back in Turul, news of the gas contract ignited talk among the locals. Alban was quick to offer his services to DuBoff's company, and his sons soon joined him on the payroll. Each received handsome advances in return for their loyalty to the project. Ayta was eager to show off her new jewelry, courtesy of Alban's frequent trips to Yakutsk, and their prosperity served as a source of pride and jealousy in the small community.

Ján avoided the conversation and focused on his own projects. He was happy for his friends, but remained wary of the consequences that they would all face. He feared that he too was at a tipping point. He was untethered, bound by his love for Sofya but disconnected to the flow of community around him. Would this be the sum of his life? Destined to mourn in obscurity a life that was stolen from him along with his family and his identity? He had the disquieting notion that an important quest loomed, a necessary and difficult task, and he worried that in that purpose, he would once again fail those he loved.

He found solace in his books. The library at the school had long ago overrun the extension they had built to house the growing collection where it served not only to expand the students' knowledge, but also to whet the appetite for reading among the town's adults. Often the youngest readers found themselves crowded out of the space, especially in the bitterly cold winter months. Success, it turned out, created new challenges.

Ján endeavored to ease the burden on the children by creating a library dedicated to more mature interests in his and Sofya's sitting room. It was a short-lived and cumbersome solution. His collection of science books, nature studies, travel journals, novels, and highly biased biographies of famous Soviets expanded after each of Alban's journeys to Yakutsk, and the number of volumes now threatened to overwhelm their small home. Not one to complain, Sofya had begun making cautious comments about the number of visitors and the lack of space. Ján listened with a heavy heart, acutely aware that she was also excluded from all the excitement that Ayta, Tuyaara, and some of her friends experienced because of the newfound oil and gas prosperity.

One morning, Sofya came home from delivering a loaf of warm bread to Tuyaara and noticed Ján's breakfast sat cold and untouched on the table. His woolly cap, seldom separated from his scruffy head, hung from the back of his chair, so she knew he was likely close by. She cleaned the table, tucking his food in a basket, and set off on a short search. She found him standing in the middle of the barn with a partial sketch and a frown on his face. Dzikusku crouched at his feet, his tail thumping in anticipation of a treat as Sofya approached. She handed Ján a hot mug of tea and gave the dog a scrap of dried meat. "I'd love to hear what is troubling you," she said simply.

"There is too much disquiet in the village. I want to create something positive, something for everyone."

Ján had an idea for a project that he wanted to do for Sofya, but it would also be their contribution to the village. He explained his vision of a library emerging out of the dark, frigid barn. He suggested carving high into the solid walls to create windows to capture the most of the stingy winter daylight. He took a stick and scratched out a spot for comfortable chairs and a table. The stick became like a magic wand as he waved it in the air, pointing out where shelves would be built against the walls to separate the books into fiction and non-fiction. A third section would be solely devoted to children's books.

In his imaginings, whole families could come together. He hoped to lay a soft rug near the smaller bookcases so that children could explore stories that intrigued them, and he would add a sturdy brick oven with a tall chimney to the center of the space to keep it warm. The more he talked, the more animated he became, but he was honest about the challenges. "It will take time and money," he cautioned. "We cannot pay any workers. Besides, all the young men are besotted with the prospect of working for DuBoff and his men."

While he conjured ideas, Sofya scribbled notes, and when he fell silent, she pulled out a ruler and drew on the paper, making crisp lines and writing notations in the margins. Ján watched over her shoulder as his dreams emerged as a design on the page. She had laid out the dimensions of the space and sketched in doors and windows. Occasionally, she asked him a question. "How wide do the stairs need to be?" and "If the tread is this wide, how tall should each rise be?" His answers were precise, and she translated his directives into the sketch.

When the drawings were complete, she sat back with a satisfied smile. "This is going to be wonderful! And we get back our sitting area in the house when this is done."

"Yes, my dear. That is my plan. A room for you to do with as you please. I cannot buy you rings like Ayta's, but perhaps this will be more practical?"

Sofya threw her arms around his neck. "Thank you, my love! This means more than any ring!"

Ján stepped back to view her drawings, astonished at her drafting skills. The project was the first glimmer of hope that he had felt in weeks.

"You are very talented," he whispered as he wrapped his arms around her. "I had hoped to do this by myself as a surprise for you. I am sorry you had to rescue me just now. I was feeling...I don't know...muddled."

Sofya sank into his embrace. "You are a stubborn old mule, you know that? I'll help you any time." And she pulled his face to hers and gave him a long kiss. She was careful to keep her thoughts to herself, but his moodiness troubled her. She vowed to watch him just a bit closer.

Alexei Turgenev sat on the piano bench as Ján stood behind him, tapping out the rhythm as the boy played. Ján could hear Sofya talking behind him but paid no mind to their visitor. His focus was entirely on Alexei until he had finished up his lesson and packed away his practice books. As Ján turned to escort him to the door, he was surprised to find Mahad standing amongst the books in the sitting room, scrunching his hat in his hands. He saw very little of the warrior in the man that had been so striking at the festival only a few months before.

Ján greeted Mahad with a hearty handshake, and Alexei, eyeing his freedom, dashed between them and out the door.

"What a surprise! I don't believe I have ever seen you in town. What brings you here?" Ján asked.

Mahad shook his head. "Can we talk? I need your help."

The men walked to the barn to find a quiet space. Snowflakes swirled in the air as cold settled into every nook and cranny. The short path from house to barn was covered in a layer of ice. Ján pulled open the big door, and they entered the cavernous space, cleared for a library that remained closer to a dream than a reality.

The two men exchanged pleasantries for a minute or two, but Ján sensed Mahad's discomfort and urged him to get to the heart of the matter.

"I wonder if I can get your help," Mahad began. "I don't know who to turn to, and I am worried."

Ján assured Mahad that he could speak openly. "Alban holds you in the highest regard," he said. "Please tell me what I can do to help you."

Mahad paused for a moment and gathered his thoughts. "You see, that's part of the problem. Alban, I mean. It's this gas business that has gotten everyone in a frenzy."

Mahad explained that his family had been dispossessed of their horse husbandry trade under the Soviet regime's push to collectivize. With the fall of that government and an uncertain future ahead, they were only just putting the pieces back together. He and his son had spent the short summer restoring the old cabin at the edge of the taiga forest and were building a strong herd to produce more milk, meat, and horsehide for the local market.

"We don't stable the horses, as you know," Mahad explained. "They are well adapted to living outdoors year-round, and they need their communal spaces to roam. It's in our blood to tend to the animals that are such an important part of this rugged community. Our family has done this for generations, and now is the critical time for animals to build up their fat reserves to survive the winter. Yesterday, our men ran into trucks and equipment in our grazing pastures. They blocked access to our herds. Said we were trespassing on their land, and they are threatening to shoot any animals that are in the way of their work." He described for Ján the bitter argument and the fight that ensued.

"Was anyone hurt?" inquired Ján.

"A few scrapes and bruises, but this was just the opening shot. The foreman came to me with a bunch of papers claiming they can prove that the pipeline has the rights to the property. He told me to move the herd. But where? We don't own the land, never have. The understanding has always been that the land belongs to all, and we have treated it with reverence. If they block our routes, our herds will die. No one has consulted with us, and we are dependent on using these paths for the health of the horses. The noise and the disruption have already spooked the animals, and they refuse to budge."

"Have you talked to Alban?" Ján asked.

"I just came from there. We argued. He insists that the project and the herds can coexist, but frankly, he is naïve!" Mahad was breathing heavily. The man who had bested all opponents in the festival games now stood before Ján looking scared and defeated. "I have never argued with Alban before. Frankly, I wonder if I still know him. It was like I was talking to a different person than the cousin with the big heart and constant smile that I remember." Mahad had finally met his match, and it turned out to be Alban.

Ján put his hands on Mahad's sagging shoulders. "What can I possibly do to help?"

"Talk to him. He trusts you."

The next day, Ján rose early. He scratched the fur between Dzikusku's ears and admonished him to stay close to home. He then kissed Sofya goodbye and walked to Alban's house. He found his friend huddled with colleagues around a large map. Red lines extended around Turul and into the countryside.

Alban motioned Ján over. "You should see this. The scope of it all! It's all very exciting!"

Ján greeted all the workers, each one a neighbor and a friend. He looked at the map and tried to discern what all the lines and markings signified. He twisted his head this way and that before he was able to glean the gist of the drawings. They signaled a vast network of roads and pipelines snaking throughout the tundra and the taiga, all for the purpose of moving the natural gas from under the ground to lucrative markets around the world.

Alban showed Ján the reference points, and true to Mahad's word, a significant juncture of roads and pipelines converged at a crucial place where the horses had traditionally pastured.

"When will construction begin?" asked Ján, stalling for time before he had to speak to Alban, a task he dreaded.

"That's the beauty of it! We've already started," Alban replied, gesturing to a cluster of red lines. "Equipment has been moved here, and we will be bringing in more supplies within the month."

The old man had described the situation with aching precision. Ján's heart sank. He was already too late, but he had promised Mahad, and he needed to try to mend fences between Alban and his cousin. He asked Alban to step outside.

"My brother," he began, seeking a conciliatory tone, "all of that planning, it is impressive. It's also vast. What will the effect be for people who make their living off the land?"

Alban folded his arms across his chest. "Who is asking?" he demanded.

"Well, I for one," Ján replied.

"Yes, but you have had little to say thus far, so there is someone else behind your questions. Let me guess, Mahad came to speak to you."

"Yes, he did, and I felt for him, Alban, I know you are excited about this work and the possibilities for this village, but are you not worried that all this development, these roads and pipelines, will destroy a part of what is so beautiful about this place?"

Alban had demonstrated little capacity for anger in all the years that Ján had known him, and his optimism and ebullience in the face of adversity were the qualities that Ján so admired in his friend. Today, another Alban faced him. Defensive and combative, he took offense at Ján's question.

"What do you know about the beauty of this place? You are here because we welcomed you and gave you a home when no one else would. Why do you wish to destroy that bond by undermining one of the most profitable businesses to come here, probably ever?" Alban leaned into Ján's face. "Surely you have figured out by now that our resilience is in adapting. People here live on the edge. There is no hospital, no cinema, no store other than the dump that Gerasim runs. This is a chance for us to provide for the health and wellbeing of everyone!"

Ján put his hand on Alban's arm and felt the rage pulsing through his friend's muscles. He knew his questions put him on shaky ground, but the image of Mahad, broken and afraid, blunted his caution. "Everyone, Alban? I thought this intrusion is what you once fought against. For God's sake, it sent you to the Dead Road! What about Mahad? Did anyone ask him and the members of his family what they needed out of this? If they cannot get their herds across, they will lose animals. They are worried about making it through the winter."

"Well, that's rich, Ján! You of all people. Someone we all took in and helped when you had nothing. Nothing! And now you wish to accuse us of crass profiteering off the backs of our families. I thought you knew me better than that!' Alban stepped toward him with his fists balled and his face twisted in anger.

Ján held up both hands, palms out. "You are right. I was nothing when I came here. Likely I am nothing still. Thank you for what you have done for me, truly I mean that. Nothing I say is meant to belittle your generosity. I just find all this unsettling."

"You know what's unsettling, Ján? Watching your sons take their wives and children and move away because they cannot make a living in this little village. It's unsettling to see people suffer with bad teeth, poor health, and substandard houses. Why, if we had a proper doctor here, your children might just be here to support you and Sofya instead of lying in that cemetery!"

Ján could not have been more shocked had Alban punched him square in the face. The trauma that had lain dormant in him like a sleeping snake now uncoiled, fangs exposed. He seethed. "Alban, I never thought you capable of such cruelty."

The two men faced off like two provoked bulls, huffing and

puffing in vapored breaths. Alban stared at Ján, daring him to speak further, but Ján backed away and began the long walk toward home. Alban watched him go with no words of brotherhood or reconciliation shared between them.

When Ján returned to his house, he walked right past Sofya and Dzikusku, grabbed a bottle of vodka from the cabinet, and exited through the back door without speaking. She called after him, but he went into the barn and shut the door.

Ján sat in the dark in his shirt sleeves, welcoming the punishing cold. His head was tilted back against the rough wood siding as he watched the dust motes float in the scant morning light that leaked through the sole window. The rift with Alban threatened to overwhelm him. This was supposed to be his grand library, his gift to the village, but all he could imagine right now was grief. His heart was shattered as though all the losses he had suffered reignited the pain within him accompanied by toxic recrimination. Blame. He was responsible for all this. Loss and self-loathing swirled around him like a poisonous fog, and he couldn't envision where the promise of him ended and the wall of sorrow began.

He closed his eyes and suddenly he was back at the No. 15 Special Home for Children, lying on the filthy mattress and listening to the rattling breaths of the boys suffering in the room with him, all of them cold and hungry. He heard Mrs. Kotova's voice, the disdain soaking through all her words.

Ján picked up the bottle and drank deeply. If he could numb himself enough, maybe the ghosts would go away. Instead, he found himself remembering the train. He was reaching out to Otto over the cold body of his mother, promising him that they would stay together. He was reaching out to Maks, promising him that he would send help. He was holding little Lara in his arms, urging the tiny infant into life and then watching her slip away. He was pleading with Ada to fight back and stay alive. He looked at his hands with contempt. What good was he to Sofya? To himself? The pain was just too much. He drained the bottle, and as the room began to slide, an idea coalesced in the corners of his tortured soul. They would be better without him. Not only Sofya, but all of them, those living and those not.

He walked out of the barn and observed Sofya through the kitchen window. He thought about how lovely she was and how that was somehow a further indictment against him. Her beauty served only to remind him that he was undeserving. He took a right turn and walked away from the house. He staggered along the lane, past the school, in front of Gerasim's store, through the village and past the cemetery, planting one foot in front of the other until he found himself at the banks of the river, teetering at the precipice of a steep cliff. He stared down the rocky façade that plunged in a straight line toward the frothing, ice-rimmed water. He heard the plaintive howl of a wolf and the rhythmic cracking of the ice, newly born in the arctic fall. He imagined himself sailing off the cliff and hitting the water, hard and punishing, then sinking downward through the icy river. The pain would be deserved. His last sensations would be that of punishment. He was scared, but he was convinced that the retribution was earned and necessary.

He inched forward, uncertain of just how close to the edge he was. The wind whipped around his ear, and he heard echoes from the water lapping against ice down below. He shuffled his right foot forward, and a small shower of rocks fell away. He counted the time it took for them to hit the icy patches. One second, two seconds, three seconds, crack. He hovered with his toes in the air and his heels on the ground.

"I always knew you were a coward," said a voice behind him. Tuyaara stood on the lane, holding a shovel and pail. Dzikusku hovered in her shadow. He cocked his head and offered a low growl.

Ján hesitated, but continued to face straight ahead. He had no desire to talk with her and lacked the courage to face his loyal companion.

"I saw you leave and followed you, carrying this ridiculous

bucket all the way and fending off your scruffy friend. Why? I don't know except I know my sister loves you for some odd reason, and I don't want her to suffer any more than she already has."

"Go away, Tuyaara," Ján said firmly. "There are things you don't know."

"Oh, I'm sure of that, and honestly, I don't care. I'm not here for you. I'm here for her, so back away and come home." She set down the bucket and walked slowly toward him. Dzikusku crept forward, matching her steps. Ján remained on the edge, barely anchored to the cliff. He heard them approach and steeled himself against her touch, but she and the dog kept their distance, standing just off to the side. He could see them waiting in the edges of his vision.

"All of us wonder why you came to Turul. What brought you here and what kept you here. You are a mystery to us, but many admire your kindness and your talents. Personally, I find your music annoying, but when Sofya married you, I saw her as a happy person for the first time in her life. Now, you have vexed her to no end since then, but she still loves you. Does that mean nothing to you?"

"I don't mean to hurt her. I love her," Ján stated, wanting only for Tuyaara to go away.

"You put yourself on a mighty high pedestal if you think that by throwing yourself off this cliff, you'll somehow free Sofya up to pursue a better life. You'll just turn the pain into something new, and forever on, you'll be remembered as the man who was selfish enough to shift the burden to others."

"That's not fair," Ján insisted. "There is so much you don't know."

"True, but I don't need to know what you've been through. We've all been through hell and back. I'm just amazed that you think you are special in that regard. Step back and talk to me. Then I'll leave, and you can do as you wish."

Ján turned his head in Tuyaara's direction and moved back two steps.

"Hear me out, Ján Balik. I don't want to know anything about you. I want you to know about Sofya because she needs you, and she cares for you. The fact that you cannot see how blessed you are is astonishing to me.

"I'm sure she told you that our father sold her to Michil. Like a bag of flour or a poker chit, he put his daughter's life out on a card table for the taking. The worst thing is that I was jealous. He didn't think I was pretty enough to settle a bet.

"And that's not all. Before he auctioned her off, he abused her over and over. He was a horrible man, and I was jealous. Yes, jealous. I am that awful person who can't see anyone else's pain because of my own selfishness. All I saw was her beauty and her usefulness to our father. Now we can dwell on that, or we can take stock of where we are now. Sofya sees something in you. Maybe she sees a man who will treat her well." Tuyaara laughed darkly. "She doesn't deserve to come down to this freezing river and wait while they haul your ugly, bloated carcass out of the water. She doesn't deserve to have to make funeral plans for a man who didn't care enough to say goodbye."

Ján turned to face her, and he pictured Sofya standing by the river with tears in her eyes. He couldn't follow through, but he didn't want to go back. He was frozen in his suffering and indecision. His chest pounded and for the first time in decades, he heard his mother's voice. *You are better than this, Ján. Go home.* The deep core of pain fractured within him, and he crumpled to the ground, sobbing uncontrollably. Dzikusku curled at his side as Tuyaara knelt down and drew him into her arms, rocking him back and forth.

Sofya watched as Ján walked up the lane with Tuyaara, followed by the dog.

When Ján reached the gate, he paused briefly to place his hand on the sergeh, standing as a silent sentry in front of his home.

Home, thought Ján. *This is my home.* He had lived here longer than any place in his life. He belonged here. Without looking up, he said, "Thank you."

Tuyaara shook her head. "Don't thank me. Just don't disappoint. You are capable of good, as much as it pains me to say it." She left Ján alone and went inside her house. He looked toward the light coming from the window of his little cottage, and he could see Sofya's outline framed by the warm glow of the oven inside. He lifted his hand to wave, ruffled the thick fur on Dzikusku's head, and walked up the path to greet his wife.

Chapter 13

Alban's Song

Turul, Yakutia, Russia
October 1992

Sofya held Ján close while he told her everything, stories of grief and loss couched in terms of his guilt over what he had failed to do to save those close to him. He opened his raw and bruised heart, exposing layers of denial and trauma, yet her patience and lack of judgment blunted his fear of rejection. Through the trauma of confronting his past lay the seeds of healing, and he was mindful of his great fortune to have her as his wife.

Sofya left his side only long enough to slip into the kitchen. She brought back two cups of steaming broth, and Ján accepted the nourishment gratefully. "I do not deserve your forgiveness, but I hope that one day, you can extend me some grace for the way I have taken you for granted."

Sofya cupped his head in her hands and drew his face close to hers so that he could see her kind, black eyes and soft mouth. "I forgave you for everything when I married you, and nothing has changed. You are a good husband, Ján. It hasn't always been easy, but you are my love, and I will not abandon you. You must promise not to abandon me, ever again."

Ján nodded, and the tears ran unchecked down his bearded cheeks. He embraced Sofya and allowed himself to fall under the spell of her soft curves and warm hugs. They had been up most of the night, and although the sun wouldn't rise for hours, the day would be starting soon. Sofya prepared a plate of fish and a few pickled vegetables, and while they ate, she scribbled a note on a piece of paper, and tied it to the front door. *The library is closed for today and Mr. Balik will not be available for lessons. Please come back tomorrow. Thank you.* She looked at Ján. His tears were dry, and he returned her attention with a kind smile on his weathered face.

"You will do something for me today," she said.

"Anything," he promised.

"You will take that book, the one that captured the bullet meant for you, and you will play for me. Every one of the melodies. And as your songs reveal themselves, you will tell me again what that person did to deserve being honored by you."

He played while she sat beside him on the scuffed piano bench. She met Ján anew, a prodigy who could turn a broken down piano into a masterful feast of notes. He immersed them both in a foreign world, transporting her to the elegant suburbs of Warsaw, the storied stage of Königsberg, where he experienced fame then fear of the invading army, and to the desolation and danger of the Dead Road. She watched him with reverence, awe, and deep sadness for all that had been wrenched from him, and while it was just the two of them in the room, they were joined by Ján's mother, his father and sisters, his aunt, Herr Kippels, Maks, Vera, and a cast of people from Ján's past, all of them necessary to understand the patchwork quilt of his grief. He saved two for last, their children, Lara and Artur.

"I didn't get to know them, so I have to imagine them, what they might have been like had they lived. Lara became a younger version of her mother, beautiful, clever, and a bit stubborn." This elicited a wistful smile. "And Artur became the better version of me. A musician with strength and resolve. In my mind he became a concert pianist and traveled the world."

"That is not a better version of you. That is the version you would have been had a war not intervened. But I can't mourn that, because if none of this had happened to you, I would never have known you. So, who's to say?" She kissed his forehead. "You are still writing your story. Who's to say what your future holds?"

Ján grasped her hands, kissed her fingers, and then pulled away from her embrace. "I am reconciled to the future, counting my blessings that I get to spend it with you. Only–" he hesitated. "I must come to terms with this." He turned to the next page. It was blank except for a title. "Alban," it read simply. "I need to express my grief over the end of our friendship, but for the first time, the melody will not come to me."

"I think it's because the story is unfinished and the situation remains unresolved. You must try again, Ján. You cannot write a song to mourn the end of a friendship that can be repaired. You cannot write it because you know what you must do."

Sofya returned home from a walk to the cemetery to find Ayta sitting on her front stoop. She had a basket by her side and was shooing Tuyaara's curious kitten away. Snowflakes danced in the air between them and settled like a crown on Ayta's fur hat. "I've been waiting for you," Ayta said. The new snow had already filled her footsteps; she had been sitting there for some time.

Sofya hugged her coat tighter and watched her friend. She couldn't read her expression. Things remained brittle between the two families, their frosty relationship mirroring the winter around them. "Hello." It was all she could muster in reply.

Ayta's heart found a measure of hope at seeing Sofya, yet she had avoided this meeting. She feared confirmation of the end of their friendship, a worry that held her back from speaking of her affection for Sofya. She had never been this parsimonious with love, and it felt cruel. "Oh, Sofya! Are you horribly mad at me? Do you hate me?" she blurted out.

"What? Of course not! Are you angry with me?" Sofya responded.

"Angry? No! I miss you!" Ayta said as she lurched forward and drew Sofya into a bear hug. "The men…I just don't know what has caused this rift. That's not true, I know all too well, but it shouldn't pit us against each other, should it?"

Sofya burst into tears. "I don't know how to fix what has happened. Ján and Alban need to talk this out, but I think Ján is so afraid that the friendship will end. He exists in a state of doing nothing."

"Alban isn't much better. He's just so aggrieved that Ján doesn't see things his way, and in truth, I think he feels judged by Ján. Perhaps Ján is voicing the doubts that Alban has buried in himself?"

The women locked arms, and Sofya drew her friend inside the house for warmth and a long overdue chat. They shed their coats and sat at the kitchen table while Sofya brewed a pot of tea and pulled her chair close to her friend.

"This rift threatens to undermine the whole village. Ján finally shared with me what happened to him in the past, and Ayta, it's just awful. I cannot say more because it is his story, but he needs to patch things up with Alban. He's the closest thing to a brother that Ján has."

Ayta shrugged. "I don't know what to do. Ján and Alban saved each other's lives in that dreadful camp. They became family, and now they can hardly look at one another. All over money or land or something that probably doesn't matter anyway."

Sofya shook her head. "We must force them to do the right thing, but how?" A fresh round of tears ensued for both women.

Ayta pulled out her basket, forcing a change in the conversation and an end to the tears. "Here, maybe this will cheer you up. When Alban went to Yakutsk last week, I gave him strict instructions to bring this back. From me to you." She pulled out a parcel wrapped in newsprint and began peeling away the layers. Sofya took each piece of crumpled packing and smoothed it out as Ayta unwound the cocooned surprise. The face of a porcelain doll emerged as Ayta pulled back the final layer of newspaper.

Sofya gasped. It was beautiful. The head was a creamy alabaster with rosy cheeks and jet-black painted hair covered by a miniature fur-trimmed scarf. She was wearing a buttery leather ceremonial dress embellished with traditional Sakha embroidery. Sofya gingerly ran her fingers over the delicate beads that were arranged in symbols of nature and spirituality. "Oh, Ayta! She's...she's...I just don't have the words. I have never owned anything so lovely." Suddenly embarrassed, she blushed. "Is it really for me?"

"Well of course it's for you! I saw it in the shop window last summer, and it's been on my mind ever since. You know, I think she looks like you. She has your serene eyes and flawless skin. I want you to have it."

Sofya held the doll reverently, afraid to move with such a fragile treasure. Ayta allowed herself to breathe. This was good. They were together again, unguarded in their conversation, and the gift had been well received.

Sofya positioned the doll high on a shelf where it could be viewed safely while she prepared meals. From her perch, the doll peered down across the sparse little kitchen with her regal black eyes and elegant clothing. Sofya backed up a bit to view her new treasure and bumped into the table, spilling tea and sending the pile of newspapers cascading to the floor.

"Oh, I'm so clumsy!" she exclaimed as she bent down to sort the mess, apologizing profusely. Ayta helped mop up the spill and stack the papers. Sofya ran her hand over the freshly rearranged pile to flatten it, and then she froze, her fingers poised over a headline. She stared intently and brought the paper closer to her face.

Ayta was concerned. "What is it? Are you alright?"

"I'm just...I don't know." She put the crumpled sheet in front of Ayta and pointed to an article at the bottom of the page. "This is a sign. I just know it. What do you think? Is this meant for Ján?"

Ayta pushed her glasses up on the bridge of her nose and read aloud, "Tchaikovsky, Rimsky-Korsakov, Rachmaninoff, Shostakovich, Prokofiev all honored Mother Russia with their musical genius. Who is the next great Russian musician?"

Sofya said, "It's a contest! What if I entered Ján? He has dozens of original compositions in this magnificent old book of his. What if he won? He might have been a concert pianist if the war hadn't happened. Maybe this is a way to reclaim that! It might be the lift he needs!"

Ayta was wary of the idea. "You would have to tell him that you sent one of his songs in, wouldn't you? I mean, they are his songs, right? He has never shared them. What makes you think he wishes to have them published for all to hear at the Moscow Festival?"

Sofya was undeterred. She wouldn't tell him, not yet anyway. Better he doesn't know so he isn't disappointed if he doesn't win, she rationalized. "He's out in the barn all day, and he has that book with him, but if I can get a hold of it at night or something, I can make a copy of one of the pieces and send it in."

Ayta had to admit that Sofya might be onto something. What's the worst that could happen? The two women hatched a plan. Sofya just needed to get her hands on that book. She carefully folded the paper and hid it under the skirt of her new doll, a guard acting in silent complicity.

Sofya tried without success numerous times to sneak Ján's book away, so when the opportunity arrived like a whisper, she almost missed it. It came as a tentative knock at the door, a slight rap rap rap that the wind threatened to carry away. Sofya heard the gentle tapping, but she thought it might be Tuyaara's cat again. That overfed mouser was making itself quite at home these days. Sofya peeked out the window prepared to shoo it away only to find little Alexei Turgenev shivering on the stoop, bundled up for the walk from the village for his lesson.

"Goodness, lad, you blew in on the wind!" Sofya pulled him inside and gave him a glass of warm milk while she went to get Ján. She found him in the barn, sitting with Dzikusku amongst a collection of tools but attending to none of them. His back was propped against the oven, newly installed and as yet unlit. He gripped the paper drawings Sofya had made for their library plans. Lumber was stacked nearby, and a few pieces lay to his side, ready to be cut.

"I am making progress cutting the boards for the stairs, but it will go much faster if I have help. At this rate, it will be a year before we have a library here."

"Oh, Ján!" She sighed. "We will figure this out. This town owes you some help, and we're going to see to it that this library gets built. In the meantime, Alexei is here and he has walked through the snow for his lesson. He deserves his time with you." She shivered and pulled her wrap tighter against the cold and her uncertainty.

Ján smiled gratefully. "Duty calls. I can always count on my little friend Alexei." He pulled himself up, brushing away the dirt from his trousers, and looked at Sofya through watery eyes.

"Go!" she ordered, and she took the plans out of his hands and gently nudged him toward the door. Ján and Dzikusku shuffled out into the wind and across the lot to the house. She heard the back door rattle on rusty hinges followed by the sound of Alexei playing his scales. She turned to head back into the house when she saw it out of the corner of her eye, lying on the dirt next to where Ján had been sitting. His leather book. She gingerly picked it up and tucked it under her wrap.

Back in the kitchen, she peeked into the music room. Ján sat next to Alexei counting out the rhythm as the boy played. The child was making remarkable progress, and Ján was beginning to think he had the determination and talent to call himself a musician.

Sofya took the book to the kitchen and set out a sheet of blank paper and a straight edge. Meticulously, she drew in the bars, the treble clef and the bass clef and thus created a template for the composition. Then she pulled out the book. Sofya couldn't read music and as she looked at the cryptic markings on the pages, she hesitated. How would she know which of these melodies was his best? She remembered listening to him play each, and they all evoked such strong emotions. What if she positioned a note incorrectly and ruined his chance for recognition? She looked up at the doll who stared into the kitchen with an expression of benevolent authority, and Sofya drew from it a slight rebuke for her indecision. She would be careful and transcribe the notes as they were written. Fate would govern the rest.

She fanned the pages and set it on the table. It fell open, and Sofya saw "Barabanicha on the Dead Road." She remembered this piece from when Ján had played it before, and the sorrowful melody had brought her to tears. She carefully copied the notes and added Ján's notations, including all the mysterious symbols. She didn't understand the significance of the markings, so she labored to get the drawings just right. Spying Dzikusku's watchful eyes, she put her finger to her lips and slipped out of the house to return the book to the barn where Ján had left it.

This will be it, she thought. *This will be the start of something new.* She read over the competition rules one more time and was dismayed to see that instructions for submission had been torn away. How should she proceed? She looked again at her copy of Ján's elegy to the prison, and she was satisfied that she had copied the score with precision. One thing was for sure, if she didn't send it in, there would be no accolades for Ján. She decided to take a chance and send it to the reporter, care of the newspaper, and hoped that either her note arrived in Moscow in time or they would give her some grace. Sofya penned a letter of explanation and then bundled it all up. As soon as she could slip out of the house, she took her letter to Gerasim's store, bought postage using her meager pin money, and kissed the envelope twice before dropping it in the post bin.

Sofya went to Ayta's house before returning home. She knocked tentatively on the door, hoping to avoid seeing Alban. To her relief, Ayta appeared and ushered her inside.

"Alban is out at the pipeline site," Ayta assured her. "He won't be home for hours."

"I feel like I am sneaking around behind Ján's back," Sofya confessed. "We have to do something to heal this rift between the men."

They huddled in Ayta's kitchen, plotting a way to bring the two men together, but they couldn't settle on a reasonable plan.

"They are both so stubborn!" Ayta lamented. "Alban won't even speak of it, yet I know he is troubled by the last time they argued. He regrets what he said, but he won't admit it."

"Ján is reluctant to make the first move. I think he would rather exist in a world where they *might* reconcile than reach out and have everything go wrong," Sofya said.

"Stubborn mules," Ayta said with a smile. "So how goes it with the library? I need to come by. We can't make it through winter without Ján's books."

"The books are still inside our house, and with the return of cold weather, there is always someone there. I can't wait to get the new library built in the barn—" Sofya squealed, startling Ayta. "That's it! The library! We'll invite the community to come and build the library. Alban will have to come, won't he?"

"It will put pressure on him and the other men to show up. I'll do my bit to get them there if you promise not to scare me like that again."

Sofya returned to the store and asked the young clerk to post a notice on the community board.

Turul needs a bigger library!
Bring your tools and help build a new gathering place in the Balik's barn
Saturday, 31 October in the morning
If you have questions, ask Sofya

Ayta waited until Alban had settled in his comfortable chair after returning from the pipeline. She brought him food and a mug of warm tea, and she sat next to him. Gently, she explained that she would be going to Sofya's house to help build the library. "I think you should come with me," she said.

Alban set his food aside and breathed deeply before responding. "I think you should leave well enough alone," he said quietly.

"You're still hurting, and I understand, but Ján was your family for so long."

"He should have thought of that when he accused me of turning my back on this community."

Ayta stood and put her hand on Alban's shoulder. "Well, you know where I will be on Saturday next. I hope you will come too, but I won't mention it again."

Ayta and Sofya cooked plates and platters of food and created a meticulous plan for the library work day. When the day dawned, Ayta arrived at the house early with more baked goods and Alban's tools. Ján was eating breakfast in the kitchen. He stood when Ayta walked in and offered her a chair and a cup of coffee. He asked after Alban as though there had been no unpleasantness between them.

Sofya told Ján about their plans. When he protested, she was firm. "We are not asking you. We are telling you that we have friends coming to build your library. You will either be a help or a hindrance, but it's going to happen."

Ján relented and, knowing he was outmaneuvered, gave Sofya a hug, and thanked Ayta. "Well let's see what happens."

The three went to the barn where Ján lit the oven, and they arranged the lumber and supplies for a crowd. As Ján cut the boards to precise measurements, Sofya and Ayta blocked out the pieces for the staircase and the loft, peeking out the door for additional workers each chance they got. Each time they peered down the lane, there was no one there.

They tried to press on, but they needed to hoist the beams to position the loft in place. The work demanded more than the two women and Ján could manage. They sat on the floor and passed a thermos of coffee around, defeated. Ayta prepared to leave. "I would stay, but I don't think I can be much help. We need young folks and men to do this work," she said with a hint of anger.

As if on cue, the barn door slid open, and Tuyaara entered. She looked at the dejected group and said, "This is a sad, sad picture. What are you doing sitting around?"

Sofya responded glumly, "No one came. We asked but no one came. We cannot do the work."

"Says who?" asked Tuyaara as she pulled the barn door wider. Behind her stood at least a dozen women. "The men are either at the pipeline construction site or wary of getting caught in the middle, but the women want their books. We're here to help, so put us to work!"

As Tuyaara barked instructions, the women wasted no time transforming the gloomy and cavernous space into a semblance of a library. Ján explained the tasks, and Sofya organized the ladies into work crews. Soon, the barn was humming with activity. The beams were lifted and secured in place, the staircase rose to meet the loft, and the space overhead grew board by board. One crew constructed the bookcases to Ján's specific measurements. With the extra help, they were even able to break out part of the side wall and install a window to let the autumn light seep in while the little oven endeavored to battle the rush of cold air. By late afternoon, they had carried some of the bookshelves up the stairs and arranged the rest on the ground floor, forming the sections that Ján had envisioned.

They were ready to start bringing out the books, but several of the women begged to go home to prepare dinner ahead of their husbands' return from work. They promised to regroup the following day to move the books to their new home. It would be a drafty, rough-hewn space, but they could embellish it over time. For now, it was the biggest library the town had ever seen. Ján and Sofya bid the women goodbye with hugs and appreciation for achieving the first steps of a dream space.

Ján and Sofya watched Ayta walk down the lane toward her home and, long after she disappeared around the curve, they remained outside. The sky was uncharacteristically clear, and the bright stars glittered against the black velvet of the sky. Ján wrapped a blanket close around them, and Sofya leaned into his chest. His heart beat steadily, and as tired as they both were, they rejoiced in the achievements of the day.

As they looked heavenward, the undulating green waves of the Northern Lights appeared. They watched the spectacle with wonder as it rippled across the vast expanse of the Siberian plain. "Oh, Ján, as many times as I've watched it, it still takes my breath away!"

"Yes, my dear, it's a good sign indeed." He felt her shiver, so he coaxed her inside, and they stoked up the fire in the brick oven and sat nearby to eat a small supper and absorb the warmth.

Ján watched Sofya as the firelight danced about her face. The years only made her more beautiful in his eyes. Her long, black hair had traces of gray that wound through her braid like a river of silver. The crinkles in the corners of her eyes and mouth imbued her face with a soft kindness and wisdom. He reached out and touched a flyaway lock that had worked itself loose, and he gently tucked it behind her ear. She lifted her hand and placed it over his, bringing his fingers down to her cheek.

"Sofya," he said gently, and she shushed him by leaning in and drawing him into a long kiss. The unspoken tension of life lived in a community plagued by conflict eased in their shared sense of accomplishment and the camaraderie of the day. They huddled together and talked of small things. Sofya thought about the music competition and decided that now was the time to tell Ján what she had done. "Dearest," she began.

"Yes?" Ján responded sleepily.

"I have something that I want to tell you, something exciting." Sofya twisted herself out of Ján's arms. It was easier to tell him by facing him straight on, but when she glanced over his shoulder, she noticed a flicker of brightness in the room. Curiously, it was coming from the back of the house. She followed the flashes of light to the kitchen, and peering out the window, she spied the flames leaping out of the newly installed window in the barn. Inside, all was glowing with fierce heat.

"Ján!" she screamed, "the library is on fire!"

He was immediately on his feet, scrambling for his coat and shoes, and together they dashed out the back door. Tuyaara and Dabyn were already outside along with several of their children and grandchildren. Ján tried to run into the barn, but Dabyn caught him and pulled him back. "Nothing you can do, brother. Don't harm yourself on a fool's errand. All we can do now is make sure the embers don't fall on our houses."

"We can't just sit here and watch. We need water!" Ján shouted, and they gathered buckets and raced in and out of their homes to collect the water supplies that weren't frozen.

The family huddled together in the yard, shivering with cold and fear as the structure disintegrated before their eyes. Sofya buried her face in Ján's coat and cried.

When there was enough light in the sky on the following day, Ján went outside to survey the damage. Dabyn walked over and put his hand on Ján's back. "It's a total loss," he said, "I'm sorry. I know it meant a lot to you."

Ján was numb. He couldn't think of anything to say, so he stood his ground and tried to make out details through the fog of smoke and charred wood that coalesced in his field of vision. Dabyn urged him to return inside and left him alone to contemplate the weight of what had occurred.

Sofya busied herself cleaning. The stench of the fire seemed to pervade everything in the house, and it was much too cold to open windows to release the acrid odor. Ján returned to his piano and sat with his leather book in his lap, furiously scribbling notes and pounding out chords. At one point, he walked into the kitchen and spied Sofya angrily scrubbing the worn wooden table in the center of the space.

"Sofya dear, don't push yourself too hard," he said gently, and he teased the rag out of her rough, red hands. Remembering her last words before the fire, he asked, "You said you had something important to tell me. What is it?"

She sighed, defeated by the enormity of the disappointment that lay between them. "Oh, it was nothing, Ján, really nothing. I was caught up, that's all."

He drew her into a tight embrace and kissed the top of her head. "I like that you were caught up. We'll figure this out."

The next morning, Ján awoke early and tiptoed into the dark kitchen to stoke the fire in the stove. He saw that the stars were once again glittering brightly overhead. He set the kettle on the fire and took his hot tea to the table, the flickering melody of the flames playing out in his head. He had written it in his book, but it lingered as an endless loop in his mind, accusing and exhausting him.

In the quiet of his solitude, he thought he was hallucinating when he heard a horse whinny, but the rattles and creaks of the attendant wagon were clearly not from his imagination. The grating sound of an engine joined the cacophony. Alarmed, Ján grabbed the iron poker from beside the oven, pulled on his coat, and stepped out into the yard. In the predawn mist, the icy landscape reflected the jarring onslaught of brash headlights from a procession of vehicles. Vibrations in the frozen ground portended more wagon wheels and motorized transports.

Sofya joined him holding a broom and a flashlight. "A convoy making its way toward us on the road. Looks like there are at least four wagons and two trucks, maybe more." She grasped the broom in both hands, ready to repel any invaders.

The wagons and trucks proceeded past the astonished couple to stop at the barn. The door to the first truck opened, and Alban stepped down onto the hard, icebound yard. He approached his friends.

Ján's heart began to race. He folded his arms across his chest and steeled himself for a confrontation.

Alban walked straight up to Ján and pulled his scarf down from his face. "Ján. Sofya. I'm sorry about the fire," he began. He thrust his hand toward Ján as if for a handshake, but when Ján extended his hand in turn, Alban drew him into a fierce hug. Then he stepped back and carefully considered his words. "This was not an accident. The fire, I mean. I should have been here the other day, and I allowed my stubbornness and my pride to get in the way. So, while I didn't set the fire, I hold myself responsible. For all this." He extended his arm to point toward the silent pile of charred beams and melted glass. "For all this, I am so very sorry."

Ján was confused. "You mean someone did this deliberately? Burned down my barn for no reason?"

Alban cleared his throat. "We were out at the pipeline site. Many of the men complained that their wives were here, helping to build a new library. They got to joking." Alban paused.

"Go on," said Ján in a determined voice.

"There was a good bit of teasing about the women thinking they could do a man's job, and then the joking turned into more serious complaints about friction between the men and their wives over this argument in our community, whether the pipeline was a good deal for the town or not. Many of the men feel aggrieved, as do I, that anyone would question our motives for trying to bring prosperity to this forgotten corner of the world." Alban fell quiet again.

Sofya was puzzled. "Where is all of this going, Alban? How did the men's grievances turn into a violent attack on our home?"

"It's complicated, Sofya, but the men, well, many of them resent being cast as threats to our community, and they blame Ján here for stirring that up. They still see him as an outsider and don't think that he should have the ability to criticize the local folks. I admit that in my anger over our differences, I allowed that talk to flourish unchecked."

"Allowed?" asked Ján pointedly.

"Okay, I may have egged it on a bit. I was feeling powerful, and I let it go to my head. It angered me that you didn't approach me again. Try to patch things up. I felt like we all welcomed you to this community, and then you created this...this situation. Anyway, some of the lads went home and took to the bottle. By the time they were thoroughly drunk, a few of them decided to come out here and teach you a lesson. I heard them bragging, and well, it was a realization to me of how complicit I had become in creating this misunderstanding."

"Misunderstanding?" Ján shot back. "A misunderstanding is when people get their feelings hurt. My property is destroyed, and my family could have been killed. Thank God we ran out of time and didn't move the books over. At least my family is unharmed and the books are safe."

"All true, my friend. All true," conceded Alban. "Ján, you and I have a lot of talking to do. You are part of my family. I am truly sorry for the way I have treated you these past months, and I am desperate for you to understand what I want to do for this town. But now, we need to set things right. These lads here, they may have been a part of the grousing, but they didn't strike the match. They want to help. We are here to build you a new library."

Ján's relief at hearing Alban's truth threatened to overwhelm his fragile balance, and he reached out to his friend to steady himself. Tears welled in his eyes and a lump formed in his throat. He missed his friend, and he was grateful that he had an opportunity to mend fences and restore his library.

He pulled Alban into a wobbly embrace and murmured into his shoulder, "Well let's get started, shall we?"

Chapter 14

Song of Reckoning

Moscow, Russia
November 1992

The snow had begun to fall in earnest, blanketing Pushkin Square and filling the streets with black slush. Harper's stories on the festival had drawn an enthusiastic response, and, although she was loath to admit it, the entries were highly entertaining. She had tracked down a man who styled himself as a *skomorokhi*, a type of minstrel who played the balalaika; a woman who specialized in Roma ballads; and a man who claimed to be a reincarnation of a Russian Orthodox monk. It was colorful work, but it didn't satisfy Harper's ambitious streak, and she was relieved when the deadline for entries passed and the performers had been chosen.

Angelica threw a steady stream of new stories Harper's way, everything from the absurd to the compelling, and she accepted each assignment without complaint, working diligently to impress her boss and cement her reputation. She managed to meet deadlines while grabbing precious spare minutes to help Tom with research on the fate of children in the Soviet State, often arriving in the early morning and staying glued to her desk into the wee hours. She had no social life, but Poli, the chatty cleaning lady, took pity on the serious young reporter and often brought home-cooked *pirozhki* to tempt Harper away from her desk with the prospect of a fluffy filled bun accompanied by a quick chat in the evening lull.

Harper had amassed a trove of resource material, and she needed to bury herself in the bits and pieces to discover the lines of the story. She had promised Tom a solid narrative, so she arrived at the office early, pleased to find the conference room empty. She glanced at Tom's cubicle where every inch of his desk groaned with files and stacks of paper. The newsroom was quiet, still awaiting the usual frenzied rush, and the few journalists hunched over their desks were buried in their own tasks.

Harper stepped into the conference room and pulled all the files out of her satchel. She then carried the stacks of documents from her own cubicle, and soon she had commandeered the space and organized her findings. Maps, photographs, census reports, arrest reports, and trial documents were separated into neat piles. Harper pulled a few photographs and taped them to the glass wall just as the elevator door chimed, and Alina stepped off carrying a stack of mail.

"What's all this?" she asked as she poked her head around the heavy glass door. Harper was staring at the collage on the wall and didn't respond. Alina crept into the room and whistled. "This is a lot. I mean, how do you sort through all this?" She moved to stand beside Harper to better take in all the images. In some, children in happier times posed with their families or their treasured pets. Later photographs showed dire conditions in work camps far above the Arctic Circle. The children's cheeks, once rosy and cherubic, were drawn tightly over sharp bones.

Harper pointed to the piles on the table and explained that it was likely that no one knew how many children had been killed or traumatized after accusations against their families. Children were assumed to inherit their parents' proclivity for anti-Soviet thoughts and deeds and thus could be killed, deported, or jailed alongside a parent, usually their mothers. The fathers often disappeared, never to be heard from again. Other children—orphans, foundlings, the ill and the infirm—were shipped in from the Soviet satellite states. They found themselves in State homes, forgotten in a purgatory of despair.

"Heartbreaking!" Alina offered a bundle to Harper. "And as if you didn't have enough to read, the mailroom dropped this off with me yesterday. They tried your desk but it was already too cluttered." Then she added, "Angelica gets back midafternoon, so call me if you need a hand moving all this." She winked and returned to the elevator.

Harper tossed the mail in her bag and delved back in the documents and notes. Tom arrived with the gift of fresh coffee and pastries, and together, they sorted out their findings.

For his part, he had conducted dozens of interviews and reviewed hundreds of official documents. At best he had a muddled picture of the system, and he and Harper tried to connect the dots and find an angle for telling the story. They were so absorbed in their work that they failed to notice the elevator chimes, the gradual quieting of the typewriters, and the darkness that surrounded the windows at the end of the day. They were startled when the glass door whooshed open.

"What the hell?" Angelica stood in her fur coat, her cheeks rosy from the cold.

"Oh, Angelica! We must have lost track of time!" Harper reached down and grabbed an armload of files and envelopes, stuffing them in her satchel.

Tom looked up and offered a weary smile. He pushed his reading glasses back on his head and rubbed his face. "We'll give it a rest for the night and clear out your conference room in a jiffy. Boy Scout promise."

"Stop." Angelica shed her coat. She picked up some of the

papers off the table and looked at the photographs that Harper had taped to the wall. "Talk to me. What story does all this tell?"

Harper and Tom took turns laying out their notes and recordings. Harper picked up a copy of an old map, drawn by hand and labeled in tiny, almost indecipherable handwriting. She thrust it at Angelica who stared at the scribbles, attempting to read the faded penmanship.

"Transit stations? Interminable train travel halted periodically by stops at stations for sorting. Are we talking about sorting people?"

"Absolutely," Harper said. "They must have been horrifying. Look at this vast network where families were split apart and dispatched. Fishing, logging, and mining camps in the punishing tundra of the far north seem to have been a popular punishment for being undesirable. Gulags were an option for adults and children. Sometimes, the children accompanied their parents to the prison camps or were sent to camps on their own. Others were separated from their families and sent to orphanages." Harper pointed to tiny dots on the map. "Vologda. There's another one between here and Kursk. They seem to be way stations for the system to discard those deemed not Soviet enough to benefit the new order."

Angelica frowned. "Do you have first-hand evidence of any of this?"

Tom confirmed that the interviews thus far had been raw and gut-wrenching. They had met men and women who carried the trauma of their experiences as though it had all happened yesterday. Some were old and infirm, others were barely middle-aged, but their recollections were frighteningly similar. Ominous knocks at the door in the middle of the night, guards forcing them to grab whatever clothing they could to leave within the hour, long train rides, separations. Years spent in the harshest conditions enduring unimaginable deprivations.

"One old man still bore the scars of virulent infections. Another recounted his time in an orphanage where there was rarely enough food and never enough clothes, but always crushing cold."

Harper was satisfied that they were making good progress with their investigation, but the stories were heavy, and the burden of the experience, still writ large on the faces of the survivors, was haunting. She looked to Angelica with a determined set to her jaw. "We need to go to some of those places, take pictures," she said, "and wouldn't it be brilliant if one of the survivors would go with us? Help us revisit the place and talk about their history?"

Angelica mulled that over. "Hmmm. Might be a difficult journey back, but you need a focus for the story. Burrow into the account of one of the survivors and tell the story from his or her angle. Really take the readers deep into how nightmarish this all was."

"There was one thing that struck me today," Harper offered, searching for a more expansive view, "the resilience. These folks went through hell and back. They lost their families, their connections, their identities, and yet they rebuilt their lives. They pressed on. There was this old woman; her name is Maria, and she must be in her eighties. She wants to go back to Siberia and find her sister's grave. Imagine traveling all that way at her age. It's been decades but she still feels a responsibility."

Angelica grabbed her coat and turned toward her office. "You two just might be onto something. Go home. It'll all be here tomorrow. The files, the data, and the pain. Don't worry about the room; we'll adjust."

Harper returned to her tiny studio apartment and checked the cupboards for something edible. A bottle of cheap wine, a can of potted meat, stale bread, and a couple of eggs were the sum total of her larder. She managed to toast the bread and boil the eggs. Too tired to set a proper place at her little table, she ate standing up.

Sufficiently fortified, she poured herself a glass of wine, curled up in her overstuffed chair, and turned on the radio. The dulcet tones of late-night songs soothed her, and, ignoring an angry protest from her downstairs neighbor, she tapped her toes to the beat of the music. Her foot knocked over her satchel, which she had tossed to the floor, and several envelopes spilled out.

"Ah yes, let's see what the postman brought," she said aloud as she emptied the bag into her lap. She was annoyed to see more applications for the festival. Several cassette tapes were in the mix, and Harper bundled them with the entries and set those aside. She would make quick work of sending them a rejection note in the morning. She briskly sorted through a few short letters and invitations before turning to a thick envelope, the last parcel in the stack. Harper picked it up and felt the heft of the folded sheets inside. Intrigued, she sliced the envelope and pulled out the contents. Fanning through the pages, she saw that it was a carefully written letter with impressive penmanship accompanied by the score of a song written in the same precise script.

> *Turul, Siberia, 10 October 1992*
> *Salutations to Harper Burns,*
> *My name is Sofya Balik, and I hope that you receive this letter in time to consider my husband's work for the Moscow Festival competition. He is an extraordinary musician–*

Harper set the letter aside, making a mental note to add it to the rejection pile, but her musician's heart was curious about the accompanying composition. She took a sip of wine and grimaced as she swallowed. *Bleh*, she thought, *tastes like a gulp of vinegar*.

She set her glass on the floor and teased apart the thick pages of a melody, lovingly transcribed. She was only a few bars in when she realized she was holding the work of an extraordinary talent. She returned to the letter and read further, her heart racing as she took in the import of this man's story. *If what Sofya Balik writes is true*...she thought, then she read a line that caused her to bolt upright in her chair and knock over her wine glass. She ignored the spill as the liquid pooled on the scuffed floor. She read the letter through, examined the accompanying score, and then she read it all a second time. "Oh, my Lord," she repeated over and over, for once at a loss for words.

Tom arrived within the hour, his hair uncombed and his shirt inside out. Harper spied him crossing the street under the flickering glow of the unreliable streetlights, and she tiptoed down the stairs to meet him in the foyer.

"Shhhhh," she warned as she wrestled with the creaky front door. "Thin walls and nosy neighbors."

"I see you're in one piece, and there are no knife-wielding intruders hiding in the corner. What the devil is this all about?" he whispered.

Harper motioned for him to follow, and they crept up the three flights of stairs to her cramped quarters under the eaves. It would be at least eight hours before sunrise, and the old boarding house was cloaked in shadows set to the cadence of snoring.

"Jeepers, you really can hear everything in this dump," Tom groused.

She eased the door shut, motioning for him to sit in her chair. "I'd offer you something to drink, but the cupboard is bare at the moment except for a sorry bottle of wine."

Tom ran his hands through his scraggly hair and shrugged his shoulders. "Don't worry, missy, it's clear you live a Neanderthal existence. Let's get to the point. Why am I here?"

"Because of this." Harper pulled the letter out of the thick envelope, smoothed it against her knee and handed it to him.

Tom fished in his pocket for his reading glasses and grasped the paper.

Turul, Siberia, 10 October 1992
Salutations to Harper Burns,

My name is Sofya Balik, and I hope that you receive this letter in time to consider my husband's work for the Moscow Festival competition. He is an extraordinary musician, and it would be wonderful to finally have one of his original songs featured. You see, he was destined from childhood for a life on the stage, and then the war happened. He was robbed of his talents, and though he does not complain, I know he carries the weight of loss and disappointment in him.

My husband's name is Ján Balik, and he is from Poland where he was born to a family of great wealth and talent. We have been married for many years now, and I just learned the details of his youth. Can you imagine the burden of that silence? He has kept all of his early life bottled up inside him because it is too painful to think about the people that he lost and the life that was taken from him.

Even as a young child, his talent was obvious and his skills were quite advanced. In the summer of 1939, his parents put him on a train to Königsberg to study with his aunt Ada, who was a famous soprano. While he was there, the Germans invaded Poland, and his entire family was killed. He was still in Königsberg when the Soviet army arrived, and he was horribly injured trying to escape. He was captured and spent the next many years in places too horrid to imagine including an orphanage and a doomed labor camp.

He has this leather book in which he compiles all his compositions. I am not an educated woman. I am simple but my husband is not. This book has the musical memories he imagined as tributes to people that died in those awful years of the war and after.

He poured his heart into each of these songs, hoping to capture the soul of the places that tested him and the people who are lost. The melodies are beautiful and deserve to be heard. They are trapped in a cracked leather journal with a bullet hole pierced through its heart, a bullet that was meant for my

*husband. Please give this music a stage so that his stolen
childhood can find meaning and the people who were so dear to
my Ján can be celebrated and remembered.*
   Humbly asking,
   Sofya Balik

Tom whistled long and low under his breath and reread the letter.

Harper whispered, "We're onto something here, I can sense it. We have to follow up, Tom. How did this man end up in Siberia, and where the hell is Turul?"

"Not a clue. What else is in that envelope?"

"It's a musical composition of sorts. A crude copy that looks like broad strokes with notations, but there's a gifted musician in these lines."

"Can you make some sense of it?"

"I can try."

"Grab that fiddle of yours, we're going to the office."

They began their search at the newsroom fueled by Poli's treats and the gift of multiple pots of hot coffee. They worked through the early dawn hours scouring their notes for any information that matched the scant clues in Sofya's letter. Later, they stood shivering at the door of the State archives until the custodian jangled the keys in the lock and let them in. As the employees filed into their stations, Tom and Harper were already exploring the dusty shelves searching for Ján Balik in records from the People's Commissariat of Enlightenment or its more common moniker, Narkompros.

Harper put her head in her hands to ease her growing headache. "So help me get this straight. This Narkompros. They had oversight of education and culture?"

Tom nodded. "Supposedly this agency, which became the Ministry of Education, was tasked with eradicating illiteracy while also supporting cultural expression. That meant approving the repertoires of performers. A rather broad mission, eh? The orphanages would have fallen into their crosshairs for improving schooling, but it appears they fell far short in their oversight."

The official files from the former Soviet State were poorly organized and often in fragile condition. Digging through the archives over the next two days, Harper struggled to decipher the cryptic handwritten records, and Tom chipped in with insights from his more experienced eye.

With persistence and a fair amount of luck, they pored over enough documents to link Ján to the No. 15 Special Home for Children. Tom unearthed a map showing the location of the facility, which placed it south of Moscow and a few hours outside Kursk.

Harper established that the home had closed in 1955 after official charges had been brought against the administrator, Manya Kotova, and several of the employees for siphoning off food and supplies intended for the children.

"It appears that Mrs. Kotova enriched herself at the children's expense," she noted. "She literally took food right out of their mouths!"

Tom contacted a former colleague in Berlin and confirmed that in the early years of the war, a well-known prodigy named Jan Richter was a featured performer at many concerts sponsored by the Königsberg Academy of Music, a highly regarded school run by Erik Richter. "The maestro was married to Ada Richter, who was a native of Poland. Seems likely that this is our boy Ján Balik using his uncle's name," Tom theorized. "From there it gets even murkier." He described how as German Königsberg succumbed to wartime deprivations, ultimately reemerging as the Russian city Kaliningrad, references to Jan Richter faded; indeed, all mentions of concerts and musical endeavors disappeared from the news reports.

"This is the part that separates the amateurs from the

professionals," Tom replied with a wink. "We're going to track this story down. If it were easy, everybody would be doing it."

They regrouped with their notes back at the newspaper, bypassing the domestic desk and decamping downstairs in the basement library where they startled Khristina, the resourceful archivist. As soon as they filled her in, Khristina dug into the newspaper's files, cross-referencing their notes, and looking for any possible clue about the activities at the No. 15 Home for Children.

Evidence of Mrs. Kotova's fall from grace was documented in small dispatches, buried deep in the coverage. Clearly, it was not the type of information that the government was eager to share. She had been removed from her post, but any reference to an arrest or censure had been thoroughly scrubbed from the documents.

Harper rubbed her eyes and battled fatigue as she considered their next steps. "This is probably a dead end, but what if we expand our search in Soviet newspapers for Ján Balik? I can't imagine any scenario in which he might have made the papers, but the piece his wife sent is titled 'Barabanicha on the Dead Road'. What is that?"

Tom asked to see Sofya's letter again. "I've run across information about this place, Barabanicha. A hellhole if memory serves and a half-brained scheme to connect northern ports through the worst possible terrain above the Arctic Circle."

"What if his arrest and sentence to that prison appeared in a footnote or list somewhere?" Harper asked.

"Not likely, missy. The sheer numbers alone. Those poor souls were meant to be forgotten."

Khristina left to enter his name in her databases, and Alina poked her head in. "So here you are! You two have been as scarce as hen's teeth lately. Very secretive. Sorry to interrupt, but Angelica is here, and she's been on the hunt for you both."

They stood before Angelica's desk and watched her read. She stared at the letter for a long time and said nothing, but her expression reflected the grief in Sofya Balik's words. She handed the paper back to Harper, dabbing at the corner of her eyes and clearing her throat.

"What else is in there?" Angelica asked softly.

Harper carefully refolded the letter and handed her the brittle sheet of music, painstakingly copied by hand. There was a weighty hush in the room while Angelica pored over the song. "Is it any good?" she asked.

Tom turned to Harper. "I for one would love to know how this sounds. Isn't it about time you have a go at it?"

Harper studied the music and nodded her head. "I can make an educated guess. It was written for the piano, and Mr. Balik has only put the broad strokes here, but I think I can get the gist of the piece." She retrieved her violin and began to play. In Harper's tentative and halting interpretation, the notes emerged as mournful and poignant, a song of loss and pain. It was a simple arrangement, yet the tune evoked overwhelming grief.

She lowered the bow and looked at her colleagues with tears in her eyes. "What kind of man can write this about such a horrific experience? If I am making the appropriate guesses, it's chilling and yet there is a sense of grace. Angelica, there is a heartbreaking and compelling story here. We know the name and location of the orphanage where Mr. Balik was sent. We know where to find him in a Siberian village. So much to uncover here. What are his injuries? How did he end up on a train from East Prussia to the USSR? How did he end up living in Siberia? I'd like to go with Tom to interview Mr. Balik and his wife."

Tom concealed his surprise. He and Harper had not discussed traveling to the far Siberian east together, but it was an intriguing idea. *This gal is fearless*, he thought.

"So let me get this straight," Angelica said, "you two are calling in chits to get information about a boy who is one of thousands who ended up in an orphanage and a prison, a boy who later married and whose wife wants him in the competition where the winners have already been decided. Am I missing something?

Maybe there's a hook here, and the man has a story to tell, but I am not convinced that we're ready to send you to the edges of nowhere to work on it."

After spending days digging in dusty files on little sleep, Harper felt the bitter slap of rejection. How could Angelica be so blasé about this unfolding story? On the verge of a meltdown, she turned to dash to the bathroom, determined not to give Angelica the satisfaction of seeing her cry. She was startled to find Khristina hovering by the door. She choked back her tears as the archivist thrust a folder toward her and then stepped back into the shadows. Harper pulled out a photocopy of the front page of old edition of *Pravda*, the official newspaper of the Communist Party, and searched the columns while Angelica leaned in, anxious to know what she was seeing.

The paper, dated October 2, 1946, proclaimed "The Verdict of History" in an arresting font. Harper quickly scanned the article. "The Nuremberg Tribunal? What does this have to do with—" She gasped when she saw the bottom corner of the page. A photograph of a terrified boy, blinded by the flash of a photographer's camera while surrounded by a crush of admirers. His youthful face was disfigured by a hideous scar where his ear should have been. The caption read "Ján Balik, pianist, is lavished with praise after a stellar performance to conclude the summer tour of The Besprizornye Musicians."

Angelica was the first to break the silence. "Figure out where Turul is and get on the next plane." She turned to Khristina. "Get me everything that's available on The Besprizornye Musicians."

It took six hours for the stalwart Tupelov jet to fight the dual threats of turbulence and fog in its path from Moscow to Yakutsk. Harper gripped her armrest and summoned every schoolgirl prayer she could remember to sustain her on the flight. Tom held their drinks and nibbled on the stale airplane food, unperturbed. As the plane circled the airport in Yakutsk, Harper was struck by the pervasive whiteness of the thoroughly frozen vista.

On the ground, the cold was as brutal as advertised. Harper emerged from the plane to find that her eyelashes froze together as soon as she stepped onto the tarmac, and her tiny bit of exposed skin burned with a fierce intensity from the subzero temperatures. *It's only November!* she thought as the sharp pains shot across her face. Tom grabbed her arm, and they made their way into the city.

Getting to Turul was another matter altogether. After several fruitless inquiries, they managed to arrange transport with a trucker who was shuttling supplies to a gas pipeline. He welcomed their company for the two-hour journey. "Good thing you're here now," he chuckled through a gap-toothed smile, "the trip takes twice as long in summer. Frozen rivers and lakes are the speedy highways this time of year."

Indeed, the drive was an unbroken icy expanse, and Harper marveled at how the trucker knew where he was going. By the ebbing light of the afternoon sun, they rolled into Turul, and the trucker dropped them off at Gerasim's store, promising to return for them the following afternoon. Harper and Tom hustled inside, catching the young clerk off guard. With the exception of Gerasim's shady contacts, visitors were an oddity in this part of the world. When Harper inquired as to how she might find Sofya Balik, the clerk laughed and pointed down the lane. "That would be her house right there."

As daylight faded, Ján shelved the last of the books and banked the fire in the oven before he pulled shut the heavy doors of the library. Since its dedication, the library had become a community hub, far beyond Ján's expectations. Dzikusku darted out into the field, skidding on the ice in search of critters, and Ján spied a truck idling in front of the store. He wondered if his newest books had arrived from Yakutsk and made a mental note to check with the clerk in the morning. He called for Dzikusku as he let himself in the kitchen, stomping the ice off his shoes, and storing them by the door. Hearing voices in the sitting room, he peeled off his coat and hat to see who might be visiting. He found Sofya talking with two strangers, and she jumped when he entered the room.

"Ján! You startled me!" Sofya blurted out, uncharacteristically shrill.

"Hello," he said to the visitors. "What brings you to the edge of the world?"

Harper watched Ján enter the little room. She saw a slightly built man with sparkling blue eyes set above a full beard and long curly hair that covered the sides of his head before it was gathered into a low ponytail. She leaped to her feet and thrust out her hand.

"Mr. Balik, it is a pleasure to make your acquaintance. My name is Harper Burns, and this is my colleague, Tom Rainey. We are with the *Moscow News*, and we have come all this way to meet you. We hope to learn more about your story."

Ján's heart skipped a beat and he felt all the air leave his lungs; he struggled to regain his composure. "Miss Burns, I do appreciate all the effort on my behalf, but I am afraid that there is no story to tell. I am a humble carpenter, librarian, and piano teacher. That is all. I am sorry to waste your time."

Sofya said softly, "Ján dear, they are here because I invited them. Miss Burns wrote an article about a competition for the Moscow Winter Festival, a musical competition. I entered you." She went into the kitchen and returned with the carefully folded newspaper. "I sent them a copy of your composition for Barabanicha."

Ján tried to hold his rising panic at bay as he scanned the announcement. The walls and the heat pressed in on him, and he wanted to run far away. How could Sofya have gone behind his back and how might he extricate himself from these reporters? He looked at Harper. "Is this the sum of it? You came all this way to hear me play the piano?"

"Well in a manner of speaking, perhaps," Harper replied,

equivocating for the moment. "We would be honored to hear you play the piece that your wife chose, *Barabanicha*."

Ján moved to the niche that held his precious Red October, and settled himself on the bench. He put his fingers on the keys, closed his eyes, and paused before he began to play. He needed neither a lamp nor the music in front of him. The haunting melody conjured the image of a man lost in his despair, surrounded by an impenetrable world of death and isolation. Despite the suffering, the piece also spoke to hope and shared survival.

Tom steadied his camera and surreptitiously snapped photographs. Ján's taut posture betrayed his repressed emotions, and Sofya hovered protectively nearby with her arms tightly crossed in anticipation of Harper's reaction. Tom lowered the camera when Ján played the last stanza and let his hands drop to his sides.

Harper had gleaned some of his angst in her attempts to render the piece, but in Ján's hands, the music was magnificently evocative. He remained glued to the bench, his head lowered in contemplation as Sofya and the reporters stood in silence, reflecting on the weight of the notes. Harper broke the spell. "Extraordinary, Mr. Balik. Do you mind sharing with me the story behind this piece?" Ján didn't react. He remained focused on the keys, his gaze distant as if lost in a trance. "Mr. Balik?"

"I heard you, Miss Burns," said Ján. "And I believe that I have concluded what you came for. I have no story that I wish to share."

Harper reached into her bag and pulled out a folder. She approached Ján and withdrew an enlargement of the photograph from *Pravda*. Switching from Russian to German, Harper said, "*Es tut mir Leid, Herr Balik*. I am sorry. I truly do not wish to upset you, but this is a photograph of you, is it not? You are a man of immense talent and, I fear, broken dreams. Can you tell me what happened?"

Ján looked at Harper with watery eyes and accepted the

photograph she held out to him. He peered into his own youthful face, and he recognized the expression of fear that took him back into the mind of that boy, caught up in forces he couldn't understand or control. It was as though a lightning bolt shot through his body. He put his hands to his face, turning inward and shutting out everyone in the room. He was back on that stage, a boy performing his best. He heard the pop of the flashbulb before the people in the audience called his name. He saw Comrade Novikov and then the visage of Mrs. Kotova appeared. He remembered his mother's dreams for him and felt the crushing realization that she would be disappointed to see him now.

Harper saw the disfigurement on the man that matched the boy's scar in the picture, and she knew that, despite the enormity of the physical assault, there was a deeper well of trauma lurking within Ján Balik. What had this man endured?

Sofya went to him and wrapped her arms around his shoulders. "Ján dear, talk to me."

He shook her off and rose from the bench unsteadily. "*Es gibt nichts zu sagen*—there is nothing to say," he replied. He moved to the kitchen to retrieve his coat and boots, and he went out through the back door with Dzikusku at his heels.

Harper followed him, and though the cold knocked the breath out of her chest and attacked her face like a thousand needles, she pursued him as he walked the short distance to the barn behind the house. He pulled open the heavy door, walked to the middle of the space, and plunged a log into the belly of the oven.

Harper entered the building and gasped. Expecting to see a collection of tools and scraps, she was met by meticulous rows of shelves lined with books. A staircase, simple but ingenious in its design, wound around the back to a loft above where more shelves waited for Turul's readers.

"You built a library!" she blurted out. "How absolutely amazing! Mr. Balik, surely you must realize that you are a man with a compelling story. A man of immense talent and dedication. Look at this place!"

"I am afraid that you mistake me for someone else, Miss Burns. I am certain that you must have come a long way, but I have nothing to offer you. I ask only that you leave me and my wife in peace. The music? It is mine, and I do not wish to give it away. The memories too. They are mine alone."

"Mr. Balik, I implore you to reconsider. Your story will touch many people. There are those who are still traumatized from the war and the atrocities committed in the years since. Your story could bring hope, perhaps resolution."

Ján moved to the door and grasped the handle. "Miss Burns, I do not know what you think you know about me, but I assure you that your knowledge is incomplete. There is nothing of comfort that I am able to share. Experience has taught me that I bring only pain in my wake. I ask you to respect that and leave me be." He pulled the door open and a rush of biting wind swept in. "You may stay the night in the house, but I'll ask you to leave us in peace tomorrow."

Ján awoke to Dzikusku's insistent prodding. He stretched out his legs and popped another log on the smoldering embers, his joints stiff and painful from sleeping on the library floor. Dzikusku licked Ján's face and sat back, wagging his tail.

"Yes, yes, I know. You need your morning scamper." Ján limped to the door and opened it just wide enough for the dog to wiggle out and hone in on the fresh tracks in the snow. Ján looked to the house in time to see Sofya walk down the lane with the reporters from the newspaper. What had Sofya been thinking when she wrote to that woman? He was glad to see that she was sending them off and hoped that she would return soon. He would have a talk with her about putting all this business about music competitions to rest.

But Sofya didn't return shortly. Ján ate the breakfast that she had left for him and then hovered by the door, wondering where she had gone. Her absence unnerved him. He was impatient to set things straight with her.

While he waited for her, he sat down to play the piano, delving into the book of sheet music that he had received just last month. He chose "Three Movements from Petrushka", the wildly enthusiastic piece that Stravinsky himself had struggled to play. Ján flexed his left hand for the calisthenics involved and launched into a frenetic version of the Russian ballet. Ján's mood turned a joyous piece of music unto a tumultuous and complex rendition, and when he finished, the exertion left his chest heaving. The workout had purged his anxiety over the previous evening's confrontation, and he had managed to tamp those emotions back into their safe hiding spaces.

He heard the rusty hinges squeak as the back door opened. "Sofya?" he called.

Tuyaara stuck her head around the door frame. "Not Sofya, just me. What's the godawful jumble of notes coming out of that box? You'll wake the dead with that racket."

Ján checked his annoyance. "May I ask if you know where Sofya is?"

"As a matter of fact, I do." Tuyaara had a smug grin on her face. She was like a cat toying with a mouse.

Ján's patience was sorely tested. "May I ask you to tell *me* then?"

"She's at the school, and she needs your help. She sent me to ask you to come right away." Seeing his alarm, she hastened to add, "For heaven's sake, don't worry. She just needs you for a minute, that's all." Tuyaara turned on her heels and exited the house, leaving Ján to scramble into his coat, hat, and gloves.

On the quick walk over, Ján looked toward the store where the truck idled, its motor humming against the harsh elements to keep the whole inner workings from freezing up. No sign of those newspaper people. *Gone at last*, he thought as he let himself into the school and walked along the familiar scrubbed floors. He turned the corner, hoping to find Sofya, and was confused to see a crowd gathered at the end of the hall. The people turned to watch him approach, and although no one spoke, several reached out to pat him on the back as they moved back and created a path for him. Ján followed Dzikusku through the crowd and into a classroom, shocked to find it filled with more people. The elders sat at the desks while the younger ones filled in around the edges.

"An inquisition?" Ján mumbled. That's when he spied Sofya standing by Alban with Harper and Tom right behind. Sofya dabbed at her red-rimmed eyes with a handkerchief. She immediately moved to take Ján's hand and draw him in, but she couldn't speak, and fresh tears began to flow down her flushed cheeks.

Alban stepped forward. "Ján my friend, we—and by that I mean all of us—are here for you. These good people from Moscow have come to record your story, and we want you to know that we admire you, we appreciate you, and we support you. We are also here to say that it is time, my friend. It is time to make peace with whatever brought you to us."

Ján felt the catch in his throat as all the nightmares flooded back. The shield that he kept so firmly fastened against the memories shifted, and he struggled to keep his armor intact. His heart was pounding, and panic threatened to overtake him. Sofya gripped his arm and led him to the front of the room, helping to keep him on his feet.

Ján looked out over the crowd. He found Ayta, Tuyaara, and Dabyn. Gerasim was in the back as was Mahad and his sons. The teachers from the school were wedged together with some of their students, their faces full of curious concern. His piano students were clustered to the side, many holding their parents' hands and watching Ján closely. This was Ján's whole world of friends and family, all gathered around him and squeezed into this modest space. His shoulders shook with the effort needed to keep his composure.

Alban put his arm around Ján and drew him close. "We have loved you for many years, and I, the longest, from our time on the Dead Road when you gave away that sorry guitar to save my sad life. Look out over there, Ján. There are my children and grandchildren. They owe their lives to you. The rest of us have loved you ever since you wandered into town with that scruffy she-wolf by your side. You have listened to our joys and our squabbles. You have comforted those of us who needed a friend, and you have embraced the memories of the ones we have lost. You committed them to music so that we may be comforted by their spirits. You did all that, Ján. You." Alban put his hands on either side of Ján's face. "It's time, my brother. It's time to confront the pain you have carried all these years. These people from Moscow are here to help you do that."

Ján was openly weeping, his heart cleaved into brittle shards and the raw pain of loss seizing his soul. Alban enveloped him in a tight hug and then stepped away. Behind him stood Alexei. He wrapped his fingers around Ján's hands.

"Mr. Balik, you believed in me. You taught me how to use music to express what is in my heart. You had patience when I didn't, and you made me into a musician. And you never complain when I hit the sour notes. Thank you." He shook Ján's hand and moved on.

One by one, everyone in the room came forward and expressed their love and gratitude to Ján. They gave him little gifts and left him handwritten notes until the room had emptied out, and the only ones remaining with Ján were Harper, Tom, Sofya, and Alban. Ján was spent. His emotions had roiled throughout the morning, and he had no reserves. He looked at Sofya, hoping she would save him, but she stood firm, rubbing his hand but offering him no opportunity for escape. Alban stood to the side, waiting patiently.

Harper was the first to break the silence. "Mr. Balik? The No. 15 Special Home for Children. What happened?"

Ján crumpled to the floor, too exhausted to weep further. "I couldn't save them," he repeated over and over.

Harper leaned down and put her hand on his shoulder. "Who, Mr. Balik? Who were you supposed to save?"

"Ada, Otto, Vera, Maks, the children," he said. "All of them."

Chapter 15

Song of Truth

Turul to Moscow, Russia
November 1992

The trucker was dispatched back on his route to Yakutsk alone with instructions to relay a message to Angelica that the reporters would be in Turul longer than expected. Ayta and Tuyaara set to work arranging guest quarters for Harper and Tom.

Tom pulled Harper aside as the truck roared across the ice on its return journey. "Impressive display of tenacity, Miss Burns."

"Oh, Tom, I'm not the brave one here. Ján Balik is the tenacious one, but his story is pulling me apart. The journalist in me wants to push all Ján's buttons and air his story out. The daughter in me sees the same haunting trauma that ate away at my father. It's paralyzing and frightening. I can't believe I'm saying this, but Angelica was right. I'm too close. You have to be the one to get Ján to open up."

Tom blew on his hands and shivered. "Listen, Harper, I don't have time for long drawn-out negotiations. It's frickin' cold out here, makes Moscow seem like the damn Riviera. Mr. Balik needs to tell his story, for his own healing and for all the damaged souls from this godforsaken time of pain. You've worked your butt off and deserve to take the lead. Now get in there and put this guy out of his misery."

They arranged themselves around the kitchen table to begin the interview. Harper reached into her satchel and pulled out a recorder, a pen, and a thick pad of paper while Tom reloaded his camera and adjusted the settings for the low Siberian light. Ján sat quietly and watched the proceedings, his hands clenched tightly in his lap.

Sofya busied herself at the stove and produced a pot of tea in mismatched cups that she laid out with much ceremony. This was the first time she had ever entertained visitors in this cottage that were not from Turul. She glanced up at the doll holding court over the kitchen from her lofty perch, and Sofya drew a measure of confidence from her silent gaze.

Harper positioned her recorder in front of Ján. "Mr. Balik, thank you for agreeing to this interview," she said. "In our reporting of this story, it is clear that much is unresolved from a period of heartbreak and great trauma, for you and many others who were trapped in the system of Soviet orphanages."

Ján simply nodded to acknowledge her statement, his unspoken actions respectful and dignified.

Harper continued. "We will report this story with sensitivity, but our priority is fairness and honesty. We will not shy away from asking you questions we deem necessary to get to the truth nor will we seek your permission before we run the story. Do you agree with our stipulations?" She looked at Ján with unwavering directness, hoping he couldn't tell that her insides were quivering like jelly.

"Madam, I would expect nothing less."

Harper established the date, times, and participants in the interview, and then the questions began. Harper had clearly done her research, and as Ján spoke, she added notes on events or people that would require follow up searches and corroboration. When

Ján described his earliest memories of family and life in Warsaw, Sofya retrieved the book with the picture of Ján's family, and they all noted the opulent surroundings and elegant family grouping. Tom snapped a picture.

Ján then recounted his trip to Königsberg, including memories of his close relationship with Ada and his fraught experiences with his Uncle Erik. He described the heady days of piano lessons and performances and the experience of being fitted for a tuxedo, its collar stiff and confining. He then shared the tragic story of hearing about how his family had been killed and his realization that he would never again return to Warsaw.

"I had to go right back on the stage. There was a worry, you see, about what the authorities might think of me, and by extension, of my aunt. It was decided to hide me in plain sight, on the stage, and music became my refuge. My family existed with me as a collection of notes that represented what they had meant to me." When he reached the part where he and Ada were attacked by the Russian soldiers, he spared no detail describing the terror of her death and his injury.

Ján had prepared himself mentally for this exposure, but Sofya had not anticipated the horror of his responses. When he described Ada's death and the shot that destroyed his ear, she openly wept, and Tom brought her a glass of water and offered his handkerchief to calm her, fearful that her reaction would derail Ján's willingness to participate.

Ján remained resolute. It was as though he were no longer in Turul, but instead back on the train packed with desperate, dying prisoners. Having ventured this far into the minefield of his memories and emotions, he was committed to telling the truth. Harper ceased asking questions and listened as Ján described a journey of unimaginable horror.

The bedlam at the train station was a difficult story for Ján to relate. "I was consumed with pain, and I remember only bits and pieces in disconnected fragments. The world was falling apart and there was so much evil, so much screaming, so much death, yet I was still alive. Why? I began to hold myself responsible for my failure to save those around me. Ada, then the children on the train. If I could have done things differently, perhaps–"

He choked, momentarily unable to speak, and Sofya pushed the handkerchief toward him. He took a deep breath and pressed forward with his story. He described falling in the snow as infection raged in his head, and he produced the leather journal from inside his jacket, demonstrating how his music had absorbed the bullet meant for his heart. He described meeting Alban, the importance of their friendship, and how he had traded the guitar to save his friend's life, an act of sabotage that thrust him into punitive isolation when the rest of his group was sent out on a doomed mission.

Sofya stood and wrapped her arms around Ján's neck. The room was hushed as they sat with the heavy truth of Ján's raw testimony and the realization of the courage, determination, and occasional twists of fate that it took for him to survive. Harper, sensing the need for a respite, offered to help Sofya prepare a meal, and she eagerly agreed. She needed an outlet for her nervous energy and was comforted by the companionship of a shared task. Together, they assembled a simple but filling meal of pickled fish and vegetables.

Harper watched Ján and Sofya from across their table. He was patiently helping her navigate this novel experience of entertaining strangers while she protectively guarded his emotions. Harper was enchanted with the couple's tenderness and reluctant to break the spell of their devotion, but she was mindful that they faced a giant chasm in his story. Ján had withheld his account of his time at the orphanage, and Harper knew they needed to tease that out and broach the necessity of taking him back there. She glanced at Tom, and he responded with a nod. He was thinking the same thing.

Ján quietly cleared his throat and said, "It's been a long day for all of us. If we may, I would like to take 'Kusku for a walk, and I invite you to join me. I wish for you to experience this beautiful place that welcomed me home."

Harper leaned forward. "Understandable, Ján, but we must get to the matter of your time at the orphanage. As you may recall, that is the heart of the story that we need to tell."

Ján reached for Sofya's hand and offered a wistful smile in response. "Yes, I have thought about that. You see, I have lived in fear of those days, and if I am truly to confront them, I must do it in my own way and in my own time."

They bundled up in their coats, and Ján called for Dzikusku. Harper and Tom followed him out the door and into the harsh Siberian afternoon. Ján seemed unfazed by the cold, but Harper found she could barely breathe as they walked through town toward the cliffs and the frozen river. Along the way, they passed by Alban's house, set among other colorful dwellings, and proceeded to the cemetery where Ján pointed out the graves of his two children.

When they neared the river, they could feel the pulse of the relentless current under the thick layer of ice. Ján said, "This place is the root of our sustenance and the source of our pain. In its flowing abundance, it provides access while also forming barriers. My wife's people have great respect for the contradictions that govern life here. You would think that in view of such power, I could shed the ghosts of my past and sink into the tragic if beautiful rhythms, but my demons have followed me. I thought my silence would shield others from my sins, but it was not to be." He stared out across the frozen expanse deep in thought.

Tom said, "We carry the memory of our injuries on our bodies and in our hearts. I have learned that our pain does not live with us alone, but is passed in some way to those whom we love."

Ján thought about that for a bit. "Perhaps you are right. I cannot shake this sense of having let others down. It is the weight I carry and the fear I have that I am simply not strong enough to protect those I love."

When they returned to the house, Sofya greeted them warmly and gathered their coats while they clutched the hot mugs of tea she had prepared for them. The fire blazed in the oven and helped to dissipate the cold that clung to their clothes and their skin as they each resumed their place around the recorder.

Harper said, "Ján, we need to talk about the orphanage and what happened to you there. Are you ready to talk about that time in your life?"

Ján leaned forward and put his elbows on his knees. He looked up at Harper, and she saw a fierce determination in his eyes. She feared that it indicated a line he would not cross, so she was caught off guard when he said quietly, "I will answer all your questions. I must, but there is something I must do first, and I need your help."

"Of course, but what can we possibly do to help?"

"You must find out if Mrs. Kotova is still alive."

Ján and Sofya pressed their noses to the window of the jet and watched the frozen landscape of Yakutia disappear into the low-lying fog. It was their first time on an airplane, and Ján was incredulous that they would be in Moscow in six hours when it had taken him months to make this journey overland. The flight attendant brought them snacks and a warm towel, and Sofya giggled like a young girl when, for the first time in her memory, another person served her.

In the flurry of activity that involved getting them packed and on the road to Yakutsk, Ján had said little. He was quietly deferential and attentive to Sofya, almost as though he was supporting her through a transformative moment. He had teared up only once, when they had walked Dzikusku to Alban's house. "I wish I could take you, my friend," Ján lamented to his companion. "I'll be back." Now as they prepared to land, all eyes were on Ján to see how he might react.

Angelica was waiting for them at the airport, and she wasted no time in getting to the heart of the matter. "We have located her, Mr. Balik. Manya Kotova, the former administrator of the No. 15 Special Children's Home is alive if not exactly well. She lives in a facility for former Soviet government workers on the outskirts of Moscow. I called and they are expecting you tomorrow."

Sofya sat on the edge of the bed and marveled at the luxury of the hotel room. Angelica had insisted on booking a room at the storied Hotel Metropol, and it was shockingly opulent in contrast to the simple life they led in Turul. Sofya was aghast at the bathtub with water on demand, the enormous king-sized bed, and the telephone that could summon a cup of tea or a twelve-course meal. She had stood at the sink turning on the taps, hot water then cold water, awed by the ease and luxury. It seemed like a dream, and yet she watched Ján closely for fear that she had unleashed a nightmare for him, a journey that might tilt his fragile balance.

He stood at the window with his back to her and stared down at the lights along Teatral'nny Proyezd, his thoughts far away. He was remembering his childhood of privilege in Warsaw with the elegant parties his parents had hosted at their home. For the first time in years, he could summon the memory of his father's laugh, a deep-throated guffaw that was a mark of his ebullient personality.

"Ján?"

"Yes, my dear."

"Come sit with me and tell me your thoughts."

Ján turned and looked at his wife. She was the one person who had shared more of his life than any other. He took in the full measure of her: a short, softly plump woman wrapped in a pristine white hotel robe that was at least two sizes too large. He saw her dark, kind eyes, a long, silken braid of gray hair falling over her shoulder, and her tiny feet dangling off the bed, not quite reaching the floor. She looked lovely and vulnerable, and he longed to scoop her up, hold her close, and protect her from the horrors he carried, the brutal truths he had worked so hard to keep hidden. How could he regret the circumstances of his life that had brought her to him? And yet that twisted journey haunted him, and she deserved to know why.

"Please excuse me, dear. I need to attend to an important errand." He picked up his room key and bent to kiss her lightly on the head. "Don't fret. I will be back."

He let himself out of the room and gently closed the door behind him. The hallway seemed to stretch for miles, and he proceeded with the confidence of one who knew exactly what he planned to do.

Sofya burrowed under the covers, the lights from the streets below casting an eerie glow in the room. She refused to lie down, determined to stay propped against the overstuffed headboard until she knew where Ján had gone and what the implications were. Was he standing on the roof, his feet tipping precariously over the edge? Was he at the bar, tossing down one vodka after another? Had he simply walked out the massive revolving door into the teeming crowd rushing by, never to return?

After a long time imagining the worst possible scenarios, she heard footsteps in the hall. They paused in front of her door, and the knob twisted. Ján tiptoed into the space like a cat burglar blending into the shadows.

"I am awake," Sofya said. "Don't ever leave me wondering like that again."

"I am so sorry, my dear, I should have been more thoughtful. I needed to get ready for tomorrow." Ján switched on the light.

Sofya gasped. Somewhere in the maze of the hotel, he had found a barber. He stood before her with a clean-shaven face and a short, neatly trimmed haircut. She had never seen him like this. He was stunningly handsome to her, and his scar, angry and twisted, was exposed. He moved to sit next to her on the bed and reached for her hand.

"It's time that I faced up to the facts of my life. If I am to confront my past, I will do it with my head held high. I won't hide my scars, or wrap myself in a cloak of obscurity." He reached to draw her into an embrace.

Harper, Tom, and Angelica were taken aback on the following day when Sofya and Ján emerged from the car that the newspaper dispatched to ferry them between appointments. Ján, looking like the celebrity his family had envisioned, strode with quiet dignity toward the conference room. Angelica was waiting to talk to him, but as he walked along the hallways, reporters lined up to shake his hand. His haircut made for a remarkable transformation, and yet his frightening scar was now impossible to overlook. For the first time, Sofya saw him as the child of aristocrats, a man who, if he had lived the life planned for him, could summon the world with a flick of the wrist or the arch of an eyebrow.

After introductions, Harper and Tom climbed back in the car with the Baliks for the ride to the Center for Joyful Aging, an ironic moniker for such a ghastly place. Ján led the group as they entered the building, and there was nothing joyful about the dilapidated facility in an industrial area near Moscow. The stench of urine wafted out into the parking lot, and once inside the grim facility, they encountered men and women languishing in wheelchairs or walking aimlessly throughout the hallways, tripping over the peeling linoleum and dragging their feet through flakes of cracked paint.

"This is criminal!" exclaimed Harper as she pulled her scarf up over her nose. Sofya was close to tears over the blatant neglect, and Tom glanced around, determined to accost anyone who appeared to be in charge. "This will surely be our next story, Harper," he said, "an investigative piece about elder abuse."

Ján plowed ahead, politely cornering a harried attendant and getting directions to Mrs. Kotova's location. They fell in behind him as he proceeded deep into the maze of hallways and approached a large room filled with dozens of patients, some muttering to themselves, others in various states of undress, the lot of them soiled and forgotten. Ján stood in the doorway and surveyed the space. His jaw clenched and his shoulders stiffened when he saw her. She was hunched in a chair against a far wall. Greasy white hair, clinging to her scalp in ravaged patches, hung down to her shoulders, and her glasses tilted precariously across her nose. Despite the years, he would have recognized her anywhere. He marched toward her and crouched down until she had no choice but to look at him. Harper turned on her recorder, and Tom pulled out his camera.

"Mrs. Kotova?"

She peered at him through filmy eyes. Her teeth were gone, giving her face a sunken appearance as though she were slowly imploding, and her hands were covered in sores. Sofya couldn't look at her, choosing to listen to Ján while she focused her gaze on the weedy lot beyond the grimy windows.

"Who is asking?" Mrs. Kotova replied in a raspy voice, garbled by disease and impediment.

"You should remember me," Ján stated, his voice even but firm. He inched closer and Mrs. Kotova made a futile attempt to adjust her glasses. Her hands were shaking, and she let them drop to her lap.

"You look familiar," she wheezed. "One of the vermin from the home, I assume." She waved one of her hands as if to dismiss him.

"That's right. Ján Balik."

She hardened her mouth, and her face reflected fear. "You're supposed to be dead."

Ján hovered in front of her, his expression unchanging. "Yes well, you tried and failed. I survived."

"Who are these people with you? The police?"

Ján shook his head. "We are not here to hurt you, Mrs. Kotova. A long time ago, I consigned you to God for justice. I am here only to ask you a question. What happened to them? The ones who arrived but never left? I need to hear you say it."

She waved him off. "I don't know what you are talking about. You need to take this drivel somewhere else."

"No, not this time. I have spent my whole life regretting that I didn't do more to expose you. Where are they?"

She pointed a bony finger in his direction. "You were a troublemaker from the minute I picked you up from that hospital. I should have left you to die." Her mouth contorted into a semblance of a smile. "Your uncle would have approved."

Ján felt like he had suffered a gut punch, but he held his ground. He was not going to let her get the upper hand on him again. "You are telling lies. I need the truth."

"Oh! That's the truth, alright. You had a paper in your pocket with an address at the top. Your uncle's family in some backwater German village. The authorities contacted him. He asked us to keep you."

Sofya moved to put her arm around Ján, but he waved her off. "We're not here to talk about my uncle. We're here to talk about the children. For the last time, I need you to say for the record what I already know. Their families deserve closure."

She leaned back in her chair and put her face in her hands. She was out of ammunition now. It was just her and the naked truth. "It was a hard time for more than just you and the rest of the little miscreants that washed up at that hellhole of a house. I'll not remember any of that just to satisfy you."

Ján said nothing in reply. He continued to stare at her, unmoving. His heart was racing, and he was gasping for breath, but he would not let her see it. Not now. Not ever again.

"Leave," she mouthed. But he remained rooted to the floor, commanding what little view she had through her rheumy eyes.

Finally, she leaned toward Ján, her breath rancid and malignant, but Ján was unmoving, insistent. "Why don't you ask that stone-faced angel? Your answers are in his gaze." She cackled.

She was so amused at her joke that she laughed until she coughed uncontrollably. She grabbed the hem of her soiled robe and tried to pull it in front of her mouth. "Help me," she gasped.

Ján stood and walked away, the others following in his wake. They heard her calling after him as they exited the foul room.

Back in the parking lot, Sofya sucked in cleaner air, while Harper and Tom watched Ján for his reaction.

Harper said, "Oh, Ján, that was unbelievably awful. I don't know what to say about your uncle. I am so sorry that woman is still so vindictive. You'd think that in that dreadful place, a person would seek some kind of redemption."

Ján put his arm around Sofya. "To the contrary, that place isn't nearly as bad as the No. 15 Special Home, and she confirmed exactly what I suspected."

They spoke little on the drive back to the newspaper, each of them processing the appalling meeting with the vindictive Manya Kotova and all but Ján reeling from the shocking conditions of the home.

"I was prepared for a dreadful old woman, but she exceeded my low expectations of a soulless human," Harper whispered to Angelica when their entourage arrived back at the newspaper offices. "I'm going to have nightmares for weeks over her festering spite."

Ján appeared more concerned with the effect on Sofya, keeping his arm around her as they settled into the conference room. He requested a glass of water for her before he sat in the chair offered by Angelica. He was unfazed by the scrum of reporters crowding the room and remained calm as he answered Harper's questions about his time at the orphanage.

He described finding the boxes containing records of deaths and learning about the children who had gone missing. "It's hard to imagine how people like Mrs. Kotova can exist in this world unable to comprehend the humanity of others, steeped in their own cruelty. I thought I had escaped with The Besprizornye

Musicians, but I was sent back to what amounted to my death sentence. Mrs. Kotova was aware of what I knew. The children hadn't run away, as their families were told. They hadn't been adopted. They were neglected, starved, beaten, and molested until their bodies gave up. Those responsible enriched themselves with the stingy resources meant for their care. She had been unable to silence me, so she turned me out to the Dead Road to finish what she'd started." He looked at Angelica, his body burdened with fatigue and the weight of revisiting trauma, but his expression was resolute. "I need to see this through."

Angelica met his gaze. "What does that mean, Mr. Balik? You asked us to find Mrs. Kotova, and we have honored your request."

"I must go back. I must find them, my friends. I will not rest until I see this through. If Mrs. Kotova was telling the truth—and I believe she was—then I must find Vera, Maks, and all the innocent children. I owe them that much."

No one spoke as the toll of his revelations settled over them, and they each pondered how a child could navigate the horrors that he had endured.

Angelica broke the silence. "You will go tomorrow. Harper and Tom, you're going with him."

They got an early start, piling in Tom's car with a basket of food, flashlights, lap blankets, and plenty of film and camera equipment. Tom and Harper had huddled with Khristina in the archives before they left, and she promised to keep digging while they were away.

As Tom drove, Ján checked the map and plotted their best approach. Sofya and Harper sat in the back seat, pensive and subdued. Putting feet on the ground at the site of an orphanage was the scenario that Harper had been working toward. Now that they were in the car with the implications of Ján's story in their thoughts, she wondered if this journey was a good idea. It was hard to imagine a more emotional experience than the meeting with Mrs. Kotova, but they were headed back into the jaws of Ján's nightmare. Sofya reached across the cracked seat and grasped Harper's hand. They traveled in that way, two women in an unspoken alliance, both determined in their own way to protect Ján and uncover the secrets that would give him peace.

The urban sprawl of Moscow gave way to more rural areas, but little of what they passed was familiar to Ján. A fresh layer of snow covered the landscape as they drove over rivers and skirted the rolling hills, making it difficult to discern much difference from place to place. For Ján, it brought back unsettling memories of sitting behind Mrs. Kotova as they motored through the frozen countryside from the hospital.

The map indicated that they should leave the M2 and take back roads to the No. 15 Home. Ján watched out the window lost in his thoughts and said little as they motored through village after village. Tom tried to lighten the mood with friendly banter, but his charisma was no match for the tension in the car, and his jovial asides fell flat. They sat together in a palpable mood of anxious anticipation as they entered the town and drove straight to the local police station.

They were met by a junior officer, an eager young man barely out of school. "I am Lt. Volkov." He looked directly at Ján. "I understand you were at the orphanage up on the hill?"

"It was a long time ago."

Lt. Volkov sighed. "My grandparents tell me there were once nasty rumors." He insisted on collecting their papers. With a shrug, Ján offered up the crumpled forms belonging to the long-deceased Evgeni Baburin, but the policeman waved him off, choosing to turn a blind eye while muttering about forms and bureaucracy. With a curt tip of his hat, he climbed in his car and led the way past an industrial complex and a sprawling train station. Ján's heart pounded. This he remembered.

"Just watch, he'll turn left up ahead and climb that hill," Ján said, his voice cracking with emotion.

They wound their way up the incline and followed the lane through a stone arch that appeared just past the crest of the hill. Below lay a crumbling chapel surrounded by buildings. Ján pointed to the statue ahead.

"St. Seraphim, the angel presiding over the convent."

They stopped near the chapel, and Ján climbed out of the car. Fifty years of memories collapsed, and once again, he was a boy, trapped and frightened. He clenched his jaw and balled his fists, insistent on maintaining his composure. He was certain that if he listened hard enough, he could hear Maks calling for him, but the abandoned convent lingered in silence, save for the occasional screech of birdsong. Sofya moved to his side, and Ján pointed out the lane that led to the house and outbuildings beyond. He explained that there was a third cluster of structures hidden in a copse of trees they could see in the distance. Harper shuddered at the thought of what had happened on this spot.

Ján walked away from the group and stared up at St. Seraphim whose ancient face had been scoured expressionless by the ravages of the harsh Russian climate. The towering hunk of stone loomed over the deserted buildings and gazed toward the chapel with benign indifference. Ján considered all the vile assaults that had happened under the watchful eye of the saint and wondered how much evil had soaked into the pores of the granite elder. Without taking his eyes off the statue, Ján spoke. His words were barely a whisper, and the group strained to hear him. "There was once a girl here; Vera was her name." Ján pointed with his finger and traced a line from St. Seraphim's cold eyes to the chapel.

Lt. Volkov followed Ján's outstretched hand and approached the door. He found it locked, but a quick rap with a hammer easily broke through the corroded metal. They crowded into the vestibule where the muted afternoon light filtered through dust-covered windows, illuminating the lazy motes that hovered in the stale air. Vines snaked through cracks in the stone, trailing up the walls and across the floor. The stubborn tendrils wrapped around the legs of the altar and twisted around the pews. Several of the benches had succumbed to rot and lay in a heap of imploded wood while others remained stubbornly bolted to the floor, their once smooth seats riddled with scars from busy rodents. Tom ventured toward the front, examining the altar. He found more evidence of animal infestation and decay, but little else in the way of clues to the children's disappearance.

He turned to walk back to the others who were still clustered together in the rear. "Do you think she meant the children were brought here to be picked up and then taken some other place?" Tom asked, his voice echoing off the ancient stone. "Doesn't look like anything has happened in here since Peter the Great was in charge." He leaned against a pew to think, and it scooted out from under him, causing him to fall flat on his back. Harper and Ján rushed to help him up.

Harper noticed that the pew had not been bolted to the floor like others in the chapel. "Hey, look here!" she called.

They were able to push that pew aside as well as the two in front and the two behind. Underneath, they discovered flagstones with chipped borders, arranged in an irregular pattern. They differed from the rest of the floor where the stonemasons' precise artistry endured in stones worn to a smooth undulating finish from centuries of foot traffic.

Tom turned to Lt. Volkov. "Looks like you're going to need a crew with shovels here."

Police cars and forensic vans soon clustered on the hilltop. While crews entered the chapel and prepared to dig under the stones, Ján walked with Sofya and Harper down the lane. The main house stood much as Ján remembered it. Even the poster of Stalin, nefarious in its projection of benevolence, remained on the water-stained wall of the room that had been Mrs. Kotova's office.

Ján crept up the stairs and entered the space where he had

hidden so long ago. The closet door was open, and they could see the empty shelves within. Ján ventured through to the other room. The piano remained, propped against the wall. A cat peered out of the top of the case and more purring could be heard inside. Mice skittered along the floorboards. Ján placed his fingers on the keys but could not produce a note. The inner workings had succumbed to rot.

They wandered out back, and Ján noticed that the punishment huts were gone, bulldozed to a pile of rubble and pushed to the side in a crude attempt to destroy the evidence. The cabins remained, some with soiled mattresses still scattered about the concrete floor and surrounded by heaps of filthy stuffing. Animals had taken over what the people had left. Ján then led them down the lane behind the copse of trees, but the whole mysterious complex where he had last seen Maks had also been razed. Wildflowers had reclaimed the spot, and only a single chimney remained to bear witness to whatever appalling activities had occurred.

Harper ventured into the woods, looking for discarded furniture or files that may have been added to a landfill or pyre, and Sofya linked her arm with Ján's as they walked back toward the chapel.

"Is it awful being back?" she asked.

"It was awful being here, and it has haunted me for years," Ján said, "but there is nothing to hurt me here now. This place is steeped in sadness and heartache, but the pain is old and has settled in my bones where I must carry it. Hopefully those who suffered have found peace."

"Have you found peace?" Sofya asked.

"I'm trying," Ján said. He reached for her hand and gave it a tender squeeze.

Tom ran toward them. "You need to come with me."

They arrived back at the chapel to see a fleet of vans displaying official police insignias parked in double lines around St. Seraphim.

A woman emerged from the back of one van and began unloading tall lamps. Tom snapped more photographs as a man in uniform walked out of the chapel and extended his hand to Ján.

"Mr. Balik? I'm Major Bugrov." He pointed at the chapel door. "There are shallow graves. I can't speculate just yet, but we are finding bones, likely children." He shook his head. "One is bad enough, but there are so many."

After years of haunting neglect, the crime scene at the former orphanage now bustled with official activity. Major Bugrov quizzed Ján thoroughly to see what he remembered from the files he had found a half century ago, astonished at Ján's ability to recall even the most minute detail of his discoveries. Uncovering the whole truth from decades of abandonment promised to be a long process, and mindful of the enormity of the evidence at the No. 15 Home and the tedious nature of removal ahead, Harper and Tom brought the Baliks back to their lodgings in Moscow as soon as the police allowed. Tom returned alone to cover the investigation.

Sofya grew weary of the Metropol. She found the crisp service oppressive and dreamed of being back in her own kitchen, vowing never to complain about cold baths or Tuyaara's gossip. She was especially perplexed by Ján. She had expected him to make peace with his tortured past, even if it meant confirming his worst fears. She assumed closure was preferable to mystery, but to her frustration, he pulled into himself. Courteous but sullen, gentle yet distant.

Harper arranged for Ján to have access to the beautiful piano in the hotel ballroom, and the staff lingered to listen as he played for hours on end. He proved to be a mercurial performer, brilliant but prone to breaking off suddenly, slipping away, and disappearing for long stretches. "I am walking, merely clearing my head," he would respond quietly to Sofya's entreaties.

Ján dwelled in aching solitude, the void of someone who was casting for a purpose, for meaning. He could put notes around his emotions, but the words were elusive. He had done his best for

Maks and Vera, but he was being pulled toward something he couldn't ignore, a frustratingly ill-defined but urgent calling that hovered before him. He longed to return home with Sofya to his library, his beloved 'Kusku, and warming cups of tea with Alban, yet something lurked unresolved, nebulous but pressing. The music in his head grew louder, but he struggled to understand the meaning while fragmented images of Warsaw haunted his dreams.

Harper saw in the Baliks a raw vulnerability, a desperate reach for emotional purchase without the support of anything familiar. Despite her vow of maintaining a professional distance, she had grown quite fond of the couple and despaired to see them so diminished. With Angelica's approval, she booked flights for their return to Yakutsk and dreaded having to say goodbye. She was pleased when Angelica proposed a final dinner at the Metropol to properly bid them farewell.

Harper pushed through the heavy glass and brass doors, welcoming the rush of warm air from the Metropol's opulent lobby. She spied Ján and Sofya sitting on a large sofa and smiled at the sight of their quiet dignity and affection. Ján stood and greeted her kindly, insisting that she take his seat beside Sofya. They endeavored to make small talk as they waited for Angelica, and Sofya passed the time quizzing Harper about her personal life and any possible suitors. After a perplexing delay, the concierge approached them with news that Angelica had called with instructions to start dinner without her.

"How odd!" noted Harper. "Angelica is never even a smidge late!"

They settled themselves at the table, and Ján quietly observed as the two women chattered in companionable conversation. When the waiter brought their bottle of wine and poured a serving for each, Harper raised her glass and toasted the Baliks. "Ján, you have been generous with your memories and revelations, and I am inspired by your courage." Ján moved to dismiss her praise, but she continued. "Wait before you protest. I wasn't finished. I want to thank you both. The love that Sofya poured into her letter inspired me. I have family here somewhere, and you have spurred on my commitment to finding them."

Sofya raised her glass in return. "We hope you find them, and we also hope that you will think of us as part of your family. Come visit again, maybe in the summertime?"

Their laughter was interrupted by Angelica's arrival, and they were surprised to see that she was accompanied by a gentleman with the refined nature of one who has lived a privileged life. Ján and Sofya looked puzzled, but Harper leapt up from her chair. "Mr. Verenich! It's a pleasure to see you." Angelica wore the smug expression of one who has brokered an exceptional deal.

Pasha Verenich reached across the table to shake Ján's hand. "Mr. Balik, it is truly an honor to meet you. I am the chairman of the Moscow Winter Festival, and I understand that your wife wrote to nominate you for our musical competition. I am so sorry to report that we have already selected our ten finalists. It simply wouldn't do to upend the competition at this point."

Ján hastened to put him at ease. "Mr. Verenich, you are kind to deliver this news yourself. I do not wish for anyone to make exceptions on my behalf."

Ján's graciousness annoyed Sofya who failed to hide her dismay. Verenich held up his hand. "Ah, but it is not disappointment that I wish to discuss. You see, Miss Turner showed me your wife's letter. Your story needs to be told, and I have seen a rough version of your composition about the Dead Road. In my humble opinion, it is the work of a truly gifted musician, one whose talent is too extraordinary for a simple music festival. Your gifts deserve a special performance, and thus, I have a proposal to make."

Ján battled a wave of emotion as he struggled to interpret Verenich's request. In his hesitation, Sofya jumped in to fill the void. "Of course, he will play! And you won't be sorry. He's a magician at the piano."

"Wait," cautioned Angelica, "there's more. Please, Pasha, continue."

"Well, if you agree of course, we propose a special concert featuring you and your compositions. As an added feature, we would like to include an encore performance of The Besprizornye Musicians. It will be the highlight of the festival, assuming we can find some of the other children who performed."

Ján wiped away a tear and allowed himself a broad smile. The thought of seeing his old friends again was a glimmer of hope that cut through his stubborn malaise. He motioned to the empty chairs, "Please, Miss Turner and Mr. Verenich, join us. Tonight, we celebrate. Tomorrow, we search."

As Angelica and Pasha took their places, the waiter scurried over to bring them place settings and supply a second bottle of wine.

Ján raised his glass. "If you will indulge me, I would like to offer a toast. I remember something my father used to say, an old Polish proverb, I believe. 'You meet your true friends in a time of need.'" He glanced at Sofya, his eyes glistening with tears. "Here's to our new friends and the possibilities ahead!"

Chapter 16

Song of Family

Moscow, Russia
February 1993

Ján and Sofya returned to Moscow, boarding their plane in Yakutsk with less anxiety than their earlier maiden flight. Harper's story had been picked up by the wire services, and when Ján stepped off the plane, he was recognized by enthusiastic fans eager to get his autograph. Harper whisked them through the airport and settled them back at the Metropol.

Harper and Tom were still working on the full feature about Ján. His life story demanded more than a single article to do justice to his history. Several installments had been published in a series about his extraordinary life, and they were besieged by calls and letters from families searching for their own long-lost relatives. Former residents of the No. 15 Special Home also contacted the paper with their own accounts of ghastly conditions, neglect, and suspicious disappearances consistent with Ján's recollections.

Four of The Besprizornye Musicians, Irina, Emil, Borya, and Leo, had been found and were eager to be a part of the performance. The other children were either lost or had died in the intervening years, but to have five performers for the event exceeded all their expectations. They would rehearse for a week with a sold-out performance scheduled for the final night of the festival.

Harper clutched a steaming cup of coffee as she shivered on a bench in Novopushkinsky Park and watched pedestrians navigate the wintry landscape in early morning darkness. Snow had fallen throughout the night, softening the angular features of the fountain and dusting the bare branches of the trees that ringed the plaza. She mulled over preparations for the concert and plans for her next piece about Ján's story. Tom's photographs had captured the complexity of emotions in Ján's interviews, and he and Harper had made several trips to the No. 15 Special Children's Home, chasing leads to complete a more expansive account of the horrors that had happened there.

"Penny for your thoughts, missy," Tom said, joining Harper on the cold bench.

"We did well," she replied with a smile.

Tom looked away and rubbed his gloved hands together.

"What is it that you're not telling me?"

"It's time, Harper. Time for me to go back. I'm feeling the pull of the Lone Star State, and it's calling me home." He met her gaze, and she saw determination with a hint of sadness in his eyes.

She breathed in deeply, the cold air stinging inside her chest. Her eyes filled with tears, and she moved to brush them away. "I hear it's hot in Texas. You're going to be quite sweaty and miserable."

"Yeah, I hear you, darlin', but I've learned a thing or two from this adventure with the Baliks. You gotta hang on to the people you love. Maybe I am just one more soul that Ján has softened with his magic touch. I have a daughter in Corpus Christi that I hardly know. The divorce was brutal, and I fooled myself into thinking that running away made things easier for everyone. I need to mend those fences."

"I hope it works out for you and for her. If you decide you prefer your winters extra frosty, remember that you'll always have friends here."

"Will you be here if I decide to come back?"

"If Angelica doesn't fire me. I'm not sure I'll ever be finished torturing her with my ideas." Harper offered a wistful smile. "Truth is, I'm going to search out my father's relatives, learn more about my grandparents and what happened to them. I guess we've all felt the urgency to seize the moment and rebuild bridges."

"Promise me you'll do your best to be safe. Don't take chances that you don't need to."

"Well, Tom Rainey, man of mystery, practicing your paternal skills on me? One thing, non-negotiable. You have to stay long enough to see Ján's story through. Promise?"

It was settled. Tom would remain for the concert, and then he would start packing up.

They returned to the newsroom to gather their equipment before the morning rehearsal. As they entered the office, Alina motioned them over. The switchboard was lit up with a frantic display of blinking red lights, and she pushed a stack of messages to Harper. "All the same guy," she said while transferring a call. "He says it's important."

Harper looked at the slip of the paper on top of the pile. It was from Igor Zajak with the *Gazeta Wyborcza*. She showed it to Tom. "It's from Poland. Ring any bells?"

Tom shrugged. The name didn't register with him.

Harper dialed the number. Why would a Polish reporter be contacting her? It had to have some connection to her stories about Ján, but what? A young man with a pleasant voice came on the line, and Harper listened with increasing interest. "Are you sure? Really, Igor, you have to be absolutely certain!"

Tom pulled up a chair and tried to glean what this man, Zajak, was saying.

"Igor! Brilliant! Hold on, and I will work on getting Ján and Sofya there. I'll call you back as quickly as I can." Harper hung up the phone and grabbed her coat. "Change in plans. I'll explain on the way."

Harper and Tom stopped by Angelica's desk on their way out and left a note with instructions for her to meet them at the rehearsal venue. They also pleaded with Alina to help them with information about flights to Warsaw. She peppered them with questions, but there wasn't time to explain. They raced out the door and hailed a cab.

They arrived to find the rehearsal well underway. Irina had completed her part, the last of the other Besprizornye Musicians in their practice rotation. A stocky woman with voluminous bleached hair and ample amounts of rouge on her cheeks, she stood beside Leo, a slight man with a balding pate, wearing an oversized suit. Both cradled their violins. Gray-haired Borya waited in the wings with his trumpet resting on his belly, and Emil, fit and athletic with a toothy smile, held his flute.

There was an atmosphere of easy camaraderie that pervaded the venue, and as Ján entered the stage, a hush fell over the sparse crowd. Harper thought back to the bearded man she had confronted in his library and was amazed at his transformation to the performer she saw before her. He had a charm and a charisma on stage that was spellbinding, and he hadn't yet played a note. Sofya acknowledged their arrival and hurried to join them in the back row just as Ján made his entrance. Angelica arrived shortly after, and Harper pulled her aside to share the developments in Ján's story.

Ján sat at the piano and rested his hands on the keys. There was no music in front of him, but as soon as he began to play, Harper recognized the piece as the first in his leather book, the composition to his mother.

"Whew-ee, every chord that man plays is a doozy," Tom whispered.

They waited until he had finished his entire set before Angelica motioned them all toward the stage. Ján was surprised to see them. "Did I sound alright?" he inquired, unsure of what to make of this gathering.

Harper spoke first. "Ján, that was beautiful, and you sounded more than alright. You're an inspiration, and I can't wait to hear you play more on this magnificent stage, but there is something you need to know." Ján looked at her with alarm, and Sofya moved to stand next to him, dreading the delivery of bad news. "Everything is fine, really, I just have some rather shocking news. When we published the article searching out members of The Besprizornye Musicians, it got picked up by the wire services, and it ended up running in the *Gazeta Wyborcza*–"

"Poland?" Ján interrupted. "Why?"

Harper replied, "It was you, Ján. You're a child of Poland, and there is considerable interest in celebrating you, but there's something else. About a week after the story ran, one of the reporters received a call from a woman who saw the article. Ján, she says she is your sister, Magda. She survived the war and is living in Poland, and we are prepared to take you to her. Today."

Ján stared at Harper as if in a daze. Sofya glanced from her husband to the expectant faces of their journalist friends, wringing her hands as she processed the weight of the moment.

"Ján," Harper repeated, unable to conceal the urgency in her voice. "We need to go."

"I can't," he said in a voice laced with grief.

Sofya laid her hand gently on her husband's arm. "Of course, you must. We will do this together."

"No, I can't. We can't," he insisted in a voice close to panic. He locked eyes with Harper. "I am a ghost, a man with no identity and no papers unless you count the worthless scraps Alban stole off the corpse of Evgeni Baburin decades ago. Sofya has papers, but still no passport. We cannot leave."

In a stunning show of dogged campaigning, *The Moscow News* managed to secure the Baliks' documents in a week, deploying Alexander Stein's connections and Angelica's persistence against the vanity of two ambassadors and the stubbornness of countless diplomats. Harper marveled at Ján's composure during seven long and intense days of emotional turmoil. His carefully composed façade cracked as soon as he held his and Sofya's passports, his Polish and hers Russian, and tears of joy flowed as he contemplated embracing Magda once again.

Once they had left for Sheremetyevo Airport, Angelica was on the phone planning promotions and interviews. Harper was charged with covering the siblings' meeting, and for maximum exposure, Angelica had suggested trying to wrangle the Baliks' former home for the reunion. Although Ján was reeling from the news, he had the presence of mind to insist that his initial conversation with Magda be held off the record, just the two of them in a neutral site. On this point, he was firm.

As the plane circled Warsaw, Ján kept his nose glued to the window. His memories of leaving this place as a young boy bubbled up, and as he looked out over a sprawling city, he struggled to find any bit that seemed familiar.

Igor Zajak greeted them at the airport with assurances that the arrangements were set. They would be meeting Magda and her husband, Stefan Nowak, later that afternoon in a suite at the newly reopened Hotel Bristol. The entourage piled into a van that took Ján and Sofya on a tour of the city with Harper in tow.

As they entered Mokotów, the driver turned down the thoroughfare that led to the Baliks' former home, and Ján felt his heart quicken. Part of him was eager to see his old house, but he dreaded the sight of the building without the family that made it a home. The driver had explained that much of Warsaw had been destroyed in the war and painstakingly rebuilt, but what of his house? Ján twisted the seatbelt between his fingers while he nursed the fear that their gracious home was one more Balik family tragedy.

The serene street radiated the aura of old money and refined elegance. Spacious gardens with mossy stone walls and long, tree-lined driveways allowed glimpses of the dignified houses sitting behind the imposing gates. Ján relaxed into the familiarity as he recalled running along these sidewalks with nannies chasing after him. The memory made him smile. The van pulled to the side of the road and came to a stop.

Sofya squealed. "Oh, Ján! This house! It's just like the picture from so long ago; it's still so beautiful!"

He kissed her cheek and climbed out of the van, walking across the street to get an unobstructed view in front of the open gate. He stood very still with his hands in his pockets, and Sofya moved to stand quietly beside him. He was staring at a snowy expanse across what would surely be a manicured lawn in warmer weather. Clusters of shrubs were strategically planted to frame the vast expanse of the stone house. A broad porch with thick columns dominated the front, and massive wings extended out from both sides. Ján saw none of this. He saw his mother, standing at the door to inspect deliveries for a fabulously extravagant party; he saw his sisters walking up the drive with their friends; and he saw his father, motoring out in his fancy sports car to hobnob with Warsaw's business elite.

A smartly dressed woman emerged out of the entryway and made her way up the drive towards them. In her hand, she held a small red box. She greeted them all and then turned to Ján.

"My name is Agnieska, and my husband and I live here now." She spoke in a nervous rush, and Ján realized that she might be worried that he would contest ownership.

Speaking Polish haltingly after so many years, he replied, "It is nice to meet you, Agnieska. I am Ján, and this is my wife, Sofya. It looks like you are taking care of the place."

Agnieska smiled and seemed to relax a bit. "Yes, we bought the property just last year and have embarked on a renovation. It was broken up into apartments after the war, lots of cheap partitions and awkward divisions. We have worked hard to bring it back. Perhaps you will join me inside and share stories of when your family lived here?"

Ján shook his head. "That is most kind of you, but it is your home now. I want my memories to remain those of my family inhabiting these rooms. Thank you for your hospitality. It is most appreciated."

Igor and Harper shared a look of disappointment over the realization that there would be no footage of Ján walking through the luxurious rooms while adding nostalgic commentary, but Agnieska nodded in understanding.

"I will leave you alone with your memories. Take all the time you wish, wander about the property, and if you change your mind, please do come inside." She handed the box to Ján. "You should have these. During the renovation, we found these hidden behind a wall. We didn't know who to give them to until now."

Back in the car, Sofya eyed the box, urging Ján to see what was inside, but he demurred. "It is for me and Magda to see together."

"Yes," she agreed. "That is as it should be."

They assembled in a richly appointed suite at the Hotel Bristol and soon thereafter, a waiter appeared at the door pushing a cart brimming with tea and sumptuous treats. Sofya insisted on serving everyone to have something to do with her nervous energy. Ján declined any refreshment. He stood at the tall windows overlooking the celebrated Royal Route. His mind was searching for memories of Magda, trying to imagine how the headstrong, flirtatious girl he knew had matured into a woman. She had lived a full life without him.

The phone rang in the suite, and Harper answered it, speaking English. "She is here now, on her way up." Sofya peeked at the mirror one last time, checking her dress and smoothing her hair. She wanted Ján to be proud to introduce her.

A knock at the door, and Harper trained her camera on Ján as he turned his back to the window and prepared to greet his sister, an expression of exuberant anticipation radiating from his face. Everyone held their breath, and then she was in the room. Magda. She was lovely, a septuagenarian with alluring blue eyes and a pile of thick white hair twisted into a bun at the nape of her long neck. Her delicate stature and patrician features left little doubt that she and Ján were indeed siblings.

Ján drew her into a tight embrace, almost as though he were afraid that she would slip out of his sight again.

Magda leaned into his shoulder and then pulled back, holding his face in her hands and taking in the exquisite sight of the brother she believed long dead. Her fingers met the knobby scar on the side of his face, and her expression clouded.

"Ján? Oh, Ján. My darling boy."

"We will talk," he promised. "First, please allow me to introduce my wife, Sofya, and to greet my brother-in-law."

Introductions were made all around, and hugs were shared freely. The conversation flowed in bits of Polish, Russian, and English, and somehow, they closed the circle.

Ján reached for Magda's hand and turned to the gathering. "We will be stepping out for a bit. Please allow us some time to become reacquainted. We will return." He looked at Sofya, and she winked at him.

"You two go," she said. "Stefan and I have some talking to do." She glanced at Harper and Igor. "We'll have plenty of help getting acquainted."

Stefan gave Magda a kiss, and then Ján picked up the little red box and led his sister out the door. They walked the short distance to Saxon Garden where he spied a bench. Snowflakes began to drift aimlessly in the waning light.

Magda wore a deep purple wool coat, but Ján had only his thick sweater.

"Are you sure you won't get too cold out here?" she asked in a motherly fashion.

Ján tilted his head and smiled. "I live in Siberia."

They both laughed. He reached for her hand. In her company, the burden on his heart lightened into exuberant joy. They sat companionably for a few minutes, trying to determine where you pick up the conversation with someone you have thought about every day of your life but about whom you know almost nothing.

Magda broke the silence. "Sofya adores you, it is clear at first glance. I am glad to know that you are loved. That haunted me more than anything all these years, hoping that you had been loved before you died."

"You thought I died?" Ján asked.

"Oh, for the longest time, I knew nothing and had no means or opportunity to find you, and when I did, finally, reach out to Aunt Ada and Uncle Erik, I heard through the tracing service that Uncle Erik had reported your and Ada's deaths."

"Hmmm, it was not so. Ada died horribly, but here I am, you see. I survived."

"Yes, you survived, and I survived too. The memories sit uneasily on me at times. There is much that haunts me about the years gone by," she reflected. "At the end of the day, we made it back here. Perhaps Mama, Papa, and Hanna know we are together now."

Ján said, "Yes. I hope that they can see us. Tell me. Whatever you want me to know."

She hesitated. "It is a story that I have never shared with anyone, not even Stefan. When I realized I was alone, I became a new person. I had two skills: I could speak several languages and I could seduce a man. I used those skills to survive, always intent on getting revenge on everyone who killed our family. I am not proud of the things I was forced to do. To this day, I cannot give voice to the life I had to live.

"After the war, I worked as a teacher, living quietly and keeping my head down. There were reprisals against women who collaborated with the enemy, and I feared that my work in the resistance would be misrepresented. Best to say nothing, go along, get along. That is what I did." Magda looked at Ján with a piercing gaze. "I never stopped thinking about you. Never. I was afraid to find you because I worried that you would be angry at me."

"Angry? But, Magda, no!" Ján protested.

"It seemed to me at the time that I had abandoned you," she insisted. "I kept trying to think of ways that I could find you, but..." Her voice trailed off.

Ján patted her hand. "We all carry that. The guilt. I have not carried it very well, myself. I cannot imagine how you could have found me."

Magda nodded. "I met Stefan at the school where I taught. I've kept my secrets, my shame, yet he is patient. Oh, Ján, he is such a kind man. One day, I told him about you, and he helped me write a letter to the tracing service inquiring about you, Ada, and Erik, hoping I could rebuild a bit of the family I lost. That's when I got the letter back from Erik's family, telling me that you and Ada had died at the end of the war. I gave up after that."

Ján told her extra bits of his story that she would not have read in the paper. "Uncle Erik was no family to us, Magda. He left me to die. Like you, I didn't believe I deserved to be loved. I had failed so many people. I couldn't reconcile my worth in such a broken world."

"Just tell me this, Ján. Have you been able to find comfort in music? You were so gifted. Mama and Papa died knowing you were safe at the time, and I am sure that brought them peace."

"I have an old piano, an upright with a scratched case and a history of abuse. We are alike in that way. It is my friend of sorts, and yes, I play every day." Ján reached under his sweater and pulled out his leather book. Magda took it and ran her fingers across the cracked leather binding. Then she opened the pages and looked at the compositions, each piece unique and remarkable in its own way. She found her own name scrawled across a yellowed page.

Ján drew out the red box. He explained how he got it, and then he tugged at the string and lifted the lid.

Magda beamed. "Photographs! Oh, Ján! I have none. These are beautiful."

They spread them out, all ten. Mostly they featured images of Hanna's friends playing tennis or posing in their bathing costumes by the river. There were two of their parents, and they held them reverently, willing their voices to emerge from the sepia prints.

"One for you and one for me," said Ján as he tucked them back in the box. "Shall we return and face the cameras? I would like to greet Stefan and thank him for loving you all these years."

They embraced, two older people, dusted with snow. Few of the passersby took note as they strolled past after a long day.

Moscow

Ján stood in the wings of the elegant concert hall of the Gnessin Academy of Music and stared out at the vast expanse of the stage, empty save for the magnificent Bösendorfer grand piano. He listened to patrons filling the hall, chatting eagerly as they filed into their seats, and he thought that if he closed his eyes, he might be able to conjure Ada to stand by him with her hand on his shoulder. *You will be brilliant*, he heard her say, and it brought him a smile.

He adjusted his bow tie and tugged at the tails of his formal evening attire. Sofya stood next to him, resplendent in her borrowed gown. She had eschewed any cosmetics but relented when Magda insisted on taking her to get her hair styled. Now she waited eagerly with Ján, her long hair twisted into an elegant updo and crowned with a sparkling headpiece of paste stones. In her gloved hand, she held the program printed on thick cream paper. Ján Balik in concert with a special appearance by members of The

Besprizornye Musicians. The lights flickered, a soft bell chimed, and chatter in the seats quietened.

"I should find my seat," Sofya said as she leaned up to kiss his cheek. "Are you nervous?"

"Not as long as you are here," Ján replied.

The lights dimmed until only a bright spotlight remained. Ján walked to center stage and stood in front of the microphone. Applause erupted in the packed house, and Ján lifted his hand to acknowledge the enthusiastic welcome. He looked out over the front row as Sofya took her seat between Ayta and Magda. Stefan sat beside Magda with his arm protectively around her shoulders. Alban, to Ayta's right, was almost unrecognizable in his tuxedo, his black hair, shot through with gray, trimmed and combed back. Flanking Alban were Harper, Tom, and Angelica.

Ján cleared his throat, and a hush fell across the vast concert hall. "I want to thank you all for being here this evening. To my sister, Magda, I thought I had lost you, and I am so grateful for the gift of having you here. To my Turul family, Alban and his dear Ayta, I am humbled that you traveled so far to join us. To the persistent journalists at the *Moscow News*—Harper, Tom, Khristina, Angelica—without you, none of this is possible. Finally, to my wife, Sofya, I owe you everything."

In the glow of the stage and wrapped in the encouragement of the audience, Ján heard a beautiful sound, one that he had thought long buried in pain. His mother's voice came to him as clear as if she were standing right beside him, delighting in this gorgeous assembly. *You are meant for great things, Ján.*

He choked back a tear and paused a moment to regain his composure before continuing. "Tonight, I will play my own compositions for you. They were written to honor the sacrifices of those who suffered. Each is dedicated to one special person or place, and holds within its rhythms a reminder of what made them remarkable.

"To my fellow performers—Irina, Leo, Borya, and Emil—I

have missed you, and you remain in my heart as brothers and a sister from a time when I needed you desperately. And to my dear mother, who long ago dreamed of my destiny, this is for you."

Ján turned and nodded to those who remained in the wings. Irina, Borya, Emil, and Leo stood with their instruments, awaiting their turn on stage. Then, to thunderous applause, Ján walked to the piano and took his place on the gleaming bench. He picked up his worn leather book and set it on the music rack, unopened. He placed his hands on the keys, closed his eyes, and lingered there for just a moment. Then he began to play.

Epilogue: Ján's Song

South of Moscow
1995

The cross was large but simple and roughly cut. A gray slab of common Precambrian rock, it carried the history of millennia in its veins of speckled silver with the occasional glint of coppery brown. Sitting atop a low hill dotted with scrubby grasses and a profusion of wildflowers, the silent stone faced out over the village and its tangled railyard below.

On the opposite side of the hill stood the walls of the Convent of St. Seraphim, presided over by the stained and pitted statue of its patron, a man revered for his mystical and solitary life. The stony visage of the ancient elder, chiseled in the long-ago days when rulers were fierce if not beloved, watched over the chapel, his frozen gaze pensive and unreadable in his lonely vigil over this haunted place.

As the final load of black soil was tamped down at the base of the cross, the leaden clouds parted overhead, and brilliant crepuscular rays emerged. The clutch of people huddled together gasped in unison as the light glinted off the plaque secured at the base of the cross. A sign, surely.

The priest waited until the men and machinery had finished their task and retreated down the hill, disappearing around the curve on the weedy road. He was a very patient man. When the sound of the grinding motors died away, he began his litany, rhythmically swinging the thurible and intoning God to sanctify the grave and bless the souls of the interred.

Ján wore his flat wool cap in defiance of the unseasonably warm day and stared intently at the cross. He had long since given up on prayers. He closed his eyes and pictured their faces instead. A mournful melody filled his head, a tribute that only he could hear. He put his arm around Sofya and reached for Magda's hand.

It had taken over a year, but a diligent task force had identified the human remains and handled them with the respect they had been denied in their brief lives. The new Russian government, anxious to distance itself from Soviet-era abuses, had returned the convent, including the chapel, to the Russian Orthodox Church. The bishops, equally eager to purge the nefarious history of the place, had acted swiftly to renovate the buildings under the gaze of St. Seraphim and demolish of all traces of the No. 15 Home.

Ján had little interest in the workings of the church beyond fulfilling his promises to his friends. With the money raised on his celebrated tour, he had purchased from the bishops a little plot of land to create a resting place for the children. He conceded only two points: the church could bury the remains according to their sacred traditions, and the monument would be in the shape of a cross.

Once the bones were released by the police, any unclaimed remains were brought to the little plot for reburial. No longer a place of pain, the sun-warmed earth at the top of the hill, a patch graced by the somber monument and encircled by a sturdy iron fence, welcomed the memory of the children with a brilliant display of blue forget-me-nots, a sign of renewed hope.

Ján removed his cap and twisted it in his fingers as he listened to the prayer for the dead. He mulled the priest's words as he conjured images of his friends, Vera and Maks, and those children whose pictures were seared into his memory. *A place of brightness, a place of abundance, a place of rest, where all sickness, despair, and sorrow are gone. Yes,* thought Ján. *That is what they deserve.* He was long past believing in a benevolent God, but he was willing to hope that there was a place where the innocent souls, so horribly wronged on earth, could find joy and serenity.

When the priest had finished his prayers and closed his book, Ján knelt down and placed his hands on the warm mound of dark soil. "Rest well, my friends, and know you are not forgotten. Your presence is a song in my heart, and your notes will be lifted up so that all can rejoice in your release from pain."

As they walked down the hill together, Ján hummed a calming melody.

"A song for your friends?" inquired Sofya.

Ján squeezed her hand. "A song for hope amidst pain. A song about finding beauty."

She smiled. "Ján's Song."

THE END

Author Notes

Ján Balik is a product of my imagination, but his story is gleaned from accounts of very real children who suffered as orphans, outcasts, or enemies of the State under a brutal Soviet regime. For my novel, *The Refugee's Daughter*, I delved deep into first-hand accounts of the grim realities for children who were forced out of East Prussia in the final days of the Second World War, many of whom were packed into filthy trains bound for work camps, orphanages, and the gulags.

Ján first appeared in that story as a nameless victim of the purges, and he represented the brief but intense bonds between strangers necessary for survival in the most traumatic moments of separation and grief. Even though his presence was mysterious and fleeting in that first book, Ján's story was quite full to me. He was tenderness amidst cruelty, beauty in the face of squalor, and brilliance in a time that rewarded only an impoverished and feral will to live.

During the years of Josef Stalin's iron-fisted control over the Soviet Union, the authoritarian government stripped the people of thirteen entire nationalities of their assets and deported them from

AUTHOR NOTES

their homes to faraway and forbidding regions. They were accused of treason, painted as undesirable. The children of stigmatized minorities and the offspring of enemies of the State shared their parents' culpability for perceived crimes. The dreaded knock on the door signaled an unimaginable journey through the grief of dispossession, arrest, exile, resettlement, forced labor, discrimination, starvation, trauma, or all too often, death. Those who survived were tainted for life.

In the years after the Second World War, the near impenetrable walls of the Iron Curtain closed around those in the conquered territories with destruction meted out as revenge for the horrors suffered by the Soviets in the war years. Children of the defeated were, like their parents, war criminals. They were tossed into an abyss of terror and deprivation. They were subject to deportation to Siberian prisons or forced labor camps. If the men, women, and children survived the treacherous journey, they were separated, put to work in mines or fisheries in the far arctic north, and dumped without provisions to survive in one of the Earth's most brutal climates. The toll on human lives was staggering. In *Children of the Gulag*, Cathy A. Frierson and Semyon Vilensky note that deaths from political repression during the Soviet era likely exceeded 20 million people with conservative estimates of 10 million children becoming orphans as a result.

In a heartbreaking paradox, success of the Soviet State depended on molding its children into enthusiastic cheerleaders for the transformation of society. Propaganda cast Stalin as the benevolent father figure under the oft-repeated slogan "Thank you, dear Comrade Stalin, for a happy childhood!" The reality was a markedly different story. Of all the people targeted for repression, 40 percent were children. Infants and toddlers were required to accompany their mothers to the gulags and camps where they languished in bleak and sordid wards with high mortality rates. Many that survived suffered developmental delays.

Author Notes

For many orphaned children including those irreparably separated from their families, a horrific reality was the Soviet system of orphanages. Records are incomplete but evidence points to a vast network of State-run institutions that received little support or scrutiny. For millions of victims, starvation and malnutrition were common including reliable reports of children scavenging trash bins for something to eat. They lacked adequate clothing and shoes in overcrowded facilities where it was not unusual for one squalid mattress with no sheets or blankets to serve as a bed for as many as four children. Heat, medicine, and kindness were in short supply, and afflictions such as typhus, malaria, dysentery, scurvy, rickets, ringworm, and lice were rampant. Mortality rates were grim with rare inspections documenting and then ignoring facilities that did not practice proper sanitation procedures to bury the dead.

Ján's experience at the No. 15 Home reflects the official reports as well as interviews from those who survived as wards of the state.

Beginning at age sixteen, children were sentenced as adults, a fate that could be applied to those as young as twelve. These children were often dumped into adult prisons where they suffered rampant abuse. This ultimately became Ján's fate, and the Dead Road project where he labored in the story was a real and horrifying place. Known officially as the Salekhard to Igarka Railway or the Transpolar Mainline, it was a doomed component of the gulag system with the singular purpose of building a railway across the hostile and forbidding terrain of northern Russia. Labor was supplied by convicts, both men and women, the majority of whom were political prisoners convicted of acts against the Soviet State. The extreme climate and ghastly conditions earned the project its nickname, the Dead Road.

The Barabanicha Labor Camp was one of the prisons built along the route. It was an enormous facility designed for up to a thousand prisoners and featured a hospital, color-coded barracks,

Author Notes

dog kennels, and the ubiquitous solitary punishment cells. Remains of the Barabanicha camp still exist deep in the far north where they remain almost impossible to reach without detailed planning and specialized equipment.

Anne Applebaum's prize-winning *Gulag: A History* is a sweeping exploration of the hellish experience in Soviet gulags. Hidden deep in this monumental work is a drawing, roughly sketched by Benjamen Mkrtchyan in 1953 and captioned "In the barracks: inmates listening to a prisoner musician." Depicting five men huddled around a sixth strumming a guitar, this poignant image inspired Ján's transformative journey through Barabanicha.

Catriona Kelly's *Children's World: Growing Up in Russia 1890–1991* and Cathy A. Frierson's and Semyon Vilenskey's *Children of the Gulag*, both published by Yale University Press, are excellent resources for authoritative information on gulags and orphanages.

Claudia Heinermann's *Siberian Exiles* trilogy is a brilliant compilation of vintage and contemporary photographs along with stunning interviews with survivors of the exiles. Her dedication to celebrating the stories and identities of those who suffered such cruelties adds a needed human touch to the staggering and overwhelming statistics of loss.

Sophy Roberts's *The Lost Pianos of Siberia* tells an astounding tale of artistry and beauty in exile. I found her book after I had written *Songs of the Dead Road* and was delighted to see in her gorgeous descriptions of Siberia a reference to Leonid Kaloshin, a man living in a remote village who cobbled together a library in his home for his neighbors and who dreamed of adding a concert hall complete with a grand piano to his modest dwelling. She also introduced me to the story behind the Red October pianos.

My gratitude to them for their copious research into primary documents and the countless interviews they conducted to offer a full picture of this terrifying chapter in human cruelty and the beauty that managed to grow through the cold and the cracks.

Author Notes

While Ján Balik's artistry is fiction, there are some gorgeous musical compositions referenced in the book. For a link to a playlist of the real works featured in the story, please visit my website, carolynnewtonauthor.com.

Also by Carolyn Newton

The Refugee's Daughter

Amid wartime brutality and unimaginable suffering, a teenager in flight from the Soviet Army struggles to survive, find her brother — and hold on to hope...

BUY NOW

Acknowledgements

Launching a novel is equal parts exhilarating and terrifying, and I am so very grateful to all my cherished helpers who shared their advice and expertise to lift *Songs of the Dead Road* from a clunky manuscript to a published work of historical fiction. I am indebted to these treasured friends and colleagues for their generosity and honesty.

Gaia Banks who, when we discussed the story in *The Refugee's Daughter*, asked insightful questions about the boy on the train. At her suggestion, Ján's story bloomed, and I will be forever grateful to her for giving him space to shine.

Clare Law, an eagle-eyed editor whose astute observations and attention to detail sharpened the narrative, and the entire team at Bloodhound Books, including Betsy Reavely, Fred Freeman, Hannah Baxter-Deuce, Tara Lyons, Lexi Curtis, and Trish Dixon. They are dedicated advocates, and I am thankful for their support and thoughtful guidance.

My mother, Suzella Newsome, my sister, Laura Pittman, and my sister-in-love, Kim Newsome, all beautifully perceptive readers. My dear niece, Lollie Newsome, a gifted, exquisite musician.

Claudia Heinermann, whose work remains an inspiration to me.

Jill Muti, an accomplished flutist, discerning educator, and cherished friend.

Madeline B, whose clever map of the Dead Road points readers in the right direction.

My lovely fellow writers who pitched in with blurbs, reviews, and a sympathetic ear. The sharp-penned Ron Rash is a generous and brilliant writer, and Sophy Roberts is as gracious as she is adventurous and talented. Tracey Dodson Buchanan and Deb Jordan, veterans of the new writer and publishing roller coaster, have been delightful companions on this journey. Cathy Rigg Monetti is a fabulous discussion partner; Valeria Wenderoth wraps a supportive community around historical fiction writers in the Carolinas; and Stacey Hettes leads the pack with fearless writing. I treasure my chats with them.

Independent booksellers who have offered me a podium, an audience, and a space on their shelves for my books.

All the vibrant, curious, and gracious book clubs who have invited me into their homes, churches, galleries, and zooms.

The readers who have championed my work, shared recommendations with friends, purchased copies to read or as gifts, and written lovely reviews.

And above all, my treasured family: Newt, Callie, David, Laura, Hillary, Jimmy, Levi, Ellie Ruth, Eden, Beau, Addy, Anna Ruth, Evie, and Ava. You are my lights and my guiding stars. I love you dearly.

Thank you.

A NOTE FROM THE PUBLISHER

Thank you for reading this book. If you enjoyed it please do consider leaving a review on Amazon to help others find it too.

We hate typos. All of our books have been rigorously edited and proofread, but sometimes mistakes do slip through. If you have spotted a typo, please do let us know and we can get it amended within hours.

info@bloodhoundbooks.com

www.ingramcontent.com/pod-product-compliance
Lightning Source LLC
LaVergne TN
LVHW090306181225
828083LV00007B/140